H.M.S. UNSEEN

PATRICK
ROBINSON

HarperCollins*Publishers*

H.M.S. Unseen is a work of fiction set in the near future. The premise of the novel and descriptions of naval operations and protocol are grounded in fact. However, certain liberties have been taken in the interest of creating a compelling narrative.

HarperCollins books may be purchased for educational, business, or sales promotional use. For information please write: Special Markets Department, HarperCollins Publishers, Inc., 10 East 53rd Street, New York, NY 10022.

FIRST EDITION

Designed by Ruth Lee.

Maps by Justin Spain.

Library of Congress Cataloging-in-Publication Data

Robinson, Patrick, 1939–
    H.M.S. Unseen / Patrick Robinson.
        p.   cm.
    ISBN 0-06-019315-8
    I. Title. II. Title: HMS Unseen. III. Title: Her Majesty's Ship Unseen.
PR6068.01959H2   1999
823'.914—dc21   98-42775

99 00 01 02 03 ❖/RRD 10 9 8 7 6 5 4 3 2 1

This book is respectfully dedicated to the military Intelligence services of both the United States and Great Britain, the men who watch the oceans and skies, and whose diligence and brilliance are often unheralded.

ACKNOWLEDGMENTS

F OR THE THIRD TIME, ADMIRAL SIR JOHN WOODWARD was my principal technical advisor in the construction of a novel. *H.M.S. Unseen*, a stealthy Royal Navy submarine, now being leased to an overseas government, was chosen for the title as it represents the central area of the book.

The Admiral was obliged to use all of his considerable ingenuity to convert it into precisely the kind of boat we required for the plot. He was also obliged to "invent" a missile system which would (a) stand some chance of working, and (b) not take us too far into the realms of the impossible.

Loyally, my supersonic flight advisor said it would never work, could not achieve its objective. The Admiral disagreed . . . maybe not today . . . but in six years?

Their good-natured disagreement, conducted over several high-tech weeks, has, I hope, brought *H.M.S. Unseen* (the novel) home with suitable grim reality, and I thank them both.

My thanks, too, to my two Scottish advisors (rural, geographic, and social), Penelope Enthoven and Olivia Oaks. For insights and religious advice concerning the Muslim faith, I am indebted to the kindly and patient Syed Nawshadmir (Ronnie), originally from Dhaka, Bangladesh, and now of Dublin, Ireland.

—PATRICK ROBINSON

PROLOGUE

January 17, 2006.

IT WAS A MORNING OF SAVAGE COLD. THE RAW, ravenous January wind hurled snow at the driver's side of the car as it crunched along a freezing man-made ravine, between drifts plowed 12 feet high. It had been snowing now for more than three months in Newfoundland, as it usually did. But Bart Hamm did not care, and he chuckled at the local radio DJ's banter as he pressed on through the howling polar blizzard of his homeland, heading resolutely for the big transatlantic air base outside the eastern town of Gander.

Bart had been working there for ten years, and he was used to the steadiness of the job, the routines, and the regimentation. Unlike most of the coastal population of the island, he never had to worry about the cold. All through the autumn and winter, the weather in Newfoundland is unthinkable, except to a polar bear, or possibly an Eskimo. But Bart was guided by one solitary

1

thought. *Whatever the disadvantages may be to this job, whatever the freedoms I have sacrificed, it's a helluva lot better than being out in a fishing boat.*

Bart was the first male member of his family in five generations not to have gone to sea. The Hamms were from the tiny port of St. Anthony, way up on the northern peninsula. Down the years, since the middle of the nineteenth century, they had treasured their independence, earning a harsh living from the dark, sullen waters that surge around the Labrador coast and the western Atlantic.

In the past century, the Hamms had been saltbankers, sailing the big schooners out to the Grand Banks for cod; they had fished for turbot from the draggers; trapped deepwater lobsters; hunted seals on the ice at the end of winter. A lot of teak-hard, rock-steady men named Hamm had drowned in this most dangerous of industries, three in one day back in the early eighties, when a fishing boat out of St. Anthony iced up and capsized in a gale east of Grey Islands.

Bart's father was lost in that incident, and his only son had never quite recovered from the ordeal of waiting helplessly, with his mother and sister, for six hours in the snow on the little town jetty. Every thirty minutes, in a biting nor'easter, they had walked up to the harbormaster's shed, and Bart had never forgotten the old man speaking into the radio, repeating over and over, "*This is St. Anthony . . . come in* Seabird II . . . *come in* Seabird II . . . *PLEASE come in* Seabird II." But there had always been just silence.

That had been twenty-three years ago, when Bart was thirteen; it was the day when he knew that, whatever else, he was never going to become a fisherman.

Bart was a typical member of the Hamm family: thoughtful, quiet, accepting, and as strong as a stud bull. He was a good mathematician and won a scholarship to the Memorial University of Newfoundland in St. John's, where he earned two degrees, one in mathematics, one in physics.

He had the perfect temperament for an air traffic control

officer, and he settled into a well-paid place in one of the warmest most protected modern buildings in the entire country. Stormswept ATC Gander was where they checked in every incoming transatlantic flight to Canada and the northern U.S.A., the big passenger jets heading back into the world from the huge freezing sky that umbrellas the desolate North Atlantic waters of the 30-degree line of longitude.

That day, driving through the snow, at 0630 in the morning, headlights cutting through the endless winter darkness, Bart was starting a seven-hour shift with an hour's break midway. He would begin at the busiest part of the morning, because anytime after seven, they would be talking to a different airliner every three minutes. You had to stay alert, on top of your game, every moment of your shift. The Gander Station was a key ingredient in Atlantic air traffic safety, inevitably the first to know of any problem.

Bart loved the job. He had excellent powers of concentration, and his rise to supervisor would not be long in coming. His shift began at 0700, which was 1200 or 1300 in western Europe. And he began to talk into his headset almost immediately upon arriving at his station, connected on the HF radio to the great armada of passenger jets trundling westward, identifying themselves in their airline's code, then reporting their height, speed, and position.

At 0717 he was talking to the copilot of a Lufthansa Boeing 747, out on 40 West, handing him a weather check, confirming the position of an offshore blizzard to the south, off the coast of Maine.

Two minutes later he picked up a new call, and his heart, as always, just skipped a beat. This was Concorde, British Airways supersonic star of the North Atlantic, streaking across the sky at 1,330 m.p.h. Bart heard a calm British voice saying, *"Good morning, Gander . . . Speedbird Concorde 001 . . . flight level five-four-zero to New York . . . MACH-2. . . . 50 North, 30 West at 1219 GMT . . . ETA 40 West 1241 GMT. . . . Over."*

Bart replied carefully, *"Roger that, Speedbird 001 . . . we'll be waiting 1241 . . . . Over."*

The information was entered on his screen, and at 0738 Bart was waiting. Concorde was usually a couple of minutes early calling in because of the high speed at which she crossed the lines of longitude. To cover the 450 miles between 30 West and 40 West, she required only twenty-two minutes.

At 0740 he was still waiting, but nothing was coming through from the cockpit of the packed British superstar racing through the skies out on the very edge of space.

Bart Hamm already had a distinctly uneasy feeling. He watched the digital clock in front of him go to 0741 and knew that Concorde must be well past 40 West. But where the hell was she? At 0743.40 he opened his High Frequency line and went to SELCAL (selective calling), the Concorde's private voice-frequency channel inside the cockpit. But there was no reply.

Transmitting directly, he had already caused two warning tones to sound in Concorde's cockpit to alert the pilots to his signals. Seconds later Bart transmitted a radio signal designed to light up two amber bulbs, right in the pilot's line of vision.

"Speedbird *001 . . . this is Gander . . . how do you read?* . . . Speedbird *001 . . . this is Gander . . . how do you read?*"

By now Bart Hamm's heart was pounding. He felt as if he were driving the supersonic jet himself, and he willed the voice of the British pilot to come crackling onto the headset. But there was nothing. "Speedbird *001 . . . this is Gander . . . how do you read?*" Unaccountably frightened now, Bart raised his voice and departed from procedural wording . . . "Speedbird *001 . . . please come in . . . PLEASE come in.*"

He checked his own electronic connections, checked every step he was taking. But he could not remove the lump in his throat, and, unaccountably, a new image stood before his mind. The one that still awakened him on stormy nights, the image of that terrible morning on the quayside at St. Anthony, when he stood in the snow, and then in the radio shed, clutching his mother's hand, praying for news of his lost father, the skipper of the missing fishing boat *Seabird II*.

He tried one more time, calling through to the cockpit of *Speedbird* 001. And his hand was shaking as he finally pressed the switch to summon his supervisor. At 0745 Concorde should have been more than 100 miles beyond 40 West, and continued radio silence could only be the dread harbinger of disaster because this aircraft was nothing short of a flying high-tech masterpiece, in which electronic backup was layered *threefold*.

At that precise time, Gander Air Traffic Control sounded the alarm that a major passenger airliner was almost certainly down in the North Atlantic. They alerted British Airways, plus the international search and rescue wavebands. They also alerted the Canadian and U.S. Navies.

The drills were routine and precise. Commanding officers were ordered to divert ships into the area where Concorde must have hit the ocean. And as they did so, the haunted face of Bart Hamm was still staring into his screen, listening through his headset.

And his urgent, despairing voice was still broadcasting, unanswered, on a private frequency, out toward the edge of space "Speedbird *001 . . . this is Gander . . . this is Gander Oceanic Control . . . please come in* Speedbird *. . . PLEASE answer . . .* Speedbird *001.*"

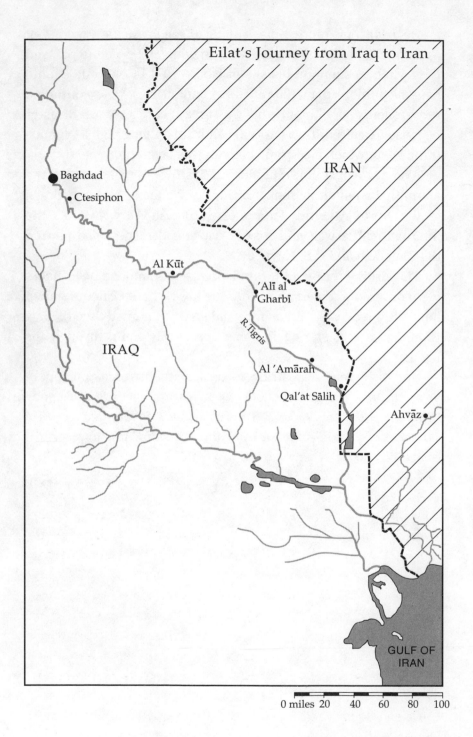

May 26, 2004.

THE LIGHT WAS FADING ALONG HAIFA STREET, AND IT was almost impossible to spot any Westerners in that seething, poor section of Baghdad. Men in *djellabas*, long loose shirts, occupied much of the dirty sidewalks, sitting cross-legged, smoking water pipes, selling small items of jewelry and copper. On one side of the main thoroughfare, dark narrow streets ran off toward the slow-flowing Tigris River.

Tiny car workshops were somehow crammed along there between the cramped decaying houses. The stifling smell of oil and axle grease mingled with the dark aromas of thick, black, sweet coffee, incense, charcoal fires, cinnamon, sandalwood, and baking bread. Not many children wore shoes, and the dress was Arab.

He should have stood out a mile, wearing a smoothly cut, grey Western suit, as he hurried out from the inner canyon of a green-painted garage. The club tie should have given him away; certainly the highly polished shoes. But he turned around as he walked out, and he embraced the elderly, oil-coated mechanic with warmth and affection. And he stared hard into the man's eyes—an unmistakable Arab gesture, the gesture of a Bedouin.

No doubt, the man was an Arab, and he caused few heads to turn as he headed back west toward Haifa Street, cramming a length of electrical wire into his pocket. He seemed at home there in that crowded, sprawling market, striding past the fruit and vegetable stalls, nodding at the occasional purveyor of spices or the seller of rugs. He held his head high, and the dark, trimmed beard gave him the facial look of an ancient caliph. His name was obscure, foreign-sounding to an Arab. They called him Eilat. But, in the circles that knew his trade, he was formally referred to as Eilat One.

He made just one more stop, at a dingy hardware store 40 yards before the left turn onto the Ahrar Bridge. When he emerged ten minutes later, he was carrying a white box with a lightbulb pictured on the outside, and a roll of heavy duty, wide, grey plastic tape, the regular kind that holds United Parcel packages together all over the world.

Eilat kept walking fast, sometimes straying off the sidewalk to avoid stragglers. He was thickset in build, no more than five feet ten inches tall. He crossed the bridge into the Rusafah side of Baghdad and made his way up Rashid Street. In his left jacket pocket there was a small leather box containing Iraq's national Medal of Honor, which had been presented to him personally that morning by the somewhat erratic President of the country. The coveted medal counted, he feared, for little.

There had been something in the manner of the President that he had found disturbing. They did not know each other well, but there had been an uneasy distance between them. The President was known for his almost ecstatic greetings to those who had served him faithfully, but there had been no such display of emotion that morning. Eilat One had been greeted as a stranger and had left as a stranger. He had been escorted in by two guards and was escorted out by the same men. The President had seemed to avoid eye contact.

And now the forty-four-year-old Intelligence agent experienced the same chill that men of his calling have variously felt over the years in most countries in the world—the icy realization that no matter what their achievements, the past had gone, time had rolled forward. The spy was being sent back out into the cold. Or, put another way, the spy had gone beyond his usefulness to his master. In the case of Eilat One, he might simply have become too important. And there was only one solution for that.

Eilat believed they were going to kill him. He further believed they were going to kill him that same night. He guessed there was already a surveillance team watching his little house, set in a narrow alley up toward Al-Jamouri Street. He would be wary, and he would be calmly self-controlled. There could be only one possible outcome to any attempted assassination.

Still walking swiftly, he reached the great wide-open expanse of Rusata Square. The streetlights were on now, but this square needed no extra illumination. A 50-foot-high portrait of the President was floodlit by more voltage than all the city streetlights put together. Eilat swung right, casting his eyes away from the searing dazzle of his leader, and he pressed on eastward toward the great adjoining Amin Square, with its mosques and cheap hotels.

He walked more slowly, tucking his white box under his arm and staying to the right, hard against the buildings. The traffic was heavy, but he had no need to leave the sidewalk, and unconsciously he slipped into the soft steps of the Bedouin, moving lightly, feeling in the small of his back the handle of the long, stiletto-bladed tribal knife, his constant companion in times of personal threat.

He followed the late shoppers into Al-Jamouri Street and slowed almost to a stop as he reached an alleyway beside a small hotel. Then he quickened again and walked straight past, with only a passing glance into the narrow walkway, with its one dim streetlight about halfway along. He saw that the alley was empty, with two cars parked at the far end. They were empty, too, unless the passengers were curled up on the floor. Eilat had excellent eyesight, and he was good at remembering pictures in his mind.

He stopped completely, standing, apparently distracted, outside the hotel, looking at his watch, checking the passersby, watching for someone who hesitated, someone who might slow down and stop, just as he had done. Twenty seconds later, he moved into the alley and walked slowly toward the narrow white door that opened through a high stone wall and led across the courtyard into the Baghdad headquarters of Eilat One.

He heard with satisfaction the rusty grind and squeak of the hinges on the outside gate. He walked past an old bicycle and opened the door to his dark, cool house noiselessly. *I wonder if they'll come in friendship,* he wondered to himself. *Or will they just come busting in with a Kalashnikov and blow the place apart.*

He turned on the light in the wide downstairs hall and checked the setting on the low laser beam he had installed to inform him whether *anyone* had entered during his absence. There had been no one. And the white light on the wall panel, which flickered red if anyone opened a window, was steady.

On reflection, he thought, *they will probably try to take me out in the small hours of the morning. Stealth will be their method, and I suspect they will use knives. Messy, but silent. At least, that's what I'd do, were I a simple paid assassin. I can't see them risking gunfire, and I can't imagine them confronting me, even in friendship. Not with my current reputation.*

It was after eight o'clock, and Eilat went to work with two screwdrivers, a large one for driving a bracket into the wall, a small one, for electrical connections. "The key to murder in the dead of night," he muttered, "is vision. Night vision."

When his tasks were completed, he placed a solid wooden chair behind the door, turned out every light, drew the shades across the windows, and there, in the pitch-black, settled down to wait. With his eyes open wide, straining through the dark, he tried to make out shapes, but it took a full twenty minutes before he could distinguish the curved outline of the water pitcher on the table at the end of the hall.

Midnight came and went. And still Eilat waited calmly. He hoped there would not be more than three of them . . . but . . . if there were . . . Well, so be it. At 1:00 A.M. he stood up and walked to the pitcher and poured himself a drink, splashing the water into a stone cup without spilling it. Then he walked back to his chair behind the door without crashing into it. His night vision, which was perfect now, he would use to best advantage. The last thing he wanted was equal terms.

They came for him at precisely nineteen minutes after 2:00 A.M. Eilat heard the gate squeak and the doorknob turn. The first man entered silently, dressed in dark combat gear with desert boots. A second man, sensed rather than observed, followed the first; and Eilat remained by the door, standing with his eyes clenched shut, his hands covering his face, protecting his night vision from the glow of the city outside.

Suddenly, very suddenly, without opening his eyes, he moved. Raising his right foot, he booted the door shut with a shuddering impact. Then he turned toward the wall again, his eyes still clenched tight.

The two visitors turned automatically to the slammed door, and, as they did so, the big theater lightbulb set above it came on with blinding brightness, catching them in its ferocious glare. For a split second the two men stood transfixed, like rabbits in a spotlight. Their hands flew to their faces, but it was too late. The bulb had been on for only two seconds, but their night vision was completely lost, at a vital moment for them both. And Eilat still had his.

He moved quickly behind the unseeing first man and crashed a smooth, heavy glass paperweight into the critical nerve center behind the right ear. Then he delivered the same blackout blow to the second assassin, after which he turned and softly opened the door. "I suppose they have a lookout," he muttered. "I may have to kill him as well."

Walking swiftly across the yard, he ignored the gate and climbed to the top of the wall, using an old wooden bench. For two minutes he scoured the alley, watching for a movement, any movement, a person, any person. But there was nothing.

Finally, he stepped down and walked back into the house, into the main room, switched on a small desk light, and collected his roll of sticky plastic packing tape. Slowly, with steady efficiency, he bound together the wrists and ankles of the unconscious intruders, using layers of tape. Then he placed one wide, thick piece right across each of their mouths and arranged the two inert bodies to his satisfaction. One, he dragged down the middle of the hall. The other, he lifted and carefully arranged, resting the man's head and shoulders across the first man's chest.

Right after that he went into the kitchen and poured himself a cup of coffee that had been percolating for several hours. It was exactly eleven minutes since Eilat had floored his assailants. He returned to the hall holding his knife and positioned himself right behind the head of the uppermost man, who was just regaining consciousness.

Leaning over, he made a small incision in the left-hand side of the throat. With a surgical twist of the knife, he severed the jugular vein, stepping back quickly to avoid the spurting blood from the third largest blood vessel in the human body. Then he walked back to the kitchen and finished his coffee.

Grunts from the prostrate man on the floor drew him back to the hall a few minutes later. The lead assassin's eyes were wide-open with terror, as his colleague bled messily to death all over him. There was almost a half gallon of blood now saturating the two men, and it was still pumping out of the neck wound.

"*Salam aleikum*—perhaps sooner than you think," said Eilat. "I expect you've noticed I just cut your assistant's jugular in half. In a few moments I shall have absolutely no hesitation in doing precisely the same to you. That would give you about eight minutes to live. It takes that long, you know . . . I mean unloading six pints of blood. He's just about gone now. I should wish him well in the arms of Allah."

Eilat walked away, seemingly indifferent to the frenzied head-shaking, two-footed kicking, and muffled screams of the man who still lived. But when he returned he was once more carrying the knife.

Again he leaned over, careful to avoid getting blood on his suit, and placed the sharp tip of the weapon firmly against the assassin's neck. And now he spoke with a hard edge to his voice. "If you want to live, you will tell me precisely who sent you, you will tell me precisely who issued your orders, and from where they came. You will speak softly when I remove the tape on your mouth. If I suspect a lie, you'll be off to join your colleague. If you speak too loudly, you'll meet him even quicker. It takes about eight minutes, you know."

With his left hand, he slowly ripped the tape-gag from the man's lips. Then with his right, he pressed the knife harder into the neck, without making a cut, and said,: "Speak, softly and truthfully."

"President, sir. He ordered it," he blurted. Trembling uncontrollably, gibbering, and begging, he poured the facts out. "Nossir . . . please don't kill me . . . I have wife . . . children, please not, sir . . . yes, President . . . he tell my boss . . . I saw you in the office today . . . the man you kill on top of me was one of your escorts . . . yessir . . . President . . . yessir . . . he say you die after midnight . . . quietly . . . please, sir . . . please don't kill me . . . I had no choice but to obey."

Eilat removed the knife and stuck a new piece of tape hard across the man's mouth. Then he walked back into the main room and took from a drawer three passports and some documents from a travel agent. He straightened his tie, buttoned his jacket, and moved back into the hall, putting the passports and documents on the table by the water pitcher, in plain view of the blood-soaked, but still-living, assassin.

He went into the bathroom and collected his shaving gear, toothpaste, and soap, and reemerged holding a small smart-looking leather case. Then he turned out all the lights and sat quietly in the dark for fifteen minutes while the irises in his dark eyes slowly grew larger, restoring his night vision. Eventually he stood up, and said casually, "Well, I'm going now. And I won't be back for a while . . . rather a long journey . . . I expect they'll send someone for you in a few hours . . . By the way, you don't have a lookout posted in the alley, do you? Don't lie to me, because if I have to kill him, I'll return immediately to this room and kill you."

He felt the man shake his head feverishly. "Very well, old chap," said Eilat. "I expect you won't want to see me again. Nor will you, unless, of course, you have lied to me."

The petrified palace guard nodded firmly. Eilat stepped out into the courtyard and swiftly took off his suit, shirt, tie, and shoes. From a cloth bag behind the bicycle he produced old, soiled Arab robes, with a turban and leather-thong shoes. He stuffed his Western clothes into the sack and slung it over his shoulder. Then, adopting the stooped posture of an elderly man, he pushed the bike out into the alley and made his way, limping painfully, to the far end, away from Al-Jamouri Street.

The disgustingly dirty little garret he had rented for more than a year was on the top floor of a small block of apartments, less than 50 yards from his house, on the same tiny street. Within moments, Eilat had left the bicycle in the downstairs hall and climbed the three flights of stairs.

Once inside, he shaved his beard, leaving just a thick black moustache, and prepared his mind and person for his chosen new life—as a street peddler—which would see him plying his wares in Rashid's copper and gold bazaars for at least the next month.

During this time, the president's security men would place an iron grip on every airport, seaport, bus and rail terminal in the country, while they tried to run down Iraq's most wanted Intelligence officer. The one with the three passports.

If they searched this land for a thousand years, mused Eilat, as he cleaned his razor, *I suppose they'd never, ever look for me along the street in which I vanished. My last-known position.*

One Month Later.

Baghdad had simmered for four days in flaming June temperatures of around 110 degrees. Not even the nights had brought in a
cooling breeze off the eastern edges of the Syrian desert. There
had been terrible dust storms out in the central plains all week,
and the winds were hot, and Baghdad's population of four million was wilting under the anvil of the sun. Nonetheless, Eilat
had to go.

He waited until ten o'clock on the night of June 26, then gathered up his heavy cloth sack and cleared his room. He collected
his bicycle from the downstairs hall, and the heat hit him like a
blast from a furnace as he shambled out into the dark alley.

By the time he reached Al-Jamouri Street he was already sweating heavily. But once on the wide thoroughfare, he mounted the old
bike and set off slowly, in a southeasterly direction, heading for the
great bend in the Tigris, where it suddenly swings west around the
university, and then east again, in a 9-mile loop out on the southern
edge of the city.

Eilat was fit, but he was deliberately overweight. In the past
month he had gained 14 pounds on a careful diet of chicken, lamb,
rice, and pita bread at least twice a day. Finally, he was leaving,
and, as he had remarked to the man whose life he had so carefully
spared a month before, he might not be back for some time.

He pedaled gently, making for the long sweep of the Dora
Expressway, right where it crosses the river. The city was darker
and quieter down there, along Sadoun Street, and only a few people were walking in Fateh Square. Eilat kept going until he could
make out the huge yawning overpass of the expressway, just as it
becomes a truly spectacular bridge.

He dismounted there and turned off the public roads, pushing
the bike in the dark until he came into the shadow of the bridge,
where he dumped the bike under a clump of bushes and began
his long lonely journey on foot, down the banks of the Tigris. It
was the great river of his boyhood, and he was aware this might
be his last walk beside its quietly flowing brown waters.

It would be a long journey downstream, 225 miles, the route laid out in detail, but without one name penciled in, on a hand-drawn map he carried in the pocket of his robe. It was a critical drawing to him, but complete gibberish to anyone else. He also carried with him a tiny military compass he had owned for many years. He intended to proceed at the speed of Napoleon's army on its way to Moscow—four miles every hour with full packs and muskets. If he could find shade, he would sleep by day and walk through the dark, which was a little cooler, but not much. As he proceeded south toward the marsh, the humidity would become stifling, and he guessed he would lose weight every day. If there was no shade, he would keep walking, beneath the glare of the desert sun.

Eilat was a Bedouin by birth, and he possessed the Bedouin pride that he alone could survive in the pitiless summer climate of his homeland, that he could go without food for days if he had to, and that he was not intimidated by even the worst dust storm. Water he carried with him, but he would not require so much as other men.

He wished, not for the first time, that he still had access to one of his father's camels. If he closed his eyes, he could easily imagine the tireless, swaying rhythm of the stride, the endless beat of the wide hooves on the desert floor. But that was all in his long-lost youth, out on the rim of the central plains, a long way north up the river, when life had been simple, and he had been a true son of Iraq.

Iraq—the country that had used him for years, often under circumstances of unthinkable danger, then betrayed him in the most brutal way possible.

Eilat inwardly seethed at the injustice of the treatment handed out to him by the President. He had seen the coldness in the man's eyes when he presented the Medal of Honor, and he still failed to understand why he should have been singled out for summary execution, after all he had done to achieve greatness for his nation.

In the past, they had paid him, and paid him well. He still had close to $1 million on deposit in four banks around the world.

And he had some cash with him, dinars and rials. But the thought kept returning: The President had not just rejected him, he had wished him dead. And in the space of just one month, he, Eilat One, had redirected all of the hatred in his soul, the hatred that had sustained him through the loneliest years, to a new enemy.

In the Arabian mind, the great flagstaff of pride stands tall. In the Bedouin mind, it is unbending. The biblical concept of revenge is universal in Iraq, accepted by all. Time is no barrier. There is no time. In a land which has survived for 6,000 years, a year is only a heartbeat, a decade just an interval. Eilat would have his revenge. Of that he was certain. He had spent his life in the service of his country, never marrying, never loving, except once. And the realization of the years wasted, squandered on an unfaithful master, burned into his mind as he walked steadily along the eastern bank of the dark Tigris.

The moon was bright by midnight, and it lit his way. Out to the left he could see car headlights in the distance, on the main road connecting Baghdad to the southern port of Basra. If he had crossed the sparse sandy flatlands between the river and the highway, he could probably have picked up a ride, or even a bus, and the flat terrain of the road, and its hard shoulder, would have been easier to walk upon. But Eilat was a wanted man, on the run in his own country, and he did not wish to be seen up close by anyone. He supposed the Army and the police had descriptions of him, and that he was now branded a murderer and an enemy of the state. Which, he considered a bit depressing but considerably better than being dead.

He smiled when he imagined how long and determinedly they must have searched for a smartly dressed, bearded businessman, in Western clothes, heading abroad. The chances of anyone connecting such a man with this scruffy country Arab, walking south, with his peddler's sack and the stooped gait of an old man, were, he knew, remote. But Eilat was not into remote. He operated only on cold-blooded near certainty. If no one saw him, he could not be recognized. And he continued through the hot night, moving over the sands as swiftly as he could, but not so fast as Napoleon.

The sun came throbbing up into the eastern sky shortly before six. In the distance Eilat could see the ancient remains of the Parthian city of Ctesiphon, which lay on the banks of the river, 20 miles south of Baghdad. The great vaulted arch that was built in the second century B.C., still dominated the ruins, and he could just make it out in the dawnlight. He still had forty-five minutes more to walk, and took his first drink of the new day, swallowing almost a pint of water. He could, he knew, refill his two leather flasks somewhere in the old city.

By eight o'clock the sun was high, the temperature on its way to 110 degrees. Eilat found the only café deserted, and he sat alone in a corner facing the wall, devouring a large breakfast of eggs, toast, and chicken with rice. He drank orange juice and coffee, and paid them to fill his water holders. The price was minimal compared to the city.

The next stretch of the river, winding all the way down to Al-Kut, a distance of 100 miles, was not a walk which held any appeal for Eilat. The flat landscape, hammered brown by the sun, was practically bereft of life, human or plant. He knew he would occasionally pass scattered date palms close to the water, tended by kind and generous rural families, who would perhaps offer him a drink. And they would want to talk. But he had nothing to say to them anymore. The President had made him an outcast in his own land, and he already felt foreign, as if he must hide all of his inner thoughts even from simple country people, people for whom he had once been prepared to die.

But perhaps that had been inevitable anyway, because he had spent so many years away, and now the men in power felt he could never be completely trusted. He could understand that thought process; just. But the blind injustice of it represented to Eilat a violation of his honor. And that he was unable to live with.

He left the café before ten and wandered out to the ruined outskirts of Ctesiphon, avoiding people, searching for a quiet, sheltered, north-facing place to sleep until the late afternoon, when he would eat and drink again, before setting off on his second night trek.

He found a small, low, dusty building of only three stone sides and a roof, a building that faced back up the river, the way he had come. It was hot and gloomy inside, but it was in deep shade. Eilat was exhausted, and breakfast had made him sleepy. But first he turned toward the back wall on a bearing of two-zero-five, a line down which, more than 800 miles distant, lay the most holy Muslim city, Mecca. Eilat faced that way as he knelt in the dust and humbled himself, seeking the forgiveness of his God.

He slept for eight hours, undisturbed, his head on his soft water bags, his right hand on the handle of his desert knife beneath the robe. The ground was rough and hard, but he lay still and ignored it.

Because the deprivations of life are the heritage of those who spring from the sands of Arabia, no matter how far he had journeyed, Eilat was always aware of that unspoken truth, that he could withstand anything in this wild, burning hot land of his birth. It was as if some distant call from the Syrian desert of his forefathers could still be heard within him . . . *Remember who you really are. You will always be a Bedouin.*

By eight he was under way, walking along the river, wishing it ran a straighter course, hoping not to meet anyone, cursing the ground upon which the President of Iraq walked. Eilat wondered what the future held for him. He had a plan, but it might not work. For the first time in his entire life he faced the world alone, entirely alone. The cord that had joined him for so long to Iraq was severed, and it could never be repaired.

He walked generally southeast with the river—and he walked for almost four days, alone and, so far as he knew, unobserved. He spoke to no one, and eked out his water and his pita bread. The sun was pitiless during the day, but shade was so sparse his planned schedule went awry almost immediately. And so he just slept when he could and walked the rest of the time, making on average 25 miles a day, without incident, and with the loss of some 10 pounds in body weight.

On the first day of July, late in the afternoon, six miles north of the riverside town of Al-Kut, he spotted up ahead his first potential problem. There on the edge of a small grove of date palms was a camouflaged Iraqi Army jeep. He could see no sign of local farmers, there was no house, and the area seemed completely desolate. But there were two uniformed soldiers leaning against the vehicle, about 200 yards ahead of him. It was just too late to stop or turn off the path. They must have seen him, and, despite the comforting sanctity of his Arab robe, complete now with the customary red-checkered headdress, Eilat knew they might very well ask to see his identification documents.

By then he was walking with a long wooden stick he had cut, and he slowed slightly as he made his approach, limping, stooping forward. He did not avert his gaze and continued walking, straight at the jeep, straight toward the soldiers, each of whom carried a short-barreled machine gun, probably old-design Russian.

He was almost level when the senior man spoke, brusquely, with authority.

"Hey, old man . . . Iraqi?"

Eilat nodded and kept going, moving past them, exaggerating the limp. For a split second, he thought they would ignore him, but then the soldier spoke again.

"WAIT!"

Eilat was not surprised. He was moving into a particularly sensitive area of his country. Al-Kut was the town where the Tigris splits, and where the great drainage program to dry out the marshes had been in place for many years. It was a program designed to destroy the wild wetland homes of the ancient Marsh Arabs, who were believed to have lived there for the entire 6,000 years of the region's history. In the opinion of Saddam Hussein, those watery miles had become a haven for deserters from the Army, and even for Iranian insurgents. Gangs of ex-Army personnel still roamed the vast overgrown areas where water remained. Eilat knew the place was crawling with soldiers because it was still believed to be somewhat out of control. Drier, but still out of control.

He obeyed the command of the Iraqi officer, turning slowly and saying softly the traditional greeting of the desert, "*Salam aleikum,*" Peace be upon you.

The officer was a man of around thirty-five, tall and thin, with a hooked beak of a nose, hooded dark eyes, and a full mouth. He did not smile.

"Documents?"

"I have none, sir," replied Eilat in Arabic. "I'm just a poor traveler."

"Traveling to where?"

"I'm looking for my son, sir. I heard from him last in An-Nasiriya three years ago. I have no money except for a few dinars, enough for some bread in Kut."

"And then you plan to walk right down the Shatt al Gharraf . . . 120 miles?"

"Yessir."

"On a loaf of bread, on your own, with no documents?"

"Yessir."

"Where do you live?"

"In Baghdad, sir. In the south of the city."

"A city Arab with no documents?" His tone was questioning. "And what do you carry in that bag?"

"Just water, sir."

"Show me," said the officer, uttering the two words that would end his life.

Eilat turned away, but he came back as fast as a striking cobra, jamming the end of his stick with colossal force into the small space between the officer's eyes above the bridge of his nose. All three men heard the bone of his forehead splinter, but it was the last sound the Iraqi soldier ever heard. Eilat slammed the butt of his right hand upward into the great beaked nose, effectively ramming the bone into the man's brain.

The younger soldier just stood there, his mouth open with total amazement, as this elderly, crippled traveler killed his commanding officer in two seconds flat. He held his hands open wide, trying to speak, perhaps to surrender. But it was too late for that. Eilat was on him with his knife, thrusting it between the ribs straight into the young man's heart. He was dead before he hit the sand.

Eilat kicked and rolled the two bodies under the jeep, located the toolbox, and shoved that under there with them. Then he cut and sliced three long strips of material from the front seat, tied them together, and shoved them into the petrol tank. He pulled them out and made a jury-rigged strip, about six feet long, going back into the tank. He lit one gasoline-soaked end and hurled himself into the sand 20 feet away as the jeep blew up in a blast of flame and black smoke. Then he picked up his bag and stick and fled the blazing wreck, racing along the river for more than two miles before he finally slowed and resumed his careful, stooping, old man's gait. He hoped the burned-out jeep and corpses would not be discovered for a few hours, but he did not bank on it.

"Anyway, who would suspect me?" he muttered. "It'll take them a few days to run an autopsy on the soldiers—a few days before they find out they were taken out by a professional." But he thanked God for the training of the military in which he had served—especially for the courses he had attended in unarmed and armed combat. He had finished first in both of them, as he had finished first in every course he had ever taken.

He reached Kut by nightfall, limping into the city. Food was easy to find, and he purchased grilled lamb and rice with extra pita bread from a street trader. He refilled his water bottles from a hose at a gas station and slept on a bench in a dark corner of the bus depot. So far as he knew, only the curbside cook had seen his newly bearded face, and even then he had kept his head well down, mumbling his order and offering no conversation.

Eilat left before dawn, following the river as it swung east away from the city toward the Iranian border. His little map marked the spot 80 miles farther on at the oasis settlement of Ali Al Garbi, where the wide stream would turn southward again, toward the Gulf—and the marshes.

For four more days and nights he walked and slept intermittently, both under the raging desert sun and through the unbearably hot and clammy nights. He saw few travelers, spoke to no one, and ate and drank only what he carried with him. His ration was three pieces of bread and four pints of water every twenty-four hours. Twice each day he would move down to the river and immerse himself in the waters. Then he would walk on, in cool but heavy robes, which dried out all too quickly.

He arrived exhausted and dehydrated in Ali Al Garbi just before midnight on July 5. He located a water pump in the middle of the town and stood drinking alone in the dark for almost ten minutes. He filled his water bags again and found an abandoned market stall on the sand, where he slept until dawn. He was two days away from al'Amarah, which was a much bigger town, but there was nothing along the route. Thus Eilat could not leave Garbi without replenishing his food supply. And he hoped there would be a café that opened early.

His luck, which had held for a long time, ran out there. Nothing opened until nine, and Eilat was obliged to wait around for three hours. He finally ate breakfast, drank copious amounts of fruit juice, and found another shop to buy bread for the journey. Because of the heat, he was wary of taking even prepacked meat, but he risked a few tomatoes and some tired green local lettuce leaves. In the second shop he had noticed a newspaper which carried a front-page photograph of a burned-out Army jeep, under the headline:

IRAQI SOLDIERS DIE REPAIRING ARMY VEHICLE.

It took him another three and a half days to reach his turning point at Qal At Salih, deep in the eastern marshes, only 30 miles from the Iranian border. It was easily the most hellish part of the journey. The unforgiving sun beat down from morning to night, the days grew hotter as he went south, and the humidity became worse. He was now 16 pounds below his regular weight, and the insects that hovered above the still waters were vicious. Eilat used his spray sparingly, when the mosquitoes were at their worst. He stuck to the river, and he knew that out to the east were the surviving ancient lands of the Madan, the Marsh Arabs.

Away to the right, on the west side of the river, Saddam Hussein had drained hundreds of square miles of the marshes right down to the confluence of the Tigris and the Euphrates. For hundreds of years those wetlands had provided a haven for slaves, Bedouins, and those who had offended against the state. The area was accessible only by small boats, and no army, however determined, had ever successfully operated in that treacherous swampland. Saddam had a solution to that. He diverted the rivers and built a couple of gigantic canals to cut off the water supply to the entire al'Amarah Marsh. The result was a dry, arid, silted-up land, in which an entire ecosystem was decimated. A huge range of wading birds, storks, pelicans, and eagles—not to mention another vast range of fish, small mammals, and people—lost their homes.

Marsh Arabs, whose families had lived there for thousands of years, were forced to leave, as the Army of Iraq in the 1980s drove through the dried-up swamps, laying down great causeways for armored vehicles to move more easily to the east, to Iraq's smoldering enemy across the Iranian border.

Eilat did not approve of the drying program. But at that moment he was much more concerned with his side of the river, where the great surviving marsh stretched for 50 miles, to the border and on into Iran, toward the foothills of the Zagros Mountains.

He rested for a whole day at Qal At Salih, regaining his strength after his sixteen-day march from Baghdad. He ate chicken, lamb and rice, fruit and vegetables. But he still risked no other human contact except for the two elderly street traders who served him. And in the late afternoon of July 12 he turned away from the Tigris for the first time and set off through the marshes for the border. His little map marked the causeways he could follow, but there were no road signs, and his navigational guides were simple. The Pole Star would show him due north, and so long as the sun rose dead ahead, he was on the right bearing.

Eilat intended to walk until dawn, until he could see the watery landscape. That meant eleven hours, including three stops, and he expected to cover close to 25 miles in the long humid night. He knew that the moon, sixteen days after it was full, would be no help at all. And he must take care not to walk over the edge of the path, into the swamp. But he was a man with excellent night vision.

Unsurprisingly, he met no one throughout the walking hours. The waters were low at that time of the year, and many of the nomadic buffalo herders had moved to the rivers. Occasionally, Eilat would spot the dim lights of a small cluster of houses set on poles above the water—*sarifas*, with their ornate latticework entrances. Outside in the shadows, moored in the high reeds, he could see the long, slender poling canoes—the *mashufs*, which are just about the only boat that can operate efficiently in the long lagoons and shallow lakes. Not many designs hold up for 6,000 years.

When the sun rose, dead ahead, thankfully for Eilat, he was seven miles short of Iran. The causeway he now walked was wide and firm. For it was along here in September of 1980 that the great armored division of Saddam's army had mounted its opening attack on Iraq's Persian neighbors, roaring through to the old capital of the border province of Khuzestan—the city of Ahvaz, to which Eilat was headed.

However, a patrolled frontier lay directly ahead, and the former Iraqi Intelligence officer had no wish to cross swords again with forces of the government of Iraq, or indeed Iran. He had an Iranian passport, but he nonetheless elected to lie low all day, then make his crossing by night, heading for the tiny border town of Taq-e Bostan. He ventured no closer in the daylight hours and finally made his move at 11:00 P.M. Two hours and forty-five minutes later, in the small hours of July 14 in the year 2004, he slipped into the Islamic Republic of Iran, crossing illegally the unseen line dividing two of the world's most implacable enemies.

He was still in the marsh, but soon the land would rise and become drier. Ahvaz was 60 miles distant, with two towns along the way, Taq-e Bostan and Susangerd, where he could eat and find water. Ahvaz was more appealing. He had arranged to pick up a letter there, and he could purchase new clothes, Iranian dress, find a decent meal, and board the train for the long journey to Isfahan, almost 500 miles away across the great range of the Zagros.

It was eight o'clock on the evening of July 17. Directly to the south of where he walked, Eilat could see clearly the bright lights of the sprawling industrial city three miles away. All along the north side of Ahvaz were huge oil refineries, burning off excess gases twenty-four hours a day. These towering beacons lit up the city permanently. It never got really dark in Ahvaz.

Eilat changed back into his Western clothes a half mile from the city's boundary. He dumped his Arab robes and bag, and strolled up to the main square, Meidun-e Shohada. From there he located the Hotel Bozorg-e Fajr, checked into the best room he could find, at $75 a night, immersed himself in a hot bath, and made one phone call. Then he persuaded a rather sullen room-service waiter to bring him sandwiches and coffee while he awaited the arrival of the *talabeh*, the young theological student who would take him to the meeting place.

That took another forty-five minutes, and it was close to eleven o'clock before Eilat and his guide, a twenty-four-year-old bespectacled Iranian named Emami, left the hotel. They turned immediately west, walking quickly through the shadowy, still-busy streets. Ahvaz was a late-night city, and many shops and restaurants stayed open until after midnight, probably because of the endless twilight caused by the flaming oil beacons.

But less than a mile from the main square, Ahvaz was very gloomy. The streets were like those of most industrial towns, poor and dirty, and made even more melancholy by the proximity of the factories and refineries, in which most men worked. The heat was oppressive, and the smell of oil pervaded the atmosphere.

They turned onto a small, deserted square, surrounded on three sides by high, dark walls, and the young *talabeh* led the way to a tall, wooden gateway. He tapped softly, twice, then said quietly, "Eilat," before tapping twice more. The gate was opened by a guard, who led them across a courtyard and into a small house, situated behind an unprepossessing city mosque. Inside stood a tall, elderly cleric, dressed in the long dark robe of his calling, wearing a white turban. Eilat knew that as an Iraqi Sunni Muslim, he would have some adjustments to make. Standing before the Iranian Shiite, he raised his left hand to his forehead and lowered it in the traditional greeting of Islam, "*Salam aleikum.*"

The Iranian wasted little time. He nodded, and said, in Arabic, "Your suggestions have aroused curiosity in certain places. The *hojjat-el-Islam* will see you in Isfahan. I will give you a letter of introduction, with a phone number. You should call it, and a student will take you to him. You must explain everything to him. But it is better that you leave now. The train departs at eight in the morning. You must sleep. Allah go with you."

Eilat bowed again and took the letter that was handed to him. He offered his thanks and followed his student guide back across the courtyard and through the gate to the square. Fifteen minutes later he was in the hotel, in bed by midnight. And before he slept he assessed his progress. *Out of Iraq. Good. Into Iran. Satisfactory so far. But will they listen, before they kill me? It's beginning to look as if they might . . .*

The following morning, after a deep six-hour sleep, he rose early, badgered the hotel staff for tea, bathed, shaved, and wished to hell he had a clean shirt. But that would have to wait. He had someone call a cab to take him to the railway station, and there he bought himself a first-class ticket to Isfahan, for which he paid in cash. The journey would take twelve hours, with a stop at Qum. Iranian trains are fast, and the first-class section was comprised of comfortable compartments for four passengers. The seats could be converted into beds at night, and the guard came around often, taking orders for meals and tea.

Eilat's compartment was otherwise empty, and the train pulled out of Ahvaz only ten minutes late, heading north across the southwestern desert, 70 miles to the town of Dezful. From there, they climbed into the high peaks of the Zagros, steaming through rough but often spectacular country along the route to the mountain town of Arak, a religious center in which, in 1920, the young Ayatollah Khomeini began his theological studies.

Arak was almost the halfway point, and Eilat's train pulled in at two o'clock. From here it was a fast downhill run of almost 100 miles to the sacred Shiite city of Qum, a place where non-Muslims are banned from entering the holy shrine of the gold-domed Astane, built over four hundred years ago in honor of the Imam Reza's sister Fateme, who died in 816. Non-Muslims are not even admitted to the hotels around this shrine, and photography in any form is absolutely forbidden. Ayatollah Khomeini studied there for fifteen years under the legendary Muslim theologian Shayk Abdul-Karim Ha'eri.

The train waited in Qum for only a few minutes, and, four hours later, Eilat arrived in Isfahan, checked into the great, ornate Hotel Abbassi, and made his phone call. He agreed to meet the student he had called at 11:00 A.M., and together they would find the *hojjat*.

Early the following morning Eilat purchased a soft leather traveling bag and some new, expensive robes in the Iranian style. He also bought a turban, new underwear, socks, and shirts, and laid siege to a city pharmacy, acquiring after-shave, toothpaste and toothbrush, shaving foam, *eau de cologne*, and expensive bath oil. On reflection, he decided, he was glad to be shut of the life of a traveling Bedouin peddler.

When he met the *talabeh* at the correct time in the hotel foyer, he was wearing the new robes and feeling clean and comfortable for the first time since the night he had dealt with the Iraqi government's assassins, more than seven weeks ago. The new student was taller than he, a slim youth of just twenty-one, from Tehran, who walked along reading an open book, saying nothing whatsoever. Eilat saw no reason to disturb these theological ponderings and stayed just behind, taking in the sights of a place he had known only in Muslim folklore.

Isfahan was once the most glorious city in the Middle East, and it still contained the greatest concentration of Islamic buildings in Iran. Beautiful, translucent blue tiles decorated much of the architecture. Like most tourists, Eilat had never seen anything to match the ancient splendors of the city.

Eilat and his guide walked along winding streets, to Imam Khomeini Square, a majestic shop-lined area of 20 acres, right in the middle of the town, the second most dramatic urban square in the world, after Tiananmen. They crossed its entire length, and Eilat actually thought he had walked enough by now, and asked in Arabic how far to the meeting place.

"One more mile, sir," replied the *talabeh*. And Eilat considered it would have been churlish to quibble since he had just walked more than 300 miles without a word of complaint.

They kept heading north for another fifteen minutes, and finally turned into the precincts of the Great Mosque of Isfahan, the *Masjed-e Jame*, a truly monumental building with its twin minarets towering over the pale blue-tiled exterior. This most glorious of mosques is unique for many reasons, particularly its unfathomable eleventh-century north dome, which is still regarded as a geometric miracle, and was designed using structural theories developed at that precise time in Isfahan by the eminent local mathematician and poet, Omar Khayyam.

Eilat and his guide entered from the east and walked across the great courtyard into the large covered area in the southeastern quadrant. It was cool in there, and some parts were in deep shade, almost darkness. Standing beside one of the ornate stucco pillars, his face completely hidden, was the *hojjat* whom Eilat had come to meet.

He did not move from the shadows, but did offer a formal greeting, and Eilat stepped forward to enfold the eminent cleric's outstretched hand in both of his, in the ancient Muslim way. The *talabeh* was dismissed somewhat curtly, and the learned man moved swiftly to business. "It's quiet in here, and private," he said. "We will speak in Arabic. If that's agreeable?"

"Perfectly," replied Eilat. "How would you like me to begin?"

By now he could see the face of the *hojjat*. And it was the face of a masterful man. Even with the white turban, the high intelligent forehead was obvious. The mouth was thin and even, the dark eyes steady but alive. He might have been seventy years of age, but there was a youthfulness in his manner and an edge of wariness. Eilat would not have been surprised if the man had carried a revolver, as he himself carried his desert knife.

The holy man walked slowly between the great supports in the vaulted area, and the Iraqi fell into step with him. "Perhaps," began the cleric, "you should begin by telling me why I, or any of my colleagues, should trust you."

Eilat smiled. Then he said slowly, "In my line of work, there must always be some risk. But I am here to offer you my services for an extended period of time. I expect to be highly paid, because I have a unique service to offer. But you may feel I ought not to be paid until my tasks for you are complete."

"That was not quite what I meant," replied the *hojjat*. "I was asking, Why? Why should we listen to you? Who are you? How can we know you are not working for a foreign government? How can we know you are not an enemy of Iran? What proof have you that we should confide in you in any way at all?"

"Sir, I will tell you as much as I can without placing myself in more danger than I already am."

"Very well, please do."

"I have spent almost all of my working career operating on behalf of my government under deep cover in other countries. I have taken some very large risks, and I have occasionally struck a savage blow against the West on behalf of the Nation of Islam."

"Are you a terrorist?"

"Nossir. I am always connected with the military."

"Are you Syrian, or perhaps Libyan?"

"Nossir. I am an Iraqi."

"And do you intend to return to Iraq should your mission for us be completed?"

Eilat elected to use a term of high respect, and he replied, "No, mullah. I will never return to Iraq. I would not be permitted to do that, except for them to kill me. And anyway, I hate Iraq. I would rather be dead than ever set foot in the place."

"So would I," replied the *hojjat*. "And what has happened to make you so bitter? What have they done to this loyal servant of Saddam's regime who stands here with me today?"

"They presented me with a medal, sir, for my long, untiring

efforts on their behalf. And that same night the President sent two of his palace guards to assassinate me."

"I see they were not successful?"

"Nossir. They were not. But it was close. I had to kill one of them in order to escape."

"Are you publicly wanted?"

"I do not believe so, sir. They would never admit anything like that. But I imagine you have sources in Baghdad. And I expect someone will confirm to you that Eilat One is missing, and wanted, and is believed to have left the country."

"Do you have a valid passport that I can see?"

"I do. Iraqi and old. But for obvious reasons I have placed tape over my real name. I do not wish you to know that yet, but the photograph and other details are all accurate."

"Very well. Might I ask you also whether you seek to engage in terrorist action against the U.S.A. and the West for fundamental reasons? Or, because you intend to carry out your attacks in such a way, the blame will surely be leveled at Iraq."

Eilat was momentarily shaken by the directness of the question, and indeed by the acute observation of his interrogator. But he knew that to hesitate would be fatal. He replied instantly. "Both."

The cleric walked slowly forward. But he was silent for more than a minute before he asked, "Have you ever attacked a target in the West in, shall we say, a high-profile way?"

"Yessir."

"Do they search for you? Are you a man wanted not just in Iraq, but by nations all over the world?"

"I cannot say, sir. No one ever mentioned that I was wanted by the United States. But I should not be terribly surprised if I was. Although I have no idea whether they have any clue as to my identity."

"I share that with them, of course."

"Yessir."

"Well, Eilat . . . I must tell you that I shall recommend that our source in Baghdad substantiate your story about your . . .

er . . . demise in that country. Could you give me a time and date when it happened?"

"I could. In the early hours of May 27 . . . the time was around two-fifteen."

"How did the man die? What did you use?"

"Knife, sir. Throat."

"Quieter . . . mmmm?"

"Exactly so, sir."

"Any other details?"

"Yes. After a long manhunt, they were unsuccessful in finding me."

"Very clever, Eilat."

"Just professional."

"Would you have any interest in telling me precisely what you intend to perpetrate against the Great Satan?"

"I should prefer not to. Unless I was in the presence of the man making the decision, and in the presence of the military commander with whom I would have to work."

"I understand. But would you propose the targets be military ones?"

"Not necessarily."

"On the question of Fundamentalism, would you say our religious beliefs are your prime reason for wishing to carry out such operations?"

"No. That was so when I was an idealist, serving my country abroad. But no longer. I have simply come to the realization that I know no other trade. It is all I have to sell. And every man has to earn a living. I believe my talent is valuable, and I see your country as a place that might use me in a way that would put Iraq in the worst possible light on the world stage. Especially in the Pentagon, which would be likely to move against them."

"I do agree with you. The idea has considerable appeal for me personally, and I suspect it will have for several others as well."

"Yessir. Might I ask who will make the final decision?"

"Oh, the Ayatollah himself. In association with one or two senior military commanders."

"The fewer people who know the precise nature of the missions, the better."

"Correct, Eilat. That is correct."

They walked in silence for a few minutes, pacing through the great stone vault in the southeastern corner of the mosque. Then the *hojjat* spoke again. "Is there any further evidence available to us, that you are who you say you are?"

"Sir, I have written my address—the address in which the killing took place—on this piece of paper. I am sure you could send someone in to make inquiries. You will find bloodstains on the floor in the main hall, and you will find holes in the wood above the door where I attached a bracket to the wall. I expect my possessions have been removed."

"Thank you, and yes, we will conduct those checks in Baghdad immediately . . . and if you are lying, we will, of course, not contact you again. If the checks are correct, as I suspect they will be, we will be in communication very quickly, because you obviously could prove extremely useful to us. Whether or not you are able to conduct the military operations you plan will be for others to decide. When and if you wish to divulge them."

The two men shook hands as before, and Eilat walked back outside, where the student waited to escort him to the hotel. Instructions were succinct—remain in place until we contact you again in the next few days."

At $80 a night in the Hotel Abbassi, I trust they'll be quick, he thought, as they strolled back through the vast expanse of Imam Khomeini Square.

The next three days passed slowly. Eilat spent his time sleeping and regaining the weight he had lost. And then, on the morning of July 23, the phone call came. It was from the young student guide, who said simply, "Please catch the noon train to Tehran. A room is booked for you at the Hotel Bolvar, under the name Mr. Eilat. You will be contacted this evening." At which point he replaced the phone.

The train ran into Tehran on time, shortly before four in the afternoon. Eilat wore his Iranian robes and turban and carried his leather bag. He settled down in the modest room on the third floor to await his call. It came at 5:06. It was another theological student, who announced he was in the downstairs lobby, and would Mr. Eilat come down at once. There were important people waiting for him.

Outside the hotel an orange taxi was parked with its meter running. And in the heavy evening traffic, they wended their way, north through the city—straight up the Vali-ye Asr, the world's longest urban road, lined with shops from the Tehran railway station on the shabby south side, all the way to the former Shah's summer palace up in the select, rarefied hills of Shemiran, a distance of 16 miles.

Eilat's taxi did not go that far. Instead it veered off to the right at Keshavarz Boulevard, past the Iraqi Embassy, and ducked into the Kheyabon area. From there it traveled less than 200 yards before stopping opposite an elegant city mosque. The *talabeh* paid the fare, and they walked down a narrow street beside the building, 50 yards to a white gate with a doorbell on the side. It was answered immediately, and Eilat was escorted into a shaded, completely walled courtyard, containing a slender date palm and a great awning of a tamarisk tree. A stone water fountain splashed quietly in the center, and beyond stood a tall house the color of sandstone, directly opposite the west entrance to the mosque.

The door to the house opened into a large, stone-floored hall, similar in design to that of Eilat's former residence in Baghdad, except about three times larger. Seated on a heavy wooden chair, attended by two robed disciples, was an Ayatollah. He wore a black robe and a black turban, which contrasted with his white beard. Seated next to him was the *hojjat* who had first interviewed Eilat in the Great Mosque of Isfahan.

Both men rose as the Iraqi entered, and one of the disciples poured him water from a large, dark green ceramic jug, which Eilat estimated would hold about one and a half gallons. The *hojjat* made the introductions, and the Ayatollah offered his hand to his visitor.

"You caused a commotion in Baghdad," remarked the *hojjat*. "We had your story checked by two sources, and one of them knew all about it without having to make even one inquiry. The other man was actually in Syria, but he telephoned back in five hours. Mentioned that Iraqi security forces are still watching all airports and seaports. They even have men on buses and trains, searching for the Intelligence officer who murdered a palace guard and fled with all his secrets."

"I suppose no one mentioned the fact that two armed men entered my house at two in the morning, and on the admission of one of them, entered with intent to assassinate me? Direct orders from the President."

"Yes. As a matter of fact our first man knew everything. Apparently there are many people who are angry at the Iraqi government's propensity to have people quietly executed. And quite a lot of them thought the President deserved what happened. Eilat One is a name on every insider's lips. But nothing has been officially announced."

"No. I thought probably not."

"I would like to ask you two things? Firstly, how did you make one of the assassins tell you what he was there for? And secondly, how did you get away."

"To the first question, routine persuasion. To the second, I walked."

Both and *hojjat* and the Ayatollah smiled. "You mean you killed one of them, and threatened the other with a similar fate?"

"Well, yes, I suppose I did. It seemed reasonable since both of them were trying to kill me, and, for all I knew, there were others outside with a similar brief."

"And about this walk. How long did it take?"

"About twenty-two days from Baghdad to the train station in Ahvaz. I suppose I averaged around 15 miles a day. It was fiercely hot, and I walked at night when I could. Parts were very slow. I stuck to the river, but in places there was no hard surface, and sometimes it took almost an hour to cover a mile. Other places were much better."

"Well, Eilat. You are a man of considerable resources. Before we ask you to outline your plans, there is one further question I would like answered."

"Please?"

"Did your President have any reason whatsoever to mistrust you?"

"No. He did not. Except for the unavoidable fact that I had been away for a very long time. And he may have felt that I had become distant and could never really be trusted. But I gave him no cause, and I worked only on behalf of Iraq. For my entire working life."

"I see," replied the *hojjat*. "But it has been very hard to discover anything about your career. No one appears to know exactly what you have been doing, or even where you have been doing it."

"For that I should perhaps be congratulated, sir," replied Eilat. "Secrecy is, after all, the difference between life and death in my trade."

"That and your sharp knife," added the Ayatollah. "By the way, do you have it with you?"

Eilat smiled. But he was not afraid of the holy men with whom he conversed. "Yessir. Yes, I do."

"Perhaps you would do me the honor of placing it on the table until you leave. We, of course, are not armed."

Eilat recognized a test of trust when he heard one, and he walked across the room, drew his knife from inside his robes, and placed it next to the water jug. One of the disciples chuckled, archly, at its size. "You are Crocodile Dundee," he said, betraying the terrible truth that he had been watching Western videos. "In disguise," he added.

The Ayatollah looked puzzled. But he ignored the young man's remark and spoke only to his visitor, offering simply, "Thank you, my son." It was, Eilat knew, an expression of trust, and for that he was grateful. For he also knew that he would need to tell these men more about his life than he had ever told anyone. They were plainly going to check him out ruthlessly, and if he wanted to earn their confidence, he would have to level with them. Otherwise, the entire exercise would become futile. There were risks attached to telling the truth, but he might face death as a spy should he attempt to conceal his background from the Iranian Ayatollah.

"And now, Eilat, the *hojjat* and I would like to hear your plans."

"Sir, may I begin by suggesting that we are dealing with two acts of revenge here? Mine and yours. And by that I refer to the occasion, almost two years ago, when all three of your Russian Kilo-Class submarines were mysteriously destroyed in Bandar Abbas. I realize from the newspapers that the Iranian Navy put the entire thing down, officially, to an accident. But I am sure we all know it was no accident. And, when you think about it, no other nation, except the Satan, could possibly have done it. They had the motive, the power, the finance, and the know-how."

"And what was that motive?" asked the *hojjat*.

"I do not really know, sir. But I would guess they secretly blamed Iran for the destruction of that aircraft carrier in the Gulf a few weeks previously. They always said that was an accident. But I don't think so, and I believe you were innocent of that"

The Ayatollah nodded. "Please go on."

"I am therefore proposing that we hit back three times. One blow against the U.S. for each of the lost submarines."

"But why do you think they will not blame us again? And perhaps launch an air strike against Bandar Abbas and wipe out the rest of our ships?"

"Because, sir, we will arrange our actions to coincide with irrefutable evidence that it must have been Iraq."

"Such as . . . ?"

"We will hit them on a selection of the following dates: January 17, the day the American Army launched its opening attack on Iraq in the Gulf War; April 6, the day Iraq was forced to accept the terms of surrender as laid down by the American puppets in the United Nations; and July 16, the anniversary of the day Saddam Hussein became President of the Republic of Iraq."

"I see . . . yes, I suppose that would be irresistibly persuasive for a U.S. Intelligence officer."

"And, of course, there is one other method we could employ, sir. Once I am clear, and back in Iran, where I hope I'll be welcome . . . we could leak some judicious details to the CIA field officers in Baghdad—details which could only have been known to the mission commander, who just happened to be a serving Iraqi Intelligence officer, now in hiding."

"Yes . . . you have given this considerable thought, have you not?"

"I have, sir. And I am, of course, assuming that I am speaking to one of the Imam's closest advisers."

"Two of them, Eilat," replied the Ayatollah. "On matters such as these."

"Are you yet prepared to divulge the broad outline of your plan?"

"Not quite yet, sir. Not until we have an agreement in principle. Save to mention that I shall require quite substantial refitting work to be carried out in one of your military bases. And that I anticipate using a surface-to-air missile, possibly a regular Russian SAM. My advice is that you order four such systems, on the basis of improving your antiaircraft defense on your surface ships. It will cost about $300 million, but I think it might prove a bit of a bargain. The system I have in mind has a vast array of radar, and I will merely require certain parts of one of them."

"Will you take charge of this work yourself personally, or will you leave it to our people?"

"I shall take charge, sir. I do not know of anyone else in the Middle East who would be qualified. Which brings us to a minor point. I shall have to be seconded into your armed forces, with appropriate rank."

"Yes, you will. But I do not anticipate that being more than a formality. However, there is one aspect I should clear up. Might you have any idea of costs?"

"Not really, save for the value of time and people. I am looking at big hardware costs, but not as much as you may think. And there is the question of my own fee."

"And where might you put that, Eilat?"

"I think $3 million would be fair. I shall ask you to put $250,000 in my Swiss account when we start, followed by $750,000 when the initial stage of the mission is accomplished.

"Then I shall require $500,000 when we set off. The final $1.5 million will fall due only when the three objectives have been achieved. That way I will have been on half pay if we fail, which I do not anticipate."

"And what, Eilat, if you should be caught? And my country is held up to ridicule in front of the entire world as a bunch of lawless international gangsters?"

"Sir, we will not be caught. Cannot be caught. But if the million-to-one chance came up and we were, suffice to say death would be preferable to me. I have no fear of it. And suitable arrangements to that end would already be in place."

"Eilat," replied the *hojjat*, "you come to us with a vague and expensive scheme. I can take it no further without a much clearer plan from you, and I shall, naturally, have to consult with the Imam and the military. However, you may assume we are agreed in principle to explore this project with you, and that you will remain here as our secret, honored guest for as long as that may take."

"Thank you. I am grateful, and may Allah always go with you. Just one thing, sir, before I leave . . . and I hesitate to ask . . . but I have been alone for a very long time. I wonder if we might pray together?"

"Of course, my son. You have been very badly used . . . let's walk together across the courtyard . . . Ayatollah, you will join us?"

"No, I have some writing to finish. I will pray in an hour."

The *hojjat* and the Iraqi entered the courtyard together and crossed it, walking slowly past the fountain. At the door to the mosque, they each removed their shoes. And the learned man turned around to ask his final question.

"Eilat, I wonder if you are yet ready, as we prepare for prayer . . . perhaps to tell me your real name?"

"Yes . . . you have been very kind to me . . . and I think I am ready now. My name is Benjamin . . . I'm Commander Benjamin Adnam."

September 12, 2004.

THEY WERE 9,000 FEET ABOVE THE DESERT FLOOR, flying low in the thicker air. The big Iranian Navy transport aircraft, a C130 Hercules transporter, was making 240 knots through crystalline skies. Down below, along the northern edges of the Dasht-e Lut, the Great Sandy Desert, temperatures hovered around 114 degrees. The Air Force colonel at the controls of the Hercules made a course adjustment to the south as they inched their way over the old city of Yazd, which has been trading silk and textiles, in the middle of Iran's vast, broiling wilderness, for 1,000 years.

"Can you imagine living in a place like that, Commander?" muttered Rear Admiral Mohammed Badr, the Iranian Navy's most senior submarine expert, as he stared down at the desert city, all alone in thousands of miles of sand.

"Only in the line of duty, sir," replied Benjamin Adnam, elegant in his new Iranian uniform with the three gold stripes on the sleeve.

The Iranian admiral smiled. "Where's your family from, Ben?"

"Oh, we've lived in Tikrit for generations."

"Where exactly is it?" asked Admiral Badr. "Close to Baghdad?"

"Well, it's also on the Tigris, about 110 miles upstream, on the edge of the central plains. You start heading west from Tikrit, you will encounter precisely nothing for 150 miles, all the way to the Syrian border."

"Sounds like Yazd."

"Not that bad, sir. To the south, heading for Baghdad, it can be quite busy. We're only 34 miles from Samarra . . . and of course you know Saddam Hussein's hometown was Tikrit. His rise to power gave the town a new life and new prosperity . . . half his cabinet came from there. My father says the old rural feel of the place vanished once it became known as a cradle of government power."

"Did you spend much time there as a boy?"

"No . . . not really . . . I went away to school in England, and when I returned I was drafted into the Navy . . . the Israeli Navy actually."

"The *Israeli* Navy?" exclaimed Admiral Badr. "How did you manage that?"

"Oh, there was a group of us, the chosen Iraqi youth, fanatical Fundamentalists, which I was. When everyone thought I was sixteen, I was really eighteen. We were all placed with families, operating under deep cover in different countries—I was sent to Israel and ordered to join the Navy. But everything was arranged for me. I was spying for Iraq for years."

"You were a submariner, weren't you, Ben?"

"Yes, for several years I was. Trained in the Royal Navy, in Scotland, after Israel bought a diesel-electric boat from the Brits."

"Think they'd train a few of our men if we bought a submarine from them?"

"Probably not. You guys are generally regarded as dangerous outlaws in the world community."

"And soon we show them how dangerous, eh Ben?"

"Yes. Except they'll think it's Iraq."

Both men laughed. They were the only passengers in the big, noisy military aircraft, as it thundered on to Bandar Abbas. But such was the deadly nature of their business, they still spoke in the guarded tones of strangers, despite having worked closely together in Tehran for more than three weeks. The two officers were already kindred spirits, mainly because of Ben Adnam's certainty that it had been the U.S.A. that destroyed the three Iranian submarines.

Admiral Badr had been the project manager for the entire Kilo-Class program in 2002. He had been at his home in the Bandar Abbas dockyard when the American hit squad had struck, smashing all three of the Russian-built submarines onto the bottom of the harbor. For Admiral Badr it represented ten years of work in ruins. He was fortunate not to have been dismissed from the Navy, but the Ayatollahs liked the big, bespectacled submariner from the south-coast port of Bushehr, and he was held in great respect by his fellow admirals. No one in Iran knew more about submarines than Mohammed Badr. At least, not before Commander Adnam arrived.

In the months after the attack, the admiral had concluded, like almost everyone else in the Iranian Navy, that the American President had blamed the Ayatollahs for the loss of the *Thomas Jefferson*, and acted accordingly. But the Americans were wrong. Iran was innocent, and the gnawing desire for revenge against the Great Satan seemed only to grow with each passing month. Especially in the mind of the man most affected by the loss, Admiral Mohammed Badr.

For him, the sudden appearance of Benjamin Adnam represented a beacon of light in the murky waters of naval sabotage, that no-man's-land of world politics, where no one admits anything; neither the criminal, for obvious reasons, nor the victim, for fear of humiliation.

But in this former Iraqi Intelligence officer, Admiral Badr could see a man with a plan—a plan of such monumental dimensions it would be a miracle if it worked. But the ex–Israeli submarine commander seemed coldly sure of his own abilities, and Iran had the money and the will to make it happen.

The admiral smiled again. It was a good-natured smile, indicating contentment with his new colleague and anticipation of the future.

"You know, Ben," he said, "I really admired your planning for these missions. But one thing puzzles me. Why did you turn down their offer of becoming a rear admiral?"

"I suppose I'm a purist about some things. Remember, I earned my rank in the Israeli Navy. I was Commander Benjamin Adnam, and I was CO of a submarine. I'm very proud of that. And I'm proud of my rank. It does me honor, and I do not want to be a fraud admiral. I am Commander Adnam. I expect you heard me tell them I'd accept rear admiral when the project was successfully completed. Because then I will have earned it."

"Very admirable," replied Admiral Badr. "And now I have a question. I heard you say twice in that last meeting that the West believes you are dead? How can they? They don't even know you? Who told them you were dead?"

"The Mossad, I expect. There was a pretty serious hunt for me after I deserted the Israeli Navy. But they thought they found me."

"Can you explain that, Commander?"

"Well, I suppose I can now. Okay. This is what I did. I had known for many months a professional forger, an Egyptian who specialized in passports and official documents. He lived in Cairo. He did the most exquisite work . . . and I had used him often in the past. The strange thing was that he bore the most remarkable physical resemblance to me. Same height and build, same complexion. He even walked like me, the big difference being a very slight limp, and he always walked with a black cane with a silver top.

"And so, I set him up. Phoned him and asked him to meet me,

privately, in a secluded place, at night, up in the precincts of the Citadel, on the southeast side of the city. There I would hand him a small attaché case made of soft leather, in which were several documents I wanted him to copy for me. I would also hand him $300 in American currency as a down payment.

"I made the time 1930, because I knew he would walk straight down the hill to the mosque he attends every night at 2000. Then I called the Mossad in Tel Aviv and spoke to a duty officer. Told them I was a sympathetic member of the *sayanim* and that I had valuable information which would cost them $100,000 if it proved to be accurate. I gave them the number of a Swiss bank account, and told them I had many contacts, and that I might be able to inform them of important matters . . . but right now, however, my information was this . . . that the missing Israeli naval officer, Commander Benjamin Adnam, was to be kidnapped and interrogated that evening by an Iraqi hit squad. The Mossad had one chance, to take him out themselves on the dark and lonely lower part of the hill leading down to the Mosque of Sultan Mu'ayyad Sheikh.

"Obviously, I told them the man would be wearing Arab dress and walking with a slight limp, using a black cane with a silver top. Their men should wear Western suits and approach under the guise of Egyptian secret police, requesting to see his papers. I was working on the theory that a criminal such as this would carry no papers of his own. That would leave only the attaché case, and right there it was up to them. Because in that case was every one of my most valuable documents . . . you know, Navy record, passport, driver's license, birth certificate . . . not to mention my cigarette case and my precious Israeli submariner's badge.

"After my own transaction was complete, I slipped away and followed the forger from a distance. I watched two men approach him and examine the contents of his briefcase. Then I watched one of them kill him instantly from behind with one shot from a silenced pistol. I watched them leave, taking the briefcase with them.

"It was ample evidence for the Mossad, and there was thus no doubt in their minds about who the dead man was. Someone found the body a few hours later, and the Egyptian police took over. But, of course, they knew nothing. There were no documents left on the corpse. . . . Two weeks later the Israelis sent $100,000 to my account in Geneva."

Admiral Badr burst out laughing at the sheer brass of the scheme. "Ben, I guess a lot of people in Tel Aviv think you are dead."

"Yessir. And they will undoubtedly have informed the Americans."

"But Commander, what had you done, precisely, to make the United States so interested in you?"

"I don't think I can reveal that. Except to say that I know your country had nothing to do with the elimination of that U.S. aircraft carrier."

"My God, Ben. Was that you?"

But the Iraqi just smiled, and said, "Admiral, let's look to the future . . ."

Admiral Badr, however, remained thoughtful. "Is your vision of the future the same as ours, Commander?"

"I believe so, sir. If you are referring to a general belief that one day the Nation of Islam must dominate the earth, to the everlasting glory of Allah."

"That is our dream, Ben. That is our dream. And there are many of us in the military here in Iran who believe that the only way to achieve this aim is to cause chaos in the West."

"You mean, sir, if we frighten them often enough, they may begin to fall apart?"

"I believe they will, Ben. Because unlike us, they are a Godless society. They have no central rallying point except money. In fact they have nothing except money. Their God is material possessions. They have no ideals.

"Great wars of the past have often been won behind a religious banner. But in this millennium, Allah alone can inspire brilliance and courage. Because Allah is great . . . and Allah is all-powerful . . . Allah makes us great . . . and when we attack, we attack behind his power, for a common cause. In the end, nothing can withstand us. Certainly not the infidels of the United States.

"We must strike hammerblows against them, over and over, until their will dissolves . . . as it must. Because they have no God. They are just overfed disciples of a lesser God—the God of money . . . and country clubs . . . and huge cars . . . and beautiful houses. But in the end they are nothing. Because they believe in nothing . . . and they have no true God. The Koran does not guide them. Nothing holy lights their way.

"They are the rampant heathens of the twenty-first century, sucking the world's resources dry. Taking, grabbing, using, claiming the rights of other countries, treating our own Gulf of Iran as if it were theirs. But one day, we will rise up and claim what is ours, what has been ours for thousands of years. And when that day comes, the power of the United States will be returned, finally, to the Nation of Islam."

The two men sat in silence after that. But to each of them the words possessed unfathomable meaning. Not everyone in Iran agreed with such thoughts, nor with Admiral Badr's preferred course of action. But there were senior military figures who did share his views, very firmly. Which is why he had been singled out to work with the newly arrived Benjamin Adnam, the world's most wanted terrorist.

The big Hercules began descending toward the Bandar Abbas airport, slipping down through the hot clear skies. Ben could see from his window the submarine docks in the distance. There would be much activity in there during the week, with the arrival from St. Petersburg of the first replacement Kilo, Russia's special export model; the 636 AIP, *Yunes-4* (Jonah-4, named for the prophet who was swallowed by a whale but saved by God).

Ben could imagine her quietly berthed in the submarine pens, the 235-foot-long 3,000-tonner from the Baltic, and as he did so he imagined himself in the control room, as once he had been. Admiral Badr also wore a faraway look, remembering, as he so often did, the black night of August 2, 2002, around the midnight hour . . . the scene of absolute devastation that had greeted him at the Iranian submarine base. The confusion. The fear. And the desperate, unavailing attempts to save the men on board the two hulls that had been sunk alongside the jetties.

He would soon have his first sight of an operational Kilo in the harbor of Bandar Abbas since that most terrible night. And it gave him heart. For he assumed that under the guidance of this quite brilliant Iraqi officer, with whom he now shared a common goal, they would harness the new Kilo to attack the hated, imperious enemy from the Western hemisphere. Admiral Badr liked it.

A Navy staff car greeted them as they disembarked and drove them immediately to the base. Ben put his few possessions in the house provided for him, next door to the admiral's residence. Twenty minutes later they were in the Special Ops room, which comprised the entire top floor of a small executive block. Each man had a private office, with secure phone lines. There was a wider conference room between them, which contained drawers full of Navy charts, reference books, architectural plans, a fax machine, a copying machine, and three computers, one containing all of the world's naval charts, another a myriad of marine engineering and design information. Ben guessed most of his work would be done on the third computer.

There was no sign of any staff or assistance in any form. But there were four armed Iranian Navy guards in the upstairs corridor, beyond the big locked wooden doors. Ben approved that, and checked that the guards would be on duty twenty-four hours a day. Every day. He also requested that the two-man guard on the main entrance be trebled.

"You like security, hah?" said Admiral Badr.

"Admiral, the consequences of a foreign agent breaching our defenses and ascertaining our plans would represent your very worst nightmare. If they happened to work for the CIA, I think you could assume a full-scale U.S. air strike on this port from one of their carriers within forty-eight hours. We, you and I, probably would never know what hit us. But, should we survive, we would be rightly blamed and executed. I don't care how many guards you deploy—40, 60, 100. The consequences of not having enough of them are utterly unthinkable."

"You're right, Ben. You're usually right, hah?"

"Mostly. Which is why, essentially, I'm still breathing."

The admiral nodded, gravely. Then he hit his beeper to summon his regular chauffeur, for a tour of the dockyard to inspect the work in progress, in readiness for the Three Strikes against the Great Satan.

The two officers each wore the new summer uniform of white shorts, socks and shoes, dark blue shirts, short-sleeved, with epaulettes and the insignia of rank. They each carried a 2-foot-long officer's baton. All of which set them apart as they stood on the dusty edge of the massive construction site being dug out of the shoreline on the southeastern corner of the harbor, directly opposite the regular submarine docks, facing inland, with the road and the open waters of the Strait of Hormuz behind them.

There was a fleet of forty trucks moving sand from a hole almost 300 feet long, 150 feet wide, and 120 feet deep. It was separated from the harbor waters by a 50-foot "beach," and as they hauled away the mountains of sand, more trucks were grinding their way in and emptying tons and tons of hard core and rubble onto the floor of the hole. It would be a mighty foundation.

"Just as you instructed, Ben," said the admiral. "One reinforced concrete submarine dry dock. Walls 30 feet thick to withstand the impact of a 10,000-pound bomb. The boat will just float in, we'll pump out the water and get to work."

"Very impressive," said Commander Adnam. "Did you decide yet where to build the model room?"

"Right here, Ben. We build it 300 feet long, scaffold and wood. Right now we're just waiting for them to pour the concrete foundation for both buildings. Maybe a week, then we'll have it erected inside twenty-one days. You have preliminary plans ready for the model?"

"Almost. By the way, how is your man at the Vickers shipyard in England? I need his details now."

"I don't know off the top of my head whether we have them

here quite yet, but I'd be surprised if we were not very much on the case. We have men in all of the big submarine bases in Europe. Our man in place at the greatest submarine builders in the world will be very efficient. Let me check later."

September 17, 2004.
Barrow-in-Furness, England.

The afternoon was drawing to a close in the brightly lit drawing-office block, out on the edge of the sprawling yards of Vickers Shipbuilding and Engineering. Most people there left at five o'clock sharp.

Vickers, whose engineers had built the spectacular Trident missile submarines, was experiencing something of a morale problem. People did not work late there anymore. There was hardly any point. All successive governments ever wanted to do, it seemed, was to cut programs, scrap submarines, and generally run down one of the finest engineering firms in the world. Some thought *the* finest.

Up in the drawing office, desk lights were going out. Young draftsmen were preparing to leave. The big computers, which contained the database for all the submarines built there, were switched off. In the outer offices, where the senior engineering draftsmen worked, only one light was still burning.

John Patel, a tall, sallow-faced man of thirty-eight, with two outstanding degrees from the University of London, was busy, working quietly, as he did, on the leading edge of new submarine design. John was widely regarded as the most important man in the department.

He was a brilliant engineer, with a spectacular career ahead of him, either at Vickers, or possibly in the United States, where such men were valued far more highly than they were in the United Kingdom. For the moment, however, he belonged to Vickers, and that was greatly to their advantage.

Except for one unknown factor. John Patel was not what he seemed, a youngish married man of Pakistani parentage living on the outskirts of Barrow, in the village of Leece. He was an Iranian who, along with his father, had been skillfully inserted into England in the 1970s when John was still a schoolboy.

Both father and son had beaten the immigration system using Pakistani passports. They had lived in the UK for twenty-seven years, the father, an ex–Iranian naval officer, working undercover for the regimes of both the late Shah, and subsequently for the burgeoning Navy of the Ayatollah.

The young John Patel had succeeded beyond anyone's wildest dreams, obtaining his job, after graduation, deep inside the Vickers corporation. Taught by his father from an early age, he was one of the shrewdest and most valuable field operatives in Tehran's worldwide spy network. For his specialty was the one area in which Iran nurtured overwhelming ambition—the formation of a strike submarine fleet that could blockade the Gulf of Iran, their own historic waters.

When John Patel finally returned to his homeland, it would be as a rich man. They had paid him well for the previous six years, during which time he had literally raided the Vickers computerized database, copying for his government high-tech secret documents involving submarines and their systems. That night he would do so again. In the next fifteen minutes he would be the only man left on the floor, as he often was.

The room which housed the database was in darkness and securely locked. No one had access except between the hours of nine and five, when the office was staffed. Six years previously it had taken John Patel approximately fifteen seconds to take an impression of the key in a piece of window putty and have a duplicate made. But such was his eminence in the department, no one would have given it a thought had he been observed working at the computer after hours.

He waited until the cleaning staff had completed its tasks before he made his move, at 6:30 P.M. Then, carrying his own powerful Toshiba laptop computer, he walked softly through the darkened main floor and quietly opened the door to the database room, closing it softly behind him. He turned on the light above the consul and heard the hum of the big corporate computer as it moved slickly into life. He tapped into the database for the section that dealt with the now-extinct Upholder-Class diesel-electric submarine, a program killed off by the government in the 1990s to the fury of the Royal Navy.

Only four of them had been built, at Vickers's Cammell Laird yard in Birkenhead, 50 miles to the south. But they were excellent ships, highly efficient, as good, probably better, than the Russian Kilo-Class, and they were the only diesel-electric submarines the Royal Navy had built since the "O"-Class back in the 1960s. They were called *Upholder*, *Unicorn*, *Ursula*, and *Unseen*. The government planned to sell all four of the stealthy 2,500-tonners to foreign governments, a course of action most British admirals considered to be somewhat shortsighted.

John Patel hooked up his Toshiba on the laplink system and hit the copy and start keys. The operation would take possibly four hours, but he would not have to monitor it. The Toshiba, with 4.3 gigabits on the hard drive, would silently absorb every last sentence and diagram of the thousands and thousands of details contained in the computerized library that represented the Upholder-Class submarine.

Every working part, every system, the propulsion, the weapons, the generators, the location of the switches, the valves, the torpedo tubes, and the air purifiers. The entire blueprint of these miraculous underwater warships would be copied, and it would take up almost the full capacity of the hard drive. It was the biggest request John Patel had ever received, and he wondered what on earth Iran's Navy could want with such a mammoth collection of data.

But the note, delivered personally by his father, had contained an air of urgency, highlighted by the rare inclusion of the specific amount of money he would receive—$50,000, payable as usual to his numbered account in Geneva. John thanked Allah for the general weakness of Vickers's security. For he planned to spend the night in the building rather than risk being searched if he left via the main gate around eleven o'clock. If he spent the night, hidden somewhere in the building, the chances of being discovered were virtually nonexistent. There was only one security guard on duty in the drawing-office building. And he was normally asleep or watching television. His name was Reg, and he was not vigilant. He usually took a walk around at ten-thirty, right after the evening news on ITV. It was not a long walk, however. Reg liked to be back in his little office for the late movie at ten-forty-five.

At nine o'clock John checked the computers, which were still running flawlessly, the little Toshiba siphoning off the priceless data from the database, turned out all of the lights, and locked the door. Then he slipped through the main floor and into his own office, which he also placed in total darkness. Finally, he sat behind his desk, looking out through the door and beyond to the unlighted corridor along which he expected to see Reg advance in ninety minutes.

It was a boring wait, but at 10:35 the lights went on in the outer corridor. John Patel softly closed his office door and positioned himself directly behind it. He could hear the security man opening and shutting doors swiftly, each one sounding a little closer. When he reached John's office he opened the door and stepped inside, but he did not bother to turn on the light, and he certainly did not bother to look behind the door. He was gone inside ten seconds, and John heard him check the next office immediately.

Reg skipped the computer room altogether, but even had he entered he would not have tampered with a running program. His brief was to locate intruders, nothing else. And, anyway, the late movie tonight was an old 1997 comedy called *The Full Monty*, which he thought was the funniest film he had ever seen.

John Patel entered the computer room at eleven o'clock, disconnected his laptop, and switched off the main system. Then he retreated to his pitch-dark office, placed the Toshiba in his briefcase, locked it, and spread out on the floor behind his desk, guessing correctly that Reg was done for the night. At eight-fifteen the following morning, he opened his office door, switched on his desk light, and began work. No one would appear before nine. No one ever did at Vickers, not anymore.

That night he would leave on time with everyone else, and he looked forward to that. In the evening he and Lisa were driving over to his father's Indian restaurant in Bradford, 80 miles away across the high Pennines in Yorkshire. That was always fun. But while he and his wife drove home, Ranji Patel would journey through the night, 175 miles south down the M1 motorway to London, taking the Toshiba laptop to the Iranian Embassy at 27 Prince's Gate, Kensington, special delivery to the naval attaché. Old friends would be up, waiting for him there in the small hours. And the little computer would be in the Iranian diplomatic bag on board Syrian Arab Airways' morning flight from Heathrow to Tehran.

November 2, 2004.
Bandar Abbas Naval Base.

In two months there had been immense progress on two fronts. Commander Adnam had mastered the rudiments of the Farsi language, using every modern computerized technique. And the Iranian contractors had completed the foundation for the concrete dry dock. They also had in place the 30-foot-thick wall on its left-hand side facing the harbor. It towered 60 feet high. The wall on the other side was nearing completion, and the great steel girders of the roof were in place. Against the long left-side wall the 300-foot model room was already under cover, and teams of carpenters were hammering home the sidewalls.

Beneath the roof concealed by sheets of tarpaulin, a huge, full-scale, cylindrical model of a diesel-electric submarine was being created out of wood and grey plastic. Commander Ben Adnam spent several hours each day in there with Iran's senior naval architects and submarine experts. The boat could have been a Russian Kilo, but it was not quite so big, and it contained many significant differences, particularly of internal layout. To the expert eye, it was several degrees more sophisticated.

Commander Adnam had been careful not to reveal the precise type and class of submarine they would use on the mission, other than to Admiral Badr. He had thus slightly irritated the Iranian Navy hierarchy by brushing aside their questions of when, how, and the Special Ops submarine was coming from? Will you require the new Kilo?

To every question, the commander answered the same. "I am not yet ready to reveal the whereabouts of the submarine we will use. But you may trust me implicitly. The entire plan depends on it—and at the correct time I will inform you how I propose to acquire it."

"But Ben," they had protested, "we must know how. Do you intend to rent one, borrow one, or even buy one? If so, from whom? We must be told the costs and who the provider might be. There may be great political ramifications."

"Not yet," the commander would reply curtly. "When the time comes I will, of course, present you with a detailed plan and report. At that time you will be free to accept or decline, as you wish. Bear in mind I do not anticipate your declining, because that would cost me $2,750,000, which I consider to be an unacceptable consequence."

Out beyond the model room, work continued under the wilting rays of the sun by day and under lights at night. Security was phenomenal. It was impossible to reach the buildings without crossing a cordon of armed guards, placed 200 yards from the new dock. Miles of barbed wire protected all approaches to the site. Every worker wore a plastic identification badge. Every man on the site was photographed and fingerprinted, checked, and searched both incoming and outgoing. A simple sign on the main gate along the road to the base read:

AUTHORIZED PERSONNEL ONLY.
INTRUDERS WILL BE SHOT ON SIGHT.

Three drivers who had arrived without their badges had been incarcerated in the Navy jail for a week as suspected spies. Special patrol craft crisscrossed the waters of the inner harbor with unprecedented frequency. A frigate remained on permanent patrol outside the harbor entrance, ready to intercept and, if necessary, sink an unauthorized visitor.

By the year 2004, the Iranian Navy was 40,000 strong, 20,000 regular personnel, and a further 20,000 members of the Islamic Revolutionary Guards Corps, special forces loosely modeled on the U.S. Navy SEALs, or the British SAS. They managed some heavy practice during the war with Iraq, but had never achieved the sophistication of the Americans, and the British would probably have been amused by their efforts. Nonetheless, the young Iranian Naval commandos were tough, fit, and quite incredibly brave, believing as they did, that in the end they were fighting for Allah and that he would protect them and lead them to glory.

From the ranks of these men, Commander Adnam would handpick two hit men for his mission. The other eighteen would be recruited directly from the submarine service—men who had been essentially without ships since the U.S. attack two years before.

He spent long hours in consultation with the commanding officers of the IRGC, poring over the records and finally selecting five outstanding veterans for interview, of whom he would reject three. He spent, of course, even longer with the submarine commanders, looking for the men who would one day man the watches on a long submarine journey.

When he was not involved in selection, Ben spent many hours alone in the Black Ops inner office, studying the superb data on the little Toshiba computer that had come from Barrow-in-Furness. Then he would consult his designers and go to the model room, to help build and perfect another corner of the phantom submarine he had masterminded.

By early December the model was almost complete, and the commander had selected his personnel. In company with Admiral Badr he had made his way out to the building site to meet the busload of twenty young men with whom he would soon go on a mission of justice for their country.

Both officers stood and watched as the select few disembarked and formed two lines of 10 men in each. The admiral and the commander walked carefully along each line, addressing each man by name and rank, talking for perhaps two minutes with each of them. They then ordered everyone into the air-conditioned conference room, set beyond the stern end of the 200-foot-long model.

And there the world's most notorious terrorist outlined their duties for them. Most of the men had some Arabic, but Ben spoke mostly in Farsi, using phrases he had learned especially for this talk. "Most of you," he began, "are already familiar with the workings of a Kilo-Class submarine, and you will understand that I have deliberately selected officers who have worked in specialist areas—I mean, of course, those who have been in charge of propulsion, electronics, generators, sonar, hydrology, communications, navigation, and hydraulic systems.

"The submarine I shall acquire for our mission will be one with which you are not familiar, and in anticipation of that, we have constructed here this full-scale model. In the coming three weeks I want each of you to familiarize himself with the workings of this submarine. Every switch, valve, and keyboard. And when I say familiarize I mean that I would expect you to go on board the real submarine in the pitch dark, find your area of operation, and work your systems without error, and possibly without light.

"It is likely that during the course of the next four weeks some of you will not measure up, and we may have to replace you. That, however, will be up to you. This is a time of extensive study, note taking, and memorizing. Pure concentration. I have selected each one of you because I know you have the precise characteristics this mission demands.

"It will not be without its dangers, but I am confident in our skills, and I am confident in the abilities of each one of you. Now perhaps we should go and make a tour of the model."

January 6, 2005.
Office of the National Security Advisor.
The White House, Washington, DC.

The national security advisor himself, Admiral Arnold Morgan, was in deep conference, studying satellite photographs with Admiral George Morris, director of the National Security Agency, located in Fort Meade, Maryland.

"What the hell's that, goddammit?"

"Er, a building, sir. A large building."

"I can see that, for Christ's sake. What kind of a building is it? Looks like a fucking indoor football stadium. What the hell's it doing in a Navy dockyard? Eh?" Then warming to his theme, as he was always prone to do, the admiral added, "Fucking Arabs taking up football? Nah, bullshit . . . they ain't big enough. Betcha you couldn't find a halfway decent lineman in the whole Middle East. Come on George, what kind of a building is it?"

"Sir, at a guess, I'd say it was a concrete dry dock for a submarine, but it has another big building on its left-hand side. Which seems to have a steel roof judging by the sun glinting off it. I have no idea what's inside, because there are massive doors at the seaward end with a thick concrete wall at the landward end."

"Hmmm. But let me ask you this. If it's gonna be a dry dock, how come it's not connected to the water? Look . . . you can see the land runs right across the entrance."

"Yessir. I do see that. But these buildings are pretty complicated, and I would guess they are fitting all the flooding systems right here where this excavation is. I'd say they would remove the strip of land along the shore, right at the conclusion of the project. That way the submarine could just float in and settle; then they just pump the water out."

"Correct."

The two men had worked together for years. Lifelong Naval officers, they were as different in character as it was possible to be. Morgan, tough, hard-looking, irascible, brilliant, rude, and, curiously, admired by many, many people. Morris, an ex–Carrier Battle Group commander, was soft-spoken, lugubrious in delivery and appearance, thoughtful in the extreme. He had followed Morgan into the position as director at Fort Meade, and his biggest problem was that Morgan frequently believed he was now doing both jobs. But the concentrated attention the president's chief security advisor focused on the ultrasecret Fort Meade operation gave the place a greater importance than it had enjoyed for many years.

"I wonder why the hell they've built a big secure dry dock," Arnold Morgan mused.

"Possibly, old buddy, because they don't want us taking out their new Russian Kilo. They're . . . er . . . a bit short of submarines these days. You wouldn't have thought it necessary, would you?"

"Not unless those stupid fucking Russians have agreed to sell 'em an entire new fleet of Kilos," he rasped. "And if they have, we'll remove them. Even Rankov understands that. When we saw the first new one in BA last week, I made it clear to him on the phone that the U.S. would not stand still while the Iranians hold up half the industrial world to ransom because of some mad fucking Muslim belief that they own the Gulf of Iran."

"Absolutely, sir."

"Anyway, George, I guess that new building is big enough and serious enough for us to take an interest. Thanks for bringing the photographs. I think we better get a couple of guys in there to take a look, since the satellite can't do it for us . . . You better get back. I'll talk to Langley."

Five hours later the CIA's Middle East chief, Jeff Austin, was on the secure line to the White House imparting the news that the Agency was well aware of the new building, but were at a loss to find out what precisely was going on.

"Admiral," he said, "everyone in the area is aware of the construction. Apparently they dug out a foundation half the size of the Grand Canyon and dumped the sand back in the desert.

Caused a daily dust storm. Our best guess is a dry dock, possibly for submarines. I believe they lost their little fleet . . . er . . . coupla years back in some kind of an accident."

"Oh, yes . . . that's right. I remember reading something about that."

"Well, sir . . . I'm not sure how strongly you feel about it . . . and the security at the Bandar Abbas base is very hot right now. But I could try and get a couple of guys in there to take a look. Trouble is they'd have to swim in, and even if they reached the building, I'm not sure they could get close enough. Even then, they wouldn't really know what they were looking at."

"Uh-huh. I see that. Do we have anyone inside the base?"

"One man, an Iranian, white-collar guy in the procurement office . . . middle level . . . useful, too. We find out most of the ships they're buying before the order gets placed."

"Didn't find out about the new Kilo, did he?"

"Nossir. He did not."

"Could he get one of our top guys into the base?"

"Possibly, sir. Leave it with me. I'll get back to you in the morning. It's the middle of the night in Iran."

"Okay, Jeff . . . make it early. I don't like submarine activity among the towelheads, right?"

"Nossir."

At 0830 the following morning Jeff Austin reported back. "They're working on it, sir. There is, it seems, the possibility of a VIP pass to the base. Our man in there has used it before. He thinks the pass might just get him through the gate out near the building . . . but he's not sure. They'll be back to us in a couple of days."

"Fine. Keep at it. I'm concerned about the Iranians."

"Yessir."

Midday. January 14, 2005.
Special Ops Room.
Bandar Abbas Naval Base.

"Did you see this report, Admiral. The one just in."

"Not yet, Ben. What's it say?"

"It's brief, from the security chief out on the main gate to the new dock. It reads:

In accordance with your instructions, I am reporting on two men we turned away at 1052 this morning for having incorrect identification passes. One of them was an office executive, Abbas Velayati, who has some clearance but not enough to enter the site. The other was a VIP guest with a correct pass, but again without clearance to the site. He said he was from Ukraine. I believe both men may be found in the procurement office, according to Velayati's identification pass.

"We must place them under immediate arrest," snapped Admiral Badr. "Neither of them could have any reason for going out there except to snoop around. We should interrogate them both. Harshly."

"I would be inclined to do none of that," replied Commander Adnam. "In fact I'd prefer to do the exact opposite. I think we should apologize for treating a guest here in such a brusque manner, then issue the correct documents for them to go out and visit the new dock, and even the model room . . . perhaps at around 1800 when the day shift is packing up. Then we can shoot them both. It would save a lot of time . . . and we would be confident our secrets were safe."

"My God, Ben. You mean I should instruct one of the guards to execute them?"

"Absolutely not. Say nothing to anyone. I intend to deal with them myself. Out by the new pumping station . . . in my new capacity as tour guide. I believe they're pouring the concrete foundation in the morning. Most convenient, don't you think?"

January 19, 2005.
Office of the National Security Advisor.
The White House.

"Bad news I'm afraid, Admiral," said Jeff Austin, even before he pulled up a chair to Admiral Morgan's desk.

"Lay it on me."

"We've had a disaster in Bandar Abbas. Lost two men, one of them our only insider in the Naval base; the other one's Tom Partridge, senior field officer, speaks Russian and Iranian. They both disappeared five days ago."

"Where?"

"Out at the base. Our man at Abbas got Tom in, on some kind of a VIP pass, and neither of them have been seen since. The Iranian's wife has kicked up a huge fuss, but the military police say they have no knowledge of anything. They say both men left the base at the regular time. The civilian police say it is nothing to do with them. My guess is they were both caught, and shot."

"Jesus Christ, Jeff. That's bad. Did it get in the papers out there?"

"Not a word. Ever since that building got started, the security's been cast-iron. We have a man in the local newspaper, and he knows absolutely nothing. Nor is he planning to investigate. We only found out when both men missed their check calls, two days after they went missing."

"Hmmmmm. We better sit on this for a few days. See if anything pops up. One thing we do know . . . they're pretty damned touchy down there, whatever the hell it is they're up to."

January 20, 2005.
Special Ops Room.
Bandar Abbas Naval Base.

"Okay, Ben. We got a communication back from Moscow. They've agreed to sell us the systems . . . four of the new SA-N-6 Grumble Rifs . . . the one you suggested in the first place. It took 'em long enough . . . and it's not cheap . . . $300 million, including 50 SAMs."

"All of those Russian missiles are pretty reliable. I'd say a 95 percent chance of a successful launch and flight. Kill probability depends on target maneuvers and countermeasures. But this one is very fast, hits Mach-2.5—1,700 mph—almost immediately. It's good to altitude 90,000 feet. Carries a 90kg warhead. The export version may need minor modification."

"Are the Russians using 'em?"

"Uh-huh. I think they're replacing a lot of the old SA-N-3s with them. I read somewhere they completely tested it on one of those old Kara-Class cruisers. The *Azov*, I think. She's in the Black Sea. What do they say about delivery? You know what they're like."

"Well, Ben, I think we can look forward to something in the next month. This system is fairly new, and it's in production, and we are very good customers. All four of them are coming on a freighter, direct from the Black Sea, and through the canal. According to this, it will clear Sevastopol in four weeks, pending receipt of our money."

"They do not, of course, have the slightest idea why we are buying Grumble-type surface-to-air missiles?"

"No. They do not. We told them we live in fear of an air strike against us from the U.S.A. We require the missiles strictly for anti-aircraft defensive purposes, to protect our navy base here in Bandar Abbas. These things could take out an incoming American fighter bomber . . . and the Russians had no reason to question us further. Anyway, I think they'll take the money from anyone these days."

The admiral looked at his watch. "Ben, we have to go. The flight's taking off in a half hour."

"Since we're the only passengers, I expect they'll wait for us," the commander said, smiling. But he stood up, quickly tidied his desk, checked out with security downstairs, and joined Admiral Badr on the upstairs landing.

1700. January 20, 2005.
The home of the Ayatollah in the Kheyabon area of Tehran.

One of the disciples opened the side door to the courtyard for the two Naval officers. He touched his left hand to his forehead and brought it down in an elegant arc. "Admiral," he said, nodding with respect. And to Ben he added, "Good afternoon, Mr. Dundee," barely suppressing his overwhelming joy at the keenness of his wit. Commander Adnam smiled, turned to the admiral, and said, "Sir, in the Royal Navy that would be described as an in joke."

They walked past the fountain and into the cool stone-floored room in which the Ayatollah sat, accompanied by the *hojjat-el-Islam* and a robed Iranian politician from the Ministry of Defense. Greetings were exchanged with grace and eloquence, as is the custom among the educated classes of Iran. But there was an edge to this gathering, and both Ben and the admiral sensed it immediately.

The Ayatollah was anxious to begin, but he did not rush into the most pressing aspect of the discussion. Instead, he began carefully, summarizing the progress report he had received from the top-secret project down on the south coast.

He confirmed that he understood the team had been selected from among the best men in the Navy. The dry dock was just about complete and would be flooded inside ten days, and the new missile system would leave the Black Sea on a freighter within a matter of days. Everything was slightly ahead of schedule, and there had been no serious outside inquiries as to the nature of the operation, save for two CIA spies who had tried and failed to gain entrance to the building site.

For all of this he congratulated his admiral and his new commander. But then his face took on a look of concern, and he spoke very quietly. "Commander Adnam," he said, "before I approved this project, you told me you intended to fit this missile system to a submarine. You even undertook to provide one. As you know, I authorized the expenditure because the dock would always be useful for our new Kilo, and the SAM system will serve as strong air defense for the base. However, before I authorize further funding, I need to know a great deal more detail about how you intend to proceed from here.

"For instance, upon which vessel do you intend to attach this extremely expensive Russian missile system? I think the time has come for us to know that."

"Sir, it will be engineered onto a submarine, right behind the fin for vertical launching."

"I see. Is this liable to be a difficult operation? I refer to fixing a surface-to-air missile system onto the deck of a submarine."

"I don't believe so, sir. It's just that it has never been done before. You see it's not the same as the big intercontinental ballistic missiles, with their extremely complex systems. We are operating with a much smaller, simpler beast, a wickedly accurate guided missile that travels at two and a half times the speed of sound, but only for around 40 miles."

"Well, Ben. Why do you think no one has ever before wanted to fire such a weapon from a submarine?"

"Oh, I think it's been talked about often, but there was never a very strong reason for doing it. They fit better on surface ships. Nonetheless, I have always considered it the most formidable possibility. A missile fired, as it were, from nowhere."

"Commander, do you envision using our only suitable submarine, the new Kilo from Russia?"

"Nossir. The Americans will be watching that too vigilantly. I am afraid we will have to be a great deal more subtle than that."

"You mean we must acquire another submarine, one which the Americans do not know about?"

"Yessir. I do."

"Then my colleagues and I believe that now is the time for you to explain precisely how you propose to obtain it. Are you suggesting the British, of all people, will sell us one? Or are you asking us to rent one, an old one from some moribund navy around the Gulf or North Africa? You have never told us, you know. And, so far as I can see, the entire project depends on the acquisition of the right submarine and the skill of our engineers."

"Yessir. It does."

"Well, Benjamin? Will you tell us your plan now? Then we can proceed to release the funds to go ahead. It may take a little time . . . you realize the new Kilo now costs $350 million?"

"Sir, had I intended to involve you in high expenditure for a submarine, I would have advised you accordingly many months ago. But I do not intend to do that."

"Then you are proposing we contact the British and make some attempt to lease one for a year, or something like that?"

"Nossir. I was not planning to do that either. I think that would be impossible, as would another expensive purchase."

At that point Admiral Badr stepped in, sensing the meeting was approaching an uncomfortable level of frustration.

"Ben," he interjected, "you have drawn me to the inescapable conclusion that you intend to use the plastic model submarine we have in the shed!"

Ben shook his head, and said gently, "Not quite. Actually, old chap, I was intending to steal one."

March 23, 2005.

2 30200MAR05. 31.00N, 13.45W. COURSE 060. SPEED 12."
Commander Adnam carefully wrote down the date, time, position, course, and speed in the manner of a lifelong Naval officer. He made the note only in his own diary, for he was a guest on board, but the old disciplined habits of the Navy, the endless recording, the blunt accuracy of even the smallest detail, never fade from the mind of a senior sailor. And for good measure the commander added, "Weather gusty, *Santa Cecilia* rolling forward, in a long swell."

They had been out for forty-seven days and had run nonstop for 13,500 miles, all the way from the Gulf of Iran, down the coast of East Africa, around the Cape of Good Hope, up the endless coast of West Africa. They were plowing north, 200 miles off the shore of Morocco, where the Atlas Mountains sweep down to the ocean, south of Marrakech.

The quarters were not comfortable, just a converted freight hold in this aging Panamanian-registered coaster of 1,800 tons. That was not much room for 21 fit men to sleep in, but the Iranian Navy had done its best. Bunks and hammocks had been rigged, there was plenty of water, the decks were roomy but sweltering hot, and the food was excellent. The rolling motion of the half-empty ship had caused some seasickness among the submariners, and the throb of the big diesel engines, so noisy in the hold, was with them twenty-four hours a day. Crossing the equator, it had been too noisy below, and too hot on deck. But the iron discipline of Ben's men held. No one complained.

The second of the two holds was full of fuel, so the freighter would not need to put ashore. That had been Ben's idea, during a daylong argument when everyone wanted to turn northwest through the Red Sea and steam straight through the Mediterranean, thus cutting the overall distance by almost a half. But the commander had been immovable.

"One visit by Egyptian customs at the canal," he had said slowly. "Just one visit. And they find a freighter, with a full crew, plus twenty-one other guys below, and a hold full of fuel. It's just too unusual. All right, I know we could be tourists, fishermen, a crew going to pick up another ship. But in my line of work, you never take that kind of a chance. And you certainly do not leave half a dozen customs officers wondering who the hell you really were. Gentlemen, I am sorry, but we go offshore in our freighter and make the voyage around the Cape. In private. No customs. No intrusions."

In the dark, windy, early-morning hours of March 23, out in the Atlantic, Ben Adnam was calculating, leaning on the starboard rail, gazing to the east, watching for lights. In his mind he was working out precisely when they would arrive at the selected spot in the middle of the English Channel, and now he jotted it down, heading back to the ship's radio room, which was empty.

He tuned to medium frequency, encrypted, and began transmitting his call sign, speaking clearly: *"Calling Alpha X-Ray Lima Three. This is November Quebec Two Uniform . . . radio check. Over . . ."*

The radio crackled a bit but remained silent. Ben transmitted again. *"Calling Alpha X-Ray Lima Three. This is November Quebec Two Uniform . . . radio check. Over . . ."*

Then, suddenly, after a delay of only a few seconds, *"Roger. This is Alpha X-Ray Lima Three. Over . . ."*

Ben spoke again. *"Two-eight-two-two-zero-zero Mike Alpha Romeo zero-five. Four-niner-five-zero November . . . zero-four-two-zero Whiskey. Over . . ."*

Then he repeated it, slowly and carefully. And the transmitter crackled again.

"Roger that. Out."

By then it was 0220, and the commander returned to the hold to sleep the rest of the night. The rendezvous was fixed.

241100MAR05.

By any standards she was a beautiful boat, a traditional white cruising yacht, which looked as if she might have once belonged to the Great Gatsby, or at least his French equivalent. Moored alongside, in the port of St. Malo, on the picturesque northern coast of Brittany, the bright teak door to her magnificent wheelhouse glinting in a pale wintry sun, the *Hedoniste* was a splendid sight. Eighty feet long, she had two staterooms, an exquisite, covered quarterdeck with an outside bar, a canopied helm above the wheelhouse, and luxurious sleeping quarters for ten. Her big twin screws were powered by two big diesels that could propel her through a good sea at 20 knots. Her call sign was Alpha X-Ray Lima Three.

On board the *Hedoniste* were the three men who had chartered her for one week, at a cost of $20,000, off-season rates. Perfectly dressed in designer yachting kit, they had arrived in St. Malo in a chauffeur-driven Mercedes limousine, each carrying expensive leather luggage. They had brought with them, in another car, their captain, an engineer, and a chef-butler.

The French agent took a cursory glance at their Turkish passports, and the three addresses either on, or close to, the avenue

Foche, in Paris, and rapturously handed over control of the boat to Arfad Ertegan, whose current French Masters' certificate fully entitled him to command the *Hedoniste*.

"You will be very 'appy, gentlemen," the agent had said, pocketing the banker's check for $20,000 cash, 15 percent of which was now his. "See you in one week."

The six young Iranian Naval officers, posing as Turkish millionaires, and their staff, had never had such a wonderful time. This was a very beautiful boat, built in England by Camper and Nicholson. They all appreciated that. They were ready to set off on the voyage across the Gulf of St. Malo, making an overnight stop at St. Peter Port on the Channel Island of Guernsey, then pressing on to the meeting point.

Essentially they had four days off, and the only dark cloud on their horizon was that Abdul Raviz, the "chef," was in fact the gunnery and missile officer in Iran's *Houdong*-Class fast-attack craft P307, out of Bandar Abbas. He had never actually been in a galley. Neither had any of the other five.

Hedoniste was laden to the gunwales with the finest French cuisine, but the combined culinary talent of its guests and crew would have had serious difficulty producing a piece of buttered toast.

They resolved to make a fast run to St. Peter Port and dine in the hotel. They carried with them a leather pouch full of French francs. The world, they knew, could be their oyster, if they could just work out how to shuck it.

282120MAR02. 49.50N, 4.20W. Course 020. Speed 7.

The *Santa Cecilia* was making a racetrack pattern on a dark cloudy night. The moon was completely hidden, and the westerly wind gusted occasionally over the short sea. Commander Adnam could see no ships anywhere along the horizon. He could hear only the hiss of the spray slashing back off the steel bow as the old freighter shouldered her way forward.

He had been on deck for half an hour, staring out to the southeast, watching for the running lights, listening for the deep throb of the twin diesels of the French-based luxury yacht. Twice he had thought he heard something, but the sound came from too far east. He knew the bearing for her approach, and in the darkness of the English Channel he stared through binoculars, straight down bearing one-three-five. But there was nothing out there, so far. Below in the sleeping hold, his men were ready, each of them in black wet suits, each of them variously armed, the two hit men from the Islamic Revolutionary Guards Corps rather better than the rest.

At 2145 he picked up the running lights of the *Hedoniste*, her white hull visible half a mile away. She was bang on time, making good headway through the bumpy sea. Ben ordered the captain to reduce speed to two knots, and huge fenders were hung off the starboard side, as the "Turkish millionaires" maneuvered alongside.

The sea was a thunderous nuisance, and the 80-foot yacht was rising and falling through 6 feet during the transfer. They used a climbing net and two rope ladders, but it was dangerous in the dark. Ben noticed that the two men from the IRGC waited for the right moment and jumped straight onto the *Hedoniste*'s foredeck. The other nineteen, including the commander, made the transfer less adventurously. Ten minutes later, Captain Ertegan revved the starboard engine and reversed away from the Panamanian freighter, which was about to head southwest.

He set a course of zero-two-zero, and the overloaded cruising yacht swung around to the north, making her way toward the great lighthouse standing guard over the legendary sailor's graveyard of the Eddystone Rocks, 25 miles away. At 8 knots Ben calculated the 133-foot-high, white warning beacon should be a couple of miles off their port beam by 0045. But they would see its two bright flashes, every ten seconds, long before that.

Meanwhile, the men were making their own introductions, though most of them had been acquainted before back at Bandar Abbas. Ben Adnam went briefly through the plan with the "Turkish playboys," and everyone could feel the atmosphere tightening as the team began to run last-minute equipment checks, paying particular attention to their breathing apparatus.

By midnight, the Eddystone Lighthouse looked very close, off the port bow less than 3 miles away. "Hold that course zero-two-zero," ordered Ben. "Make your speed ten, remember we're just a luxury yacht running in late from the Channel Islands . . . keep the decks clear for the moment . . . we have plenty of water and we're well clear of the rocks."

By 0100 the towering light, which has warned sailors of the dangers since 1698, was slipping behind, brightening the black water off their port-side quarter. The sharp white flashing light was certainly more efficient than the 60 great tallow candles of the eighteenth century, but Ben would have been glad of pitch-black just then, as *Hedoniste* drove forward toward the coastline of southwest England.

He had chosen a craft such as this because it was unlikely to attract the attention of the notoriously vigilant English coast guard, who were always apt to stop an old foreign freighter making its way to port in the small hours of the morning. There were still around 9 miles to run, but the sea was almost deserted along the inner east-going traffic lane. The men had started to blacken their faces with a special oil, and little was said as they prepared for their mission. They had gone over the plan a thousand times. No one was in any doubt about what was expected of him.

At 0155 Ben spotted the line of red lights on the radio masts high up on Rame Head. He estimated they were 4 miles away, right off the port bow, one of them flashing a warning to aircraft. The light on the western end of the breakwater was dead ahead.

Ben Adnam and his navigation officer, Lt. Commander Arash Rajavi, aged thirty-one, were alone under the canopy of the exposed upper bridge while Captain Ertegan steered from the warm wheelhouse below. Both men were protected from the chill March night by their wet suits, and on their heads they wore dark balaclavas, which they would keep on under the tight-fitting black-rubber hoods they would need for the mission.

Suddenly, in his naturally soft voice, the lieutenant commander said, "Sir, can I ask you a question?"

"Fire away," replied Ben.

"How do you actually know the submarine is there?"

"I know," said Ben.

"But how?"

"Well, first, I read last August that the Brazilians were negotiating to buy one of the Royal Navy's Upholder-Class submarines, HMS *Unseen*, and they hoped to take delivery in the submarine base in Rio de Janeiro around May 15. I calculated twenty-eight days at 9 knots for the 5,500-mile journey, so they probably intended to clear Plymouth Sound around April 18.

"I knew there would be a six-week workup period for the Brazilian crew right out here in the Channel beginning around March 7. That would mean the submarine would arrive in the Devonport Navy dockyard for maintenance three weeks before that. On February 1, just before we left, I asked our agent in England to check when HMS *Unseen* was scheduled to leave the base at Barrow-in-Furness. That part was easy. They were having a little ceremony to say good-bye to her on February 14. So I knew everything was right on schedule. She has been sighted since then . . . working down here.

"So . . . Arash, you will find that *Unseen* will be right out there where I say she'll be. Moored on the big Admiralty buoy, 440 yards inside the breakwater. The buoy is huge . . . they say it could hold an aircraft carrier in a full gale. But that's where she'll be, three weeks into her workup, with about forty Brazilians on board. I know. I've moored on that buoy in a submarine while I was training here. That's where all Royal Navy workup submarines tend to spend their weekday nights if they're not out at sea."

"Sir, you are very smart man."

"Still breathing," said the commander absently.

By 0220 the sea was calmer in the lee of the Rame Headland, and Ben ordered an increase in speed, to 12 knots. They looked like a typical big motor yacht with nothing to hide, charging in from the Channel Islands, running late, anxious to make Oliver's Battery, the big marina, northeast of Drake's Island, deep in Plymouth Sound. Innocence, thy name is Benjamin, and to underline it, he personally called the marina on Channel M to check their berth and give an ETA.

The sky was brighter, the streetlights of Plymouth casting a glow in the sky to the north. Through his glasses Ben could make out the old familiar breakwater that guards the sound—right out in the middle, more than three-quarters of a mile long, a low man-made construction of concrete and rocks, with a lighthouse on either end.

Ben could see the light flashing at the western end, and as they drew ever closer, he picked up the little intercom, and snapped, "*Stand by!*" No reply was needed, and now they were right opposite the light.

"Four hundred meters," said Ben. "Lead swimmers prepare to go . . . reduce speed . . . make it eight knots for the next half mile."

He lifted his night-vision binoculars and could make out the dark hulk of the submarine out on the buoy, a quarter mile off the starboard beam.

"This is it . . ." he said. "Lead swimmers . . . GO." And he heard a soft splash as the flippers of the first two Islamic Revolutionary Guards hit the dark waters of Plymouth Sound together.

"Okay everyone, let's go . . . Six at a time over the port side. I'll go last . . . then we'll regroup and swim in together . . . 50 yards behind Lieutenant Commander Ali and his man. They're well on their way now."

Ben pulled down his face mask, fixed his breathing gear, and dropped over the side of *Hedoniste*. He checked with all three group leaders that everyone was safe, then gave the order to swim forward, using flippers, just below the surface. And the nineteen-strong Iranian Naval hit squad began to kick slowly through the water toward HMS *Unseen*.

Out in front, Ali Pakravan heard the motor yacht head on up the sound, lights still on full, the noise growing fainter. But he kept swimming: kicking and gliding, no splashing, no arm movement, just the legs, just as they had trained. His colleague, Seaman Kamran Azhari, swam just behind him, the rifle with the night sights clipped to his back.

After seven minutes Ali came to the surface and tried to see the submarine. It took a few moments for him to focus; then he saw her, about 100 yards ahead. In a few more klicks he would be able to see on the fin the white marking S41, the individual identifying mark of the jet-black, 230-foot torpedo and mine-laying patrol submarine, now a part of the Brazilian Navy.

They made their way slowly to the steep, slippery slope of the bow, hidden by its curve, and in the water they prepared the special electromagnetic clamps. Seaman Azhari placed the first two a foot out of the water, then hauled himself up and softly placed two more, three and a half feet higher up *Unseen*'s bow. Next he unclipped the rifle from his back, as the lieutenant commander began to work his way up beside him, moving the magnetic clamps one at a time to give himself purchase.

It took Ali two minutes to reach a point where he could safely lie on the downward curve of the bow. High above he could see the fin, on top of which, he knew, was the night guard. According to Ben, he would just see the man's head and shoulders above the rail of the bridge. And he would see it very clearly through the night-vision telescopic sight on the rifle.

Ali moved one of the clamps and took up his sniper's position on the casing. Ben was right. He could see the sentry up there, but the man was standing sideways, hunched against a light rain that was beginning to fall, and made a very difficult target. Ali, the best marksman in the Iranian Navy, was uncertain whether to wait or fire, but he decided that time was a luxury he did not have, so he lined up the crosshairs of the rifle sight with the guard's left temple. He steadied himself, held his breath, and shot Seaman Carlos Perez dead, from a range of 110 feet. As it made its exit, the snub-nosed bullet blew away the entire right side of the Brazilian's head. There was no sound save for the familiar soft pop made by a big rifle fitted with a silencer.

With the night guard taken care of, the Iranian lieutenant commander stood up on the casing to signal to the rest of the swimmers it was safe to work their way around to the port side of the submarine. Handing the rifle back to Azhari, he moved along the casing and unclipped the rope ladder he had carried with him. He made it secure, then slid it silently down the hull and into the water. Almost immediately he saw the black-hooded figure of Commander Adnam coming through the water, and Ali Pakravan called out softly in the night, "Here, sir. Right here."

Ben came up the ladder, still using his breathing gear. Right behind him were two other submariners, both of whom had previously served in the old Iranian Kilos. They moved swiftly to the door at the base of the fin and unclipped it gently. Ben opened it and led the way inside the fin to the top of the conning tower, still undetected. He pulled from his pocket a sealed grenade, a special chlorine grenade, which he prepared and threw straight down the tower hatchway. He waited for what seemed an age after it had gone off with a soft fizzing noise. But it was only a minute, and he climbed down after it, followed by his two henchmen in the full breathing gear.

At the bottom of the tower, in the control room they separated, one man heading forward and one aft, rolling more grenades ahead of them. Ben stayed right where he was, acting as communications number to the men above as they gathered silently on the casing, under the supervision of Lt. Commander Ali Pakravan.

Of the thirty-eight Brazilians aboard, none survived the first two minutes. Those asleep never awoke. Those awake gasped, choked, and quickly died. The massive level of concentrated chlorine released into a confined space, was sudden, silent, and deadly. It took less than ten minutes to ensure no one remained alive.

With the possibility of survivors eliminated, Ben himself started the engines, running them steadily, with the ventilation and battery fans working flat out to clear the hull of the poisonous gas. They tested the atmosphere constantly until almost 0400, when Commander Adnam declared the ship clean so the cold men on the casing could safely come below. There was some nervousness among the team members who did not have full breathing gear, but they all wore small chlorine-proof gas masks and went about the depressing business of dragging the bodies to the torpedo room, where they would be stored, each one zipped tight in a waterproof

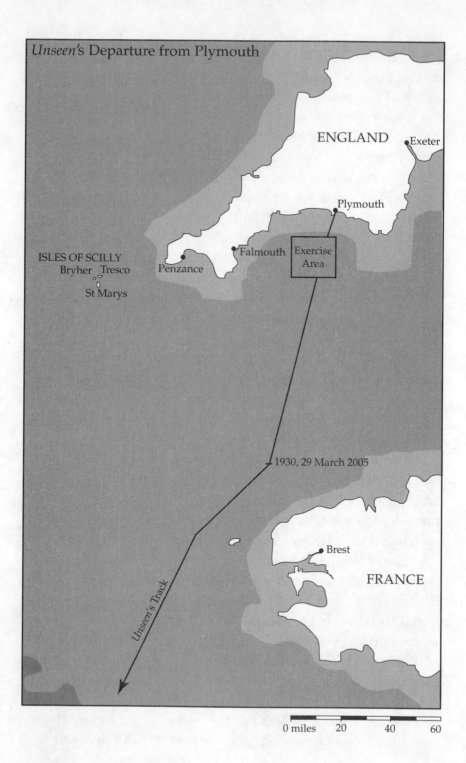

Unseen's Departure from Plymouth

ENGLAND

Exeter

Plymouth

ISLES OF SCILLY
Bryher   Tresco
St Marys

Penzance

Falmouth

Exercise
Area

1930, 29 March 2005

Brest

FRANCE

Unseen's Track

0 miles   20   40   60

body bag the team had brought with them. They would be disposed of at the first fueling stop out in the cold Atlantic off Gibraltar. There was, of course, no question of dumping them out into Plymouth Sound.

By 0400 Commander Adnam had located the ship's weekly Practice Program and the daily signal log. These two items had told him what to expect. Even the names of the four British training staff. The dreaded Sea Riders, he remembered, were due to come back on board at 0755 that morning. Same team all week. He noted that the Brazilians were a little behind where they should be at this stage of the proceedings. The previous day the crew had been practicing routine snorkeling drills, starting, running, and stopping the diesels while submerged.

"Should have finished that last week," he murmured, as he turned the pages, trying to find out what they were scheduled to do today. "Good job old MacLean's not training them. He'd have made them walk the plank by now."

As he had guessed, *Unseen* was due to sail at 0800. This was listed alongside the Exercise Area, Stop Time, and Type of Exercise. The day's activities were simply listed as INDEX—Independent Exercises. But there were some scribbled notes in the margins that told him they had been scheduled for emergency maneuvers: matters such as the avoidance of oncoming shipping; plane breakdowns; steering failure; failure of the systems that govern seawater, electronics, hydraulics, mechanics. Breakdown drills. Fire drills. Flooding drills . . . etc., etc. But there was also the most blinding bit of luck—the submarine was to stay out overnight, getting some much-needed practice on special drills, in particular night snorkeling

Ben read the Orders slowly and carefully, then located the previous day's Next-of-Kin signal, the one every submarine captain sends to his shore-based headquarters immediately before departure. This details all changes to the crew list in the NOK book held ashore; the final update, ensuring accurate names and addresses of the next of kin of *every* man aboard, just in case the submarine should disappear.

At 0500 he called a short briefing for his officers, while the rest of the team continued to familiarize themselves with their specialist areas of the ship. Of course, everything was more real than it had been in the Bandar Abbas model, where they had practiced so intensely for many weeks. But, with very few exceptions, every switch, valve, and keyboard was exactly where it had been in the model; the precious data from the big computer in Barrow-in-Furness had taken care of that.

"Gentlemen," said the commander, "I am sorry for the delay, but I have been trying to read up on procedures. Our sailing time is, as planned, 0800, three hours from now. I have the Next-of-Kin update, and the Squadron Standing Orders. At about 0755 we are expecting four Royal Navy Sea Riders to arrive from the dockyard to supervise the day's exercises. And we will take care of them as planned. We will allow them to arrive safely and go below. Lieutenant Commander Pakravan, well-done tonight. You and Seaman Azhari did an outstanding and difficult job. I know I can leave you to silence the Sea Riders as soon as they come below.

"The only major change to our plan is that I intend to send *Unseen*'s diving signal to cover today and tomorrow's program, because she's not due back until tomorrow evening. However, we must send in a Check Report every twelve hours because this ship is still in Safety Workup. I intend to comply with all of the external procedures when we depart, and it is vital that we make no errors. I also intend to *walk* out of Plymouth Sound with this ship, not run. When we leave here I do not want one shred of suspicion left behind us. That way we have many hours to get free. And once we are free, they'll never find us."

Like all of the Iranians, Lt. Commander Arash Rajavi listened carefully to the intensive two-hour training program they all faced. And he tried to stay calm. But it was hard to cast from his mind the overwhelming magnitude of their crime. There they were, sitting bang in the middle of the historic harbor of Sir Francis Drake, the very cradle of the Royal Navy, having *stolen* one of their submarines and killed all of the crew. Three hours from now Commander Adnam was planning summarily to murder two British officers and probably a couple of petty officers. *My God!* he thought. *If we are caught, they will execute every last one of us.*

But he fought back his fear and his natural instinct to escape from there at all costs as he listened to the cool, measured words of his leader. Not for the first time, Lieutenant Commander Rajavi decided that Benjamin Adnam was, without doubt, the most cold-blooded man he had ever met.

Two hours later, neatly dressed in Brazilian Naval uniforms, four hands, in company with a young officer, waited on the casing for the arrival of the Sea Riders. They spotted them through the cabin windows of the harbor launch, speeding down the well-marked channel west of Drake's Island, toward *Unseen* at 0750. Two more officers, plus a lookout, were on the bridge, all in Brazilian uniforms. Five minutes later the launch was alongside, and the young officer on the casing saluted, wishing the Royal Navy men "Good Morning" in an Iranian accent which Ben hoped would be assumed to be Brazilian.

The launch headed back to the dockyard, and one by one the four Royal Navy men came on board, making for the open hatch on top of the casing. There was an 8-foot steel ladder inside, and the leader, Chief Petty Officer Tom Sowerby, made his way expertly downward, his final steps on this earth. As his right foot hit the ground three of the Iranians grabbed him, with a hand clamped tight over his mouth to stop him crying out as Ali's knife cleaved into his heart. Lt. Commander Bill Colley, next on the ladder, never realized what was happening below until it happened to him as well.

Eight minutes later, all four of the Royal Navy men had joined the pile of zipped-up bodies in the torpedo room. It was 0759, and Commander Adnam was preparing to leave British waters.

At 0800 sharp, he ordered the Brazilian ensign hoisted on top of the fin. The diesel generators were still running sweetly as they slipped the buoy, and Ben ordered, "Half astern," then "Half ahead" as he turned HMS *Unseen* away from Plymouth, making coolly for the western end of the breakwater, and freedom. No one, in all of the great sprawling Royal Navy base, had the remotest idea that anything was other than normal.

The men accompanying Lieutenant Commander Rajavi on the bridge were surprised at the sight of Rame Head as they ran fair down the channel, keeping the big red buoys to starboard. The headland, steep-sided, solid rock, no trees, with a small chapel on top, looked even higher by day, visible for almost 20 miles. Ben Adnam's engineering officer had the big electric motor running steadily, with the diesels working to provide the power.

Below in the control center, the CO studied the operations area where *Unseen* was scheduled to work that day, and headed for the northeast corner of the "square," a couple of miles west of the Eddystone Lighthouse. There was almost 200 feet of water under the keel, and, with all signals now correctly sent to home base, he ordered the submarine to dive. The great black hull slid down beneath the cold gray waves, leaving behind a mystery that would rival that of the *Marie Celeste*, and which would last for many, many months.

Commander Adnam was in perfect position. He was in precisely the area he was supposed to be. He wanted to test his team in some under way drills in precisely the same way the Sea Riders would have been testing the Brazilians. In the following few hours he worked the Iranians through the electrical and mechanical systems, the sonar, the radar, the ESM, the communications, the trimming and ballasting, the hydraulics and air systems, even the domestic water and sewage systems. He checked the periscopes and low-light aids, sometimes running easily at nine knots, occasionally stopping in the water to give his Officer of the Watch experience at trimming this new and strange submarine. More than half of the time was spent snorkeling, making certain the ship's battery was well topped-up. Sometimes the commander offered quiet advice to the younger men, sometimes he pushed them harder. But there was never an edge to his voice. He was always conscious that a tired crew might make mistakes, but not so many as a tired and frightened crew.

Three times he took her deep, insisting his men grow accustomed to the diving angles. Twice, in midafternoon at the southern end of his ops area, he ran her on the surface, which Lieutenant Commander Rajavi regarded as one of the most reckless decisions he had ever witnessed. *What if anyone should see us?* At one point late in the afternoon, he actually ventured to ask if the CO considered it possible that there might be a hunt on for them. "Would you not feel safer, sir, at periscope depth?"

"There is no danger," replied the commander. "If there were, I would not be on the surface."

At 1930 he sent in his Check Report to the operating authority, Captain SM2 in Devonport, half an hour early. He was 90 miles from his diving position, and now he turned the ship toward the southwest, running throughout the night on course two-two-five, heading for the northwestern coast of Brittany, snorkeling constantly, keeping the battery well charged. They went deep only twice in the small hours, once when they detected a threatening sweep of British military radar, and once for a large merchant ship close by.

At 0700 the following morning Commander Adnam sent in his second Check Report, the last one. By then he was, of course, well beyond his ops area, but naturally it was assumed the signal was sent from *Unseen*'s correct, designated place in the ocean.

By 1800 that evening, when his Diving Signal was due to expire, he would be 180 miles away from *Unseen*'s designated area of activity. But by then, he would be running deep down the Atlantic, 120 miles west of the big French Naval base at Brest. Ben Adnam would take no chances there.

301725MAR05. Second Submarine Squadron Operations Center.

Lt. Commander Roger Martin, the staff officer, Operations, had just about had it for the day, coping as he did with the frenetic mass of tiny problems that made up this unenviable job. Aside from the endless stream of Orders coming across his desk, he had also been coordinating all the plans for exercises among the boats in the squadron. Not just the workup boats; Lieutenant Commander Martin was dealing with the exercises for all of the squadron boats based in the vast Devonport dockyard.

He took a deep swig of tea, checked his watch, and prepared to hand over for the night to the duty staff officer, Lt. Commander Doug Roper. He checked his list over again, as he always did when there were boats at sea, ensuring that every anticipated Check Report and Surfacing Signal was recorded on the State Board complete with times when ships were due to make contact.

By now he could see the fair-haired athletic figure of Lieutenant Commander Roper striding along the corridor, and he greeted him cheerfully. "Hello, Doug, we're more or less in order here . . . except for *Unseen*. She's not actually late . . . but her Diving Signal does expire at 1800, and she's been well ahead of time with communications for the past couple of days. I was just beginning to wonder . . . still, Bill Colley was her senior Sea Rider today, and he did mention he might give the Brazilians an extra hard time out there. He reckons they're slipping behind with their program. Perhaps he's keeping them at it until the last minute."

"Probably," replied Lieutenant Commander Roper. "Still, you always wonder when they cut it fine. I'll keep a close eye on the situation."

"Okay, old pal. I'll be off now . . . have a good night."

Doug Roper was a very ambitious officer, aged only thirty-one. He was not yet married, and money from his family timber business in Kent had enabled him to buy a flashy, low-slung, white sports car. In a predominantly middle-class operation like the Royal Navy this might have caused some envy, but this lieutenant commander was universally popular, and in addition to having a keen and profoundly watchful mind, he worked extremely hard.

He studied the sheets he had been handed and checked his watch. It was 1740. He checked for *Unseen*'s Surfacing Signal. Nothing. And for no accountable reason, alarm bells began to go off in Doug Roper's head. Time was running out. If *Unseen* continued to live up to her name for much longer, he was going to become the busiest man in Plymouth.

He realized that Lieutenant Commander Colley might just have forgotten to send the Surfacing Signal. But he knew *when* she was supposed to be on the surface, and by now she should be *on* the surface, close to Plymouth. *Maybe*, thought Roper, *she's had a total communications breakdown, and is right now running through the harbor, trying to contact anyone in sight to pass her signal by light, VHF or word of mouth.* But somehow he doubted that.

And at 1800 on the dot, he hit the phone to the captain, Second Submarine Squadron (SM2), to report the overdue Surfacing Signal—standard Submarine Safety Instructions (Allied Tactical Publication ATP 10). Doug Roper knew that a disaster must be considered a possibility.

The captain instantly put into operation Comcheck, a procedure that effectively means, *Hey*, Unseen, *haven't you forgotten something?* But in fact it alerted all Royal Navy ships in the area that a communication was urgently required with *Unseen*. The signal from the Second Submarine Squadron was regarded as sufficiently important for a copy to be relayed to the Flag Officer Submarines in Northwood, 250 miles away in West London.

Thirty minutes later nothing had been heard, and it was almost impossible that the submarine had not yet found some way to communicate her safety. By 1835, Captain Charles Moss was in the Staff Office. So was Lt. Commander Roger Martin. The mood was somber. The Royal Navy had not lost a submarine since the diesel-electric A-Class boat, *Affray*, had gone down in the Channel in April 1951. Everyone knew it had taken months to find her.

At 1900, they went to the next phase, SUBLOOK, because each of the four officers in the room knew that if *Unseen* was on the surface, someone should have reported in. If she was dived and anyone had survived, they'd have released the expendable communications buoys, or the main indicator buoys, situated one forward, one aft. If anyone had gotten out, their locator beacons should have been picked up. But not a word had been heard, and she was an hour overdue. The worst was feared. It always is when they issue SUBLOOK.

Because this is a very big word in the Navy. It comes in capital letters, a serious message that will alert other nations, and rescue Coordination Centers all around the English Channel. It also alerts the RN Casualty Organization and the Public Relations network. *We are very much afraid we have lost a submarine, NO SHIT.*

The word whipped around the base that *Unseen* was missing. Four available guided-missile frigates moored alongside in Devonport were ordered out to the exercise area. Royal Navy warships were signaled to stop whatever it was they were doing and start looking and listening. The senior officer out there, Captain Mike Fuller in the 4,000-ton Type-42 destroyer *Exeter* was ordered to coordinate a methodical search of the area. Two maritime patrol aircraft, big RN Nimrods, were diverted to search the waters south of Plymouth Sound, under Captain Fuller's control.

The weather was deteriorating. With the fading light of that early-spring evening, the breeze was backing southwest, and a gale-force wind was gusting off the Atlantic straight up the English Channel. The sea was rougher than it had been for a week, and Captain Fuller, on the bridge of *Exeter*, was extremely concerned the search would become impossible if sea conditions worsened much more.

Back in the Staff Office, Lt. Commander Doug Roper, as the duty officer, was dealing with the minute-by-minute reports coming in. But he also could see the looks of real concern on the faces of Roger Martin and Charles Moss. He could hear the captain saying, "Time is of the absolute essence. The quicker we find it, the better our chances of getting any survivors off."

All four men knew that a major accident seemed certain, but that Bill Colley and his men might still be on board, on the bottom somewhere, their air supply strictly limited, some men possibly injured, waiting to escape when the searchers finally arrived. All submariners realize there's no point just getting out and floating up into a raging, empty sea, where death is just about inevitable. The trick is to float up into the arms of your rescuers, who will haul you out, administer first aid, and get you into the ship's hospital, where they can at least treat hypothermia and possibly the "bends" and CO_2 poisoning.

By 2130 two of the frigates were working with active sonars, checking out known wrecks and bottom contacts, to see if a new one had appeared. Captain Moss had ordered two minesweepers into the area because their sonars are particularly well suited to wreck searches. In the next twenty minutes they began scanning the bottom of the English Channel, trying to sift out a new wreck from the thousands of others that had been there since World War II. In Captain Fuller's destroyer, and in the four frigates, the navigation officers pored over charts detailing almost all of the wrecks on the floor of the Channel. Commander Rob Willmot, in the 4,200-ton Duke-Class Type-23 *Portland*, thought they had something out on the western edge of the "square." It was not marked as a known wreck, and, but for the sea conditions, he was ready to send down two divers and a TV camera to have a closer look.

However, despite an evening full of false hopes, and false alarms, no one had anything firm. At midnight Captain Moss issued the fateful SUBMISS Signal, six hours after *Unseen*'s Diving Signal expired. There was now in place a full-scale, coordinated, international search, which would continue until the submarine was found. In the hard-edged mind of the Royal Navy, submarines do not just disappear. They might go missing, because they have sunk, or even blown up, or even been blown up. Nonetheless, the submarine, or its wreckage, had to be somewhere.

The critical issue was, had *Unseen* left her area of operations? Why on earth should she have left it? Bad navigation? Incorrect tidal calculations? Sheer carelessness? Not very likely. But the specter of the *Affray* still haunted the Royal Navy submarine operators—because that 1,800-tonner out of Portsmouth on a training exercise, full of men just in from the surface Navy, was finally found on the bottom a long way outside her allocated area, right down by the Hurd Deep, off the Channel Island of

Alderney, weeks after any hope of survivors had disappeared.

Shortly after midnight the next of kin of the four British Sea Riders were informed. A communication was drafted to the Brazilian Navy Headquarters in Rio de Janeiro detailing the men who were on board. The press were informed very quickly, because that way they could be controlled a little more, rather than having them pick something up on the Naval networks and start off by asking, *Are You Trying To Keep This A Secret?*

Nonetheless everyone knew the press would do its worst, dragging up every Royal Navy submarine that had ever been lost, starting with *Affray*, then going back a year to January 1950, when *Truculent* collided with a merchant ship and sank in the Thames Estuary, then moving back to June 1, 1939, when the *Thetis* went down off Birkenhead. It was all more than half a century ago, but still it was sufficient for the media, apparently, to conclude that submarines are not much better than iron coffins. At least that's how the news was presented by the time the headline writers had gone to work. *Should Our Bravest Young Men Be Subjected To This Carelessness?*

At 1945 (EDT) the news reached the office of the director of National Security in Fort Meade, Maryland, and Admiral George Morris was very thoughtful. He read the brief details over and looked at a chart on one of the computer screens, tapping a button that drew it in closer, then took in a much larger area. *Out of Plymouth, eh? Long time since the Brits lost a submarine. Wonder what happened?*

Ten minutes later he had reached Admiral Morgan at the White House, still in his office, and interested, as ever, in *anything* to do with submarines.

"How long's it been missing, George?"

"Seven or eight hours since its Surfacing Signal was due."

"I don't mean that. How long since they heard from it?"

"They got a Check Report in at 0700 their time. 'Bout twelve hours before her Diving Signal expired."

"Hmmmm. Where was she?"

"Twenty miles off Plymouth Sound."

"They gotta lot of ships out there searching?"

"Guess so. They've had sonars working the bottom of the ocean for several hours, but no one's found anything."

"Ocean?" replied the old blue-water submariner. "That's not a goddamned ocean, it's some kind of a fucking mudflat. The English Channel's only about 20 feet deep. I bet the fucking periscope's sticking out of the water! Incompetent Brits. Couldn't find an elephant in a chicken coop."

George Morris laughed politely. "Anyway, they have found literally nothing. No buoys, no signals, no wreckage, no oil slick, no survivors. Damn thing just vanished off the face of the ocean. Sorry, Arnold . . . off the face of the mudflat."

Admiral Morgan chuckled. "They asked us for help yet?"

"No. At least no one's told me. But SUBLANT will know."

"Okay, George. Keep me posted on it, will you? And if the Brits do get in touch, would you have their Flag Officer give me a call . . . he's an old friend just got promoted. Admiral Sir Richard Birley. 'Course when I knew him he was Commander Dick Birley, trying to drive a Polaris boat. We shared a few laughs in London . . . too long ago. So long, George."

Arnold Morgan was late. It was after eight o'clock, the exact time he was due at a small French restaurant in Georgetown for an assignment to which he increasingly looked forward. It was only dinner with his secretary, which might almost have been mundane for a sixty-year-old, twice-divorced admiral. Except this secretary, the thirty-six-year-old divorcée Kathy O'Brien, was possibly the best-looking woman in the entire White House. A long-legged redhead from Chevy Chase, she had worked for the tyrannical Texan since first he had entered the building and almost fired his new chauffeur on opening day.

For one month she had gazed with awe at his command of the workings of the world's navies, his knowledge of international events, the intentions of various countries, his total mistrust of foreigners. For another six months she had watched him ride roughshod over men in the highest offices, contemptuous of stupidity, withering in his judgments, cynical in his appraisal of diplomats, especially foreign ones.

The President himself, a right-wing Republican from Oklahoma, trusted Arnold Morgan implicitly. He actually loved Arnold Morgan. So, fortuitously, did the beautiful Mrs. Kathy O'Brien. And the friendship had grown, hesitantly at first. For it was beyond the comprehension of Arnold Morgan, who had no illusions about his craggy lack of good looks, how any woman could be attracted to him, far less this goddess who worked as his secretary.

His failed marriages, and the endless criticisms of his wives, both of whom had summarily left him, had created a man who believed that all women were a mystery, and whatever it was they wanted or liked, it most definitely was not him. As such, he chose to "get along without 'em," and it had been so long since any woman had shown the slightest interest in him, he almost died when Kathy O'Brien said one day, "You, sir, eat too many of those damned roast beef sandwiches, and you drink too much coffee. Why don't you come out to my house tomorrow night, and I'll cook you a decent dinner?"

He was so utterly flabbergasted, he had just said lamely, "Okay, what are you going to cook for me?"

The slender Kathy, sassy to the last, called back "Roast beef," as she swung out of the door.

That had all started a year ago, during which time the admiral had discovered that this lady, who had her own money and did not particularly need the job, offered him what he had never had from either wife. She offered him total respect for what he did. In her heart Kathy O'Brien worshiped him, although she was not anxious for that aspect of the relationship to become known.

But unlike the wives, she had seen him operate first hand . . . talking to the President as an equal, laying down the law to people of incredible stature on the international stage. She had seen high officers of the CIA tremble before his wrath. She had seen top brass from the Pentagon arriving at the White House just to hear his opinion. She had fielded calls for him from the heart of the Kremlin. Even from Beijing.

As far as she was concerned, this five-foot-eight-inch, powerfully built military dynamo was the most important man in Washington. He was important not for his family background, and not just for his job. Nor even for the fact that he had been one of the Navy's best captains of a nuclear submarine. No, in Kathy's mind, Admiral Arnold Morgan was important for his towering intellect and his towering personality. He was biggest medium-sized man she had ever seen.

In turn she never minded if he was late . . . *Christ, he's probably saving the world.* She never scolded him when he forgot a gift, or failed to thank her, or was suddenly unable to accompany her to her mother's house in northern Maryland. Because she knew him. If Arnold could cram those little matters into his crowded life for her, he would do so. If not, he was probably in the Oval Office, or in the Pentagon, or visiting Admiral Morris at Fort Meade. He could be anywhere. How many girlfriends could say that? Not many. And above all, he was most definitely not a womanizer. As his secretary, Kathy *really* knew that.

And now as she waited at *Le Champignon,* nursing a *kir royale,* she smiled at how she knew he would look when he came in the door—flustered, irritated, preoccupied, worried he had forgotten something, a look like thunder on his face, frightening the *maitre d'* to death, telling him to get someone out there to park his car . . . until he saw her. And then the pent-up fury of Admiral Morgan would evaporate while she watched, and his face would light up, and he would lean over and tell her that he loved her above all else. And she almost wept with joy at the very thought of him.

He finally arrived at 2025, having fought his way up Pennsylvania Avenue in the pouring rain, cut across M Street and into Georgetown along Twenty-ninth Street. As she expected, he told Marc, the *maitre d'* to get someone to get rid of his car. But he was too late. Marc, like Kathy, was honored to be in the great man's presence, and he'd had someone out there waiting under the awning ever since Kathy was seated. The admiral always arrived and just jumped out, right outside the door, leaving the car running, with no thought for the two slightly confused Secret Servicemen who followed him everywhere in another vehicle. One of them would drive them both home to Mrs. O'Brien's house later.

The admiral greeted her with enthusiasm, since it had been all of three hours since they had seen each other. And he ordered the same drink as Kathy. The admiral was a curious dichotomy, because, for a man who professed to mistrust all foreigners, he had developed the most cosmopolitan taste in food, thanks in part to Kathy, who had lived in Paris with her former husband for almost three years in the 1990s.

Tonight they chose *pâté de foie gras*, followed by *sole meunière* for her, and *coq au vin* for the admiral. He selected a bottle of 1995 Puligny Montrachet to share with the first course, which Kathy could finish with her fish. And he chose a half bottle of 1996 Château Talbot to go with his chicken. It was an expensive dinner, and they tried to make time for it twice a week.

Admiral Morgan was financially better off than he had ever been, because his job as national security advisor to the President now carried a salary of almost $200,000, and under a new law he was also entitled to collect most of his admiral's pension while he served in the White House. The President himself had pushed that law through, because he believed it was absurd that top military people were being lost to government simply because their pensions were suspended while they worked as senior public servants.

"The pensions have been earned, over years and years of service," he said. "I expect these outstanding men to be paid entirely separately should they choose to enter another important job in government when their days in the armed services are over."

All of this was outstandingly good news for the admiral, because his two former wives had both remarried, his children were grown and earning, and, anyway, his daughter, like the wives, was not actually speaking to him right at the moment. His obligations were minimal.

Kathy, meanwhile, was noticing that her admiral was not

actually speaking to her much at the moment either. He was very much within himself, and munched contentedly.

"Is there anything the matter?" she asked.

And he looked up suddenly, "No, no . . . I'm sorry. I was just thinking about something . . . kinda bothering me."

"What kind of thing? Not me I hope."

"No, no. You don't look anything like an Upholder-Class submarine . . . entirely the wrong shape . . . and you're faster." He grinned his lopsided grin.

"What submarine?"

"Oh, it's just been announced that the Brits have lost a submarine in the English Channel. It's on all the news channels, and it'll be in every newspaper tomorrow. It's the first time they've lost one for a half century. There's a real fuss going on over there. Right now, as we sit here, half the Royal Navy is trying to find it, but there seems to be no sign."

"Oh, how horrible. Do you think it's on the bottom somewhere, and they're all still alive? How long have they got before the air runs out?"

"Not long . . . forty-eight hours at most . . . and they were last heard from about twenty hours ago. They're gonna have to move very quickly to save them."

"Look, darling, I know how awful it is and everything. But why is it giving you such concern?"

"To tell you truth I'm not sure. There's just something in the back of my mind that's bothering me. I think it's because there's been no sign of any wreckage, no oil, no buoys, nothing. Which means it went down intact. Now there could be a complete electrical failure, I suppose, but the Brits are damned good at this sort of thing, and modern sonars are damned good at sweeping the ocean floor. Chances are she's got some power, but no one's heard anything. And her area of operations was not that big. They've got God knows how many ships in there. And to me that suggests the submarine is not in its ops area. For some reason it went outside the square."

"Well is that so bad?"

"Only because it's missing. But if it did go outside the square, there are five clear reasons why it may have done so."

"Tell me what they are."

"One, they got confused, made a mistake. Two, they got careless, weren't paying attention. Three, catastrophic mechanical failure. Four, the submarine was hijacked by persons unknown who forced the crew to drive it somewhere. Five, the submarine was stolen, and the crew are all dead."

"Jesus. Are you serious?"

"Kathy, let me tell you something. When we lost the *Thomas Jefferson*, nearly three years ago, the whole darned thing started with a missing submarine. And a Navy that simply did not know where it had gone."

"I notice you always get very jumpy when there's any kind of a problem with a submarine."

"That's because I know what a menace they are in the wrong hands. And I'm not going to be all that relaxed until I know those guys in Plymouth have found it, either in good shape or wrecked. I just hate not knowing."

"You haven't spoken to anyone over there?"

"No. Not yet. But I was thinking about having a chat with FOSM tomorrow. He's an old friend."

"FOSM?"

"Sorry. Flag Officer Submarines. Dick Birley. He and I were in London together for a few months. Haven't spoken to him for a while. But he always sends me a Christmas card."

"Do you send him one?"

"Well, I don't really do Christmas cards."

"Perhaps we should think about rectifying that this year."

The admiral smiled. "Yes," he said. "I think we should. Perhaps it's nearly time we shared one."

"Then you'd have to find yourself a new secretary . . . and then I'd be the one waiting at home like all your other wives, while you run half the world. No thanks, Arnold Morgan, I'll marry you when you retire. Not one day earlier."

"Jesus Christ. It's like trying to negotiate with the Russian Navy. I'm not ready to retire."

"And I'm not ready to stay home waiting. Besides, I like to keep a good eye on you. And I can't do that if I'm Mrs. Arnold Morgan. I think things are just fine, just the way they are."

"I guess I love you, Kathy O'Brien. Don't ever go away."

"No chance of that. Are we going home, or are you going back to the factory?"

"We're going home."

310500MAR05. 47.02N 08.49W. Course 225. Speed 9.

HMS *Unseen* ran steadily southwest, almost 300 miles from Plymouth, 250 miles from the massive air-sea search being conducted, by four nations, on her behalf. The submarine had snorkeled for much of the night, and her battery was well topped-up as she made her way across the western reaches of the Bay of Biscay toward her first refueling point in the Atlantic, 500 miles off the Strait of Gibraltar.

Right there, in two days, she would locate the *Santa Cecilia*. And the crew could hardly wait to get there. Not because of a shortage of fuel, but because of the forty-two bodies piled in the torpedo room, zipped up in the bags, but decomposing and unsettling for the new owners of the ship.

Lieutenant Commander Pakravan was in favor of firing them straight out through the tubes, with the garbage, but that was principally because he had not given the matter serious thought. When he mentioned the subject to Commander Adnam he quickly realized just how little thought.

"No, Ali. Wouldn't work. Every time you use a torpedo tube to get rid of loose stuff, like an ill-fitting body bag, something always gets caught up. Then you have to get someone into the tubes to free it all up. It's more damned trouble than its worth.

"I worked out our plan of action long before we left Bandar Abbas, because I knew we would have to dispose of at least forty bodies, because that's how many Brazilians I knew there would be. The problem is they need to be weighted down. Decomposing bodies blow up with gases, and they float to the surface. Someone would plainly find one of them. So I decided we would have to be very thorough."

"You mean we have to get them up onto the casing ?"

"We do."

"But they're heavy as hell."

"Yes. I know. We'll rig up the small-stores davit, with a block and tackle right above the hatch. The blocks need to be 8 feet above it, so that each body can swing out onto the deck. There'll also be a big canvas bag, the one they use to catch seawater coming down the tower in rough weather on the surface. Looks like a huge spinnaker bag from a sailboat, but it'll do fine for us. All we need to do is get each body into it, then haul away."

"Sir, what about the weights? We don't have anything like that."

"I never thought we would. Which is why the freighter is bringing us a little gift, like 50 cubes of specially cast concrete, each one weighing 80 pounds, with a steel ring, and a long plastic belt to attach it to one of the bags. They've been aboard since we first left Bandar Abbas."

"I didn't see them."

"They don't take up much room, just a space 8 feet by 5 feet by 5 feet high. We stored them aft on the middle deck. No problem."

"Why do you want to tie them on? Why not just unzip the bags and shove a cube inside each one?"

"Have you ever smelt a five-day-old body, Ali? I wouldn't wish that on any of you. Specially times forty."

"Nossir."

Commander Adnam took her deep at 0600, just as the sky began to brighten over the Bay of Biscay. They would run all day 250 feet below the surface, and then come to periscope depth to snorkel again during the night. The same would apply during the following twenty-four hours, and Ben expected to make his rendezvous with the *Santa Cecilia* in the small hours of the next day, April 2.

011200APR05.
Submarine Staff Office. Royal Navy Dockyard, Devonport.

Lt. Commanders Roger Martin and Doug Roper were absolutely baffled. Not a sight, not a sound, not a fragmented sonar bleep. No wreckage, no buoys, no signals. Nothing. HMS *Unseen* had simply vanished. Whatever air had remained in the lost diesel-electric boat must have long since run out, and there was no longer any possibility of survivors.

The situation was officially SUBSUNK. The chilling Royal Navy signal to that effect had been put on the nets the previous day at 0900. This signal is reserved for use only when a submarine is known to have sunk. Consequently, the urgency had gone out of the search, because the ships were no longer involved in a life-or-death race to get the crew off the bottom of the sea.

Henceforth, it was strictly by the book. But HMS *Unseen* had to be found. And the area of search was being extensively widened, because it was clear the submarine had gone beyond its quite small exercise area. Three Royal Navy frigates and Captain Mike Fuller's *Exeter* were methodically sweeping the bottom with sonars, as were the two minesweepers. Eight times they had sent divers down, plus TV cameras, but there was never even a hopeful sign.

Meanwhile the press were laying it on the Royal Navy. "Experts" were demanding to know how such a thing could have happened. There were already distant allegations about bad training, poor discipline. "What on earth was the Navy thinking of, allowing a bunch of Brazilian rookies to drive this boat underwater? . . . *when it was known they were behind schedule in their training, and presumably competence* . . . was it not a fact that Lt. Commander Bill Colley was unhappy with their progress . . . was this not an accident waiting to happen . . . ?"

Every day the Navy was besieged by these simplistic questions, about a wildly complicated problem. The Public Relations department was on duty twenty-four hours a day. And Captain Charles

Moss knew that his days in the Royal Navy were probably numbered. Someone was going to be blamed for this, and there was no one else really. He could imagine what the admirals would say. *Captain Moss should have initiated SUBMISS earlier when it was perfectly clear there was no communication of any kind from Unseen. And the question of the Brazilians' competence must come into the matter. Did he or did he not know that Lieutenant Commander Colley was concerned? If not, why not?* Captain Moss, aged forty-seven, was already considering his future career opportunities out of uniform.

020230APR05. 35.22N 14.46W. Course 180. Speed 9. 240 miles due west of the Rock of Gibraltar.

Unseen continued south, in the dark, snorkeling. Commander Adnam took a sweeping all-around look for the lights of the *Santa Cecilia*. They still had ample fuel, but the CO was as anxious as anyone to get rid of the bodies in the torpedo room.

At 0240 they spotted her navigation lights, out on the southern horizon, returning from the North African port where she had refilled her massive converted diesel-fuel tanks, just in case *Unseen* was getting low. Thirty minutes later, Ben ordered the two ships together on the surface of a calm, moonlit sea.

The commanding officer explained that they did not currently require fuel, but that he would like to make a new rendezvous eighteen days hence, down in the doldrums, the hot windless seas around the equator. For now, they would just like food and water, and the concrete weights lifted over. Ben had no intention of telling anyone on the freighter what he wanted the weights for, and no one asked. There was something about Benjamin Adnam. He was not a man for idle chatter. If he wanted you to know something, he would tell you.

Ben stood up on the casing, watching as the hydraulic lifting arm on the *Santa Cecilia* hoisted and lowered the concrete cubes in a heavy-duty tarpaulin, ten at a time. His crew stacked them neatly on the unlit deck, and within a half hour the freighter captain waved them good-bye and turned back to the south.

At that point Ben's crew went to work. The davit was unbolted from its stowage in the casing, slotted into its sleeve in the deck, the block and tackle rigged ready. Down below they were dragging the sealed bodies from the torpedo room to the point where the big sail bag rested on the lower deck. Six men worked on the relocation and positioning of each body inside the hoist-bag. Two more hauled it up and out of the hatch. Then three men lashed the concrete weight to it with three turns of the plastic belt and heaved it into the water.

First to take the long 10,000-foot drop to the floor of the Atlantic were Lieutenant Commander Colley and his men, the last ones to die, and the first four out of the torpedo room. The average time taken per body worked out to six minutes, and the entire exercise took a little over four hours. But the bodies would never be seen again, and there was a thin, self-satisfied smile on the face of Commander Adnam as he, too, turned south, and took *Unseen* deep once more, just as the sun began to rise above the eastern horizon.

031100APR05.
Office of the National Security Advisor.
The White House.

"Hi, George. Anything happened?"

"Nothing in Plymouth. But we just got a new set of pictures from Bandar Abbas. I can reveal that damned great building is definitely not a football stadium. They just flooded it. It's a dry dock for sure ... here, take a look ... right here ... see where they moved that beach in front. The water just flows straight in now."

"So it does. And we can't see in from either of the Big Birds, can we?"

"Nossir. The angle's not good, and they keep the door shut. We can't photograph inside. Also, sir, we don't know much about the other building, the one constructed hard against it. I suppose it might be just a big storage area. But there must be something in it. Beats me."

"Hmmmmm. Guess so. What are they saying in Plymouth?

"Not much. There are a few reports, just detailing what the submarine's program was for the day. Funny, they were scheduled to work on emergency maneuvers . . . you know, system failures, mechanical, electrical, hydro, fire drills, flooding drills. Also they were out for thirty-six hours, practicing night snorkeling."

"I'll tell you something, George. She'd have been a hell of a submarine to steal, if the guy doing the stealing was familiar with the Brits' workup routine . . . knew how to read the signals off the Squadron Orders."

"How do you mean?"

"Well, if he sent in his signals on time at twelve hours, then twenty-four . . . then missed when his Diving time expired, Christ . . . he'da been about 300 miles away before he was missed. In another twenty-four hours, while the Brits groped around his ops area, he'da been another 200 miles farther on."

"Sir, are you sure you're not letting your imagination run riot?"

"No, George, I'm not sure. But what I just said is possible. Sherlock Holmes would not have dismissed it. Neither should we, however remote it might be."

"Arnold, they did have the signals in."

"I know. But signals do not announce where they began. Either by radio or satellite, you can send in a signal to the operating authority, and the Brits wouldn't have the first idea whether it came from Plymouth Sound or Plymouth Rock. Signals are signals. No one would bother to check, because they all know where the goddamned submarine is . . . in its ops area, right?"

"Right."

"Wrong. I do not believe the sonofabitch was in its ops area, because the goddamned British have been combing it for five fucking days with half the Home Fleet, and found nothing. The chances are it's not there. So where the fuck is it?"

"I'm not sure, sir."

"I know you're not fucking sure, George. Now let me ask you this. If you had to stake $10,000 of your hard-earned personal money on a bet, would you bet, yes, it's in its ops area, but the stupid Brits can't find the bastard? Or would you bet, no, it's not in its ops area. It's somewhere else, either by accident or design?"

Admiral George Morris thought carefully and then he replied, "My $10,000 says it's somewhere else, beyond the ops area."

"Exactly. So does mine."

April 2005.

COMMANDER ADNAM DROVE *UNSEEN* DOWN THE coast of North Africa, running southwest for 1,600 miles, past the long, hot coastline of Mauritania, where the shifting sands of the Sahara Desert finally slope down to the shores of the Atlantic Ocean. Right there, just north of the Cape Verde Islands on latitude 17.10N, longitude 22.40W, he changed course to the south, still running at nine knots at PD, all the way down to the Sierra Leone Basin.

He made his final course change there, before the refueling stop, then headed southeast for another 800 miles. *Unseen* crossed the equator at 1500 on April 20, moving silently through the lonely blue waters of the Guinea Basin toward their rendezvous point at 04.00S, 10.00W. There was 17,000 feet of ocean beneath the keel.

The *Santa Cecilia* showed up right on time at 0300 on the

morning of April 22. They were 3,600 miles and eighteen days from their previous meeting point west of Gibraltar, and the submarine was low on diesel.

It was a stifling-hot night, and there was no wind whatsoever, and no waves. But the swells were deep, and the great, flat, moonlit waters of the doldrums rose and fell in those long glassy seas that lie between the north-flowing Benguela Current surging up the coast of Africa, and the south-flowing Guinea Current.

The fuel transfer was not easy and took four hours. The goodbyes were brief, and the two ships turned south once more, arranging to meet again, thirty-two days hence, east of the island of Madagascar.

May 10.

Admiral Arnold Morgan was breaking the habit of a lifetime. He was going on vacation tomorrow. And, as a further break with tradition, he was taking his secretary with him. This, incidentally, caused no consternation in the White House, where secretaries normally remain in the office to cover for vacationing bosses.

Everyone knew about Admiral Morgan and Kathy O'Brien. Everyone had known for the past six months. Ever since the national security advisor had decided no longer to keep their secret. He had even touched base with the President, and informed him of the relationship, on the basis that the Chief Executive ought rightly to be the first to know who the third Mrs. Arnold Morgan might be.

The President was delighted for them both, but accepted that Mrs. Morgan would, for reasons of propriety and professionalism, leave the White House once they were married. He also made one strict condition, that he would be invited to the wedding.

Since then every young stud on the Presidential staff had refrained from asking Mrs. O'Brien out for dinner, which was as well, since she always said no anyway. But the subject of her discreet romance became unaccountably off-limits. No one ever mentioned it, and certainly no one risked a joke about it, possibly because there was the unseen threat that anyone who really pissed off the severe and autocratic ex–nuclear submarine commanding officer might find himself on the wrong side of one hundred lashes. Admiral Morgan had a way of exuding authority.

Two weeks previously, he'd talked to the President about the vacation first, told him he would like to take Kathy to the Western Isles of Scotland. There were a couple of people he wanted to talk a little business with in the UK, for reasons he would be happy to reveal to the President. But he would prefer to wait until after he returned.

"Arnold," said the great man, "however you want to play it is almost certainly the right way. However, for security reasons I would prefer you to travel in a U.S. military aircraft, and I hope you can make it back for my birthday on May 24."

"No trouble, sir. I'll be gone ten days max. Leaving on the eleventh. But I might have a little interesting stuff when I get here."

"Okay, Admiral. Stay cool. We'll talk soon."

He was finally ready to leave, and two White House secretaries were detailed to stand guard over Kathy's executive domain while she was gone. The admiral and his distant bride-to-be would fly in a U.S.A.F. modified KC 135 jet, the military equivalent of a DC10, manufactured by McDonnell Douglas and fitted with a secure, ultramodern communications system in case the President should wish to speak to the admiral in-flight.

They took off from Andrews Air Force Base at 0700 sharp, and came in to land at the Royal Air Force's Lyneham base in Wiltshire at 1800 local time. A U.S. Navy staff car met them and drove them 50 fast miles to a beautiful, private, hotel-restaurant, the Beetle and Wedge, on the banks of the River Thames at Moulsford, Oxfordshire.

The car that followed them contained two Secret Servicemen, plus the high-security communications system that would patch the admiral directly to the Oval Office. The hotel owner had previously worked in 10 Downing Street and understood the intricacies of such matters. Though her ex-boss, the pedantically polite and careful former Prime Minister, Edward Heath, might have found little in common with the irascible right-wing American national security advisor.

Arnold Morgan and Kathy checked into separate but adjoining rooms. "Just in case those assholes from the London tabloids have planted some ugly little bastard with a camera up the goddamned chimney."

Later they dined by the river, looking out at one of the most perfect stretches of water on the Thames. They ate fresh grilled fish that the landlord prepared for them personally, and they sipped glasses of golden Montrachet Chevalier, 1995. The admiral's long-suffering secretary had rarely, if ever, felt so happy.

"Why won't you tell me where you're going tomorrow morning?" she asked, just before they retired for the night.

"Because tomorrow, my private thoughts and fears suddenly become business. And that's classified, even from you."

By 8 A.M. the following morning the admiral was gone, driving through the little towns of Wallingford and Thame to the Oxford–London motorway, the M40. His driver sped him in the direction of Northwood, home of the Flag Officer of the Royal Navy's Submarine Service.

A young submarine officer met him at the main gate and hopped into the car for the short downhill drive to FOSM's lair. He was escorted immediately into the inner sanctum, and he was greeted personally by Rear Admiral Sir Richard Birley, a lean, slightly built man, with smooth-combed fair hair, who walked athletically, and whose smile had caused deep wrinkles at the sides of his eyes. He had not smiled much lately, however.

"Arnold! How terrific to see you . . . it's been too long. Actually . . . it's been ten years. Come and sit down."

"Hey, Dick . . . good to see you, old buddy. How's Hillary and the girls?"

"Well, they're both at university now . . . but basically everything's fine. Bit quieter without them . . ."

"Guess so . . . I forgot to tell you before, but I'm thinking of getting married again myself . . . but she says she won't do it till I retire."

"Christ, that probably won't happen for about thirty years since you're A) indestructible, and B) wedded to the security of that country of yours."

"Heh, heh, heh . . . I'll talk her into it."

"Bully her into it !"

"Heh, heh, heh."

"Want some coffee?"

"Good call, Dick. Black with buckshot."

"Black with what?"

"Buckshot. That's what I call those little white bastards that make it sweet . . . I always forget the proper name."

"Oh, I see. Well, I'll pour it while you tell me what you want to see me for. I'm assuming this isn't purely social?"

"No it's not. I came to see you because I wanted to have a chat about HMS *Unseen.*"

"Uh-huh. I've been doing quite a lot of chatting about that particular submarine just lately. But not more than about seven hundred times a day."

The British admiral poured the coffee, invited his lieutenant to locate buckshot, which caused huge merriment among the American Secret Service detail sitting in the outer office. They were very used to seeing people scurrying around looking for Hermesetas for the Big Man.

"Dick, we're old friends. And I want you to answer me straight. Was there a real problem with the Brazilians? Were they really as incompetent as the newspapers are suggesting? I mean the general impression we're getting is that your department somehow allowed a bunch of lunatics to go out and kill themselves in a Royal Navy submarine."

"Arnold, how confidential is this conversation?"

"Totally. I just want to get filled in, privately, with a conversation that will never go beyond these four walls. Not even to the beautiful lady who won't marry me."

Admiral Birley chuckled. "Arnold, the Brazilians were not

wonderful, but they were not that bad. They were a little behind in their training, but only about a week, and I had four sea trainers on board, men who we think are the best in the world.

"The Upholder-Class boats are very good. We spent a year ironing out all the initial difficulties before we were forced to put them out of service and into reserve. *Unseen* was completely sound mechanically. As a matter of fact she was in excellent shape. It is very hard for me to accept that the Brazilians did something so absurd that it sank the bloody boat."

"But what about all this newspaper stuff?"

"Christ, you of all people know what they're like. Give them just a sniff of the possibility of incompetence, and they move in like vultures, regardless of the damage they might be doing, regardless of who might be irretrievably hurt. Regardless of whether they are right."

"I suppose that's the difference, Dick, between proper executives and media executives. The proper ones have to be right, or suffer often horrendous consequences. The media guys can more or less get away with anything."

"That's how it feels from here at the moment. We've now been conducting our search for six weeks, and we've found absolutely nothing. It's bloody expensive in time and money. It preoccupies the submarine service, in return for which we are all being pilloried on a daily basis. The training captain in Devonport knows his career is on the line . . . and I have to say, I think mine is as well. The Royal Navy has not lost a submarine since the *Affray* in 1951."

"Yes. It's a goddamned bad business. You guys only took five weeks to find the *Affray*, and that was with equipment half a century behind what we have now."

"And Arnold, it's all made worse by the unmistakable fact that we have not found her, and we ought to have found her. Privately, truly between you and me, I'm just beginning to think something pretty bloody odd might be going on."

"I've been thinking that since around April 5."

"You would, cynical bastard. But I could not allow myself that luxury. Not with my whole department under fire. And, of course, we've had all this grief from the Brazilians. *Where's my submarine? Where are our people? What kind of an operation are you running? This is a disgrace. We hope you don't expect us to pay for this.* Not that they paid much for her anyway . . . $50 million for a submarine that cost $300 million plus.

"Of course the damned media don't understand anything about a deal like this, and how damned difficult it would be to stop the Brazilians going to sea anyway. It is their submarine, after all, and it's awfully hard to tell a foreign Navy their chaps are incompetent, even if they are. Which in this case they actually weren't."

"Hmmmmm. Let me suggest something to you, Dick. I expect you know that when we lost that aircraft carrier nearly three years ago, we had reason to think it was hit by a nuclear-headed torpedo delivered from a Russian Kilo."

"No. I did not know that."

"Then I must ask you to please make sure this conversation never gets repeated. That particular Kilo was, in effect, stolen from the Russian Navy, although there was no suggestion of violence. For weeks, the Russians swore it had sunk in the Black Sea. And they were telling the truth as they knew it. But when the dust cleared, it had not sunk. It had been removed. And I'm very afraid we might be looking at something similar right here."

"Jesus . . . Arnold, my heart is telling me that such a thing could not possibly happen in the Royal Navy, in which I have served all of my working life. But there is a small voice in my mind that is saying yes it could."

"I've been hearing that same voice for several weeks, Dick," replied the American. "Just because I know how good you guys are. I know how thorough a job you're doing. I know that modern sonars are excellent at sorting out what's on the bottom. And you are telling me you had your own sea trainers in that boat and that the Brazilians weren't *that* bad anyway. I know all that to be true. So where is the sonofabitch?"

Both men were silent. Then Admiral Morgan spoke again. "Dick, this is the most secret information I have ever uttered to a foreigner. But when we ran the mystery of the *Jefferson* to ground, we came up with an Arab terrorist, trained as a submarine officer in Israel, and here in Scotland, where he passed your Perisher with flying colors. He was a submarine genius, and he obliterated a United States aircraft carrier.

"According to the Mossad, he's dead. But I could not place my hand on my heart and say I *know* he's dead. And I suspect neither could the Mossad. I'm scared shitless the bastard's still alive. I'm scared shitless because he's familiar with the U-Class . . . and I'm really scared shitless that he's out there, driving HMS *Unseen.*"

Rear Admiral Sir Richard Birley sucked in his breath between his teeth, an involuntary gesture made at the enormity of the American's words. "Where do you think he's going?"

"That I don't know. But if he's taking weapons on board somewhere, I guess we have to face up to the possibility that he might be planning to slam a few more warships, ours, yours, whoever. He's a Fundamentalist, working for Iraq. He hates the West . . . he'll do anything to strike against us. We've already established that. But I can't see him going home to Iraq. They simply do not have deep enough water to operate a submarine."

"Do we begin a search?"

"I don't know how. Your *Unseen* is like the Kilo, only even quieter. Can't hear it. Can't see it. I don't know where to start. And I'm afraid to instigate anything. I just can't advise the President to start looking for a submarine all over the goddamned oceans of the world when it might just have had a battery explosion and destroyed itself in the English Channel."

"No, I suppose not. But it didn't, did it?"

"No, Dick. No it didn't. And the only ray of hope we have is there's not really much he could do with it."

"No."

"I presume she has no weapons on board?"

"True."

"And the Iraqis have nothing that would fit?"

"I very much doubt it. Nor any trained crew to drive it . . . much less handle weapons."

"Then there's not much left. I guess he could fill it with explosive and blow it up somewhere it could hurt the U.S."

"You mean something like the Statue of Liberty?"

"Well, I dunno really. But I guess he could make a hell of a big bang somewhere."

"Seems a hell of a lot of trouble for a bomb. There are many better ways, easier ways, to make a major bang. I must say, it's a baffling scenario."

"Which means, Dick, we better think about it real deeply, right? Keep me posted, won't you?"

Three hours later Admiral Morgan and Kathy arrived back at RAF Lyneham, where the KC 135 was ready to fly them all to Prestwick, way up on the western coast of Scotland, just south of the great championship golf links of Royal Troon.

They arrived at 1530, and the admiral insisted on driving the Navy staff car himself with just Kathy on board. The four Secret Servicemen rode in a separate car right behind, with the communications equipment. And they headed north, as the admiral put it, line astern, up the A78 coast road, which winds along the spectacular shoreline of the Firth of Clyde until it heads back toward Glasgow along the south bank.

But the admiral was not going that far. He drove 42 miles all along the water's edge, then pulled into a small country hotel on the outskirts of the little port of Gourock, which stands on the headland where the Clyde makes its great left-hand swing down to the sea.

"We're anchoring here for the night," he told Kathy. "The guys in the back have already made their security arrangements. You and I are going for a little walk; been sitting down all day." They were shown immediately to their suite, which had a sensational view right across the water to the point of land where the Argyll Forest reaches down to the sea at the tiny fishing port of Strone.

They watched a ferry moving lazily across the calm surface, and out beyond there was a big sailing yacht, heading northeast, with a light, chilly southwester billowing the mainsail. Farther east, a black-hulled freighter steamed steadily toward Glasgow.

Admiral Morgan stood by the window, staring distractedly at the idyllic scene before him.

They pulled on big sweaters and walked out into the late-afternoon sunlight, making their way along the shore for about a half mile before the admiral stopped and pointed directly across the deserted water. See that gap over there, between the town on the left? . . . that's Dunoon . . . and the headland . . . right there on the right?"

"Uh-huh."

"That's the entrance to the Holy Loch, the old American submarine base. That's where we ran a Polaris squadron from . . . straight up there. Kept the world safe for a lotta years . . . right through the Cold War."

"You were there for a while, weren't you?"

"Sure was. Must have been thirty years ago. I was the sonar officer in a nuclear sub. We were only here for a couple of weeks . . . went right out into the Atlantic . . . right up to the GIUK Gap. It was deep cold water . . . watching for the Russian boats . . . tracking 'em . . . recording 'em. None of 'em ever got far without us knowing."

"What's the GIUK Gap?"

"Oh, that's just the narrowest part of the North Atlantic . . . the choke point formed by Greenland-Iceland and the UK. The Russian Northern Fleet boats have to go through there to get out into the rest of the world . . . and they have to go through there to get back. That's why we patrolled it all of the time."

"Why were you all so anxious to track them?"

"Because submarines are very, very dangerous, and very, very sneaky. You just don't want 'em wandering around on the loose when no one knows where they are. You have to keep an eye on them. If there's one thing that makes me real nervous, it's a submarine that's somehow gone off the charts."

"Like that British one?"

"Well, not really," he said quickly. "The Royal Navy thinks that one is wrecked on the bottom of the ocean. And we have to accept that. But I'd like them to find it."

Kathy looked at him quizzically. "Well, my darling, I don't know who you were seeing this morning . . . but I'd say your private thoughts had most definitely become business."

They both laughed. And he put his arm around her shoulders as they strolled leisurely the rest of the way to the harbor and watched the gulls wheeling in a noisy cloud at the stern of the departing evening ferry to Helensburgh.

"That's where we're going tomorrow," he said. "On the new car ferry. We're visiting an old friend of mine . . . we'll sleep late, then spend the afternoon getting there."

It was a pity the weather suddenly changed, but the clouds were beginning to roll in from the southwest, right across the Mull of Kintyre and the Isle of Arran, darkening the waters of the Sound of Bute, Rothesay, and the Clyde. By the time Arnold and Kathy reached the hotel it was raining lightly, and the water seemed misty.

It was not much better the next day. In fact it was probably worse. The rain was steady, and they sat in sweaters and raincoats, outside on the upper deck of the ferry, under an awning. "This is a most beautiful part of the world," said Kathy. "Is the weather always so miserable?"

"Mostly," replied the admiral. "A lot of people have summer homes up here on the lochs, but you couldn't *give* me one. I remember the time I was here. It wasn't much different from this the whole two weeks. And it was summer."

"But it is so beautiful. I expect they forgive the climate."

"I expect they do. There is a certain way of life up here—you know, golf, sailing, shooting, fishing. And there is a kinda coziness about log fires and whiskey, which is what they love. But it's goddamned hard work, if you ask me. Just a place to visit. Give me a warm sunny bay anytime."

"So speaks the world beach expert, who hasn't had a vacation since 1942," said Kathy, giggling.

"Jesus. I wasn't even born in 1942."

"Precisely."

"It's unbelievable, the insolence I have to put up with. You sure we oughtn't to get married? So I can keep you in order."

"Quite sure, thank you. Unless you want to use that contraption in the leather case that Charlie's carrying over there, and tell the President you've decided to bag his job and take to the hills."

"Heh, heh, heh. Come on, we're outta here . . . this is Helensburgh. Let's get in the car . . ."

They drove the black Mercedes off the ferry into the rainswept streets of the little Scottish town, with the Secret Servicemen right behind in the big Ford Grenada. The admiral did not require a map to pick up the A814. He found it with the ease of a man who had done it before, and headed north up the eastern bank of the Gareloch. "This is British submarine country," he said. "Right there, that's the Rhu Narrows . . . used to be a very narrow channel leading up to the base at Faslane, where the Brits kept Polaris. They widened it for Trident."

Kathy stared out at the black waters. Just the thought of a submarine running down there gave her the creeps, and she thought of what Arnold must have looked like thirty years ago, perhaps standing on the bridge in his uniform, bound for the dark, cold wasteland of the North Atlantic.

Arnold, too, was preoccupied, looking at the waters of the loch. But he was wondering about a trainee submarine commanding officer, who had also spent time here, learning the craft which had caused the United States Navy so much heartbreak. *I just wish I knew whether that little bastard was alive or dead*, he thought. *That way I might have a better idea whether* Unseen *was alive or dead*.

They drove on in silence for a while until they reached the small town of Arrochar, way up at the head of Loch Long, 15 miles from Helensburgh. There the admiral announced a course change onto the A83 through the forest, all along the foothills of The Cobbler, a craggy Scottish mountain that has marked the way home for submariners for generations.

"We're making a westerly course, now," the admiral told Kathy. "For about 16 miles, then we run down the coast of Loch Fyne to Inverary. I'll show you a castle there that belongs to the Duke of

Argyll. We'll go and take a look while the guys check into The George; that's a local pub."

This took about an hour, driving around to find a suitable vantage point to see the famous four round towers of the castle, and the Secret Servicemen took even longer to organize their phone linkups. They decided to have dinner at the pub restaurant in two shifts, one at 1800 and one at 2100, since two of them would be on duty at all times of the night.

Kathy and the admiral finally arrived at the big white Georgian house on the shores of Loch Fyne at 1730. It was still raining, and they were greeted by a tall, elegant-looking man of about sixty, with greying hair and a beautifully cut country suit.

Impeccably mannered, he turned to Kathy, and said: "Hello, I'm Iain MacLean, and I am delighted to meet you."

"He sells himself short, Kathy," interjected Arnold Morgan. "He's really Admiral Sir Iain MacLean, former Flag Officer of the Royal Navy's Submarine Service, and in the opinion of some people, the best submariner this country ever had."

The two men shook hands warmly. They had not met for several years since the Scotsman had served a stint in Washington. But they had been in phone contact during the *Jefferson* investigation, in which the retired Royal Navy officer had played a pivotal role, as the Teacher who had actually taught Benjamin Adnam how to command a submarine.

At this moment the introductions were cut slightly short, because the front door was opened by a classic-looking Scottish country lady, just as a pack of three black lunatics burst around the side of the house in a rambunctious trio of tail-wagging Labrador bravado. The first two, Fergus and Muffin charged forward and climbed all over Kathy, but the third one, not much more than a puppy, with feet like saucepans, took a cheerful rush at the American admiral, leapt up, and planted his muddy paws right in the middle of his white Irish-knit sweater.

"Iain! Iain! For God's sake get those bloody dogs under control. They're supposed to be trained gundogs, not street hooligans," called Lady MacLean, but it was too late for that.

By now Admiral Morgan had decided to grab the puppy and lift him up; that way he could get a better grip on him, despite having his face licked. Kathy, who had dogs of her own, coped extremely well, and Sir Iain apologized.

"Don't bother apologizing to me," said the national security advisor. "I love these guys, what's this one called?"

"He's new. I call him Mr. Bumble. Annie thinks he's an absolute bloody menace."

"Well he is a bloody menace," said Lady MacLean. "This morning he went into the loch, then rushed through the drawing room straight over one of those sofas. It took me an hour to clean it." Then she laughed, and added, "By the way, I'm Annie MacLean . . . Arnold, lovely to see you again . . . and you must be the beautiful Kathy?"

It was second nature to this very senior officer's wife to put younger people totally at their ease. She had spent a lifetime doing it, as a captain's wife, a rear-admiral's wife, and finally as a vice-admiral's wife: being charming to the wives of lieutenants, knowing their husbands were terrified of Iain.

But she made it all very easy, and the butler, the red-bearded Angus, came out and took the luggage, before showing the Secret Servicemen to a small downstairs room next to the kitchen, where they could have some tea and watch the television during the early part of the evening.

Then Annie took Kathy into the big kitchen with her, while the two retired admirals made their way to the great wide drawing room with its perfect southern aspect over the loch.

"Christ, Arnold, she's an absolute stunner," said Sir Iain softly as they settled into the sofa Mr. Bumble had done his resolute best to destroy that morning. "Matter of fact, I'm slightly afraid she might be a bit too good for you."

Arnold Morgan chuckled. He had always been extremely fond of the droll, aristocratic Scotsman, and he had much to talk to him about. Iain MacLean was one of the very few people in any navy to whom he was prepared to defer in matters of strategy, history, and intention. They were both thoroughly learned men in the art of Naval warfare, its execution, and its prevention.

Dinner that evening was substantial. They began with wild, local smoked salmon, served with a white burgundy. Then Angus brought in a large, hot, baked Scottish game pie, which Kathy thought was about the best thing she had ever tasted. She could not identify its contents, but according to Sir Iain neither could anyone else. "I've always thought it was grilled stag with slices of barbecued golden eagle," he said. "Annie's got a warlock in the village who makes them."

"Don't listen to him, my dear," said Lady MacLean. "It's a perfectly normal game pie, made by Mrs. MacKay. She also makes them for The George. I expect some of the meat has been frozen, but it's got some pheasant, grouse, and venison . . . and I think a few oysters."

"Well, I think it's delicious,", said Kathy. "And so does Arnold. I think that's his twelfth slice."

"Eighth," muttered Admiral Morgan, chewing luxuriously and sipping a glass of velvet 1990 Château Lynch Bages.

Sir Iain went out and produced a bottle of chilled sauternes, a 1990 Château Chartreuse, which they sipped with the poached pears Lady MacLean served for what she referred to as "pudding." Which her husband took pains to point out was a particularly "bloody silly English phrase for dessert . . . used mainly as a way for pretentious middle-class snobs to differentiate themselves from the riffraff."

"Well, I'm not a pretentious middle-class snob," said Lady MacLean with an edge of indignation.

"No. I know you're not, since your father's a ninth generation Scottish earl. That's why I said *mainly*. I mean . . . 'pudding.' What kind of a word is that? Bloody ridiculous."

"Well that's what our schools taught us. That's what everyone I know says."

"Most of 'em probably only say it because you do. That's what snobbery is. . . . Kathy . . . how about some sauternes . . . with your pudding?"

By 2230 the party was drawing to a close. Lady MacLean

announced that she was on her way to bed, and Kathy said she thought that was a sound plan. Admiral MacLean said he thought he and Arnold might wander over to the study for a medicinal glass of port before retiring and chat about old times for a half hour.

They walked across the hall together, and Sir Iain closed the door behind them. He put another dried log in the dying embers of the fire and poured them each a glass of Taylor's '78 port from a decanter. The log crackled into life, and they sat among the admiral's collection of books, in deep leather armchairs. Sir Iain touched a button on a music system to his left, and the unmistakable sounds of Duke Ellington drifted around the room.

"Goddamned Brits," said Admiral Morgan. "You guys have a real way of living life, which I sometimes think we have not quite mastered in the U.S."

"We've just been at it a bit longer," said the Scotsman, smiling. "Probably learned a bit more about what's important. We're not here that long, you know."

"We're too busy being successful," said the American. "Still, I guess we might get there in the end."

"Actually, I'd rather like you to get there now," said Sir Iain. "What is it, Arnold, that really brings you here? As if I don't know."

"If you do, tell me."

"It's that damned submarine, isn't it."

"Yes, Iain. Yes it is."

"And what is it that you want from me? I'm long retired as you know. Very out of touch, really."

"I know one thing. Your brain's no more out of touch than mine is. I just want to know what you think. Is it still floating? Or is it history? Is everyone really dead?"

"Well, Arnold, I thought after two weeks that they would have found it. And I'm now drawn to the conclusion that it isn't there. Look here, they found the bloody *Affray* after five weeks, without any modern equipment. My opinion is that *Unseen* is not wrecked and did not destroy herself. No one hit her with a torpedo. Otherwise, something would most definitely have been found."

"Well, where is she?"

"Three possibilities. The crew went berserk and stole her to get away from their wives. But you might have thought they'd have run out of fuel by now. The second is that the ship was hijacked, for political purposes. The third that she was stolen."

"Which one do you like best?"

"Don't like any of them. But I don't believe she's sitting undiscovered somewhere in the English Channel. And, if you press me, the third. If she'd been hijacked for some political purpose, I guess we'd have heard. So I think she was boarded and stolen, and that she's out there, and that the crew are dead. I do not believe Lieutenant Commander Colley would have left the training area. But I am 99 percent sure that submarine is not in the training area anyway. So someone else must have driven the submarine out."

"That's precisely what I think, Iain. But my real question is firstly . . . who? Who's driving her with such skill she's never been caught for nearly two months? And where did she get her fuel from?"

"We're dealing here," replied Sir Iain, "not just with a competent submariner. We are into the realm of sheer daring, ruthlessness, originality, illegality, and, not least, specialized competence in the Upholder-Class.

"There's only one man in all the world to fit that list. But, if I am to believe my American friends, that man's dead."

"If I believed that, I would not be sitting here with you. Iain, I think he's still alive, and I think he's out there, driving *Unseen.*"

"So, since you mention it, do I. Have for some time now. How about another glass of port?"

"I think we may *need* another glass of port. Since we have more or less established that some kind of an Arab homicidal maniac is riding round in a silent submarine waiting to do something big. I cannot tell you what it will be like back home if he strikes again. It will finish this Republican administration."

"Shouldn't wonder. Trouble is, I don't know how to catch him. We don't know where he is within 10,000 miles. Still, she was only on safety workup . . . she would not have much on board in the way of serious weaponry."

"Yeah, I guess so. Dick Birley and I came to much the same conclusion. But it's kinda tiresome, just sitting still, waiting for something to happen."

"I don't really think you have a choice, Arnold. What can anyone do? Unless he makes a mistake. But judging by his track record, he's not especially prone to those."

"I can get the Navy to put everyone on a heightened alert, for some spurious reason. But my fear remains, despite the apparent lack of weapons, that Adnam plans to hit another aircraft carrier."

"You think his luck might hold that long? I doubt it. I think if he tried again, you chaps would probably get him. Nonetheless, it is a worry. But there's not much to be done . . . we just have to hope to God he makes a mistake."

The two admirals retired for the night at 2330. And Arnold Morgan lay next to the sleeping Kathy, trying to think of the glorious stretches of water they would see the next day on Sir Iain's boat. Trying to cast from his mind the specter of Ben Adnam at the helm of another rogue submarine.

201200MAY05. 15.52S, 55.10E. Course 360. Speed 9.

The *Santa Cecilia* refueled *Unseen* for the final time shortly after midnight, 200 miles off the Bay of Antongil on the northern coast of Madagascar, close to the remote French Island of Tromelin. There remained just seventeen days of the journey back to Bandar Abbas, running deep up the Indian Ocean to the Gulf of Iran.

The submarine had run perfectly all the way, but they were very short of food and water, and Commander Adnam was pleased to restock the galley.

Back at Bandar Abbas, eagerly awaiting the arrival, was Admiral Badr. His plans to get the submarine home, without the prying eye of the U.S. satellite seeing them, were well in place. He was confident no one would see *Unseen* enter the new dry dock, and confident no one could possibly photograph her once she was inside.

The Iranians had a very good hold on the U.S. satellite patterns and were able to predict accurately enough the gaps in overhead coverage. The submarine must make its 14-mile surface run across the shallow water to the harbor at 0130. That way she'd be in by 0245—thirty minutes before the next satellite would pass overhead.

That was how they had landed the Russian weapons system in total secrecy when it arrived in March. The freighter had waited in the strait, right off the eastern tip of the Island of Qeshm, then run in fast across the shallows, right between satellite passes.

Admiral Badr was amused at the success of the operation, but seethed inwardly at the humiliating fact that he and his Navy had to behave in this way because of the Great Satan. It was, he said, unconscionable that a foreign nation should subjugate the ancient rights of Iran to defend herself in any way she so wished.

But all was well. One complete Russian Grumble missile system was safely installed in the workshop area at the deep-set end of the dry dock; the other three were being set up as part of the Naval air defense system. The new dock's cranes were in place, as were the long galleries that would enable engineers easy access to the submarine. High, heavy-load-lifting apparatus crisscrossed the upper airspace right below the thick concrete ceiling. There were 50 guards on duty outside night and day. The barbed wire was in closer. And there was a second notice board erected right outside. It read, like the one near the main gate:

AUTHORIZED PERSONNEL ONLY.
INTRUDERS WILL BE SHOT ON SIGHT.

Admiral Badr's missile engineers had checked the system right through and, as far as they could tell, it was flawlessly constructed. It was brand-new, tried and tested over many months by the Russians in the Black Sea in their 10,000-ton guided-missile cruiser *Azov*. All that mattered now was Ben's safe return with the submarine.

The Russian freighter had delivered a stockpile of 96 weapons, which ought to be ample for their purposes, since Commander Adnam would require only six. And the Iranian admiral looked forward to the Mission of Justice with great anticipation.

070100JUN05. 26.57N, 56.19E. Speed 2.
Racetrack pattern in 150 feet of water.

Unseen moved 50 feet below the surface, slowly, through the warm waters of the Strait of Hormuz, just to the east of Qeshm, waiting for the American satellite to slide away through the heavens.

At 0130 Commander Adnam issued the orders to surface and head up to Bandar Abbas at 12 knots on course three-three-eight.

And with that the ex–Royal Navy submarine came barreling out of the ocean, shaking the blue water from her decks in a cloud of white spray, the batteries driving her forward on her single shaft, the fastest she had moved since leaving Plymouth sixty-eight days previously.

Ben Adnam and his navigation officer, Lieutenant Commander Rajavi, were on the bridge as they raced across the bay, the hot night air in their faces. Up ahead they could already see the lights from the Iranian Naval station, and soon they could spot the green light high on the right-hand wall of the harbor. The CO ordered a reduction in speed just outside the entrance, and at 0245 *Unseen* ran fair down the northerly channel into the arms of her new Iranian masters.

They made the hard 90-degree turn to the right, at the end of the harbor wall, and two small tugs maneuvered the 230-foot hull toward the dry dock. Ben Adnam stayed on the bridge, checking the tugs. At 0256 they slid into the new dock, way in, safely away from the vigilant photographer that would drift silently past, in nineteen minutes, miles above. The massive steel double doors were now closed across the entrance to shield the lights inside, where a small team of Navy personnel were waiting to welcome *Unseen* home. The outside door was constructed to take the full force of an incoming cruise missile without caving in.

Ben Adnam walked across the gangplank onto dry land for the first time in four months. Admiral Badr was waiting, and the two men embraced, kissing on both cheeks several times in the old Muslim way.

"How are you, Ben?" asked the Iranian submarine chief.

"I'm tired," he replied. "It's been a long haul."

The admiral led him outside through a small side door to a waiting staff car, and they drove to his house. The journey was only six minutes, but the commander was asleep by the time they arrived. Admiral Badr awakened him and carried his sea bag past the six guards patrolling outside. Once inside, there were four young Iranian men to assist him.

They removed his Brazilian uniform, undershorts, and socks, the only kind of clothes he had worn since March 29, and carefully placed his knife on the table. Then they led him to a hot bath full of exotic restorative oils. Ben just managed to wash himself with a bar of jasmine soap, but he fell asleep three times in the bright steamy bathroom. Two of the servants shaved the rough dark stubble from his face. Finally, they just let the water out and helped him to his feet, drying him off with big, soft, orange towels. Then they sprayed him with scented water, dusted him with jasmine talcum powder, and helped him into a pressed white-cotton robe.

Ben Adnam fell into bed in the large air-conditioned room, where he slept for thirty hours, guarded like a pasha, protected like Fort Knox.

When the submarine commander finally surfaced it was 1000 on June 9. Admiral Badr had issued orders he was to be informed as soon as Ben returned from the undead. Shaved and sharp now, he was ready to come out at the bell, and he greeted Mohammed Badr in their private dining room, which was situated in Ben's house.

"We followed much of your progress through the English

newspapers," he said. "Benjamin, you may leave no footprints, but you are very adroit at causing chaos."

"I hope so, sir. By the way, under the terms of our agreement I am now owed $750,000, which I shall require before we move further."

"I am aware of that. The wire transfer was made yesterday morning to your numbered account in Switzerland. I have here the document of confirmation, signed by the bank. You are at liberty to check with your own bank now if you wish, on that telephone, to ensure I am telling the truth."

"That will not be necessary, Admiral," replied the commander, nodding. "And I thank you for your meticulousness and punctuality."

"As indeed we thank you, Benjamin," smiled Mohammed Badr. "Any problems with the boat? All of our engineers report her in excellent shape. Just routine maintenance, minor leak in the seal around the shaft. She's electronically perfect as far as we can tell."

"She ran fine all the way. The operation was conducted with the utmost professionalism. I expect the Royal Navy was quite confused by the entire thing."

"They have not said so, Ben. Indeed, the search goes on in the Channel. But I hear some rumblings that senior officers are beginning to wonder if she is there at all. However, nothing has been said publicly."

"No, they won't do that."

"Ben, what I really want to discuss with you is the Russian missile system. It's very large and very complicated to fit on a submarine. We could be refitting for a year."

"Look, Admiral. If we were trying to fit a medium-range SAM system for use against military aircraft, you'd be absolutely correct. Because we'd need large complicated radar and control systems to cope with military aircraft, trying to evade, ducking and diving, using amazing decoys and jammers. But we're not doing that. We're dumbing down a very sophisticated system . . . we can actually bolt the parts we need onto the submarine, right up on the casing behind the fin. Our targets are much simpler, highly predictable, with steady course, speed, and height. No defensive systems.

"We will make one modification as I mentioned before, to ensure simple, active radar homing . . . just enough to allow front-lobe approach to the target. We can't rely, for instance, on infrared, rear-lobe homing. This weapon has to go to the height we tell it, then turn to meet its target head-on. Then it must acquire the target with its own radar homing system . . . then lock on and hit, at a closing speed of perhaps Mach-4."

"Mmmmm. Still, I've never seen so many radar systems as these."

"But we don't need them on the submarine. Those are intended to give the weapon considerable guidance-update information from its surface firing platform while it is in mid-flight. I intend to feed it all the information it needs to find its target before it's fired. I'm after a sitting duck, not a swerving teal. We're going to mount our missile launcher in a specially constructed pressure-tight box, and bolt it onto the rear end of the fin. The submarine's regular radar will have to be tweaked up for long-range aircraft detection. And we need it to provide basic preflight guidance instructions for the missile. Then, in trade terms, we just 'fire and forget.' If the target's not too fast, we should have time to get a second bird away, should the first one fail."

"Ben, I've mentioned this before. You are a very clever man."

"Still breathing, Admiral. In my game that's a major plus."

"I have a distinct feeling you're likely to go on breathing for a long time. So long as you always stay a couple of steps ahead of the enemy."

"I hope to, but right now I'd like to conclude this topic by making certain you follow our principal problem, that is fitting the 'box' to the submarine without dangerously reducing her surface stability. Like she might be so top-heavy she rolls right over. But that's easily solved with a couple of buoyancy tanks, regular saddle tanks on either side of the hull.

"Our only other problem is to build our own fairly simple fire-control system to work from inside the hull. Then we need just to connect them up on a permanent and reliable basis, despite the difficulties of the underwater environment."

"And you truly believe we can manage all that?"

"Certainly I do. Otherwise, I would never have begun the project."

"But it's never been done before, has it? Not by *any* navy?"

"No. But only because there's never been an operational requirement for it. If there had been, every major maritime power would have such a system. It's just that submarines have never been sufficiently under threat from aircraft. They still aren't."

222000JUN05. 30.30N, 49.05E. Course 90. Speed 2.

The big Iranian naval barge, edged along by a following tugboat had reached its destination now, 600 miles north up the coast from Bandar Abbas in the Gulf of Iran, a little more than 40 miles offshore. Commander Adnam, Admiral Badr, and the missile director from *Unseen*'s crew were all on the barge, on the bow of which was bolted the modified version of the Russian Grumble Rif missile system, securely covered, and surrounded by four engineers. The night was clear and moonlit, with the stars shining brightly above. The test site was close to perfect.

They took the covers off the consoles, which were situated right back on the stern, and the missile director sat in the bolted-down chair in front of it. There was little swell on the ocean that hot Arabian night, and everyone was in shirtsleeves. The radar on the barge scanned the skies for aircraft but found nothing within a radius of 100 miles.

Ben Adnam checked his watch, which now showed 2025, and he knew that the pilotless target aircraft was off the ground above Bandar Abbas, banking out over the Gulf, then back along the coast, climbing all the while to a huge altitude of 60,000 feet. Soon it would head north for around 100 miles, or seventeen minutes, then turn south for the final time and come racing back at 600 mph toward the skies above the barge.

They picked it up on the search radar on the southern leg of its journey, and the missile director found it again, incoming from 40 miles out. His fingers flew over the keys as he programmed in the information to the missile's guidance system.

"Climb out position in."

"Target course and speed set."

"Target height preset at 60,000."

"Weapon One ready."

At two minutes before 2100 he called: *"Stand by."*

Then he hit the launch key, and the big Russian Grumble-Class SAM missile, in a thunder of flame and exhaust, ripped out of the launcher, dead vertical, and screamed straight up into the sky. Everyone watched it, like a huge firework, and they all saw it change course after twenty-five seconds, reaching its 11.5 miles altitude.

They saw it swerve north toward the target, still making 1,700 mph And they watched it obliterate the incoming empty aircraft in dark, but crystal-clear skies more than 20 miles from where they stood. A great sheet of flame seemed to light up the universe. It was a perfect front-lobe attack, of such awesome speed and power, no one felt able to say anything for a few moments.

Except for Commander Adnam, who said crisply, "Thank you, gentlemen. That will do very nicely. I think we can go home now."

Fifteen minutes later, the 275-ton Kaman-Class fast-attack craft *Shamshir* came alongside to take off the admiral, the commander, and the missile officer. The engineers and the Navy guards would remain on the barge for the long slow journey home.

Admiral Badr and his submariners would be in Bandar Abbas in twenty hours. They would dine on board while the French-built Iranian ship sped through the Gulf at 30 knots all the way.

Conversation at dinner, during which the admiral and Commander Adnam sat alone, had an edge of elation to it. The system had worked, which, of course, at $300 million, was only to be expected. But the question of time was important. *Unseen* needed to be back in the North Atlantic by early January, which meant the work had to be completed and tested by late October.

Ben's view was sanguine. "I cannot see it taking that long, sir. The hardest part is behind us. The modifications to the submarine are comparatively simple. It's just a matter of ordinary submarine engineering, nothing very complicated."

"And the dates, Ben, are you happy with them?"

"Well, I'm happy with one, January 17, the fifteenth anniversary of the day the allies attacked Iraq for the first time. But thereafter I think we'll avoid anniversaries. I'm afraid it might look as if Iraq were being set up. And that would lead the Americans right to us. The missing submarine, the big new submarine dry dock in Bandar Abbas, into which they cannot see. Three hits against the West plainly designed to get Iraq blamed.

"No, Admiral, I think January 17 would be nicely subtle. It might take everyone a while to figure that out, but there are better ways to persuade the Americans that Iraq is responsible. Incidentally, we must not forget to put the new Kilo back in the new dock, as soon as I sail . . . and make sure we're seen doing it for a few minutes right at the beginning of a satellite pass."

241000JUN05.
The Special Ops Room. Bandar Abbas Navy Base.

Commander Adnam had drafted a totally bogus signal, to be transmitted from Navy Headquarters in Bandar Abbas to an Iranian Navy patrol craft in the northern end of the Gulf. The message ran as follows:

Intelligence received of Iraqi surface-to-air missile test in area east of Qal At Salih. Four missiles flown. One at fast high-altitude airborne target—apparently successful at time 222101JUN05. Launch platform unknown. Investigate. 240100JUN06.

It was encoded in a comparatively low-level operational system. And, as Ben Adnam had anticipated, it was intercepted by local American radio surveillance at the time of transmission.

Fort Meade had decrypted it three hours later. Langley had a copy one hour after that. And the CIA's chief field officers in both Jordan and Kuwait had it soon afterward

Ben's plan was proceeding, as usual, with the inevitably of sunrise over the desert. This was not a drastic message, just one of several reports sent out on a daily basis. And it scored a bull's-eye, ending up in the hands of Chuck Mitchell, an Arab-speaking American from Boston, who operated under deep cover in the main telegraph and fax office on the east side of Rashid Street.

Chuck had two messages that evening. The first was from Kuwait, which quoted an inquiry about missile test-firing in the marshes, east of the Tigris. The second message was from the CIA man in Jordan, asking baldly: Anything on Iraqi missile tests in the marshes near Qal At Salih? It added that there had been an inquiry from HQ.

The CIA man had heard nothing. But that did not mean nothing was happening. He contacted another CIA field man in Baghdad, Hussein Hakim, a recruit of some twelve years, and they arranged to meet at 2000 in a dingy coffeehouse in the poor south part of the city, both in Arab dress.

Hakim was late because he thought, neurotically, that he might have a tail, but it turned out to be a false alarm. He finally found Chuck, who was also getting nervous, at 2045. They did not wish to spend long together, and the conversation was terse. Yes, the idea of a big missile-testing program somewhere new was serious. But no, neither of them could work on it specifically. Best just to keep their ears to the ground and hope the satellites could find something.

Chuck Mitchell sent a signal back confirming he was on the case, requesting a better feel for urgency and/or need for confirmation. He was not optimistic, and his communication reached the desk of the CIA's Middle East chief, Jeff Austin, shortly before lunch. He read it and ruminated on the endless problem of Iraq. If it was not one thing, it was another. That damned nation had practically caused a world war fifteen years ago, and since then there had been nothing but problems . . . possible nuclear weapons, possible chemical weapons, possible nerve gas being used on the Kurds again.

Not to mention, of course, the vaporizing of the *Thomas Jefferson* in the high summer of 2002. This was also plainly the work of Baghdad, and it had hitherto gone unpunished. Now the Iraqis were testing, in secret apparently, new antiaircraft missiles down in the marshes. There were two big questions: Where did they get them? What did they plan to do with them?

Jeff Austin's antennae were up. And he hit the secure line to Admiral Morgan's office. The two men talked for about ten minutes without reaching any major conclusions, save to keep a very careful watch on any activities by the Iraqi military in the marshes, and to be extra vigilant with the satellite cover in that area.

"Fucking towelheads," growled the admiral, as he replaced the telephone. "That's all we need. The Marsh Arabs with a nuclear deterrent. Holy shit. How about the fucking Incas? What about the Eskimos?"

What the admiral did not know was that the *only* missile of any significance that had been fired in the Middle East that year, was the big Grumble Rif in the Gulf of Iran a few days previously. But Commander Adnam had chosen his site well, way offshore, hundreds of miles from any city, and fairly close to the Iran/Iraq border. And it was all over in seventy seconds. There might have been the occasional amateur astronomer who thought he saw a flash in the sky. Possibly a group of tribesmen in the hills who thought it might be the end of the world. But no country had reported a downed plane, no one had seen a missile take off. No one had reported anything. Bar Adnam.

Meanwhile back at the Bandar Abbas Naval Base, a team of engineers was working on the new weapons system for HMS *Unseen*. Commander Adnam intended the system should be fitted as a self-contained unit, possibly as high as the top of the fin, bolted into place in an airtight and waterproof "box" and connected just by wires to the fairly basic control system already installed in the submarine.

It was cumbersome but ingenious, and Ben Adnam had

already proved, to himself at least, that it would work to devastating effect. Inside the huge dry dock, the bolt holes were being drilled into the casing and into the stern end of the fin. By late August the missile system would be completely modified for its new and relatively simple task. Not even the Russians had the remotest clue as to what was happening in the dry dock. No one knew what the thick rubber cable connectors were for, as the engineers gunned them into place on the aft section of the deck.

Commander Adnam and Admiral Badr were constant visitors, waiting for the day when the heavy-load-lifting apparatus would hoist the massive "extra fin" into place. That happened on September 14, and when it was completely fixed, five days later, they pumped the water level as high as possible and submerged *Unseen* to the bottom of the deep dock. The water still only covered the fin by about 8 feet, but it was enough to check over several hours that she was watertight at periscope depth. That was critical, as important as the test results at deeper depths, when the whole system would be pressurized inside.

The seals held perfectly, not a drop of water entered the "box." Then they deliberately overpressurized it internally, to two atmospheres. No bubbles emerged, and there was a smile on the face of Ben Adnam.

The workshop was quieter. Only the electronics engineers were still working, calmly checking circuits as the system depressurized.

That afternoon, as they walked into the dock, Commander Adnam said softly to Admiral Badr, "Soon, my friend, both your revenge and mine will be complete."

And he gazed with the utmost satisfaction at the submarine he had personally stolen from the Royal Navy, the submarine that would very soon launch an attack the like of which had never been seen in the entire history of naval warfare.

He did not, however, linger for very long. He had been busy all day, and that night he wanted to pray, and to ask the forgiveness of his God.

January 16, 2006.
Baku, the capital city of Azerbaijan.

THE GOOD-BYES WERE CORDIAL, BUT NO MORE. THE six-man negotiating team from Russia had been noncommittal throughout. The Chinese were polite but remote. And the Iranians wore the complacent smiles of those who hold all the aces and three of the kings. Four visiting Arabian sheikhs, an Al-Sabah from Kuwait, a Salman from Saudi Arabia, Hamdan Al-Maktoum from Dubai, and a representative of the emir of Bahrain, had been, like the others, essentially disinterested in the outcome of the meeting.

Bob Trueman, the six-foot-five-inch Texan leader of the United States delegation, had rarely attempted such an uphill struggle. At 384 pounds, with a tendency to sweat like a wild boar, he gravitated toward flat, even ground, both physically and mentally. Mountainous roads, without his Lincoln Continental, were not his thing. He even made his home in the great flatlands of the eastern shore of Maryland, where once he took his wife Anne for a walk, along the sprawling goose-hunting marshes. "'Bout thirty years ago, I think . . . before the boys were born anyway. Probably the last real exercise I ever took."

And Baku, this strange half-Muslim city that sits on the south shore of the great beak-shaped Apsheron Peninsula on the Caspian Sea, had proved to be a pinnacle too far for the mighty Bob Trueman. In his opinion there was no way the United States was going to win the mounting global struggle for the vast oil reserves surrounding the region.

It was all too damned late. That was the trouble. The god-damned White House and Congress had fiddled while Central Asia had, in a sense, burned; right in front of their eyes. And, in Bob Trueman's opinion, *That damned President with the loose zipper ought never to have been elected . . . just sat there . . . that sono-fabitch . . . attending to his personal problems while the rest of the industrialized Western world edged closer to the brink . . . and now look what's happened.*

In Bob's view, the entire idea of this three-day conference had been nothing less than a Sino-Iranian strategy to humiliate the U.S. The Russians, the Chinese, and the Iranians, thrown together now, as never before in the entire history of Asia and the Middle East, formed a lethal oil cartel that had effectively shut the West out of the second largest reserves on earth.

"All we need now is for the Iranians to have another shot at blockading the Gulf with their fucking Russian mines, and there could just as easily be a war," he muttered. "A real shooting war. Because if we cannot tap into the Caspian reserves, and the Gulf gets closed, even for a month, the whole fucking place is going to grind to a halt . . . Japan . . . Europe . . . and the U.S."

But these were personal fears. And Bob's mission in Baku was public. This huge, bearlike, but deceptively cunning Ameri-can, smiled and shook the hand of his Russian host. And he wished a warm farewell to his old trusted friend Sheikh Hamdan, and to young Mohammed Al-Sabah. To the Iranians he was courteous, wishing profoundly that there was some way, somehow, that the U.S. could participate in the marketing of the Caspian oil. But as he knew only too well, the pipeline across Iran would be financed essentially by China. The only other pipeline was going *to China*. In brief, the Iranians had gone for the shutout, and they'd made it.

The problem was, how to get back in. And now Bob Trueman faced the smiling head of the Iranian delegation, and the two men shook hands. They both knew there was a price the U.S. might have to pay, and they both knew it would be way too high—like finance a whole pipeline, in return for access to 20 percent of the crude oil. Only Bob Trueman knew that Congress might just have to bite the bullet on that one and pay up. The balance of oil supplies these days was just too delicately poised.

He told the Iranian that he had greatly enjoyed his visit to the old Persian city of Baku, and that the mild winter climate had been more than agreeable. He thanked him for the tour of the historic Muslim part of the city, which dates back to the ninth century. And he remarked how impressed he had been at the smooth working of this, the largest cargo port on the Caspian Sea. "Just wish you guys could find a way for us to help out somehow," he said.

"Mr. Trueman, as you well know, in the years between 1996 and the new millennium we would have welcomed your help. But your administration chose not even to speak to us. I am sure you, of all people, must understand we had to turn elsewhere. . . ."

"I do understand . . . and I am sorry that old enmities should have lasted so long . . . I guess we just had a President who thought he was still trying to get the hostages free in Tehran, eighteen years later."

"We thought it showed a lack of foresight, Mr. Trueman. There were so many people in my country who wanted a partnership with the West . . . so many who wanted to join in the prosperity of the West. But you would never listen to the voices of reason that have always existed here in Persia. We're not all Muslim Fundamentalists, you know."

"I do know that . . . and I just wish things could be different . . . but . . . well . . . you hold the aces. The best way out to market for that oil is straight across Iran to a Gulf port . . . and we coulda built that pipeline quicker and better than anyone."

"If, Mr. Trueman, you had condescended to speak to us." The Iranian smiled. "By the way, when do you leave? I have much enjoyed talking with you."

"We got a U.S. Air Force plane taking us to London in two hours. Then we're flying the Concorde home tomorrow morning . . . new service, nonstop London–New York, then on down to Washington. Probably takes that sucker about sixteen minutes to get there."

"It's a beautiful aircraft, Mr. Trueman. I have always wished to fly on it one day myself."

"Mr. Montazeri, if you can come up with a way to bring my country into the marketing of the Caspian oil, I will have my government hire one of those babies, just for you, and fly you from Tehran to Washington to celebrate."

"I will continue to think about it," replied the Iranian, laughing. "But the Chinese are very well entrenched now. As we both know, they invested billions and billions of dollars in acquiring the oil, helping us finance the pipeline. . . ."

"Guess so. And, of course, they need so much oil. What's that statistic again? By the year 2012 they will require 97 percent of all the oil in the Gulf?"

"So the economists say, Mr. Trueman. And since Beijing cannot have all of that, I suppose they will have to purchase it from somewhere else."

"I'm a little afraid they've already done that," replied the American. "So far as I can see, the entire production of Kazakhstan is on its way to the east. And there's not a thing we can do about it . . . thanks to the shrewd and farsighted way our last President helped to make them the second richest country in the world."

"No, Mr. Trueman. I do not believe there is."

Everyone was standing, making their farewells in the tall, ornate government conference room, and Bob Trueman's men were beginning to move toward the massive bulk of their leader.

His assistant, Steve Dimauro, the physical opposite of his boss, was whipcord slim, a former All-Star college baseball shortstop out of Vidalia, Georgia. Made it to the Yankees AAA in a big hurry, but lacked the patience, and maybe the size, for the final journey to the Bronx. Steve, with his degree in economics, quit in his third year as a pro and joined the oil giant ARCO, where Bob Trueman was already a towering hero, having masterminded the huge strike in the desert of southern Dubai back in 1980.

Now, seven years later, the thirty-year-old Dimauro was one of ARCO's young tigers, and his association with the formidable ex-VP Trueman, leader of all current Presidential missions to the Middle East, was powering him ever onward and upward in the corporate structure. ARCO was more than happy to lease him out for a year to gain priceless knowledge of the Russo-Sino-Iranian cartel, which today had so much influence in the running of the industrial world. When Steve returned he would do so as a vice president.

Bob and Steve were accompanied by four United States Republican congressmen, Jim Adison (California), Edmund Walter (New Hampshire), Mark Bachus (Delaware) and Dan Baylor (Texas). En route to the airport they traveled in two separate limousines, one for the two ARCO men and the former oil professional Dan Baylor. The other for the other three congressmen.

There was no particular hurry, but the driver was surprised at Bob Trueman's instruction for a first stop at the new McDonald's that had opened in downtown Baku. "Just wanna pop right in there for a coupla of Big Macs," he said. "I often do that in the midafternoon, kinda stabilizes my weight, keeps it right where it is. At my age you don't wanna start losing, suddenly. That ain't real good for you."

"You mean between lunch and dinner?" inquired Congressman Baylor.

"Right. You see I'm a guy with a big bulk," said Bob seriously, but unnecessarily. "And given the pressure of my work, that bulk is under attack from my own body. That means in about eight hours I could be undergoing some weight loss. Now that wouldn't affect a little guy like yourself," he added, staring at the beefy six-foot Texan's 225-pound frame. "But a big man's gotta do what a big man's gotta do. And right now, that's weight maintenance. McDonald's, driver."

Bob Trueman was still munching cheerfully as they arrived at the airport and boarded the Air Force jet for the six-hour flight to London that would get them in at 1900 local, in ample time for dinner, overnight at the Connaught Hotel, and breakfast with four American oil execs based in London. And on out to Heathrow for the 1100 departure of Concorde. By the time they boarded he was not only still chewing, but was also still grumbling about the shocking lack of foresight the West had demonstrated with regard to the Caspian oil.

"Even back in 1997," he was saying, "it was known that the Caspian reserves in Azerbaijan, Kazakhstan, and Turkmenistan added up to a vast field second only in capacity to the big one in Saudi Arabia. With the Chinese desperate to plug in to it, what does the West do? It does four things.

"One, our President decides to do everything he possibly can to make the Chinese even richer . . . most favored nation, export anything they want to the U.S. Hand over key aeronautical technology to them, in return for our being allowed to export to them. Whatever makes them happy.

"Two, he decides not to speak to the Iranians, thus denying us a partnership in the best oil route out of the Caspian area.

"Three, the Americans decide to expand NATO east, but not to allow Russia in, thus driving China's traditional enemy straight back into her arms, now as a friend and vital trading partner. Not to mention the head honcho in the Caspian oil. China's new best friend is the precise spot we don't want her.

"Four, the Europeans, with a blinding flash of brilliance, decide to refuse membership in the European Community to the Turks, who, because of the Bosporus, own the *only other way out* for oil tankers from the Caspian."

He stared at his five-man audience. "Is there anyone here who can enlighten me as to where precisely we get these fuck-ups who are supposed to be looking after the interests of the West. Anyone? Please . . . ?"

There were just five grim smiles on that aircraft, as the bludgeoning words of the massive Texan struck home. The lethargic behavior of the Western powers had been close to blind neglect, as China, in partnership with Iran, and the Russian oil corporations, had placed a stranglehold on the Caspian oil. It was not as if there had been any secrets.

There had been a huge public announcement when Iran had bought a 10 percent share, back in 1996. In 1997 there was another press announcement that China had wrapped up a deal with Kazakhstan for future exploration of the apparently endless oil fields in the western part of the country.

The Chinese National Petroleum Company (CNPC), under this agreement immediately invested more than $4 billion in the "exploitation" of the Aktyubinsk field—principally for the construction of a pipeline to ship oil from western Kazakhstan to Turkmenistan, and potentially, farther on to Iran."

Earlier that same week China had signed *another* four-billion-dollar deal for the exploitation of the nearby Ozen field. "This arrangement," Beijing suggested, "may even conclude with a new pipeline direct to China, because of our determination to find secure oil supplies to meet soaring domestic demand."

"Right there a three-year-old panda could've worked out what was happening," grunted Bob Trueman. "And right in the middle of it we have an ever-aggressive Iran, not just threatening but *actually telling everyone* they plan to blockade the Gulf with mines, because the seaway belongs to them. So there we have it. The Gulf might close altogether, at least until we and the Western Allies can blow the bastard open again . . . and now we're locked out of the other big world oil supply. Everyone in the industry could see it coming. And what did we do? Nothing. A great big zero. And now this. Fuck me."

The interesting part of this discussion was not that Bob

Trueman had shed the light of a prophet upon the subject. Bob was not renowned as a major intellect, even in the higher reaches of the ARCO boardroom. He was just a professional oil man, with a voracious appetite for knowledge. His staff referred to him as the Bear, his office was referred to as the Cave. He carried three brief-cases usually, and read, according to Steve Dimauro, "about 3,000 magazines a day."

He was a likable character who tended to drive his colleagues crazy because he believed there was no group of people on his staff who could provide him with as much information as he needed. His intake of both knowledge and calories, on any given day, approached the high frontiers of supply-side economics.

Above all, however, he was quick to recognize a fool. And he definitely recognized one in a position of power. Bob Trueman had been voluble in his condemnation of the White House in the dying years of the twentieth century. And he worked for America's current Republican President with all the energy of a true zealot. The cool rejection of his proposals in Baku, by the new men in charge of world oil—or at least a significant piece of it—had frustrated him almost beyond tolerance.

"And it was all so goddamned simple," he growled. "All we had to do was cozy up to Iran, mend a few bridges, offer them some assistance. Then finance a U.S.-Iranian pipeline with a big fat ARCO refinery, right at the end, bang on the Gulf. That way every-one gets rich, the world keeps turning, and Iran loses its fanatical desires to close it all down. *Goddammit.*"

The final word was the key to his abilities. Bob did not come up with solutions. He was not a creative thinker. He was an oil-industry computer with a giant database of knowledge, honed after a lifetime in the world's oil fields. He was a man who ought to be listened to, but, for two reasons, he was never going to be president of ARCO; one, because he might not find the decisive-ness to move forward in a crisis. Two, because he did not look like a natural candidate for long life.

0950. January 17, 2006.

Bob Trueman and his colleagues were ensconced happily in the big Concorde lounge in Heathrow's Terminal Four. All six men were sipping coffee, and the team leader had helped himself to a couple of Danish pastries. Steve had made an unusual request, that they would like lunch two hours into the three-hour flight. However, shortly after takeoff he asked if the chief U.S. oil negotiator might have a couple of cheeseburgers. Steve thought he might have to delve into the mysteries of his boss's weight-maintenance program, but Julie, the Concorde flight attendant had smiled sweetly, and replied, "Of course, sir, I am quite certain we can manage that."

Meanwhile, Captain Brian Lambert, in company with his Senior Flight Engineer Henry Pryor, and First Officer Joe Brody, was already in the cockpit, running through the long prestart checklist that accompanies the still-superb achievement of flying a 200-foot-long delta-winged aircraft at a speed of MACH-2, twice the speed of sound, right out on the edge of space, with 100 people on board being variously served filet mignon, roast grouse, or salmon.

Henry had already walked around the aircraft for almost an hour, making his standard visual external check. And now he sat in his seat in the cockpit, running through all the preflight tests and checks, in strict accordance with the minutely ordered written procedures. No details were skimped. No detail was so small it could be ignored. Before takeoff, Henry operated by the well-tried book.

The two pilots had studied the flight plan and the en-route chart, and, with fifty minutes to go, the flight engineer handed over his documents to the captain, who signed the log and formally accepted control of the aircraft. Now both pilots had a copy of the flight log clipped to the front of their boards. They were concerned at this moment with way points, altitudes, and radio frequencies.

Flying the Concorde is like flying no other aircraft. Everyone is always busy, such is the terrific speed and height. The supersonic empress of the North Atlantic is a demanding mistress, and the degree of care needed to bring her safely home requires the leading edge of crew diligence and perception. Her altitude is governed by barometric pressure, rather than actual feet above the ocean, and as she burns fuel at a terrific rate, becoming lighter in weight, she rises and then corrects, maybe through 500 feet over a couple of minutes.

Right now Captain Lambert was feeding the way points into the computerized inertial navigation system. These were the milestones they would call out to air traffic control all the way over the Atlantic, every 10 degrees of longitude, a distance of 450 miles. They would check in with Shannon/Prestwick (SHANWICK) oceanic control about 30 minutes after takeoff, then make another call at 4 degrees west, at the acceleration point above the Bristol Channel. That would confirm Concorde's route, which is not the same as the other big commercial jets heading west across the Atlantic.

Concorde flies alone for several reasons, the first being that all populations in all countries must be protected from her big sonic double boom as she races through the sound barrier. Thus her course takes her straight down the middle of the Bristol Channel toward southern Ireland, where she begins to wind up her speed to supersonic. Then she streaks southwest, climbing to her cruising altitude of approximately 54,000 feet, more than 4 miles above the other jet aircraft, throwing her boom out behind her across the ocean.

Out over the Atlantic she leaves the coastline of County Cork 45 miles to starboard, sticking to a course way south of the other airliners. Concorde flies over no land between Somerset in the west of England, and the immediate precincts of John F. Kennedy Airport, Long Island, east of New York City. The 3,500-mile journey will be accomplished in three hours. At supersonic cruise speed she makes 1,330 mph, covering a mile every 2.7 seconds, 22 miles every minute. She drops a little time climbing out over southern England, where her speed is strictly restricted to just less than MACH-1, but still more like a guided missile than an airliner.

Flying her today was forty-four-year-old Brian Lambert's second choice. His first would have been to watch his son Billy play rugby, in the front row of the scrum for his prep school first fifteen. They were up against the tigerish lineup of Elstree School in Berkshire, who traditionally won the game by about twenty points, but were perceived as vulnerable in the new season of 2006. Still, his wife Jane would be going, and Brian would be thinking of them both at 1430, when Billy would lead the team out for the first time. Concorde's pilot would be in New York by then.

For January, it was a good day for rugby. Cloudy, not too cold, with a softish pitch thanks to three days of almost nonstop rain. Driving from Surrey to Heathrow, on still-wet roads, Brian had already noted the westerly wind and layered banks of cloud, assembling in his mind the kind of weather he would encounter as he flew the takeoff. He wondered which particular aircraft it would be today. Not, he hoped, the one that had developed a shaky gauge in number three fuel tank last week.

Now, with forty-five minutes still to go before the new 1045 departure time, he was familiarizing himself with his two-man crew. Henry Pryor he knew. They'd flown together in December, but Joe Brody, the first officer from West London, was a mere acquaintance. It was standard British Airways procedure to select random crews, mainly to avoid the obvious problems of overconfidence, slackness, and bad habits, which occasionally evolved among men who work together all the time.

Thus the three men assembled, as a flight crew, for the first time a couple of hours before departure, in the operations office, where they went over the flight plan and studied the detailed weather information provided in a folder by the airport meteorological office. Every possible contingency was contained there . . . temperatures, pressure systems, winds, potential areas of turbulence, possible icing areas, all laid out in a coded format, incomprehensible to a layman.

In the cockpit, preparing to leave, the planning schedules focused the minds of each of the three men. The fuel tonnage, which ensured they would have sufficient to land in the event of an engine failure, was critical. Because Concorde cannot fly at MACH-2 on only three of her Rolls Royce engines, neither can she remain at her great height. And when she slides down to a lower altitude, her fuel efficiency is cut by around 25 percent, which could force her to land in the Azores, or Gander in Newfoundland, or Halifax, Nova Scotia. Henry Pryor was watching the steady filling of those 95-ton capacity tanks with a beady eye.

The trim of the aircraft was also a vital part of the preparation, because the center of gravity must be spot-right. With Concorde carrying a grand total of 185 tons in weight, it is more complicated than on any other aircraft, because of the constant transferring of fuel from tank to tank in flight, and the subsequent redistribution of the tonnage. Most of the passengers are sitting in front of the gravity center. Indeed the pilot works 38 feet in front of the nose-wheel, and 97 feet in front of the mainwheels. The loading officers, working with the crews, often make keen judgment calls. But they miss nothing, and the 384-pound bulk of Bob Trueman had been taken into account, along with everything else.

They called the flight shortly after 1015, and the passengers were all on board by the time the fueling was complete at 1028. The computerized loadsheet showing the final weight and balance of the aircraft was checked carefully by Brian Lambert, who signed it. The ramp coordinator reported formally to the cockpit, then left, securing Concorde's door behind him.

The captain and First Officer Brody then set the white markers to the takeoff speed, and pitch angles of the nose cone, for the climb-out.

"Start clearance," said Brian Lambert.

And Joe Brody contacted air traffic control, requesting permission to start the engines.

"*London Ground.* Speedbird *Concorde 001 on stand Juliet Three for start-up.*"

"Speedbird *Concorde 001, clear to start. Call on 131.2 for pushback.*"

Henry Pryor made two further entries on his checklist. Then he started Concorde's number three engine.

171054JAN06. 49.76N, 32.03W.
HMS *Unseen* in the North Atlantic.
Periscope Depth. Course 180. Speed 5.

Linked to the commercial satellite international communication system, MARISAT, the ex–Royal Navy diesel-electric ran silently. The special submarine aerial had worked perfectly when they accessed, just before first light this morning. The message from Bandar Abbas Navy HQ had been succinct:

"KING BIRDS ON BOARD SUPERSONIC FLIGHT 001, ETD LONDON HEATHROW GATE 1045 (GMT), SCHEDULED 51N, 30W APP. 1219(GMT)."

Commander Adnam, standing in the control center with his navigator, had raised his eyebrows, and murmured, "Hmmm. An interesting first test. The highest and the fastest."

Now, four hours later, he checked for surface ships, found none, and ordered *Unseen* to periscope depth in readiness to receive his next satellite communication. He also ordered the ESM mast raised and heard the hiss of the hydraulic rams as the big radar-interceptor mast slid upward. Ben checked the immediate horizon through the search periscope.

1042 (GMT) Heathrow.

Flight Engineer Pryor had all four engines running. Concorde's nose and visor were set in the 5-degree position for the taxi to the runway, during which time 30 more checks would be undertaken by the flight crew. That morning Concorde would take off from runway 27R heading 274 degrees magnetic.

The final checks completed, Concorde taxied into her holding position, waiting her turn to leave. The cabin staff were strapped in, the flight engineer had moved his seat forward and was looking over the pilot's shoulder, his left hand on the back of the captain's seat. The word came over the intercom at exactly 1100.

"Speedbird *Concorde 001 cleared for take-off.*"

"Speedbird *Concorde 001 rolling*".

Brian Lambert opened the throttles. The afterburners kicked in, increasing the acceleration.

"Airspeed building."

"One hundred knots."

"Power checked."

"V1, Captain."

This is 165 knots, the point of no return. Any faster and the aircraft could no longer stop in time to abort the takeoff. She hurtled forward, building to her ground-leaving speed of 250 knots.

"*Three, two, one, noise . . . cut the afterburners.*"

And Brian Lambert, husband of Jane, father of thirteen-year-old Billy, gunned Flight 001 westward, shrieking into the skies above London's premier airport, climbing quicker and steeper than any of her bigger, heavier Boeing counterparts.

Concorde was watched, as always, by a breath-holding crowd of onlookers in the Terminal Four departure lounges. But she was watched also by the silent Naval attaché from the Iranian Embassy, who stood behind the glass staring west, speaking crisply into his mobile phone. "*Concorde takes off 1100,*" he said softly.

171104JAN06. HMS *Unseen* at PD. Course 028. Speed 5.

Commander Adnam held in his hand the brief printout from the satellite message, direct from the Iranian embassy link.

FLIGHT 001 CHOCKS AWAY 1045, PROBABLE TAKEOFF 1100.

In one hour and ten minutes, he thought, Concorde would be a couple of hundred miles out. It was not a particularly clear day, visibility was only 3 miles, but his radar would take care of that, and, so far, the sonar sweep had found no noises to suggest any ships within a 12-mile radius. The seas around the submarine were clear. There was no one around: perfect conditions in which to commit the ultimate sea-air atrocity of the twenty-first century.

Ben Adnam's team was highly trained. When he gave the word to the radar operator to begin the tracking, his men would slip into well-rehearsed routines, which they had practiced a thousand times. He felt relaxed and unemotional, as he always did when the pressure went on. And right now the Iraqi-born CO was in his rightful element, commanding a top-class submarine, with 2 miles of water beneath the keel, out here just west of the Mid-Atlantic Ridge, watching and waiting, intending, as usual, to outwit his enemies, in the most holy name of Allah.

1104 (GMT). West of Reading.

Brian Lambert had Concorde almost at 400 knots, and with the nose raised, they were climbing at about 3,000 feet a minute. Joe Brody had received clearance for 28,000 feet, and the captain had turned off the seat-belt sign. The weather up ahead looked gloomy but settled. In any event, Concorde would race 4 miles above the nearest clouds as soon as she reached her cruising altitude.

Still at MACH-.95, fractionally less than the speed of sound, the supersonic British Airways flagship thundered across western England. At 1124, high above the Bristol Channel, just before longitude 4 degrees west, her oceanic clearance came through.

"Climb when you're ready . . . cruise between 50,000 and 60,000 feet on track Sierra November."

Flight Engineer Pryor began the rearward transfer of the fuel, preparing for supersonic flight, and Brian Lambert pushed the throttles hard forward, on full power. The afterburners were fired up two at a time, as Concorde streaked through the sound barrier, smoothly accelerating to MACH-1.3.

Many passengers felt the two gentle nudges as the afterburners were ignited, and still others paused from the morning papers to listen to the sounds of the big engines changing slightly in tone. Bob Trueman wondered if he might hear the sizzle of a couple of cheeseburgers deep in the galley. He regarded sudden loss of weight much more seriously than he would ever have regarded sudden loss of altitude.

He and his team occupied a block of seven seats close to the front of the cabin—two doubles on either side of the aisle, row four; one single on the aisle, right behind in row five; another double for Bob alone, plus briefcases, on the other side, row five C and D.

Immediately in front of them was the unmistakable figure of the 1970s British pop icon Phil Charles, who was still recording at the age of fifty-five, with a reputed net worth of $300 million. The small, balding, unshaved figure sat unobtrusively with his pony-tailed manager. Both men wore T-shirts and leather jackets. The seats to their right, row three, C and D, were occupied by two sour-looking, willowy blondes in their mid-twenties, who might have been daughters, but were probably not.

Phil Charles's long lifetime of philandering was a constant source of delight to London's tabloid newspapers, mainly because he was such an unprepossessing individual with a plain and obvious vendetta against the shareholders of Gillette. He always looked dreadful to the middle-class eye.

Steve Dimauro had recognized him immediately and nodded a greeting, which was returned with a grin. In Steve's opinion the scruffy-looking Phil might not have cut it with the willowy ones, but for that $300 million. "Sonofabitch can still sing, though," he muttered as he took his seat on the aisle opposite the chief.

Way back in the aft section of the cabin was another pop singer, also British, the piano-playing rock star Shane Temple. He and Phil Charles wore nearly identical clothes, and they sang a lot of the same music. The difference was in the bank balance. Whereas Phil had never stopped being successful, deftly changing his style with the moment, but retaining his traditional sound, Shane had floundered in the eighties, and floundered more in the nineties, being reduced to working on the northern circuit of nightclubs, Skid Row to a pop icon.

His career had been begun again with a sensational rock-opera revival in the opening months of the new millennium. But times had been hard for a long time, and Shane was still a few hundred thousand pounds light of his next castle.

Concorde trip was a big event for him; a major recording session in New York might see him right back on top this year, and he had spent at least ten minutes cooperating with the airport press corps. Nonetheless, as they boarded the flight, his longtime manager, Ray Duffield, had groaned when he saw Phil Charles slumped in his seat reading the sports pages of the *Daily Mail*.

"Son," he growled to Shane, "I've got bad news. If this fucking thing crashes, you're not gonna get the ink."

Concorde reached 50,000 feet at longitude 10 degrees west. This is the north–south meridian, which cuts through the westerly isles of Connaught, bisects the Dingle Peninsula in County Kerry and runs to the east of Mizen Head. Brian Lambert crossed it at 1136.30 flying at MACH-2 at latitude 50.49N. First Officer Brody reported their way point to Shannon, and the air traffic control center made a note to expect Concorde to come in again 450 miles later, at the 20-degree west way point. Time: 1157.

The air routes were, as always, busy at that time of day, and to the north of Concorde's flight path there were no fewer than six westbound air tracks in operation, with big passenger jets running through them 100 miles apart, but flying in eight layers of aircraft, "stacked" at different altitudes. Only Flight 001 made her journey in solitary splendor, moving nearly three times faster than any of the others.

Bob's burgers arrived at approximately the same time as First Officer Joe Brody checked in to Shannon from way point 20 West, at 1157(GMT) precisely. Out of range now on VHF, he used the High Frequency radio, confirming that the next communication would be their last before handing over to oceanic control Gander, Newfoundland, when they were 1,350 miles out from Heathrow, approaching the middle point of the oceanic crossing.

Shannon "rogered that," and signed off. Henry Pryor checked the fuel tanks of *Speedbird* Concorde 001, and the first officer confirmed the precise distance to way point 20 West . . . just a little more than 450 miles, since they were running slightly south, and the lines of longitude were edging fractionally farther apart.

171210JAN06. 49N, 30W. HMS *Unseen* at PD.
Speed 5.

Commander Adnam's radar was searching the skies to the east, the operator paying particular attention for long-range air detections. "Just keep looking," said the CO. "Anything at over 1,000 knots, that's the target." The first detection found Concorde 210 miles out at 1210.33.

"New target, sir. Moving very fast."

"Must be an aircraft."

"Fits Concorde's route plan, sir."

"SURFACE. BLOW ALL MAIN BALLAST. I want a good blow . . . maximum buoyancy right away. Officer of the Watch, keep her headed into the swell . . . avoid surface rolling as much as possible."

The jet-black submarine came bursting out of the icy depths of the winter Atlantic, water cascading off her casing. Deep inside the hull, the Russian missile systems' computer established the critical data for a surface-to-air missile attack.

"Speed 1,300 knots plus, sir."

"Approximate course two-six-zero."

"Range now 188 miles."

"Okay team," said Ben Adnam calmly. "Check the surface picture visual. No hurry, chaps . . . what do you have . . . ? Fine. Just those three civil airliners 80 miles to the north. No problem. Let's just relax and do it right."

By 1213 all the known data, the radar range and bearing, had been fed into the computer. And now they had refined the target. The CO had an accurate course, speed, and closest point of approach. The range was now 153 miles. CPA: 4 miles. Every 5.2

seconds *Unseen*'s radar completed a sweep, and every sweep signified Flight 001 was 2 miles closer.

"Officer of the Watch, sir. Submarine at full buoyancy now."

"I have an adequate firing solution within the parameters, sir."

"We have set the pressure height: 54,000 feet. CPA remains 4 miles."

"Computer estimates time of launch 1216."

1214: *"Target holding course and speed, sir. CPA same. Predicted time to enter the missile envelope 1218.12."*

At 1215: *"Computer in final prefiring sequence, Captain! Countdown now sixty seconds."*

Commander Adnam betrayed nothing. He stood motionless in the control center, awaiting the information that would confirm he had not crossed the Iranian border from Iraq in vain.

At 1216 it came. *"MISSILE LAUNCH!"*

And up on the casing, in the huge box situated right behind the fin, there was a searing burst of fire and fury, as the Russian-built SAN-6 Grumble Rif guided missile blasted into the empty skies above the ocean, making a dead vertical course, straight up through the thick grey cloud, to 54,000 feet. The 10.5-mile journey took it a shade less than thirty seconds.

Right there, guided, like Concorde, by its pressure-height barometer, it leveled out, and its preprogrammed computer brain changed its course, sending the fiery weapon 4 miles across the no-man's-land of the upper stratosphere, right onto the Closest Point of Approach of Flight 001 out of Heathrow. Again the Russian rocket swerved for its final course change, now aiming east-northeast.

The radar that lanced out of the head of the missile made a long, unseen, cone shape in the sky, and Concorde was heading straight into it. At that point, barring a spectacular malfunction, Ben Adnam's killer Russian SAM could not miss.

Back in the cockpit, First Officer Brody, checked in to Shannon, again reporting his position on the primary band of the HF radio. They were now approaching the 30 West way point, and Joe

Brody made his radio switch, changing to the secondary band to make contact with the air traffic controllers at Gander. *"Good morning, Gander . . . Speedbird Concorde 001 . . . flight level five-four-zero to New York . . . MACH-2. . . . 50 North, 30 West at 1219 GMT . . . ETA 40 West 1241 GMT. . . . Over."*

On board HMS *Unseen*, tension in the radar room was beginning to mount.

"Missile on height through CPA, heading out to target . . . it's looking good." The words of the radar operator hung in the air as the SAN-6 streaked along course zero-eight-zero, down which Brian Lambert's oncoming aircraft was 78 miles away. Concorde and the Grumble Rif were closing at a colossal speed of more than MACH-4, 3,000 mph, a mile every 1.2 seconds.

At 1217: *"Holding missile and target firmly on radar, Captain. If the bird's on the right height, it's looking good."*

Commander Adnam moved into the radar room, gazing at the screen over his number two operator's shoulder. His fist clenched the back of the chair, as Concorde entered the firing envelope at 1218:12.

At 1218:18, the operator called: *"Target and missile returns merged, sir."*

At 1218:20, Brian Lambert saw it, bright glinting in the sunlight, fire rampaging in its wake. He opened his mouth to speak, uttered the sound *"MISS—"* as Benjamin Adnam's radar-programmed warhead smashed into the underside of Concorde's nose, blowing off the entire front end of the aircraft, leaving the fuselage to rip back from the structural frame like a peeling banana.

The total disintegration of the aircraft was over in a split second, and death came instantly for the 100 passengers, as they blew into the silence of near space. The changes in the pressure caused the bodies to explode, suddenly lacking the 15 pounds per square inch of pressure that normally accompanies human life. The gigantic detonation of the fuel stored in the aircraft's wings blew even the wreckage to smithereens. Bob Trueman died with a cheeseburger in his hand.

171219JAN06. HMS *Unseen*. The radar room.

"No contacts on radar bearing, Captain. Just three civil aircraft to the north."

Commander Adnam turned away from the screen and walked back to the control center. And there he ordered the submarine dived. "Open main vents. Slow ahead. Ten degrees bow down, 17 meters." And as *Unseen* disappeared again, he ordered, "When you've checked the trim, go to 100 meters. We'll clear the datum to the southward at nine knots. Thank you, gentlemen. Thank you very much."

The world's first disaster involving a supersonic aircraft had taken place. But at that stage, as the burned-out pieces of wreckage tumbled eerily down over a wide area of the windswept North Atlantic, no one yet knew anything. And it would be a while before anyone did know anything.

It would not take as long as the great Naval brains had taken to work out that HMS *Unseen* had vanished the previous spring. But it would be another twenty minutes before an unnatural silence in one small corner of the great aircraft control room at Gander would alert the world to the shocking truth that the unthinkable had indeed happened.

By 0743 (EST) in the snowbound air traffic control center on the east coast of frigid Newfoundland, the operator in charge of Concorde was already worried. The British supersonic jet had come in a minute early at 30 West, and it was most unusual for the next call-in to be late. By now Bart Hamm knew that Flight 001 must have passed 40 West, and he had heard nothing.

At 0743.40 he went to SELCAL (selective calling), Concorde's private code on High Frequency. No reply. Transmitting direct to Concorde's cockpit, it activated two warning tones, like little bells, designed to alert the pilots. At the same time Bart transmitted a radio signal designed to light up two amber bulbs right in the line of Brian Lambert's vision.

"Speedbird *001* . . . *this is Gander* . . . *how do you read?* . . . Speedbird *001* . . . *this is Gander* . . . *how do you read?*"

At 0746 Bart Hamm called in his supervisor. At 0747 (local) Gander Air Traffic Control sounded an international alarm, alerting British Airways that Concorde was missing, instigating a massive air-sea search and rescue, informing the United States and Canadian military that a major passenger airliner was down in the North Atlantic. *"Last known position 50.30N, 30.00W. . . . British Airways Concorde Flight 001."*

There were few ships in the area on that freezing January day, but two Japanese fishing trawlers began to head south out of the Labrador Basin to the position in which Concorde might have come down. It was a forlorn hope, because survival was unlikely. There was no question of slowing down to a reasonable landing speed on the water, given its cruising speed of 1,330 mph.

In the Canadian Naval Base in Nova Scotia, the Commander Maritime Forces Atlantic, Rear Admiral George Durrell, ordered two of his 4,800-ton guided-missile frigates, the Halifax-Class *Ottawa* and *Charlottetown* to make all speed to longitude 30 West on the fiftieth parallel. Both warships carried a Sea King helicopter. For good measure Admiral Durrell also sent in his massive 14,500-ton Heavy Gulf Icebreaker *Louis S St. Laurent*, turning it east-northeast from 500 miles off the coast of Newfoundland. With a crew of 59, plus 38 scientists, this ice-busting giant had been the first ship ever to reach the North Pole. Its three-shafted props could drive it through a big sea at 18 knots. The chances were the *Louis S*, carrying two helicopters, would arrive at 30 West before the frigates. But it would still take a day and a half to get there.

Admiral Durrell's aircraft would be quicker. And by 0830, two Lockheed CP-140 Auroras were up and out of Greenwood, Nova Scotia, making 400 knots toward Concorde's crash area. They were scheduled to arrive by 1230.

In London, news of the lost supersonic jet broke before the end of the 1:00 P.M. bulletin on BBC. And it was delivered in tones of pure disbelief by the newscaster. The broadcasting corporation then announced that the BBC 2 channel would follow the story day and night for the next twenty-four hours, all other programming being canceled. Not since the death of the Princess of Wales more than eight years previously had the BBC moved into such extensive coverage.

The trouble was, of course, there was almost nothing to report. The great airliner had simply vanished. It was there one moment, gone the next. And in the aftermath of its demise there was not one shred of wreckage, not one suggestion as to the whereabouts of the black-box flight recorder, not a word from anyone, save from Bart Hamm in Gander, who was quite prepared to confirm he had heard precisely nothing.

Television, radio, and newspaper reporters had about three facts—one, Concorde had reported its height, speed, and position at 30 West; two, it had failed to report in at its next way point at 40 West; three, they had the passenger list. And Ray Duffield had been right. His man Shane had almost drawn a blank. Phil got the ink.

The London tabloids unanimously led their front pages with variations on the same headline:

PHIL CHARLES DEAD IN CONCORDE
MYSTERY CRASH

or:

CONCORDE CRASH KILLS PHIL CHARLES.

British Airways announced late in the afternoon that Flight 001 had been commanded by Captain Brian Lambert, "one of the most senior and respected pilots on the North Atlantic route." His copilot had been First Officer Joe Brody, "an ex–Royal Air Force fighter pilot who had been with BA for twelve years." Flight Engineer Henry Pryor, was, according to the BA press release, "shortly to have been promoted to the most senior engineering position in the entire Concorde fleet."

Jane Lambert, who heard of the catastrophe to her husband's aircraft at halftime in Billy's match against Elstree, was taken to the headmaster's study, where she reacted with immense bravery. "I have been Brian's wife for eighteen years," she said. "I have always been prepared for something like this . . . every time he leaves the house." They didn't tell the little boy until the game was over.

In Washington, the loss of the government's oil-negotiating team, including four congressmen, was a major story. The evening television newscasts, which had much more time to prepare than their British counterparts, were concentrating on a report from a Northwestern Airlines pilot whose plane had crossed 30 West around the same time as Concorde, some 80 miles to the north. "I thought I saw," said Captain Mike Harvold, "a small fire-flash in the sky south of my aircraft. I'd say just about on my ten o'clock. I was heading two-six-zero at the time for the coast of Newfoundland."

Questioned further, he confirmed he could not make out the shape of any aircraft so far away, "I guessed it might be Concorde, but I couldn't be sure, and I just made my report of the possible explosion in an unknown aircraft. But there's nothing else up that high. I guess it had to be Concorde. Looked to me like it just blew right out of the sky. I suppose you couldn't discount the possibility of a bomb . . . but the security surrounding that thing is unbelievable. In the trade, a bomb in Concorde is regarded as just about impossible."

By the late evening, the experts were in, extolling their opinions to a shocked U.S. audience. The possibility of a bomb was chewed over in much detail, but not in the same way as with other airline disasters. Concorde was too well managed, too small, with too few passengers, and the legendary security was as near to watertight as any security ever can be.

"Experts" who had never traveled on Flight 001 announced they thought it was possible to plant an explosive device on board. "Experts" who had actually traveled supersonic, thought the opposite. Some thought Concorde might have blown up because of a fuel leak. One source even mentioned the possibility of a missile strike, assuming at that stage it could have come from a surface ship.

But checks were made over the next forty-eight hours, and it became clear that 10 miles below Concorde's flight path, in the vast wastes of the North Atlantic, in waters so lonely the nearest land is over 1,600 miles away in any direction, there was simply no platform for such an attack to be launched. No land. No warship. Not even a decent-sized merchant ship. No one could have loosed off an accurate radar-guided missile at the supersonic passenger jet, because no one had a place for the launcher. In any event, hitting an aircraft traveling that fast, that high, was way beyond the capacities of 90 percent of the world's guided missiles, even if there had been a launching pad. The possibility seemed so utterly unlikely it was not discussed at the highest levels, even in the Pentagon.

Not even in the White House, by the zealously suspicious Admiral Arnold Morgan . . . although he was heard to mutter cynically to Kathy O'Brien that evening, "Goddamned Brits are getting a little careless, hmmm? First a three-hundred-million-dollar submarine which is never seen again . . . now a supersonic aircraft, also vanished . . . That's not like them. Not like them at all."

By midday on the morning of January 18, it was decided that since the accident had been to a British Airways aircraft, built in Great Britain and flown by British pilots, the entire thing had little to do with the United States, not in formal terms. Certainly the Federal Aviation Administration was more than interested in the world's most famous aircraft hitting the Atlantic en route to New York. But the actual investigation into the causes of the destruction of Concorde would be undertaken by the Air Accident Investigation Branch of the Department of Transport in London. The crash had, in any event, occurred slightly nearer to the UK than to the shores of either America or Canada.

And now there were two Royal Navy warships on their way out to the seas which roll over 30 West around the fiftieth parallel, where at first light that morning the Canadian Navy surveillance planes had spotted wreckage in the water. The big icebreaker was still twelve hours away from the spot, and the frigates were even farther. So the searchers would just have to hope the lighter material would keep floating. There was no sign of any bodies.

The loss of Concorde very quickly began to emerge as one of the great mysteries. British Aerospace and Rolls Royce engineers dismissed out of hand the possibility of the fuel leaking and igniting. The security dragnet that surrounds all Concorde flights dismissed as absurd any possibility of anyone planting a bomb on board.

Indeed there have been only two comparable air disasters in recent years. The first was USAIR's Flight 427 from Chicago to Pittsburgh in 1994—when the Boeing 737 plunged 6,000 feet and nose-dived into a ravine at 300 mph killing all 132 passengers and crew.

The black box explained nothing, and no one has ever offered a satisfactory reason for the crash.

The second, of course, was TWA's Flight 800, an aging Boeing 747 that burst into flames and plunged into the Atlantic off Long Island in July of 1996. There are still those who swear the aircraft was hit by a guided missile. Particularly three commercial airline pilots who reported seeing at least one missile in the air while flying over the same New York airspace where Flight 800 exploded.

The pilots, from Northwest, Delta, and US Airways, were all headed westward over the city toward Philadelphia, and they reported their missile sightings separately.

The U.S. Navy replied that they might have sighted two D5 Trident missiles being fired at the time from a submarine, USS *West Virginia*, off Florida, the night being very clear. However, those missiles were being launched toward the Azores, and the launch platform was close to 2,000 miles away. It was not terribly likely that all three of the commercial pilots would have made such a colossal error of distance judgment, especially since they were all flying the wrong way to see the Trident missiles anyway.

Pierre Salinger, JFK's former press secretary, was convinced the U.S. Navy shot down Flight 800 by accident, with a missile which somehow got away. He went so far as to call a press conference in Paris to present his findings four months after the crash. But none of it ever came to anything.

The only truth was that no one had ever explained conclusively what happened to USAIR's 437 at the bottom of the ravine, nor what had befallen TWA's 800 off Long Island.

By the afternoon of January 19, Concorde 001 had joined that select pair of great modern aviation mysteries. No one was able to offer one single clue as to what had brought down the MACH-2 thunderbolt that flies alone on the frontiers of space.

What everyone required was Concorde's two black boxes, one of which was the Cockpit Voice Recorder (CVR) the other the Digital Flight Data Recorder (DFDR). But the aircraft had gone down in such diabolically deep water, possibly almost 3 miles, right on the far northwestern edge of the Mid-Atlantic Ridge, it might prove impossible to retrieve anything off the bottom.

The British would no doubt bring to bear the most modern sonar systems and diving machines, and the Americans would no doubt find a way to assist. But it should be remembered that the finest feat of recovery ever, for black boxes, took place in February 1996, when a Turkish-based Boeing 757 from the Dominican Republic plunged into the Caribbean killing all 189 people on board.

On that occasion, four or five nations jointly financed a contract for the U.S. Navy to dive to more than 7,000 feet. On the first day they discovered that the black boxes were still emitting signals from their underwater locator beacons, which led the divers immediately to them. To this day, airline investigators still discuss that operation with awe.

But it had been carried out in warm water, in bright conditions—a far, far cry from the black depths of the rough, storm-tossed North Atlantic in January, where Concorde's black boxes might also still be emitting signals, but from an ocean floor more than *twice* as deep as the one in the Caribbean that claimed the 757.

The media's problem in covering the news story was that there appeared to be no one to blame. Certainly not the pilot, nor his crew, who were dead, and had been flying Concorde for years. Certainly not the Shannon Air Traffic Control operators, who had already said good-bye to Flight 001. And certainly not Air Traffic Control, Gander, who were 1,600 miles away, and reported no unusual weather conditions for any flight, all day, particularly for one flying 4 miles above the weather, where the wind rarely rises above 40 knots.

The tough, hard-eyed security chief on duty in Concorde's area at Heathrow made a bomb inquiry from a female reporter from London's Channel Four look ridiculous. He gruffly informed her that if she cared to put an unauthorized suitcase anywhere near *Speedbird* 001's loading bay, she would probably be torn to pieces by guard dogs, and if not, then shot on sight. He was only half joking.

201100JAN06. 43N, 38.25W. Depth 100 meters. Course 120. Speed 5.

HMS *Unseen* was running silently, and deep, the commanding officer sipping Turkish coffee in the control center, in conference with his navigation officer, Lt. Commander Arash Rajavi.

"I think we were correct, Arash. It was wise to clear the datum and make nine knots away from the firing area for a day. Now I think we are also correct to continue at five knots. At this depth and speed we are completely safe from detection. But tonight we shall have to snorkel for a few hours . . . batteries getting low. I just don't want to come up before dark."

"Nossir. I think not. The Americans are very vigilant around here. They have big a surveillance station at Halifax, as you know. That SOSUS very dangerous to us. If we stay dead slow, they hear nothing, right?"

"That is correct, Arash . . . but we'll have to snorkel by 1800."

"Then where, sir? Where do we go afterward? Can I know our next mission?"

"We will stay on the westerly edge of the Mid-Atlantic Ridge for the next twelve days. Detection is nearly impossible there.

That way we can be back in our old position on 30 West, at the fiftieth parallel in perfect time."

"We fire again, sir?"

"Yes, Arash. We fire again."

Day after day they cruised quietly, snorkeling for very short periods by night, but always keeping the batteries well charged, just in case *Unseen* should need to get away from a pursuing U.S. or British warship. It was impossible for Commander Adnam to know whether or not the military had yet been called in to assist with the investigation into the crash of Concorde, but he knew they would come in the end.

He sensed that inside the U.S. military he had a very determined opponent. Someone who, he had no doubt, would one day piece together that one maestro had sunk a carrier and downed a supersonic jet. Both times using a submarine. Ben Adnam had no illusions about his own cleverness, but he was equally certain there was at least one person, just as cunning and just as brilliant, operating on the Great Satan's side of the fence. It was that sort of assumption that kept him alive, he reckoned.

They stayed silent in the deep water, occasionally monitoring the satellite for news or orders from Bandar Abbas. And the Iranian crew awaited patiently the next instruction from their Iraqi captain.

For eight days he revealed nothing. They all knew that the next mission would be essentially the same as the first, but on January 26, *Unseen* received a terse signal: *"PR campaign launched."* And Adnam briefed his crew on what this meant.

Then, two mornings later on January 28, a highly exclusive photograph appeared in the international Iranian daily newspaper *Kayhan*, which is the much more hard-line English-language edition of the *Tehran Times* . . . designed for an overseas readership.

The picture showed up, in color, over four columns, at the top of page five. And it showed two Army trucks, full of heavily armed Iraqi soldiers, driving through the streets of the little marshland town of Qal At Salih, east of the Tigris, some 30 miles from the Iranian border. Behind one of the trucks was a trailer on which was some kind of a rounded cargo, covered with a tarpaulin.

The caption beneath it said:

IRAQI ARMY PERSONNEL ON THE MOVE NEAR
OUR FRONTIER. FEARS OF MAJOR GARRISON
BUILDING AT QAL AT SALIH.

Beneath the picture, the italicized credit line read:

AGENCE FRANCE PRESSE.

Now, none of this was particularly interesting. It was deep in the background of the photograph, slightly hidden beyond the trucks, where the writing was apparently on the wall. In daubed Arabic lettering was the slogan, DEATH TO THE OIL THIEVES. Beneath it was the unmistakable pterodactyl outline of Concorde coming in to land, nose angled down.

The photograph would have been perfectly complete without it, and indeed it really required a magnifying glass to make out the exact message of the lettering. But in Paris that morning there was someone with a magnifying glass, Ross Andrews, the CIA's chief field officer in France. And he was staring at the picture on page five of *Kayham* with profound interest.

He called the veteran picture editor at *Agence France*, and wondered if he could purchase a copy that might be clearer. Such requests from American Embassy staff officers were not unusual, and Franc Gardu said he would call back when he located the negative.

Unhappily he could find no trace of the picture, not in the printing rooms, not in the wire room. Uneasy about calling back the U.S. Embassy and admitting he had no idea where the picture was, he placed a call to the offices of the *Tehran Times*.

Franc had spoken to the picture editor there many times, especially during the various Middle Eastern conflicts of the past thirty years, and now he queried: "Are you certain you got that picture from us?"

"Of course I'm sure. It came in by wire yesterday morning. I just signed the credit to your account. It's a nice shot."

"Does it have our stamp on it, top left?"

"Wait please . . . I'll check . . . absolutely. It's right there."

"You wouldn't be good enough to wire us back a copy would you? I can't find the negs."

"Sure . . . be happy to."

And with that, Karim Meta wired a copy of a perfectly exquisite forgery to Paris, a forgery so beautifully worked that no one except a military scientist would ever be able to tell that the trucks, and the soldiers, and the trailer, had been superimposed onto a photograph of a painted wall in a back street of south Tehran.

That morning Franc Gardu received several other requests for the photograph, one from the *Kuwait Times*. By the evening, midday in Washington, there were two wired copies of the picture on the desk of the CIA's Middle East Chief Jeff Austin. One from Paris, one from the field officer in Kuwait.

Each one was accompanied by a similar memorandum, remarking how odd it was that a few remote people, from deep in the land of the Marsh Arabs in southeastern Iraq, had reason to be cheered by the loss of the U.S. oil-negotiating team that had died on Concorde. "No secret about the deaths, every paper in the Middle East carried the story. Here in Kuwait City there was even an interview with Mohammed Al-Sabah about his friend Bob Trueman . . . just seemed a bit strange that there should have been people who were pleased the Americans had died, right down there in the marshes."

Jeff Austin's mind buzzed. It was the second time he had seen that name Qal At Salih in the last six months. The first time had been back in the summer, when there had been two mild alerts about Iraqi missile testing in the marshes, though nothing had come of it.

And now this. Cheers from the Marsh Arabs about Concorde's crash and the Americans who died in it. Jeff Austin called Admiral

Morgan in the White House on the secure line and recounted his thoughts. The national security advisor was very reflective.

"How'd we get the picture?" he asked.

"Apparently with some difficulty. Two of our guys spotted it in the Tehran paper, and then had to negotiate with the French picture agency to buy it. I'm sending a copy over to you right away . . . you'll see . . . it's not that easy to read the graffiti right away. It's in Arabic. It's the picture that grabs you . . . the one of the aircraft. I thought both of our guys were pretty sharp to notice it. Ross Andrews in the Paris embassy was first."

"Uh-huh . . . yup, Jeff. I'd like to see it. By the way . . . did we get any more confirmation on that missile-testing business we discussed before?"

"Not a word, sir. Not another word."

"Qal At Salih . . . that's a goddamned funny place to be associated with world atrocities. Fucking Marsh Arabs splashing around with guided missiles hidden up their goddamned djellabas."

February 2006.

T HE LOSS OF THE THIRTY-YEAR-OLD CONCORDE, THE
sixth of the production models that had arrived onstream
between 1976 and 1980, occurred at a poignantly significant
moment for the aircraft industry. Because, at that very time, Concorde's natural successor was undergoing its final trials out on
the West Coast of America. It was the Boeing Starstriker, the last
word in supersonic flight in the opinion of its designers . . . twice
the size of Concorde, with three times the passenger capacity,
and 350 mph faster across the ocean. But, more than that, it her-
alded the reclaiming of the high aviation ground by the U.S.A.,
after thirty-five years of European domination.

Those thirty-five years had never been easy for the American
plane makers to accept. Way back in the early sixties, when President Kennedy had been determined the U.S.A. would lead the way
in the production of SSTs, Boeing had been at the very forefront of

the design developments. The great swing-wing Boeing 2707-100, built to fly at MACH-2.5 with 300 passengers, had seemed set to blow the Anglo-French Concorde right out of the game, just as the Boeing 707 had outcommercialized Vickers's beautiful, quiet VC10.

But then had come the fashionable clamor for a cleaner, quieter, less polluted world. And America's East Coast liberals waged a six-year campaign to have the supersonic transports killed off, as "too costly, too noisy, too threatening to the environment, totally unacceptable to anyone living anywhere near the airports of New York and Washington."

With JFK gone, men like Senator William Proxmire rallied support for the cause that the U.S. government ought not to be funding it. There were Harvard scientists founding outfits like Citizens League Against the Sonic Boom. All over the country a rising hysteria grew ever stronger. The East Coast press printed every outlandish claim, that the great sound-barrier boom of the SSTs would obliterate houses, destroy the American wilderness, wipe out entire species of life on this planet: birds, insects, domestic pets, possibly even liberals.

By the mid-sixties, it was clear that Concorde was in front of the Boeing 2707-100 in its development, but most experts believed the great SST from Seattle would come in late, with a more realistic economic base, and take over the world's most expensive passenger flights without much trouble. Poor little Concorde would be stampeded aside in the rush.

However the more pressing stampede was that of the abolitionists, and by the late sixties the tide had turned. Pan American and TWA, the two U.S. airlines that had been vociferous supporters of supersonic transport, canceled their orders for Concorde, and a shiver of apprehension was felt in Seattle.

And there was no help from the military, which had traditionally stood behind major aircraft development. In the old days, of the early fifties, any new American SST program would have been for the development of some huge Air Force-manned bomber, and money would have been made available from the defense budget. However, that game, too, was changing drastically, and big manned bombers were becoming obsolete in the new age of guided missiles.

Which left the Boeing Corporation in Seattle to fight a lone battle for its supersonic passenger jet, an aircraft totally impractical without government funding, an aerial wagon around which the Indians were already circling.

On the night of May 17, 1971, Congress finally finished it, voting 49–47 to discontinue funding the project. The men from Seattle were devastated. And three years later, they could only watch helplessly when a cheering crowd estimated at 250,000 surrounded Los Angeles Airport to witness the spectacular landing of Concorde prototype 02, as it came howling out of the skies on its triumphant American Pacific Coast tour to sell the concept of supersonic flight.

There were many designers, engineers, and test pilots at Boeing who never quite got over the political killing of the 2707-100, an aircraft equally as dramatic as Concorde, and probably many times more financially efficient. One of them was a twenty-eight-year-old design engineer named John Mulcahy, an ex–Boston College football star, with an engineering doctorate from the Massachusetts Institute of Technology.

On February 2, in the deep winter of the year 2006, the sixty-three-year-old John Mulcahy was president of the Boeing Corporation, and he sat at the head of the long table in the rarefied corporate conference room listening with unashamed satisfaction to the latest reports of the tests on Starstriker. This was indeed the aircraft to dominate the world in the field of high-speed business travel, transatlantic, transpacific, global. Concorde had proved conclusively there was a market for executives who need to move across the world in a big hurry, the hell with the expense. And the giant Boeing SST was ready to place the corporation right back in the driving seat of world aviation. Where, John Mulcahy fervently believed, it had always belonged.

Certainly, in the intervening years since Concorde had first taken flight, the Boeing Corporation had dominated the world of commercial aviation, the Boeing 707s, 727s, 737s, 747s and the rest had been unrivaled in their volume, their safety and efficiency. But Concorde, nothing like so commercially successful, and a financial failure on so many routes, remained the glittering flagship of air travel.

She was the capricious high-speed record holder of the airways, the passenger jet everyone loved to watch. She had always been to aviation what the Cowboys were to football, what the Yankees were to baseball, what Arnold Palmer was to golf, what the Princess of Wales was to fashion. Concorde was the supersonic jet everyone wanted to meet, preferably from a window seat, sipping champagne, transatlantic.

Which made many Boeing execs consider the world a cruel and unfair place. Because they had designed an SST just as glamorous, even more spectacular-looking, and considerably faster. And government officials, more than three thousand miles away—*American* government officials—had destroyed her.

But now things were going to be very different. Based on those long-shelved plans and designs, they had re-created it all thirty-five years later. They had advanced the systems, refined the engines, working in conjunction with Pratt and Whitney. From the old stillborn 2707-100 had sprung the twenty-first-century 2707-500, the Boeing Starstriker. Now the world's hotshot travelers would see what American excellence really stood for. And in a sense the men from Boeing would stand vindicated for all the millions of millions of dollars they had spent back in the sixties, and all the thousands of man-hours they had expended.

Starstriker represented living, growling proof, that where politicians might be quite happy to squander colossal amounts of money, which was not theirs anyway, America's heavy industry was not so inclined. Their knowledge, their research and development had been meticulously stored over the years, then distilled, cultivated, and improved. And the East Coast journalists who had gleefully added up the costs of the old 2707-100 and pronounced Boeing money managers "guilty of extravagance beyond words" throughout the first SST program . . . well . . . they could now go chew on their own long-dead, ill-thought-out feature articles. In the unlikely event they would ever be able to comprehend the depth of their misjudgments.

John Mulcahy beamed with good humor. He sat next to his chief engineer, longtime vice president Sam Boland, whom he had first met at MIT and subsequently lured from another major U.S. plane maker. To his left was the top test pilot in the United States, Bob "Scanner" Richards, Boeing's near-mythical project manager whose instinct for the smooth running of a revolutionary design venture was fabled throughout the industry. Scanner had just declared the titanium-bodied Starstriker, "about as close to perfection as anyone's gonna get an SST in this lifetime."

John Mulcahy had also listened to a report by his public relations chief, Jay Herbert, who had described, in barely controlled excitement, the events that would unfold in Washington, right there at Dulles International Airport on February 9, when Scanner Richards would take Starstriker on her maiden transatlantic test flight in the company of all of the top Boeing technicians who had worked on her for so long. There would be no passengers, just the high-tech air crew and staff. The guest list at the celebrity breakfast and reception was as glamorous as anything seen in the nation's capital since the Reagan years.

Ten minutes previously Jay had revealed that the President of the United States would arrive at Dulles, together with his wife and National Security Advisor Admiral Arnold Morgan, plus Secretary of Defense Bob MacPherson. Chairman of the Joint Chiefs Admiral Scott Dunsmore had accepted, plus the heads of all the Armed Services. Leading senators, congressmen, governors, the titans of corporate America, media tycoons, Wall Street giants, and a smattering of show-business lightweights, actresses and singers, who would probably claim most of the headlines.

The maiden transatlantic flight of Starstriker had captured the attention of the press and television as few technological subjects ever do. Orders and inquiries from at least eight different airlines, four of them American, were being dealt with on an hourly basis by the marketing department. John Mulcahy had known some great days as the man at the helm of the world's greatest aircraft production corporation. But February 9 promised to be his finest hour.

He was a tall, craggy man in appearance, inclined to look a bit disheveled even in a brand-new expensive suit. His much younger wife, Betsy, fought a losing battle to make him look like the president of the Boeing Corporation, but she could never persuade him to get his shoes shined. And no matter how many times she bought him a tie from Hermès he always managed to knot it badly, somehow too thin, and it rarely hid the top button of his shirt.

Nonetheless there was an aura of power about the man. He stood six feet three inches, and his hair was thick, iron grey in color. He laughed a lot, but he also frowned a lot, and he ruled the corporation in a stern, hands-on manner. Only his true friends understood that behind this forbidding, somewhat severe exterior there lurked a wild Irishman, dying to break cover. No one ever forgot John's sixtieth birthday party in a private room at the most expensive hotel in Seattle . . . when he stood on a table at one in the morning and insisted on singing a succession of traditional Irish revolutionary battle hymns. Upset a few local matrons, but Senator Kennedy seemed wryly amused.

John Mulcahy's grandparents were from County Kildare in Ireland, and he treasured his roots in the old country. Each year he and Betsy flew to Shannon and drove up to the family village of Kilcullen, where he stayed at the home of one of Ireland's major industrialists, Brendan Sheehan. On the way, they stopped and played golf for two or three days at Mount Juliet in County Kilkenny. In Kildare they played Michael Smurfit's magnificent golf course at the K-Club. One day John Mulcahy intended to bring Starstriker to Shannon, which housed, after all, a section of the oceanic control center that would soon be guiding the new supersonic aircraft safely across the eastern half of the Atlantic.

He found it enthralling: the very prospect of his great aircraft descending through the mists of the Shannon Estuary, its landing wheels reaching out for Irish soil, 150 years after the penniless Seamus and Maeve Mulcahy had fled the famine, survived the voyage to America, and set up home in Boston, where, two generations later, John had been born.

He was a true romantic, an Irishman of the blood, and his contract with Boeing stipulated, in italicized letters, that he was *never* required to be at the office on March 17 of any year, save for an outbreak of war, fire, or mutiny. He did not miss many of the other working days, however, and he held the daily operations of the corporation in what some people believed was an iron grip. Boeing had never had a better president.

And the meeting today found him in an expansive mood. Concorde's disaster had, of course, played into their hands, and while no one, genuinely, wanted to gloat at any airline's catastrophe, particularly that of an important customer like British Airways, it was impossible to turn back the thought that Concorde's calamity was, inevitably, Starstriker's benefit.

The specter of that splendid airliner, coming apart at the seams, way up in the stratosphere, hung heavily over the table.

"What do you think happened to it, Scanner?" asked the president.

"I'm completely bewildered, to tell you the truth, John." said the ex–Air Force fighter pilot. "I mean, what could have happened to it? There's nothing up there to hit, and nothing known to man that could have hit it. Except maybe a meteorite, or a hunk that fell off a satellite. But the odds against that have gotta be millions and millions to one."

"Then what?" persisted the president.

"Well, we do have that other pilot's assertion, the guy from Northwestern, that he saw fire in the sky right where Concorde must have been. But I don't know about that . . . I guess we must be left with internal failure of some kind. "

"Yeah, but what kind of failure?"

"I can't imagine. Both British Aerospace and Rolls Royce say a fuel leak fire is absolutely out of the question, so we have to forget that. And no one thinks it remotely possible that a bomb could have been planted. Which really leaves not much, except an engine fire that somehow got to the fuel. But to me that doesn't really ring true. Without the fire observation from the other pilot, I'd be inclined to think in terms of metal fatigue, or a structural failure at MACH-2. But I don't think either of those things would set the sonofabitch on fire. Beats the hell out of me, John."

"And me. Just doesn't add up, does it?"

"Not in this life."

"Anyway, gentlemen, we better go on. Now, when are we moving to Washington?"

"On schedule, John. The aircraft departs on the afternoon of February 7, subsonic from Seattle to Dulles, leaves at 1600, arrives in secret and in darkness 2220 local. She's being towed straight to a hangar, kept under wraps for the night, serviced thoroughly the next day ready for the 0830 departure for London on the ninth."

"Okay. The rest of us leave here at 0800 on the eighth arriving Washington 1630. Reception and dinner beginning 1900 at the Carlton. That's industry only, plus three senior U.S. Senators."

"Good. Kennedy coming?"

"Yup."

"That's better yet. He's still the best we have. Knows more. Thinks more. Does more. Even though he's a Democrat. Plus he's as funny as hell. Put him near me, willya."

"How about John Kerry?"

"Yup. He's coming as well."

"Excellent. Am I speaking?

"Yes. First draft's ready tomorrow. I believe you're working on the departure speech yourself."

"Yup. Don't want any help with that one."

Friday, February 3, 2006. London.

Great Britain's Minister of Transport, Howard Eden, was under pressure. Every day he faced a barrage of criticism over the Concorde air disaster. The media were demanding answers, the opposition benches in the House were demanding answers, and now the Prime Minister was demanding answers.

"Jesus Christ," he told his secretary, in their besieged private offices in Westminster. "You'd have thought I was driving the bloody thing."

He had just returned from a bruising session of questions in the House, during which there had been calls for his resignation. He had been publicly described as the Minister Without A Clue—a crib from a recent tabloid headline—and variously as "incompetent," "uncaring," "witless," and "Ti,"—the latter, the Tory shadow minister explained, was short for "*Titanic*," which everyone knew was a total bloody disaster.

Howard Eden was the latest in a long line of British government ministers who seemed fine while the winds were fair, but came unbuckled at the first sign of trouble. This was undoubtedly because the ruling Parliamentary party too often appointed ministers to areas where their degree of knowledge and competence was near zero. In recent years they had made bankers and lawyers into defense ministers—and appointed all kinds of political misfits into the great offices of state.

Howard Eden, in office for only eighteen months, still knew very little about modern air transportation. And he was not much better on road and rail. His job was regarded as a stepping-stone to higher office. Which was why he was all at sea, like Concorde, in his current predicament. And now he had to report to the Prime Minister who had made him transport minister in the first place, to explain precisely why his department was being made to look absurd on a daily basis, right out there in front of the entire world.

He had no answers. Everyone knew that. For the search for wreckage was going especially badly in mountainous North Atlantic seas almost 3 miles deep. The only glimmer of hope was that on the tenth day of the operation out on 30 West, a Royal Navy sonar operator thought he had heard the locator beam of Concorde's black box. Whether or not they could ever get down there to retrieve it was highly debatable. But arrangements were being made for an unmanned diving submarine to go down and try.

The Prime Minister's concern was a sharp lessening in public confidence in air travel. And, being an instinctive politician, he understood the reason for this was lack of explanation as to the cause of the disaster. What he needed was someone who could step forward, and say, *Prime Minister, we are dealing here with almost certain metal fatigue, and we are examining every aircraft in the fleet for any further signs of it. Concorde was lost due to a structural failure and we are making absolutely certain such a failure could never, ever happen again.*

The public could forgive an identifiable problem that was being fixed. They had proved that years ago when there were a succession of accidents with the Comet airliners. But the public could not cope with uncertainty, especially when the government's own experts were plainly without clues. The British Airways board was beside itself with worry. Three of their members would be in Washington five days hence to see the fanfare of departure for the big Boeing superstar that would, expensively, put their beloved Concorde out of the business of supersonic flight forever.

It would, of course, be churlish for the Prime Minister to sack Howard Eden for his current role in one of Britain's worst ever crashes—one which had killed four United States congressmen. But it might look a whole lot better if he resigned. There's nothing quite so good as a scapegoat to take the heat off everyone else.

However, in this instance, the public outrage, fanned by the press, was so intense, it seemed nothing could diminish the clamor for heads to roll. As if 115 on board *Speedbird* 001 were not sufficient.

Howard Eden had no intention of going to Washington to attend the triumphant ceremony of the American plane makers. With a weary step, he headed downstairs toward the ministerial limousine, to take him to 10 Downing Street for possibly the last time.

Not far away, there was equal depression in the offices of the Air Accident Investigation Branch of the ministry. With every day that had passed since zero plus two, the number of clues had diminished. There had been pieces of wreckage on the surface, but only from the cabin. All of Concorde's heavy-duty components, like the four engines, the tail plane and undercarriage, were on the bottom of the Atlantic. The wings seemed to have been blown into shards by exploding fuel, and they did not float. The Navy searchers found no sizable pieces whatsoever. The other problem was the height. "Normal" air disasters, which take place at the regular cruising altitude of above 30,000 feet can scatter debris over a 4-mile area.

In this case, given the 10-mile height and the terrific speed, the wreckage seemed scattered across a square of 10 miles by 10 miles, or, from the searchers' point of view, 100 square miles, made infinitely more difficult because no one actually knew, with any accuracy, precisely where Concorde had been when she came apart.

Each day the department tried to assemble a report, demonstrating that some progress was being made. But it was almost impossible. Assisted by the senior brains of British Airways, and by the British Aircraft Corporation, even by French experts from Aerospatiale, there was nothing to piece together. Not unless they could find a way to reclaim the critical parts from the bottom of the Atlantic. And no one seemed very optimistic about that, particularly since it would cost a king's ransom even to attempt it. No one had ever been anywhere near that depth in a search for wreckage. Not even the *Titanic* rested in water *that* deep.

Friday, February 3.
Office of the National Security Advisor.
The White House.

Admiral Arnold Morgan was on his "break." This was a twenty-minute hiatus he tried to take each morning at around 1100 when he checked through newspapers and magazines, "just to check no one's done anything absolutely fucking ridiculous."

He was sitting at his big desk, perusing the national weeklies, chatting with Kathy O'Brien and sipping black coffee. "This

Concorde thing's like a time warp," he was saying. "Remember last spring when the Brits were searching for the submarine? Well, they're still doing the same thing now—groping around the bottom of the goddamned ocean, and both times they are finding nothing significant."

"I could remind you," said Kathy, "that despite your fears, the submarine has never been seen, and neither has it blown up another aircraft carrier. Most reasonable people believe it must be on the bottom, wherever that may be, a tomb for all the crew, whoever they may be."

"You could remind me of that," replied the admiral. "And you could remind me that in your view I suffer from incurable paranoia, which I do."

They both laughed. But Arnold Morgan was serious. "When I was in the National Security Agency, I tried to connect apparently disconnected facts. And a lot of the time I was very wide of the mark. But not always. And I got it right more often than anyone else, which is, I guess, why I'm sitting in this chair. And I'm now pondering three totally disconnected facts.

"One, that British submarine is still missing, and I, in company with a very few like-minded paranoids, think it might be out there plotting and planning a strike against the West. I think it is possible that Commander Adnam may be alive, and that if he is, he is driving HMS *Unseen* . . . somewhere.

"Two, a brilliantly maintained aircraft, flying high, completely out of harm's way, suddenly falls clean out of the sky, for no discernible reason.

"Three, there are, in the intelligence community, deep suspicions that Iraq, possibly assisted by the Russians, is testing SAMs, surface-to air-missiles, down in the southern marshes—a strange place, where we know there was some elation over the Concorde disaster."

"Hold on one moment, Arnold, are you trying to tell me we have this homicidal maniac, who's *stolen* a Royal Navy submarine, somewhere on the loose in a submarine which can shoot down supersonic airliners at will. Isn't that a bit far-fetched?"

"Probably. At least it would be if his name wasn't Benjamin Adnam . . . but the most far-fetched part is *where* Concorde vanished."

"How do you mean?"

"Kathy, more than 94 percent of all air crashes take place on landing or takeoff. Just go over the ones you remember . . . the one in the Florida swamp, the one in the Potomac, the one at the end of the runway in Boston, the one up the mountain near Tokyo, even the TWA off Long Island, the one near Paris, the one that fell short of Birmingham airport in England. All near airports. Passenger aircraft hit mountains coming into land, they misjudge runways in bad weather, and they take off when something's not quite right. But they hardly ever blow up of their own accord, or fall apart when they are cruising through empty skies . . . because there's nothing up there."

"No . . . I suppose they don't."

"Just think about it for a minute. Here we have this beautiful aircraft, powered by four Rolls Royce engines that the Brits check thoroughly about every two days. Its safety record is immaculate, its pilots and flight engineers carry out five times more safety checks than any other aircraft requires. When that baby takes off, every working part is as close to flawless as the Brits can get it. The safety procedures are sensational . . . they even ensure sufficient fuel to land on *one* engine anywhere during their journey. . . .

"And yet, halfway across the ocean, in light winds, flying clear at 54,000 feet, not a semblance of a problem, something happens that is so sudden, so utterly drastic, the sonofabitch just self-destructs, all on its own. Neither pilot apparently had time to yell to Gander Control on the radio, 'We're in trouble.' Not even 'Holy shit!' Nothing. Kathy, that aircraft was taken out at the speed of light, and even the terrorist community would have to admit it would be impossible to get through the BA security to plant a bomb. The Concorde team security-check *every passenger's goddamned baggage in detail* . . . no, Kathy, in the absence of the black box, I'm saying something's going on."

"Do you think someone fired a missile at it . . . like they say happened to the TWA flight?"

"Kathy, I can't say that . . . because there's nowhere in that part of the Atlantic *from which to fire a missile.*"

"How about if there had been . . . a nearby island, say. Or a cruising foreign warship? What would you have said then?"

"I would have been pretty goddamned suspicious, that's what, Kathy. I'd have been drawn to the conclusion that someone had knocked Concorde right out of the sky."

"Which leaves us where."

"Nowhere, basically."

"How about Ben?"

"Well, no submarine in anyone's navy has ever possessed the capacity to fire a surface-to-air guided missile that high, that fast, and that accurately. Not even us. And Ben Adnam is a known Iraqi, working for that barbarous but kinda primitive regime.

"I suppose they might have bought and tested a Russian missile that would have done the job. But it would have needed refining. And their submarine would have required major surgery. They don't even have a submarine that we know of. They don't even have any water deep enough to float it in. Hell, the Iraqis don't even know how to *service* a submarine, never mind turn it into the most advanced underwater weapons system in the world. So I guess I just don't know. Maybe the facts are incompatible.

"The trouble is, Kathy, if we accept there is even a possibility that Concorde was hit by a missile, we have to accept that it must have come from a vanishing submarine. Because there was nowhere else it could have come from. Barring outer space."

Monday, February 6.
Office of the Chief of Naval Operations Admiral
Joseph Mulligan. The Pentagon, Washington.

"Arnold, as I live and breathe! To what do I owe the pleasure of this unexpected visit? Good to see you."

"I just wanted to have a chat with one of the very few entirely sane minds operating in this neck of the woods."

"You might have the wrong office. Bear that in mind . . . three years in here can really test your powers of logical thought."

"Not yours, Joe. How 'bout some coffee. You might need it when you hear my latest theory."

"Good call, lemme order some . . . then we'll talk."

Five minutes later the two men settled into more comfortable chairs and began a discussion that might have sounded eccentric among other Naval officers. But not between these two.

Admiral Morgan cited the two entirely separate circumstances that had seen "the Brits groping around on the bottom of the ocean." He outlined his view that the apparently deceased Commander Adnam might not be quite so dead as all that. And that, in his opinion, shared by some very influential others, it was possible that the Iraqi commanding officer might right now be at the helm of the lost HMS *Unseen*.

He then cited two other circumstances he considered to be absolute impossibilities. The first was that *Unseen* had somehow been missed by the Royal Navy after an exhaustive ten-month search, and had in fact sunk. "Not possible, not even likely; she's out there somewhere. Stolen."

Admiral Mulligan nodded gravely. Then he nodded some more after Admiral Morgan explained his theory that Concorde's disappearance was, if anything, even more mystifying than *Unseen*'s. The question he wanted to run by the head of the United States Navy was this: "Do you think it's possible that the fucking Iraqis have somehow converted a submarine into an antiaircraft guided-missile boat that knocked Concorde out of the sky, bang in the middle of the North Atlantic?"

Admiral Morgan waited for the big ex-Trident commanding officer to laugh. But Joe Mulligan did no such thing. He stood up and walked around the room, a deep frown on his face. Then he said, "If it was any nation other than Iraq—which knows zero about submarines—I'd have to say yes. But, Arnold, they don't even own one, and they never have owned one. They could not possibly produce a team capable of operating one. Nor could they possibly manage the modifications. Have you considered the possibility they may have had someone do it for them? It's just a simple missile system. It's not brain surgery or anything."

"Joe, I had, but I came up with no answers."

"Well, let's think of it now. But before we do, let me run this by you. Antiaircraft missiles on a submarine are not entirely unknown, although there's never been a diesel boat with the kind of firepower you're talking about. But there was one . . . back in the seventies."

"There was? Who did it?"

"The Brits."

"They did?"

"Uh-huh. It was kept very low-key. But it was carried out by an old friend of mine, Royal Navy two and a half, Harry Brazier, Lt. Commander H.L. Brazier. Lovely guy, smart as hell . . . painted his submarine, an old A-Class boat, with white letters SSG 72 on the fin."

Admiral Morgan chuckled, slurped his coffee, and said, "Go on."

"Well, the Royal Navy converted that boat, HMS *Aeneas* she was called. They somehow fitted an old Blowpipe system to the front of the fin. Harry told me all about it. They called it SLAM—submerged launch air missile. The captain aimed it through the search periscope . . . they had to come to just above PD . . . fired it from a mounting, a kind of big, bulbous tower which came above the height of the fin. I remember he once showed me a photo . . . told me they had to remove the gun on the forecasing because of the top-weight.

"There were four missiles inside that tower, pressurized to keep out the water. It was only a modification to the land, hand-held Blowpipe. And it didn't pack that much of a wallop. The missile only went about 3,000 yards, but they thought it might knock a helicopter out of the sky. Harry told me it was dead easy to do. The only difficulty was making it seatight. But the Vickers engineers did it, and it worked. That boat could come up, slam a helo out of the sky, and vanish without trace. You were essentially left with a guided missile that had been fired from nowhere."

"Do you think the Iraqis could have stolen *Unseen* and made such a conversion in some other place?"

"I very much doubt it. A missile system that would launch a weapon 10 miles into the air and still keep going, maybe for a total of 40 or 50 miles, would need a pretty good-sized launcher, and a very sophisticated fire-control system. To fit it, you'd need some serious engineering, and deep skills. You'd need high-tech workshops, heavy-lifting gear. All the trimmings. But if you had the system, on board a big supply ship, and a place to work, I don't think it would be impossible. If you could find a way to engineer it into place in secret."

"As I recall, Joe, the Iraqis still have that Stromboli-Class replenishment ship they bought new from the Italians. I forget her name, but she displaced nearly 9,000 tons loaded . . . she was pretty useful. I suppose a rendezvous between the Stromboli and the submarine is not out of the question . . . it's just a matter of where they could have got the conversion done."

"Guess so, Arnie. But it's still a hell of a long shot. I assume you've checked the Stromboli's whereabouts and activities.

"Yes. She's out. And I know it's a long shot. But there ain't no short shots . . . right now I'm into long shots. Maybe they got ahold of another ship."

The CNO laughed, but he was still very serious. He was about to speak again when the President's national security advisor stood up, and said swiftly, "Joe I don't wanna waste your time. But let me ask you one final question, bearing in mind that I think we have just outlined the mere possibility that Ben Adnam might be out in the Atlantic with the most lethal submarine ever built . . . the world's first terminally deadly antiaircraft submarine."

"Well, *you* have, Arnie. Go on."

"What's the worst thing that could ever happen, this week?"

"Dunno."

"Come on, Joe. Think. Right now let's assume Commander Adnam is moving east across the North Atlantic, where he's been hiding. And now he's on the move, heading for the Mid-Atlantic Ridge, right out by 30 West. He's running slowly, 500 feet below the surface. What's the worst thing he could do?"

"You mean start knocking passenger airliners out of the sky?"

"No, Joe. Not any old passenger airliner."

The big man hesitated for a few moments . . . then he said, quietly, "Jesus Christ. Starstriker . . ."

"Yes, Joe. Starstriker."

"My God, Arnie. That's a big ole bone to chew on. You think it's possible?"

"Not really. I'm still hung up on the sheer unlikelihood of Iraq being able to make that missile conversion. Besides, there's not a damn thing we could do about it. The Royal Navy's Upholder is like the Russian's Kilo, you can't hear it at all, unless it's careless. What could we do? Send out the Atlantic Fleet to hunt it down? They might try for a year and *still* not find it. No, Joe, I'm afraid it's too way-out . . . no facts . . . just supposition. And you and I can't operate like that . . . not on blind guesswork involving a thousand-to-one shot."

"Guess not. But it sure as hell was an interesting discussion . . . You leaving now?"

"Yup. See you Thursday, Chief . . . bright and early . . . and by the way, it might not be that bad an idea to fire up SOSUS to keep a wary eye out for the lost British Upholder. You never know . . . they're pretty good up there in those waters."

"We've done all that, and we got the Brits to hand over her signatures. Hey, before you go . . . there's just one thing else I recall about *Aeneas*. That Blowpipe program was not done for the Royal Navy . . . it was done for the navy of another nation who paid for the whole development in cash. Harry said the Royal Navy merely borrowed the submarine for the missile-firing trials and took the money."

"You don't happen to remember which nation it was, do you? Maybe they lent the plans to someone recently."

"No, Arnie. Harry was never told that. But he always thought it might be Israel."

0700. Thursday, February 9.
Dulles International Airport, Washington, D.C.

Marie Colton, the svelte, dark-haired forty-five-year-old deputy head of Boeing's Public Relations Department, had been in action since 0500, overseeing the transformation of the biggest room in the airport. The deadly-serious, inwardly driven California divorcée, must have walked about 300 miles throughout the first-class area before her boss, the tall, laid-back Midwesterner, Jay Herbert, arrived on the scene at 0705.

At that point, Marie was ordering a group of flower arrangers around as if she were in an armored Panzer division, moving forward on Leningrad. You could not see the carpet for blooms, petals, leaves, and cut stalks. In the background, a six-strong team of long-haired electrical madmen was wiring up an interplanetary sound system to a couple of speakers the size of the Lincoln Memorial.

"Jesus Christ!" said Jay, protecting his ears from a high-pitched shriek that threatened to render everyone deaf from one end of Fairfax County to the other. And then to Marie, he added, "Everything under control?"

He intended the question to have an edge of irony to it. But Marie had never been terribly into irony. She possessed the quintessential literal mind. Jay had a policy *never* to waste a good joke on the female Obergruppenführer of the PR department; but occasionally, in the face of chaos too great to bear, he caved in and let one slip.

She turned to face him, with a quick deep red smile designed to betray the put-upon hurt of early-morning martyrdom. "Perfectly," she replied. "I wish you had been here a little earlier."

"Oh really?" he replied, caving in to his own sense of humor yet again. "I'm sorry, Marie. I had no idea you'd be so occupied."

Thus began the busiest, most important day in the entire history of the Boeing PR department. "Sometimes I think you say things just to upset me," said Marie. "Which is very unfair when you know how difficult this has all been. And how pressed we are for time."

"Ah, but I have inordinate faith in you," said Jay. "And I know we're going to see order spring from this chaos inside the next thirty minutes. Either that, or we're all fired."

Marie turned, exasperated, back to the flower arrangers. Jay moved toward his technical director, who was testing the television satellite hookup that would relay live from the cockpit the entire flight of Starstriker 001. "We in good shape, Charlie?" he asked.

"Yessir. Looking good . . . here watch this, see that picture there, looking out at the maintenance area of the airport? That's being filmed right through the cockpit windshield of Starstriker. We got a ship out there off Long Island recording the sonic boom from below . . . we got the black box wired up to the satellite link. Everyone in this room's gonna hear every word, while they're watching the big screens . . . these guys are gonna think they're *in* Starstriker, not just listening and watching."

"Looks terrific, Charlie. Sound effects okay?"

"Yessir. We got the full Dolby wraparound digital system installed. When that baby blasts off the runway, this room is going into a gut-rumbling shudder . . . just like in a movie . . . the earth will move.

"When she breaks the sound barrier that sonic boom is going to rattle the cutlery in here. Then we're switching right back to the main cabin, where there will be total silence. The pilot is going to mention the boom right before it happens . . . then he'll explain how it slips away and how no one inside the aircraft can hear a thing."

"Perfect. No glitches, Charlie, for Christ's sake . . . we got the President in here and God knows who else. Right now the future of the entire corporation is in your capable hands."

"Yessir. Don't worry. We're not going to have a problem. Everything is very routine. And we're well organized. Just sit back, eat your breakfast, and enjoy."

"You do good work, Charlie. Keep going."

Jay Herbert held down one of the biggest PR jobs in the United States because he never wasted his time on details. His responsibilities were too diverse for that. He delegated carefully, picked his people well, and edited the minutiae out of his life on a daily basis. He did not much like her, but he had hired the Obergruppenführer because he sensed that real detail, feverish pursuit of the apparently unimportant, was her forte. She never forgot anything, her desk was a symphony of lists, and she walked around with a clipboard of the key ones, checking off, adding to, adjusting, arranging, adjudicating.

"Marie Colton," Jay would whisper conspiratorially to senior colleagues, "lets nothing through the cracks, and I mean that financially, socially, academically, and probably sexually." It always got an inexpensive laugh, which was after all a part of the corporate PR head's job.

There was just one area of his duties that caused Jay Herbert to become marginally bogged down, and that was copywriting. An ex–Chicago newspaperman, the forty-eight-year-old Jay had been out of journalism for almost twenty years, but he still had the editor's dire compulsion to cut, change, and rethink other people's words. He always said it had to do with the natural literary rhythm that ran through his soul, and he found it impossible to deal with any writer who did not march to the beat of that precise same drum.

As such he drove a succession of advertising-agency executives almost crazy with his insistence on passing, personally, on every sentence of every Boeing brochure, every headline, every cross-head, every descriptive word. He would pore over submitted copy, cutting, editing, improving, forcing advertising men to wonder why the hell he had hired them in the first place, since he plainly wanted to write the stuff himself.

That day's brochure, printed and designed in the most expensive color it was possible to use, had taken six months to put together. Jay regarded it as his masterpiece, and it probably was.

He walked outside into the corridor, to where the big boxes were being opened. Four female assistants were in the process of placing one brochure at each table setting. Another pile was being placed at the entrance table, where each guest would receive a metal Starstriker badge engraved with his or her name.

Jay could see the front cover of the brochure, glossy white with the legend: STARSTRIKER—STAIRWAY TO THE FUTURE. It was illustrated with a thin line of shooting stars that swept away to a rendition of Old Glory fluttering in the heavens. The PR chief thought it was a knockout.

It was almost 0730, and Marie Colton had the flowers under control. The horticultural mess had vanished, and the room was spectacular. The miles of electrical wires that had traversed the floor a few minutes earlier had also vanished. The two big cinema-sized screens were in place diagonally across two corners of the great room, ensuring that everyone could see everything.

Jay had a quick conference with the catering boss to make certain absolutely anything anyone could desire for breakfast was available. The top table was laid with a milk white table-cloth, on which were placed jugs of orange juice and bowls of fruit. Baskets for toast, hot rolls, and Danish pastries were every-where. All of the waitresses were dressed as international airline stewardesses, the waiters as pilots.

The sixteen guests at the top table would be the President of the United States, John Mulcahy, Senator Kennedy and their wives, plus Admiral Arnold Morgan and Robert Macpherson. Then, inter-spersed, would be seated Chairman of the Joint Chiefs Admiral Scott Dunsmore, plus the three separate service chiefs, including, of course, Admiral Mulligan, all with wives. An Air Force band was tuning up in a corner of the room. A 25-foot-long model of the new supersonic aircraft was suspended from the ceiling.

The two other main tables, each of which seated forty-eight people, were placed at right angles to the VIP group, and everyone was seated democratically, senators, congressmen, business lead-ers, potential customers, and show-business personalities. Behind these was a long narrow press table on which were seated, facing the screens, twenty-four media heavy hitters: a half dozen top columnists, six stars of television news, six editors, and six proprietors, all handpicked by Jay Herbert.

Outside, beyond the doors of the great room, was another whole press area with its own screens and tables, buffet refreshments, and a zillion telephones and computer terminals. The press and public launch of Starstriker would bang a hole in a million dollars. The place was already crawling with Secret Servicemen.

Shortly after 0735 the guests began to arrive. And, as they did so the cinema screens came to life, the one on the left showing the scene outside the door with a detailed announcement of who each person was. "Ladies and gentlemen we are pleased to welcome now Sir John Fredickson, Chairman and Chief Executive of British Airways, and Lady Fredickson, both of whom arrived last night from London . . ."

The big screen on the right was relaying the scene from the cockpit, where Scanner Richards and his co–test pilot, the African-American Yale graduate Marvin Leonard, were running through the checks with the Senior Flight Engineer Don Grafton. As with Concorde, the procedures would take more than an hour. They had been working on it since 0700. The audience could see them in the dark cockpit, following the list on Engineer Grafton's board, as he studied the cathode ray tubes that contained the critical data bank that would alert them if anything was even remotely amiss. The "Glass Cockpit's" instrumentation panel, with its six big CRTs, made Concorde's bewildering mass of conventional dials and switches seem like something out of the Dark Ages. In the deep background, caressed by symphonic Dolby sound, Frank Sinatra sang alternately, "Fly Me to the Moon" and "Come Fly with Me."

He sang until precisely 0800, when the Presidential motorcade arrived, the first car bearing the President and his wife, with Admiral Morgan and Robert MacPherson.

In two cars following came the service chiefs and more Secret Servicemen. Everyone was greeted by John Mulcahy and his wife, and the party walked into the big room while the Air Force band robustly played "Hail to the Chief."

The Republican from Oklahoma occupied a very special place in the hearts of almost all the Americans in the room, and they stood and clapped in time to the old familiar music. And as they did so, a giant Stars and Stripes slipped down from the ceiling and fluttered perfectly in the controlled breeze of a secret fan, set in the fuselage of the model Starstriker. As the music ended, the entire gathering was on its feet to clap and cheer the right-wing President from the Southwest, a man who loved the military, who loved big business, who would not permit one dime to be cut from the Defense Budget, and who had twice reduced corporate taxation.

Also insiders, and there were many in this room, were still talking about a story making the Washington rounds in the last few days, of how a national news magazine had planned to write a humiliating cover story involving a very minor indiscretion by a senior, highly decorated Army officer, who had twice been cited for gallantry in the Gulf War.

The publisher of the mag had, apparently, been marched into the Oval Office, where the President had told him that he "would not tolerate one of my most trusted military personnel being held up to ridicule in front of every tin-pot fucking dictator in the world because of your goddamned desire to sell magazines.

"Run that story, and I will use my executive power to have you charged with treason against this nation—and don't think I wouldn't do it. Try to remember one thing . . . you do happen to be an American, no matter how hard that may be for the rest of us to believe. Try to behave like one for a change . . . now get out."

The publisher was apparently shaken, visibly. Had to be given a glass of water right there in the West Wing. But the story was canceled, and the publisher now sat subdued at the long press table, and everyone in the room noticed that he alone did not applaud the great man when the music died down.

It was 0814, and Starstriker was moving out to the taxiing area. The big screens were showing views from outside and inside the cockpit, every touch of the throttle eliciting a deep, grumbling roar from the Dolby sound system, as all four engines responded slickly. Everyone saw the ground engineer disconnect the tug. The nose and visor were lowered, and Scanner Richards headed her out to the takeoff point.

Then, for the first time, Boeing's supersonic aircraft could be seen, a sleek white 300-foot-long delta-winged giant, with a wider body than Concorde's, but not noticeably so because of the extra length. Passengers would ultimately sit in 36 rows of 8, widely separated into 4 pairs of seats. The pilot was almost 60 feet in front of the nose wheel. The Dolby sound system was still picking up the words of the flight engineer as he ran further safety checks while heading out toward the nearly 2-mile-long runway 19L.

Starstriker arrived at the takeoff point three minutes early, which gave Frank time for another couple of verses of "Fly Me to the Moon" and John Mulcahy to stand and welcome everyone for the second time and assert what a very great privilege it was for him to host such an august gathering of dignitaries, all of whom, he hoped, would shortly be paying customers on his aircraft, no matter which airline's livery Starstriker carried.

Everyone heard the Dulles tower clear the aircraft to enter the runway. And then the voice came through again. *"Tower to Boeing 2707-500. . . . Starstriker 001 cleared for takeoff."*

In reply, Scanner Richards's echoing words, on the Dolby system, sounded like Shakespeare. *"Zero-zero-one rolling . . ."*

Inside the cockpit, they heard Marvin Leonard counting . . . *"Four—three—two—one—No . . ."*

And they watched Scanner Richards smoothly extending the throttles forward, as Boeing's supersonic flagship powered out of the starting gate.

"Airspeed building . . ."

"Afterburners . . . 100 knots."

"Power checked. . . . V1 . . ."

At 200 knots the nosewheel lifted off the runway, and Starstriker seemed to hang at 10 degrees as her speed built.

Inside the VIP room the big hitters held their breath, as Marvin Leonard said, *"V2, sir . . . 221 knots . . ."*

And Starstriker rocketed off the runway, accelerating to 250 knots, climbing into the cold clear skies above the Washington suburbs, tracked by the television cameras, as avidly as any space program. Scanner Richards took off to the northeast, altering course to due east for the 135-mile flight to the Atlantic coastline. There she would accelerate again, climbing to her cruise altitude of 60,000 feet, where her engines would settle into the fantastic speed of MACH-2.5, two and a half times the speed of sound, or, close to 1,700 mph.

Starstriker had to fly southeast for 50 miles, before adjusting through 90 degrees for the Atlantic crossing. Boeing's supersonic masterpiece made short work of that, and the VIP room sat spellbound, listening to the pilot call the way points. From the moment of the major course change to the northeast Starstriker, still accelerating, devoured the 300 miles up to Nantucket Island in fifteen minutes.

"Nantucket abeam, sir . . . 39.50 North, 69.00 West . . . MACH-2.5 . . ."

The words of Marvin Leonard, magnified by the sound system, electrified the gathering. The President looked over at Admiral Morgan and shook his head in sheer wonder. This thing was not a spaceship, on its way to Mars. This was a regular passenger jet aircraft, pointing the way to travel in the twenty-first century, exactly as Jay Herbert's carefully crafted sentences pointed out in the Boeing brochure.

Jay himself had pulled up a chair to the press table and was talking some of the newsmen through the flight, explaining how the captain would shortly come under the guidance of Oceanic Control, Gander, checking in every 10 degrees, or 450 miles, or, incredibly, every thirteen and a half minutes.

Starstriker was at full throttle. She checked in at the 50 West way point, right on 42 North, 10 miles above the great swells of the Atlantic flowing over the freezing Grand Banks. Relaxed, Scanner Richards faced the camera, while Marvin flew the aircraft, and he told everyone back at Dulles what a truly fantastic machine it was, and what a great privilege it was for him and his crew to make the first test flight transatlantic. He wished everyone good morning, and jauntily asked John Mulcahy if it would be okay for him to have a quick cup of coffee. It was a mild joke by Scanner's normal standards, but it laid 'em in the aisles in the VIP room, such was the depth of admiration for the job he was doing.

As the guests continued with their eggs, scrambled with smoked salmon, accompanied by Waterford crystal glasses of Krug champagne and orange juice, the minutes ticked by. And Starstriker ripped across the clear northern skies, the throaty crackle of her four engines lost out there on the frontiers of space.

The way point at 40 West was passed right on the forty-fifth parallel, and ATC Gander, in faraway snowbound Newfoundland, checked them in. Starstriker thundered on toward the next way point, the one at 30 West right above the Mid-Atlantic Ridge, where Scanner Richards would alert ATC Shannon in southern Ireland that his supersonic aircraft would check in from 60,000 feet at 30 West, in thirteen and a half minutes. Speed was steady at MACH-2.5.

Marvin Leonard said good-bye to Gander and made the 30 West contact with Shannon right on time, reporting height, speed, and position. The deep southern Irish brogue, the distinct tones of a Kerryman, came in immediately.

"Good morning Boeing Starstriker 001 . . . roger that . . . talk to you in minutes thirteen . . . over."

At which point came the first glitch of the morning. Both the big screens illuminating the flight at the VIP breakfast banquet went blank, fizzing noisily through the mammoth Dolby speakers. A collective groan went up, right out of the early days of cinema when the reel ran out. But before it died away, two things happened. The chief electrician headed across the room toward the control panel, and Admiral Arnold Morgan leapt to his feet, knocking his chair flying, and exclaiming, *"JESUS CHRIST! OH NO . . . JESUS CHRIST."*

To his fellow guests it seemed like an outpouring of fury and disappointment at the failure of the system. A few people laughed, but the President's wife grabbed his hand, and said,

"Come on, Arnie . . . it's not that bad . . . they'll have it going in a few minutes."

But her husband's national security advisor was completely distraught. "*NO . . . NO THEY WON'T. GODDAMMIT . . . GOD-DAMMIT . . . THAT BASTARD . . . GODDAMMIT . . .*" Those closest to him could see tears of anger and frustration streaming down his craggy face. And the only clue that this was no ordinary outburst was perhaps the fact that Naval Chief Joe Mulligan looked positively ashen. He excused himself and came round to Admiral Morgan, placing his arm around his shoulders, and muttering, "Come on, old buddy . . . I guess we got work to do."

Everyone saw the two military men leave the room, walking quickly, out toward the office where the Presidential communications were located, guarded by six Secret Servicemen. There were three telephones in there, and while John Mulcahy stood up and apologized for the technical interruption, the President's chief security advisor was already on the secure line to the White House, instructing them to patch him through to Air Traffic Control, Shannon, southern Ireland.

That took less than thirty seconds because Kathy O'Brien had the numbers right in front of her. When the admiral made contact, announcing himself as the senior security representative of the President of the United States, the operator put him through at once to the ATC supervisor.

And he had no idea what the fuss was about. "Sir, Starstriker 001 made contact at 30 West, nine minutes ago . . . she's not due in for another four minutes . . . how can I help?"

"*GO TO SELCAL . . . BOMBARD THE COCKPIT WITH SIG-NALS . . . GET 'EM ON THE LINE!*"

"No problem, sir. I'm sitting right here with the operator now . . . we're going through on her private call sign HF band . . . we just lit two warning lights in the cockpit and right now we have four warning bells ringing."

"Are they coming in?"

"Not yet, sir."

"*HIT 'EM AGAIN FOR CHRIST'S SAKE.*"

"No need sir, these systems operate nonstop . . . it's happening over and over."

"Are they coming in?"

"Nossir."

"How long before they're due?"

"Two minutes, sir"

"KEEP HITTING 'EM."

"I'm doing it, sir. But they're just not answering. It's very unusual . . . very, very unusual."

"GIMME THE TIME AGAIN."

"Starstriker's due in sixty seconds, sir."

Arnold Morgan waited. He waited next to his trusted friend Joe Mulligan for a full minute, then another. Then the Irish ATC supervisor said, "We're on the line. You can probably hear our operator right next to me."

And in the distance the admiral could hear a disconnected voice, and the tones were somehow hollow. *"Starstriker . . . Starstriker. This is Shanwick . . . this is Shanwick . . . go ahead with your position report. Starstriker 001, please go ahead with your position report . . ."*

The two admirals, both of them in mild shock, stood in silence, still listening for the words of the Irish supervisor to confirm that it was all a mistake, that the Boeing supersonic was still racing through the skies.

But at 1001 (EST), the operator came back on the line and delivered his message with a softly spoken jackhammer. "I'm sorry to inform you, sir, that we are now certain Starstriker is down in the North Atlantic, somewhere east of 30 West, her last-known was 50.30 North at 60,000 feet. We are alerting all ships in the area plus the appropriate United States agencies."

Admiral Morgan replaced the receiver, looked at the highest-ranking officer in the United States Navy, and said, "He got her."

Admiral Mulligan found it hard to speak. Their conversation of just three days earlier would haunt both men for years to come. But still the question remained: Was Ben Adnam really out there in a stolen diesel-electric submarine silently slamming passenger jets out of the Western skies on behalf of Islam?

"Well," rasped Admiral Morgan, "with two supersonic aircraft down, for no reason, in roughly the same patch of water, in three weeks, an accident looks pretty goddamned coincidental."

They walked back to the main room, uncertain what to do or say. But pandemonium had already broken out. When Shannon put the announcement out to the international air-sea rescue services, it took just a few minutes for the news to reach the British Broadcasting Corporation, and subsequently to be released in a news flash on the television and radio networks. This meant, broadly, that the entire world news media knew that Starstriker was down within twenty minutes of the crash.

The television people could not believe their luck. One of the great stories of all time was breaking, and there they were, in a room with the Boeing president, his PR chief, and other executives. Even the President of the United States was there. Even the head of the United States Air Force. Even the Chairman of the Joint Chiefs. They even had the chairman of British Airways, which had lost the Concorde a mere twenty days earlier. These journalists were involved in the News Nirvana of the last hundred years.

In the opinion of Arnold Morgan nothing useful could possibly be achieved by any of the Presidential party, and he recommended that everyone leave immediately, an evacuation facilitated by the Secret Service. Admiral Mulligan made the same suggestion to Scott Dunsmore, and the military top brass were also out of there in record time, leaving Jay Herbert to protect John Mulcahy as best he could. The electronic satellite links to the great aircraft had been switched off, since it was plain there was nothing to which they could connect. Starstriker was history.

The Pentagon staff car dropped Admiral Mulligan at the White House. And there in the West Wing, behind the locked doors of the office of the NSA, sat the only two men in America who had even a partial, if outlandish, theory to explain what had happened. Each tried to assemble his thoughts, trying to decide what to do about the menace that might be lurking five hundred feet below the surface, somewhere in a million square miles of the North Atlantic.

"The trouble is," said the Navy chief, "we still don't have a shred of evidence, and I can't just order a fleet to take off on some wild-goose chase. It would cost a fortune, which is not in our budget, and we'd hardly know where to start looking. Plus the operation would have to be 'black,' since we cannot alarm the populace. We'd need a dozen warships, which would alert the entire Armed Forces that something dead suspicious was going on right out there where the two jetliners went down."

"I know, Joe. Don't I just know. I think the best way forward is for us to analyze carefully the whole scenario . . . just to get it clear in our minds. That means we should assess the similarities between the two disasters, which is very simple.

"Both aircraft were maintained to the highest possible standards. Both of them just vanished off the airwaves around 30 West. Neither pilot, so far as we know, had time even to utter the word, SHIT. Which means they both blew up internally, or fell apart for unknown reasons. Or they were hit by a big guided missile, capable of perhaps a 50-mile range, at a speed somewhere between MACH-2 and MACH-3. Because of the obvious security surrounding Starstriker, there can be no question of a planted bomb. Neither does anyone think that was possible with Concorde. Which leaves us with the possibility of metal fatigue or structural weakness.

"But not on two aircraft built thirty years apart, one of which had been flying perfectly all its life, and the other judged to be the very last word in supersonic travel by every single one of the many, many world-class engineers at the Boeing plant."

"I agree, Arnold, with all that. Which leaves *only* the missile."

"Right. And the difficulty with that is simple; there is nowhere to fire it *from*. No land. No nearby ship, certainly not a warship. Unless the missile was delivered from space, which is not within present-day technology for us, it must have been fired from a submarine. A specially fitted submarine, one with a sizable surface-to-air system out there on its casing, probably in front of the fin like your man Harry's Blowpipe, only a lot bigger."

"Right, Arnold. And we have a missing submarine, nearly brand-new, whereabouts unknown, somehow taken beyond the very capable reach of the Royal Navy."

"Correct. And we have the possibility of one of the most dangerous submariners who ever lived being at the helm. I've spoken to David Gavron in Tel Aviv, and he admits, very frankly, that when you get right down to it, they cannot be certain whether Commander Adnam is dead or alive. They never saw the body, which has now been cremated by the Egyptians. They only had his papers. Could have been anyone. They could even have been forged, probably by fucking Adnam himself."

"Plus, Arnold, we have the irritating possibility that the plans for Harry Brazier's Blowpipe system are very possibly in the archives of the Israeli Navy. If they were, it's dollars to a pinch of shit Adnam has a copy of them. Christ, he served as commanding officer of an Israeli submarine. I bet he knew every inch of those drawings."

"Could be. If Harry's best guess is correct, Ben Adnam knew how to make that conversion. The only gap in an otherwise reasonably logical progression is that we don't know how the goddamned Iraqis did the engineering or where they found a trained submarine crew."

"No . . . no we don't. And it's a big gap. But he's fixed it before. I think we are going to assume they did it. And I think we have to consider ways of catching this submarine before he strikes again. I'm just not sure where to start. SOSUS came up with nothing. Do you think we have to talk to someone? Like Scott, or the President? Maybe Robert Mac?"

"I don't know. For right now I think we ought to wait for twenty-four hours and see if anything comes out in the media or in the searches going on out there. I think if we're going to propose a truly outlandish course of action, we need the boost of the continuing mystery. That way people will be a bit more ready to listen to us."

"Okay . . . shall we regroup late afternoon tomorrow, compare notes . . . here?"

"Yes, 1700 hours."

"You got it."

The Navy Chief walked out still frowning. And as he did so Admiral Morgan picked up his secure line and dialed a number on the other side of the world. Seconds later the telephone rang in the big white mansion on the shore of Loch Fyne.

"Iain?"

"Speaking."

"Arnold Morgan here."

"Good afternoon, Arnold. How nice to hear you. I'm afraid to say, you have the most terrible problem."

"I know. It's him, isn't it. Banging out airliners from a submarine."

"Yes, Arnold. Yes it is. It's him."

1500. February 9, 2006.
The Oval Office.

ADMIRAL ARNOLD MORGAN HAD JUST WALKED through the door and the President was awaiting him, sitting quietly with Secretary of State Harcourt Travis. Before the admiral could utter even a word of greeting, the Chief Executive said curtly, "National Security Advisor, you are holding out on me."

"Sir?"

"You are holding out on me. When Starstriker was lost this morning, you were the only person in that room who knew what had happened. You were expecting it. You reacted in about a half second. Too quick to absorb a mere possibility. And you were right, a full fifteen minutes in front of the world, and you said, 'That bastard.' I heard you.

"Arnold Morgan, I am sufficiently presumptuous to regard you as a true friend. And I'm not accusing you of anything. Not yet. But you better have a real good explanation for your apparent preknowledge."

Admiral Morgan nodded to Harcourt, then said, "Sir, I do have some theories. And I will not pretend I did not have a gut feeling that this *could* happen. But when it actually did I was as shocked as the next man. Just a bit earlier. And you know me well enough, Mr. President, I tend to react quickly. If there was anything I coulda done to prevent that disaster, you know I'da done it. With or without your permission."

And then, over two cups of coffee, in a talk which lasted almost thirty minutes, he recounted to the President and the senior foreign policy executive in the United States government every one of his thoughts, from the moment HMS *Unseen* went missing to the moment Starstriker was apparently blasted out of the sky.

He fitted the pieces together, and he plotted the progression of his ideas, and he made particular reference to the fact that he had no explanation as to how the Iraqis could have converted the British submarine into an antiaircraft weapon. In particular he pointed out the real gap, the real weakness in his argument: the question of *where* the Iraqis could have carried out the work, given the impossibility of their own situation; no deep water, no submarine base, and thus no home, no expertise, not many friends. He also pointed out that the American surveillance system was all-seeing but not fireproof. And the Iraqis had shown once before that they were capable of extraordinary cunning.

Finally, he talked about Benjamin Adnam and his belief that the presumed-dead terrorist *must* somehow be involved.

"I did not, sir, want to alarm you," said the admiral. "Because I did not have one shred of proof. I still don't. It's all just my own thoughts. But when you think, and half believe something, and then you get a hard-ass fact that slams it all together . . . well, right then you start to believe you may be right. Which I now do."

The President nodded. "Very well, Arnold. I understand. Two questions. One, how did Adnam know our oil-negotiating team was on board that particular Concorde flight?"

"That's easy. There was a full Iranian delegation at the conference in Baku. Bob Trueman certainly knew at least two of them pretty well. I am sure they just asked politely about his long journey home, and, being a civilian, he told 'em he was flying Concorde the next morning out of Heathrow."

"Right. And Starstriker?"

"That was Adnam's real objective, and it was one of the most publicized flights in history. Scruff, Kathy's highland terrier, knew Starstriker's ETD from Dulles this morning."

"Hmmm. I guess he did. How about the missile? Heat-seeking?"

"Nossir. Both aircraft were going too fast to risk chasing from anywhere astern. They were also damned high, and there are very strict range limits on these highly accurate SAMs. You'd only get one shot at a supersonic. My guess is that the missile was launched vertically, with preprogrammed radar. It adjusted trajectory and course automatically . . . it's called fire-and-forget in the trade . . . came in from dead ahead . . . smashed straight into the nose."

"Jesus. But Arnold, ought you not to have mentioned this to me beforehand?"

"Sir. For the past ten months I have been pondering the possibility that Adnam might be driving a stolen submarine. Naturally, my thoughts were that he might take another shot at us, even though I knew he had no major weaponry on board. But I didn't have the remotest idea where he was. I was not even confident enough to talk to the Navy. It was just a theory, mostly intuition, no facts. Then Concorde goes down. Do I connect my off-beat military theory with a crashed British passenger aircraft? Maybe. But not strongly enough to start alerting the Navy to take action. Certainly not to bother the President of the United States."

"No. I do see that. When were you going to speak to me?"

"Probably tomorrow evening. I told Joe Mulligan that before I said anything, we better wait to see that there was absolutely nothing from out of Starstriker's cockpit, like, 'We just ran out of gas.' But, not for the first time, you preempted me."

The President relaxed. "Guess I did. And you're a pretty hard guy to preempt. But Jesus, Arnold, I never saw a public over-reaction like yours this morning. People thought you'd lost it."

"Not quite, sir."

"No, Arnold, not quite . . . and now what? What do we do?"

For the first time now, the refined, scholarly Harcourt Travis spoke. But first he stood up and walked, thoughtfully, the length of the Oval Office and back. "Arnold," he said, "the trouble with theories is that they take on a life of their own. And if the very basis of their premise is wrong in the first place, they waste a thunderous amount of everyone's time. Also, they have a way of quite unnecessarily annoying foreign governments with which we are compelled to deal.

"Greatly as I respect your instincts, I am obliged to remind you that a couple of air crashes do not necessarily give credence to a scenario from a Bond movie . . . mad underwater terrorist running amok with the world's airlines."

"No, Harcourt. I know they don't."

"Plus the fact that your villain is: A) supposed to be dead, as far as anyone knows, and B) he is from a country that does not even own a submarine at all, far less the most lethal antiaircraft boat ever built."

"I know that, too, Harcourt."

"When I listen to you fit some of the pieces together, I do accept there is a remote chance you may be correct. But by God, Arnold, it is so remote. *If* the British submarine was not sunk, *if* it was somehow stolen, *if* this Adnam character is somehow still alive, *if* Iraq was somehow able to get it, hide it, convert it, man it, and operate it. *If* this same country was able to buy such a missile system from someone and fit it onto a submarine. *If* this Adnam was able to conceal himself in the North Atlantic, *if* he had been able to fire two untried SAM missiles from some kind of a jury-rigged launcher, and actually hit two of the highest-flying, fastest aircraft ever built. *If*, Arnold, your auntie had balls, I guess she'd somehow be your uncle. Count me out, pal. At least until you can provide me with one solitary shining F-A-C-T."

The President shook his head. Then he repeated his last question. "Well, what do we do?"

"I honestly don't know, sir," replied the admiral, ignoring the onslaught of skepticism displayed by Harcourt Travis. "I suppose we could accept my theory and obliterate Baghdad in retribution. But we'd look pretty fucking silly if a different kind of truth came out about the crashes. So that's out. At least for the moment."

"You can say that again," interjected the Secretary of State. "Do you have any idea what an uproar something like this could cause? Really, Arnold, even you have to get real on matters of this scale."

"Harcourt," replied Morgan, wearily, "you don't have to keep reminding me of my shortcomings, mainly because I might have to remind you of a few of yours . . . lemme just run this technical detail past the chief.

"Just assuming my unsupported theory is largely correct, the search area for a submarine is, by now, massive. Take the spot around 30 West where the two aircraft vanished. It's at 50.30 North. By the time we get out there with search aircraft, Commander Adnam could have been moving for twenty-four hours, leaving us a search area of at least 30,000 square miles. Expanding with every fucking minute that passes. By the time we get ships out there three days later, the target could be virtually anywhere.

"If you take 50.30 North, 30 West as the search-center, he could be on an 800-mile radius circle, or, stated another way, in a search area of over 2 million square miles . . . and that 2 million square miles is all water. Because the crashes happened bang in the middle of the ocean. One suspects by design.

"HMS *Unseen* could have gone north toward the coastal area of Greenland; west, way off the coast of the U.S.A. and Canada; east toward the west coast of Ireland; or south to absolutely nowhere. Adnam could be *anywhere in that area*. We'd have only one chance—that he gets careless and SOSUS picks him up, holds him long enough for MPA to get a fix. Sir, whatever, we're still looking for a poisoned needle in the Sahara desert."

"Supposition, supposition. The entire theory is one of supposition . . . we're not just looking for a needle in the Sahara. We're looking for a needle that probably does not exist. And in my book that's probably a needle not worth looking for." Harcourt Travis was on the verge of exasperation.

But the President wanted to proceed. "Arnold, how would it have been if we'd sent a fleet of nuclear submarines out there the moment we knew about the crash?"

"Better, but not much. They'd want three days minimum to get to the crash site. *Unseen* would still be more than 600 miles from the datum. That's a 600-mile radius circle, or 1 million square miles. We'd still have to trip over the sonofabitch. And we'd be just as likely to trip over ourselves."

"Who else knows your thoughts? Just Joe?"

"And our old friend Admiral MacLean. As you know, I visited him in Scotland. And I spoke to him again about two hours ago. He agrees. Adnam is on the loose, and he will almost certainly strike again. But Iain does have one thought which is useful . . . refueling. *Unseen* has a range of about 7,000 miles. He thinks it likely that Ben was topped up, say 1,000 miles out from the datum before Concorde. That means he's probably used up more than half of it, running back and forth.

"Joe's activating a search for any suspicious-looking tanker in the North Atlantic, Iraqi or otherwise, that is apparently going nowhere. If we find any, I guess we could have 'em tailed by a nuclear boat. That's how the Brits caught *General Belgrano* off the Falklands. Tracking the refueling ship."

"You want Harcourt to call some kind of council of war?"

"Not yet, sir. We better wait to see if anything whatsoever shakes out of the crashes in the next two or three days. I really think it would be crazy to start sending the Atlantic Fleet out right now. We've told 'em to maintain overhead surveillance in the immediate search area, and SOSUS has been briefed to be more than usually vigilant for *anything* that might be a U-Class signature anywhere in the North Atlantic. Meanwhile, I think we better keep our powder dry. . . . The last thing we need is coast-to-coast panic because an unseen enemy is wiping out international air traffic."

"No. We won't be thanked for causing that. But, Jesus, what if he hits another airliner?"

"Sir, I think we have to brace ourselves for that. But we'll be much more alert, and I think we should quietly send a Carrier Battle Group into the area . . . they're pretty good at finding submarines. Usually. Then we can keep land-based Maritime Patrol Aircraft working as well. Make it a general area search. But we should keep the SSN force well clear. Otherwise, we'll end up with a Blue on Blue. If we stay with surface-and-air search only, we can say they're just looking for wreckage."

"Arnold, as always it was instructive in the extreme. Keep me well posted, will you? I agree we ought not to make an early, rash move. But please, if you have any thoughts whatsoever, make sure I know about 'em. Real early."

"Absolutely, sir."

The admiral walked toward the Oval Office door, and, as he opened it, the President spoke again. "That, by the way, was not an admonishment . . . just my way of congratulating myself on my choice of a national security advisor."

"Thank you, sir."

Then turning to the Secretary of State, the President said, "You were pretty hard on him, Harcourt. I know I told you to bounce him up and down a little, find out how strong his theory was, but you came close to making him look a fool."

"Men like Admiral Morgan cannot to be made to look very foolish," replied Travis. "He's too damned clever. Also he happens to have the only theory in town about the crashes. But it is so far-fetched . . . more Hollywood than Washington . . . and I still believe it will be completely discredited in the end."

Harcourt Travis stood, gathered up his documents, and made for the door. But he was leaving behind a man in a mammoth quandary. The President had always recognized the admiral's paranoia about submarines, and he did not want to be sucked into some drastic action against an enemy that might not exist. As Morgan had pointed out, he had not one shred of proof that

Ben Adnam was out there, no proof that he was even alive, never mind at the helm of a rogue submarine. Certainly nothing but a bunch of circumstantial evidence to back up a truly majestic theory of international terrorism on an unimaginable scale. Harcourt Travis offered the easy, do-nothing, political solution, the cynical, lethargic stance of the international statesmen. Never get into a fight you might not win.

Maybe the admiral's losing it, the President thought. *Maybe he's just worked this one out a step too far, since, by his own admission, the Iraqis seem incapable of operating a submarine, much less making the missile conversion on the stolen submarine. And yet . . . and yet . . . being right has a virtue of its own. And with my own eyes I saw that Morgan was the only man in the United States this morning who was right, who was half expecting Starstriker might not make it across the Atlantic. What do they say in horse racing: keep backing him until he loses? I guess he's my man, for better or for worse.*

By the time the President had made his decision, the admiral had quickened his stride, marching back to his own office, head thrust forward, his mind locked on to one unnerving fact. *I have to get this whole fucking scenario right out of the hands of civilians and under the control of the military on both sides of the Atlantic. I just can't have some fat, dumb, and happy asshole in a Savile Row suit making some loosey-goosey remark on the BBC that is gonna send half the world into a fucking tailspin. And that is highly likely to happen. Specially if they find one of the black boxes."*

He walked into his office, closed the door, kissed Kathy, told her he loved her, then ordered her to get her ass firmly into gear and to get Admiral Sir Richard Birley on the line in London immediately, if not sooner. "He's probably at his residence. It's 2100 over there . . . he lives right near the base at Northwood . . . the number's on file . . . comes under FOSM."

Before he had finished yelling instructions, Admiral Birley was on the line from his office.

"Arnold. Hello, I was half expecting you to call . . . if our last conversation had a basis in truth, we are, shall we say, in the deepest possible trouble."

"Dick, we have more or less accepted here the truth of our last talk. I am presuming there has never been a squeak from *Unseen*?"

"You presume correctly. And we both know why. But we have to ask ourselves, what now?"

"Well, I had a purpose in this call . . . I think circumstances have thrown the Royal Navy and the United States Navy together. What may appear at first sight to be a civilian problem is now no such thing."

"Correct. I had absolutely the same thought myself."

"Are the search ships for Concorde all Royal Navy?"

"Yes. Two frigates and a destroyer. We're running a deep unmanned submarine from a civilian mother ship as well, but I can keep the lid on them."

"Great. Because we're sending three Navy ships out there to search for the wreckage of Starstriker. Also I wanna get a CVBG into the area as soon as possible. And, even quicker, some MPA. The thing is we have to keep any news of any black box we find under very tight control."

"We realize that over here. If the recording has the pilot shouting out that he was about to get hit up the arse by a guided missile . . . well, we won't want the media getting hold of that too soon. Because they would go instantly berserk. God knows what would happen then. I suppose all transatlantic flights would be in chaos, but also Adnam would know we were onto him . . . and that way he might make a bolt for it and disappear for good . . . knocking down a sodding aircraft whenever he felt so inclined."

"That's it, Dick. We have to keep this very, very tight. What I need to know is this, how can our two organizations keep a handle on it? The black boxes must be kept out of careless hands. I'm assuming your investigators won't just unpick the box and issue a press release?"

"Good God no. We're probably as tight with this information as you are. The box will be dealt with in secret at the laboratories of our Air Accident Investigation people. Nothing will be released to anyone until they are sure of their ground. But in this case I think there should be a formal military representative on the team."

"Right. I was going to suggest our CNO talk to your First Sea Lord . . . just to ensure that if either you, or we, get ahold of any one of the four boxes, we share whatever information we have. The idea is to catch this bastard, not sell fucking newspapers."

"Absolutely. I'll tell you what. I'll speak to someone in the ministry right away, and brief them as to our thoughts. Basically I think the way forward is for our Air Accident Investigation people to lock in with your Federal Aviation Administration. I'll call you back."

"Okay, I'll be waiting."

All through the small hours of the night, the Navy chiefs conferred. The First Sea Lord arranged for both the Navy and the Air Force to listen to the black-box recordings at the headquarters of the Air Accident Investigation people. Admiral Joe Mulligan, through Admiral Dunsmore, received similar clearance from the Oval Office, and by 0400 London time, the deal was done. The Royal Navy and the United States Navy would work in tandem, expense no object, in order to bring up the black boxes.

It was as well they had all worked so quickly. At 1340 (GMT) the following day, the Royal Navy's deep-submerged submarine, found one. It was still transmitting its locator signal, and *Exeter* had detected it on passive sonar. The box itself was 3 miles down, and they grabbed it with the aid of a television monitor, two floodlights, and a special small bathyscaphe lowered from the minisubmarine.

Back on board *Exeter*, they identified the black box, which was in fact orange, as the CVR, the cockpit voice recorder, that had belonged to the Concorde. In accordance with the latest orders a satellite signal was sent to both Northwood and the

Pentagon. Then the box was sealed, and *Exeter* made all speed due east to the English Channel, where she would come within the range of a Royal Navy Sea King helicopter.

The box was ultimately flown straight to the Royal Navy Air Base at Culdrose, Cornwall, and on from there by fixed-wing military aircraft. It was a long costly mission for one single word. The only sound to be heard from the cockpit beyond the reams of regular flight recordings was just one short shout from Captain Lambert. It sounded like "MISS," but there was a lot of interference. It could just as easily have been "KISS," or "BLISS."

That part of the recording was relayed to the White House immediately, where Admiral Morgan and Admiral Mulligan were waiting. Arnold Morgan suggested, "the guy either wanted to take a leak, or he was requiring, or getting, a blow job from the stewardess!"

He caught Admiral Mulligan in mid-swig, and the CNO did his unavailing best not to laugh or blow coffee down his nose, but he failed on both counts. And while the towering ex–Trident commander mopped his mouth with a big white handkerchief, the national security advisor moved into serious mode without missing a beat.

"Joe," he said, "Captain Brian Lambert saw it, didn't he? Not once in the whole recording, all the way from Heathrow, did we hear him even raise his voice for emphasis. That loud shout of 'MISS,' was entirely out of character. The captain meant to say 'MISSILE!' in my opinion. Poor guy never got the chance. The bastard was coming straight at him, closing at MACH-4, nearly 2,700 mph If he'd spotted it in clear skies even as much as 4 miles away, it would have hit him in five seconds. And that'd be my rough assessment of a totally lousy equation."

"Sounds right to me, Arnold. There is no other word that fits the pattern, especially the ones in your sexually explicit theory. He was trying to shout 'MISSILE' all right. This recording has been very useful . . . it's just about confirmed our original thoughts. And it emphasizes that if the Brits can find a small box in the middle of the Atlantic with modern equipment, they sure as hell could have found a fucking great submarine in the shallow English Channel."

Just then the telephone rang on Admiral Morgan's desk. It was a call that had been intercepted by Kathy, so it was plainly important. The national security advisor picked it up and was put through to Admiral George Morris, calling from Fort Meade.

"Arnold, hi. One of my guys just got something that might interest you. We've been running routine date checks on the computers, seeing if anything interesting correlates. And he's come up with this. January 17, the day Concorde, and our oil men, were blown out of the sky. It was the fifteenth anniversary to the day since the opening shots of the Gulf War. January 17 was the day we unleashed the first barrages of Tomahawk cruise missiles at Baghdad . . . it's not that much of a coincidence, but it's a bit of one."

"Yes, George. Yes it is. The odds against it are 364–1, and it might be a pointer. I thank you and your team." Click. As ever, Morgan had no time to say good-bye, as the problems that were ostensibly civilian crowded in, unproven, on his military mind.

That evening he and Kathy O'Brien were dining together in Georgetown, and despite all of his efforts to make it cheerful and pleasant, the silences were too long and the admiral's preoccupation was almost total.

"You always take these matters so personally," she said, holding his hand, looking into his eyes, confirming unknowingly that she was easily the most beautiful woman in the room. But he kept repeating over and over, "Darling, he's going to do it again. I know this bastard."

"Would you like to go home?"

"No. We better hang around for a bit, then get the driver to swing back through the city and pick up the first editions, see if the Fourth Estate has stumbled on something I've missed."

"Would that be a first in your long career?" she asked sweetly, fluttering her eyelashes.

"Maybe a second," he growled. "But I don't remember the other occasion."

They sat companionably, sipping amaretto on the rocks, while the admiral tried to cast from his mind the all-too-real vision of a missile, closing at MACH-4, as the one that probably hit Starstriker most certainly was. "Imagine that," he said. "You could see it 4 miles out, perhaps a glint in the sunlight, thin contrail behind . . . now count to five . . . that's it. One. Two. Three. Four. BAM. And it's gotcha. Wouldn't that be a bitch?"

"Oh yes, I think it would," she replied. "A real bitch."

Even Admiral Morgan smiled, just once.

An hour later the newspapers were in the back of the White House car, displaying practically nothing else on the first ten pages. The headlines were varied, from the staid *New York Times*'s U.S. SUPERSONIC CRASHES IN NORTH ATLANTIC to a local tabloid's STARSTRIKER STRIKES OUT.

Inside the papers were columns and columns of news and speculation, the disaster having taken place so early in the day there was ample time to interview all manner of "experts," especially those who were captive at the VIP breakfast banquet.

Every one of the publications on Arnold Morgan's lap connected Concorde and Starstriker, speculating on the proximity of the crashes, both in position and time frame, three weeks. Somewhat to Morgan's relief, no one digressed on the possibility of a missile, because the Federal Aviation Administration had stamped on that from a great height. "You would need a certain type of high-accuracy missile to achieve such an objective," their spokesman had said. "The best of them have a range of only around 50 miles, and at that point in the Atlantic Ocean there is simply nowhere to fire from . . . no land, and, the satellites confirm, no ship. We regard a missile as impossible."

Every newspaper carried that quotation. And none of them carried the theory any further. Instead they concentrated on the risks of flying that high and that fast in anything except a spaceship.

Two of them, the *Washington Post* and the *Philadelphia Inquirer* went into the possibility of a stratospheric Bermuda Triangle—trying to compare the fickle atmospherics ten miles above the earth to the strange volcanic eruptions under the sea near

Bermuda, which scientists believe release gases into the ocean water, reducing its density and causing ships simply to sink.

The *Post* hired an expert from the Woods Hole Oceanographic Institution to explain how this reduction in water density wreaks havoc with the theory of Archimedes, that a ship displaces an amount of water to equal its own submerged volume . . . "therefore if the ship is 50 percent underwater, but the water here is 50 percent less dense because of the gases, then the ship will just go straight down . . ."

The general drift was that somewhere up there in the final layers of the earth's atmosphere, there was just such a hole, and the two supersonic airliners traveling on almost identical flight paths, one heading east, one west, had just charged straight into it, spun, and powered into the ocean, with no time for anyone to correct anything. "It takes," the expert wrote ominously, "only twenty-seven seconds for Concorde to travel 10 miles, probably faster going straight down . . . Starstriker could have hit the ocean from that height in fifteen seconds."

Spokesmen from the Green Party had a field day, citing the hole in the ozone layer, caused by carbon-gas emissions, as the likely culprit for the crashes. "With the atmosphere noticeably thinner in certain areas, it seems probable that the air density may be reduced sufficiently to make the flight of a high, delta-winged aircraft impossible. It is therefore our view that all such flights should be suspended pending a scientific investigation of the atmospheric phenomena 10 miles above the earth."

"Do you believe any of this stuff, darling?" asked Kathy. "I mean the hole in the stratosphere, like the hole in the ocean near Bermuda."

"No," said the admiral brusquely.

"Why not? It makes sense to me."

"Because it's aerodynamic bullshit," he replied unexpansively.

"How do you know?"

"Because Concordes have been flying through it eight times a day for thirty years and none of them ever fell out of the sky. Now we have two in three weeks."

"Maybe the situation is worsening. Maybe it's been worsening for several years, and suddenly reached a critical point."

"Maybe. But Concorde flights have not been suspended. In the twenty-three days since Captain Lambert's aircraft hit the ocean, there've been 184 supersonic flights, from Paris and London to New York and Washington, right through, or damn close to, that flight path, a lot of 'em half-empty.

You know why they didn't flip and plunge into the sea? Because Ben fucking Adnam did not fire a guided missile at 'em, that's why."

"Oh," said Kathy, with an air of finality. "You mean he's kinda on his break?"

"No. He's just pretty selective. And I have no idea where he will strike next. But he will. Mark my words. He will, if he can. I know him."

"Oh, do you? I didn't realize. Perhaps we should have him over for dinner. How about next Wednesday with the Dunsmores?"

Admiral Morgan, despite himself, caved in and laughed, really laughed, for the first time that evening. "It is my unhappy lot to be contemplating marriage to a complete dingbat," he said; then he softened even more, while he added, "Without whom the sun will never rise for me again."

Kathy O'Brien had, however, learned from her man the joy of pressing on with a winning line. And now she had a small gold pen in her hand, and she was writing in a small leather-bound notebook, "That'll be seven now, won't it . . . ? I do hope he likes swordfish . . . some people are funny about it . . . oh my God, he's not a vegetarian, is he?"

"Thank you, Katherine," said the admiral, still chuckling. "I think I'd prefer we gave him a nice little serving of grilled cyanide since we're on menus."

By now it was almost midnight, and the car was turning into Kathy's wide tree-lined drive; the car with the Secret Servicemen and the communications system came in right behind them. Another Secret Serviceman drove the admiral's car in the rear.

Both Arnold and Kathy were used to traveling in convoy by now, and Charlie the chauffeur never worked nights.

The three men on duty spent the night watching television in Kathy's basement study, taking turns to walk around the grounds in pairs, sidearms drawn, connected to their colleague by radiophone.

Arnold Morgan's was the best-known relationship in the White House, but no one had ever tipped off the press. Not a word about it had ever appeared in any tabloid publication, possibly because both Kathy and Arnold were unmarried, but perhaps because of the reason offered by Charlie himself, "Ain't no one never gonna gossip about that admiral, because of one good reason. Terror, man, sheer fucking terror. Trust me."

HMS *Unseen*, running deep at 8 knots in the early hours of February 10, was making a northeasterly course right above the submerged cliffs of the Rekjanes Ridge in 2000 feet of water. She was on longitude 29 West heading for 51 North, 500 feet below the surface. She left no trace, and nor would she do so unless she ran right into the path of an American nuclear boat. In three days she would slow down and remain totally silent, except when she was snorkeling. On this particular night she would not even come to periscope depth.

Twenty thousand miles above her the satellites scanned the Atlantic Ocean, still searching for the surface ship that could have fired the missile that had downed Starstriker. Below them the search aircraft laid and relaid their buoy patterns. But there was nothing. And Commander Adnam was heading for shallow water, where he would be even more difficult to locate. Shallow water where his snorkel mast could more easily be lost in false echoes on searching radars.

He stood quietly in the control center with Lt. Commander Arash Rajavi, who was looking at a screen showing a North Atlantic chart.

"Right there, Arash. I want to stay right above the Ridge in the shallowest possible water. We're much easier hidden that way.

So let's make our course three-one-five for another 500 miles, then switch to zero-four-five, all the way up to the Icelandic coast, for the refuel. How far does the Rekjanes stretch? 'Bout 1,200 miles?"

"Bit more, sir. More like 1,350. We ought to be off the southern coast of Iceland by February 15, that's five days from now."

"What's our position for the course change, Arash?"

"We'll be at 54 North, 37 West . . . that's when we swing northeast at last. As you can see, the ridge is like a big V facing west. It would save a lot of trouble to go straight."

"Not if someone picked us up in deep water. Stay right over the ridge all the way."

"Aye, sir."

"You have our destination plotted . . . see it right here . . . this big fjord way east of Reykjavik. We'll still be 175 miles south of the Arctic Circle, and the Atlantic does not freeze up there. Also, the bay I have chosen is very quiet and shallow. It's deep enough to hide in, but almost landlocked, hell for a searching radar or sonar . . . I once went up there with the Royal Navy. It's where one of the big Icelandic rivers flows in . . . see it on the map . . . right here. The Thjorsa, flows right down from the central mountains to this place Selfoss."

"Will they be looking for us yet, sir?"

"If they are, they'll be in the wrong place. That's why I struck twice from exactly the same spot. That's where they'll concentrate their search, and we'll be hundreds of miles away by the time they arrive. My only worry would have been if they had gone looking for our refueling tanker. But we don't have a tanker, do we, Arash? We have the beautiful *Santa Cecilia*, registered in Panama, just an old coaster running along the shores of Iceland. They will not give it a second glance."

"You think of everything, sir."

The CO grinned. "Still breathing, Arash. That's the test. Officer of the Watch . . . hold our speed at 8 knots for another twenty hours . . . we come to PD then, access the satellite, and snorkel for 3 hours. That's all."

February 11. The White House.
Office of the Vice President.

Martin Beckman was not the kind of veep normally associated with a right-wing Republican administration. At the age of sixty-two, he was a totally unreformed environmentalist, a throwback to the anti-Vietnam marches of the sixties, a man whose secret patron saint was John Lennon. They had both wanted, with great passion, to Give Peace a Chance. Martin still did.

He had been selected as a running mate because he was probably the most left-wing member of the Republican party, and it was widely believed that he might scoop up a few million votes on the college campuses, campaigning on the hot environmental issues of the day. Martin was also one of those liberal thinkers, who, if he could, would have presented every last American dollar to the weak, the sick, the hopeless, the impotent, the pathetic, and the poverty-stricken. Tough-minded, hardworking successful Americans were not Martin's game. He believed they could get on with it by themselves.

He was a wealthy man, the recipient of a huge trust fund from his father, an old-time investment banker from New Jersey, who had made millions and millions of dollars but had successfully sired only one child. From birth, Martin had lived a life of quiet affluence.

And he had a following. There were people all over the country who believed in, and liked, the tall genial Easterner who looked very like Franklin Roosevelt and displayed similar perfect manners, a kind smile, and a large fortune. Like FDR, Martin had never done anything in his life except run for office, and to try, instinctively, to make things better for the less fortunate. However, the mere sight of the great liberal Martin Beckman, working in the clever, cynical, realistic setting of this American Presidency, was a total enigma. Like seeing Stormin' Norman Schwarzkopf in a gay bar.

But he was an important Vice President, because the Chief Executive had made him so. He had handed over for his attention every single left-wing issue that needed addressing. The veep was the main man in matters of welfare, black education, urban improvements, the environment, and peace talks in all of their forms, especially if they involved the Third World. The President was not afraid to delegate, and in Martin Beckman he had an extremely capable, loyal man who willingly represented him at all the solemn, tiresome gatherings he wished to avoid.

Martin, who had never married, was tireless. He sought no glory for himself and briefed the President often and meticulously on all matters he thought required the attention of the top man. Which was basically why this Presidency had steered clear of almost all trouble for the past five years. And why Martin Beckman was about to head off, with a full staff, to a world peace conference being held among many nations in London— including the regimes of Iraq, Iran, Libya, Syria, and China. This was a group the American President could just as easily have hung up by the thumbs, never mind talked peace with.

But it was a highly acclaimed achievement by the British to have organized such a conference. Basically it included the major Commonwealth countries, the nations of Europe, the Middle East, the old Soviet Union, the United States, Japan, Brazil, and Argentina. The Third World was not included, but all the Arab nations were, because this was essentially a discussion about money, and oil, and trade. It sought to clarify the idea of peace based on economics. More cynically stated, it represented the oldest bedrock of modern civilization: How can the rich keep the poor under control, without going bust in the process?

Martin Beckman had been nominated to chair the conference, and he rightly regarded it as a great honor. The President was delighted, and his second-in-command would travel to London with the kind of backup usually reserved for a Presidential state visit. Mr. Beckman would travel with a major staff of twenty-four people, plus two Democratic Senators, one from California and one from New York. Their London headquarters was already in place at the United States Embassy in Grosvenor Square. It was the most widely publicized gathering of international statesmen for years.

The entire American team would make the journey together in the brand-new intercontinental Presidential jet, *Air Force Three*, a lavishly modified Boeing 747. Colonel Al Jaxtimer, a former B-52 Air Force pilot in the Fifth Bomb Wing out of Minot Air Force Base, North Dakota, would fly the aircraft, assisted by his longtime copilot Major Mike Parker and his regular navigation officer Lt. Chuck Ryder. The three had flown many missions together, and in accordance with the new U.S. Air Force policy would fly the Presidential jet as a team for a period of two years.

For the peace mission they would fly from Andrews Air Force Base direct to London Heathrow. They would be met by the U.S. ambassador to the Court of St. James, who would travel with Martin Beckman in an open limousine, given a clear day. It was anticipated that a vast throng of twenty-first-century British peace marchers would line the route to the left of the north-running road through Hyde Park, to clap and cheer the Vice President of the United States, the man upon whom so many hopes were pinned. The farseeing man who seemed to hold the hope of the modern world in his hands.

The actual President of the United States, and his national security advisor, privately thought that the whole lot of them, including the Arab-sympathizer Martin Beckman, were out of their minds.

But, sane or not, the United States delegation to the four-day Peace Conference of Nations took off in *Air Force Three* on the morning of Tuesday, February 21. And the journey was everything Martin Beckman had hoped, a beautifully smooth Atlantic crossing, an impressive reception at the airport, and a rapturous welcome from the cold green lawns of London's Hyde Park, where thousands turned up and lined the route.

The great swelling sound of their anthem, *"Give Peace a Chance"* could be heard a mile away. Martin Beckman waved in greeting, visibly moved by the long-lost sounds of his youth, as the haunting bittersweet words of the song drifted up through the bare trees. He found himself thinking, irrationally, *My God, I just wish John Lennon could be with me right here. What a moment for all of us who believed then, when no one else did.*

He was right, too. It was a moment, the highest moment in a privileged life. Martin Beckman, the world's best-known liberal, might even take a run at the presidency in 2008.

During the conference, London was a city under martial law. The negotiators used the great forum of the Guildhall for their deliberations, which more or less brought the financial district to a standstill twice a day, since the Prime Minister had authorized the Army to throw a cordon around the building in readiness for a terrorist attack by the Irish Republican Army. In London this was a likelihood as powerful as ever, after the total failure of the latest round of peace talks and, in the IRA's view, the total failure of the British Prime Minister to control the intransigence of the Ulster Unionists.

All the world's major embassies were under guard from the police and the military, as were London's leading hotels. You could have mistaken the Connaught for Catterick Barracks. There seemed to be enough uniformed soldiers outside the Savoy and the Grosvenor House in Mayfair for a winter Trooping the Color. The U.S. military, in plain evidence on the great steps of the embassy, made the west side of the square look like West Point.

No one could remember security like it. But Britain's Anti-Terrorist Squad believed an attack was not only possible, it was likely. And their general view was that if any delegate, *anyone*, from any nation was injured by a bomb, the reputation of the capital city of England would be forever tarnished. Worse yet, the Anti-Terrorist Squad would get the blame. Thus no chances were being taken. The world's delegates for peace would carry out their duties protected by those who believed that real strength came from hard-assed military training, top-class battle equipment, wary eyes, and a big stick.

The conference itself was a brilliant success. The press reported it nonstop. It led every television newscast, the newspapers were filled with interviews from delegates, and the discussions which took place in the great forum were reported diligently. Even the private deliberations between nations were accompanied almost immediately by a press release. All over the world, the firm but understanding voice of Martin Beckman was heard. Matters of great moment for the Third World, and indeed the survival of a free world, without war, were debated long and hard.

They tackled the most vexing subjects of the previous decade. The crippling burden of Third World debt, which, at the turn of the millennium meant that every single person in the Third World owed a total of $400 to the Western banks. For three years now there had been suggestions that the Third World must ultimately be forgiven those debts, in some way, because most of them simply could not pay. Not if they were also to run their countries. There were penniless African nations whose repayments each year added up to more than their GNP.

Naturally the question of corruption came up, how these African dictators were running around in Rolls Royces, stealing Western aid, and hiding it away in Swiss banks. But Martin Beckman stood up in his seat for the only time in the conference and made the most impassioned plea, almost begging the nations to require their banks to forgive at least half of the debt. He ended his speech with words that were heard around the world. *"It is not just a matter of corruption, it is a matter of humanity, a plea for someone to listen to their plight, a plea to someone to respond to the heartbreaking conditions, a plea to end, in the name of God, these areas of stark, human misery."*

He got his way, too. All of the delegates agreed to recommend that their governments attack the problem, forcing banks to listen to reason: that it was not all the fault of the poor nations. Much of the problem could be laid at the door of the banks themselves, for making highly injudicious loans to those who plainly could not repay, worse, did not understand the terms correctly. Martin Beckman was on the verge of making himself a significant piece of modern financial history.

They also worked on the burgeoning grain mountains, examining ways to ship the vast tonnage of surplus cereals from Europe and the United States to the Third World. They hammered out a rota system that other nations would contribute the shipping and freight costs to match the contributions of the governments that supplied the wheat, oats, and barley.

They tackled the world oil-distribution problems. At least they tried to. But there was a certain reserve about the Middle Eastern nations, most of whom had recently mortgaged years of "futures" in order to buy warships and aircraft. China, whose voracious appetite for automobile fuel was reaching gluttonous proportions, stayed out of this discussion, despite Martin Beckman's assertion that they were currently using more refined oil than the U.S.A.

Nonetheless it was tacitly agreed that all nations at the conference would resolve to ensure that the world's tanker routes would remain open for free trade, for the greater good. Iran, the nation that strategically controlled the Strait of Hormuz, voted yes for this only after Martin Beckman made another speech suggesting that any blockade of the Gulf would cause untold hardship to the sick and the elderly and the children of the poorer European nations.

"This is a conference about humanity, for humanity," he said. "I am quite certain that all the nations here would wish to proceed in that spirit . . . I do not think anyone in this room would approve any nation making oblique threats to cause hardship for any of our fellow men. Not here, Iran. This is a forum for peaceful coexistence among nations . . . and I defy you to vote against a resolution for the peaceful trade routes of the world's principal fuel."

Thus the guardians of the Strait were shamed into joining the unanimous vote for free and open tanker routes, wherever the tides ebb and flow on the planet earth. Martin Beckman arrived in London a hero of the Left. As he prepared to depart for Washington on Sunday morning February 26 he was a hero of the people. And not just the people of Great Britain and the U.S.A. He was a hero of the people of the world. His was the voice of decency and reason, a man whose clearly defined basic goodness came through to all the delegates who dealt with him.

Certainly the world leaders present recognized that he spoke with enormous authority, as the Vice President of the most powerful of nations. But Martin Beckman never mentioned what his nation might or might not do. He came to the conference with an air of modesty, and, despite being lauded by the international press on an almost hourly basis, he departed with the same humility. Which was a considerable achievement, because it seemed that every member of the crowd that had thronged the eastern edge of Hyde Park to see him arrive, thronged into the precincts of London's airport to see him depart.

The security was massive as the American delegation arrived at Terminal Four, but thousands and thousands of students still packed the viewing galleries and the fences along the perimeter to watch the gleaming new Boeing of the U.S. Presidency take off for Washington. And as it did so, above the roar of the four giant Pratt and Whitney engines, there could still be heard the anthem of the Doves, swelling out across the airport. The unforgettable words of the slain John Lennon rose into the winter sky, lilting, beseeching, over and over, turning the commercial sprawl of Heathrow Airport into a sacred cathedral on this cloudless Sunday morning. *"ALL WE ARE SA-A-YING . . . is GIVE PEACE A CHANCE."*

260900FEB06. 53.20N, 20.00W. Depth 300. Course 180. Speed 9.

HMS *Unseen*, fully refueled and stored, had been running quietly south from the frozen shores of Iceland for four days, snorkeling for the shortest possible periods. And now, 470 miles due west of Galway, the CO ordered the submarine to periscope depth once more.

The crew raised the big communications mast and sucked down the critical message from the satellite. *Unseen* was back underwater cruising south by the time the commanding officer decrypted it.

TARGET 3. AIR FORCE THREE VP-U.S. ABOARD. ETD/LHR 1100GMT. EN ROUTE WASHINGTON DIRECT, GCR, VIA WAY

POINTS BRAVO, GOLF, KILO, NOVEMBER, PAPA, QUEBEC, AND X-RAY. SQUAWKING IFF CODE THREE, 2471.

The Sunday morning air traffic was busy, but not so busy as on a weekday. Transatlantic jetliners were using four of the northerly routes across the ocean, stacked four high. This meant that a big passenger aircraft from one of the European capital cities was passing overhead every nine minutes, flying at around 420 knots at 33,000 feet minimum. Sometime after 1210(GMT) *Unseen* would begin her target search . . . for the only one using IFF Code 2471.

The time passed slowly in the black submarine, but it came back to periscope depth and went to full alert shortly after 1200 (GMT). At 1233 they saw her IFF code on the radar screen, their first detection.

"Squawk Code 2471, sir. Bearing one-zero-zero. Range 224 miles."

At 1235: *"Range 204, sir. Track and CPA assessed. Distance off track 34 miles."*

"That's too tight. I'm going to make a fast run south," snapped Ben Adnam. *" . . . 10 down . . . 150 feet . . . make your speed 18 knots. I want to be back up and looking by 8 miles to CPA."*

The submarine drove down under the Atlantic waves leaving no mark on the choppy surface. The planesman leveled off at 150 feet; then *Unseen* accelerated, running flat out through the deep, eating up the distance, but risking detection as her electric motors powered her forward.

At 1245 the Americans caught her, picked her up on SOSUS, the great underwater electronic network that scans the oceans on behalf of the United States. It was a quiet day at the U.S. listening station at Keflavik, way out on Iceland's southwestern peninsula, and the urgency in the voice of the young operator was surprising.

"I'm getting something, sir, not engine lines, but it's a noise source of some kind . . . probably flow noise. I don't think it's weather."

His supervisor moved swiftly over to check it out. There were still no machine-originated lines coming up, but it was a very definite noise. And it was not a fish. That left the only other fast-moving creature under the sea.

The supervisor strained his eyes for five minutes, searching for a clue. Shaft count? Blade count? Not a whisper. No telltale pattern came up on the screen.

At 1256 (GMT) the marks faded, then died altogether, as HMS *Unseen* slowed down and began to head back to the surface.

The supervisor moved away, told the operator to stay sharp, and immediately sent a signal to Fort Meade, Maryland.

ELEVEN-MINUTE TRANSIENT UNDERWATER CONTACT AT 1245GMT. POSITION 50N, 20W—ACCURACY PLUS/MINUS 200 MILES. INSUFFICIENT DATA FOR CLASSIFICATION OTHER THAN POSSIBLE FLOW NOISE. ZERO CORRELATION ON FRIENDLY NETS.

The signal was on Admiral George Morris's desk by 0800(EST). The director had been there since 0700, and he read the message carefully, simultaneously hitting the secure line to the White House, directly into the office of the President's national security advisor.

At 1258 the radar operator in *Unseen*, then at periscope depth, was scanning the skies to the east. Within thirty seconds he had reestablished the track and the CPA. *"Target approaches 49 miles. Distance off track 20."*

"SURFACE! BLOW ALL MAIN BALLAST."

Unseen climbed malevolently out of the Atlantic, smashing her way through the waves, green water surging over the casing, the missile launcher stark against the empty skyline, as the radar tracked the incoming *Air Force Three*, bearing home the peace champion from the Peace Conference of Nations.

"Speed 420 knots, sir."

"Range now 42 miles, sir."

"*Check surface picture. Anything out there, inside 12 miles?. Nothing? Perfect.*"

"We have adequate firing solution within the parameters, sir."

"Target holds course and speed. CPA unchanged . . . entering the missile envelope, sir."

Commander Adnam nodded, checked his watch. "*COUNT-DOWN?*"

"Sixty seconds, sir."

At 1302:20. "*MISSILE LAUNCH!*"

Unseen's third SAN-6 Grumble Rif blasted off from the deck of the ex–Royal Navy diesel-electric. With fire roaring from behind, it streaked into the skies, climbing to 2,000 feet in three seconds, where it should have accelerated, but instead, summarily blew itself to smithereens, showering the ocean with flame, sparks, and shrapnel.

"*MALFUNCTION, SIR! MISSILE HAS SELF-DESTRUCTED.*"

But the CO had seen the sudden unaccountable destruction, and the heavy cloud of smoke that hung high above his ship. With the launch aborted, he ordered the fire-control team to program and launch missile four.

At 1303:20 it fired, screaming into the sky with a perfect vertical takeoff, reaching 33,000 feet in under twenty seconds, and angling across to the Closest Point of Approach, toward which *Air Force Three* was making 420 knots, 15 miles out.

Colonel Jaxtimer saw it through the clear skies, or at least he saw the vertical smoke trail way out in front. The ex–Air Force bomber pilot reacted instantly. He was trained for this, and he was ready, and he knew what he was seeing. His broadcast waveband was open to Shannon, ready for the 20 West way point, and he hit it instantly. "MISSILE! *This is a guided missile!*"

As he spoke the SAN-6 changed course and came straight at the Presidential Boeing. Al Jaxtimer saw it, and he was still on the line to Shannon ATC. He hit the decoy button, knowing it to be near-useless in a head-on attack, then hauled on the stick, trying to evade. But the big Boeing was not built to be a fighter plane. And the Shannon operator heard the colonel cry out, "JESUS! MIKE!" as the big Russian-made weapon came screaming in, smashed into the area right below the nose, exploded, and blew *Air Force Three* apart, along with everyone who flew in her.

In the control center of *Unseen*, the words were simple, and they signified a task accomplished. *"No contact on radar bearing, Captain."*

"Thank you, gentlemen. Nice recovery. Open main vents. Take her deep, 300 feet. Make your speed nine when you're down there. Course zero-four-five." It was precisely 1305 (GMT).

0805. Office of the National Security Advisor. The White House.

Arnold Morgan gazed at the communication from the Icelandic listening station, which George Morris had faxed over from Fort Meade. The admiral looked at the time the American surveillance team had picked up the transient contact: 1245. *Jesus! Twenty minutes ago. Not bad.* He walked over to his big, sloping, chart desk, upon which the light was permanently on, and checked the position.

He took his calipers and made some measurements, muttering to himself constantly. "Something out there on 20 West, way south opposite the west of Ireland . . . could he be out there? And if he is, what the hell's he doing? It's seventeen days now since Starstriker went down . . . but this signal is telling me the guys at Keflavik think they may just have detected a diesel-electric, and that bastard's in one.

"Let's see . . . uh-huh, he could be in that position very easily. But why's he in such a goddamned hurry? What's he doing running his boat at a speed like that for eleven whole minutes? He must know we might get onto him. Beats the hell outta me, but he must think it's worth it.

"He's too far north to be after another supersonic airliner. And there's not many warships out there. It really beats the hell out of me. But what do I know? Not much, except he got two supersonics, and he might be after a third. That's not much, but it's a whole lot more than some of these other assholes around here know."

He buzzed Kathy, and asked her if there was anything he could reasonably offer her to acquire a cup of coffee. "I'm up for anything, dinner tonight, marriage, undying love . . . whatever pleases you. BLACK WITH BUCKSHOT, DINGBATS!"

Kathy shook her head, fixed him some coffee, and walked into his office. And there she found her boss and future husband, hunched over a map of the North Atlantic, pressing the buttons of a small calculator. "He coulda gotten there . . . no doubt . . . and since George couldn't find a trace of another diesel-electric boat within hundreds of miles . . . and since even the Brits haven't the first idea who it might be . . . I guess that's gotta be him, right?"

"Right," said Kathy. "Here, drink this. Shall I presume you are still searching for your phantom Arab submariner?"

"I'm not sure I haven't found the sonofabitch," he growled. "At least a very sharp young man in Iceland may have found him."

"Iceland!" said Kathy. "I thought he was an Arab, not an Eskimo."

Admiral Morgan smiled. "No. They just caught a noise they thought might be a submarine up there. Pretty vague but plausible for the man I seek. He gives away nothing, if he can help it. And he ain't given us much this time either."

By 0820, he had finished his coffee and was preparing to attend a meeting in Bob MacPherson's office, when the phone rang. It was Admiral Morris again from Fort Meade.

"Arnold? George. *Air Force Three*'s down in the Atlantic. No survivors. It was hit by a missile. The pilot saw it, and he had time to broadcast it. I got a recording. Last known position 53 North, 20 West. I'm sticking right here."

Admiral Morgan felt the blood draining from his face. His mouth went dry, and there was a tremble deep within him. He could find no words. He just stood in the middle of the room, in total shock. Kathy O'Brien came back through the door, and she thought he was having a heart attack. "My God! Arnold, what's the matter? Here, come and sit down."

The admiral walked to his desk and sat down with his head in his hands. "Just please tell me if you're ill," she said. "Shall I get a doctor?"

"No. No. I'm okay. But I just heard *Air Force Three* has been hit by a guided missile, right where I'm guessing Adnam is, on the chart. The Boeing's down in the North Atlantic. No survivors."

"Holy Mary, Mother of God," said the Irish redhead. "Please tell me this is a joke. Was Martin on board?"

"The whole team was on board. Al Jaxtimer had time to broadcast. He saw the missile that killed everyone."

Just then the admiral's private line to the Oval Office lit up red, the signal for the national security advisor to report to the President immediately. Arnold Morgan pulled on his jacket, grabbed the chart he had been working on, and walked swiftly to the private office of the Chief Executive.

The great man was alone, pacing the room, his face, like the admiral's, displayed only numb shock and sadness. However, he had not summoned his senior security advisor to join him in grief. And Admiral Morgan knew that. Before the door was closed, he heard the President say, "Well, Arnold, that's that. You were right. That theory of yours has panned out. There's someone out there shooting down airliners. I don't think any reasonable person could arrive at any other conclusion."

"Nossir. And they have to be doing it from a submarine. And there's only one submarine that could be doing it, and that's the missing one from the Royal Navy. As you know, sir, in my opinion there's also only one man who could be doing it. And he's not as dead as we thought."

The admiral laid out his Navy chart on the table. And he pointed at longitude 20 West. "Twenty minutes before *Air Force Three* was hit, sir, right down here, our listening station in Iceland picked him up on SOSUS. They couldn't be accurate about position, and the boat was too far away to put up engine lines. But they thought it worth reporting as a possible submarine running through the water, I should think quite fast, for eleven minutes only. It had to be him, sir. . . ."

Just then, one of the private phones rang, and the president picked it up. Then he handed it to the admiral. "It's for you."

"Morgan. Hi, George . . . yup . . . yup . . . what was it? . . . merchant ship . . . Jesus Christ! We're gonna have trouble keeping this one quiet."

He replaced the receiver, and said, "This is developing into an even bigger horror story. A British merchant ship in the area, running 20 miles due south of the datum, reported in on the air-sea rescue band, that they saw the smoke trails from two missiles, one of which seemed to have exploded right above the water. Then they saw a much longer trail going very high. . . . Then they thought they saw fire and wreckage falling toward the water. They're heading into the area right now. That means the Irish and Brits know something diabolical has happened."

"They're right, too. It has. But you and I alone, Arnold, cannot have the luxury of grief. Not right now. We have to get this into line. And we have to stop this sonofabitch. I mean. . . . Jesus . . . he can't just park himself in the middle of the Atlantic and keep firing missiles at passenger jets."

"Yes he can, sir. He can in that submarine. It's just like the Russian Kilo. If he stays deep and slow, we might not find him in a year. Not if he can find a way to refuel without us catching him . . . which he obviously has done, several times already. If he can find his way to relatively shallow inshore waters, which is what that submarine was designed for, we might *never* find him. The ocean's just too fucking big, and that boat is too damned stealthy."

"Arnold, there has to be a way."

"Sir, whether there's a way or not, we sure as hell have to try. I was about to call Joe Mulligan and give him the new search datum. I'm assuming the Royal Navy is sending in a couple of ships to try and locate whatever floating wreckage there may be. I'm afraid we're running out of deep-submergence submarines. At this rate we need a new one every couple of weeks. Do you have to broadcast, sir?"

"I'm not certain. But I guess so. Tonight."

"Well, sir, I better go and establish who knows what, and who has already said what to whom. Will we reconvene in, say, one hour."

"Yes. Come right back here . . . make it ten o'clock. Give me a little time to chat with Dick Stafford and Harcourt. Jesus, this is unbelievable."

The admiral's inquiries seemed to be overtaken by a new development every five minutes. But he noted the hard, salient facts down in his log in the manner of an ex–nuclear submarine commander.

1. 261304(GMT)FEB06. 53N, 20W app. *Air Force Three* hit by guided missile fired from sea level. Destroyed. Plainly no survivors.

2. Oceanic Control, Shannon, has tape of Colonel Jaxtimer's voice confirming missile sighting. Tape removed by station chief in accordance with international airline agreements. Now held securely, pending arrival of U.S. ambassador from Dublin and U.S. naval attaché from London.

3. Shannon alerted all air-sea rescue networks to crash. They estimate it took place 470 miles due west of Galway.

4. The Irish and British press found out that *Air Force Three* was down at approximately 1330GMT. U.S. press picked up news flashes 1340 (GMT), 0840 (EST).

5. Gander ATC not involved. *AF3* had not yet checked in.

6. One Irish operator, and one supervisor heard Colonel Jaxtimer's last words. Both men reputedly senior, and reliable, and bound by classified-information rules inherent in their job. Nonetheless, they know, and they are not under our control.

7. British merchant ship saw two missile smoke trails. Broadcast this information on air-sea rescue networks. May have been heard by several ships, but we have not located *any* ships in the area. British captain bound for Cardiff docks, South Wales.

8. MOD, Whitehall, unhopeful of cast-iron secrecy even if no one else did hear merchantman's broadcast. But the captain will be met in Cardiff by MI5 agents, plus reps from U.S. Embassy, London. The captain was ex–Royal Navy, former surface ship lieutenant, which is hopeful.

9. Assessment of chances of keeping the missile attack secret—not high. We must plan for it to leak out inside a week.

10. Assessment press angle when they find out—they'll go for terrorism since we are not at war.

At which point the admiral closed his book, and called Admiral Mulligan for the third time in forty-five minutes.

"Hi, Arnold. We got two L.A.-Class boats up that way, both attached to the *John C Stennis* CVBG. They've been heading north up the Atlantic for a few days now, but they're within twelve hours of the datum. I put the whole group on high alert. But we have no idea which way the submarine will run . . . north, south, east, or west."

"I know. It's a fucking frustration, right?"

"Yeah. That, and the fact that in twelve hours, even if he's only making 5 knots, deep and quiet, he's still going to be somewhere in a circle radius of 60 miles, or, somewhere in the middle of 10,000 square miles. If he makes a fast run for it, which I don't think he'll do because of SOSUS, you could very quickly double that."

"Why do you think they heard him, Joe, just before he fired?"

"I'd say he wasn't happy with his position off track, and with the Boeing charging in toward him, he had to make his adjustment very fast. He took the risk, ran the boat flat out to get into the best firing position, and they caught him. But then he went slow again. And they never heard him again."

"You know the problem with this bastard, Joe? He's a perfectionist in a submarine. Hardly ever takes a chance, never makes a mistake. I must say I'm filled with foreboding about this . . . but we have to catch him, Joe. I'm just afraid he'll strike again before we do."

T HE DEATH OF MARTIN BECKMAN WAS A STAGGERING blow to the morale of the Western world. The United States was stunned, coast to coast, and it was the kind of public grief hitherto reserved for John F. Kennedy, and his brother Robert, and for Martin Luther King, Jr. For men whose vision had given great swaths of the populace a reason for hope, and optimism. No Vice President in the entire history of the nation had ever come close, in death, to causing such a widespread outpouring of mass despair. In London, the former New Jersey senator had touched a chord of high, unselfish principle and reasoned promise, just as the Kennedy brothers, and the Reverend King did, most every time they spoke publicly.

Late Sunday afternoon, in churches of every denomination, all over the country, services were concluded with renderings of John Lennon's everlasting song. And all through that night, thousands and thousands of ordinary American people would keep a candlelit peace vigil outside the White House. By six o'clock the vast crowd was already massed all the way back to the Washington

Monument. Huddled together in coats, parkas, scarves, gloves, and fur hats, they crowded the icy acres of West Potomac Park, along the Reflecting Pool, right to the steps of the Lincoln Memorial. And each time the bells of nearby St. John's Church behind the White House tolled out the hour, a thunderous chorus of the dead Vice President's beloved anthem lifted up through the black winter skies of the American capital. . . . *"ALL WE ARE SA-A-YING is GIVE PEACE A CHANCE."*

Martin Beckman had touched the soul of a nation. Those people, gathered on that freezing evening, believed that somewhere out there, perhaps on the mystic foothills of heaven's Mount Olympus, the Great Champion of Peace still stood tall. And they believed that his voice would never be silenced, just as the voice of the Reverend King had never died away. They believed the memory of Martin Beckman would always remind the most powerful nations of an iron-clad world, to listen to his plea . . . for the plight of the Third World poor, in the name of God, to the plain, heartrending face of stark, human misery.

Perhaps in death, the Vice President's avowed cause would grow even greater. But back in the Oval Office, where the President, his national security advisor, Bob MacPherson, and Admirals Dunsmore and Mulligan, wracked their collective brains, the talk was not of peace. It involved the massed resources of the United States Armed Forces taking up secret battle stations against the great underwater terrorist from a distant desert.

It was Secretary of State Harcourt Travis who would now bring the voice of the cold-blooded detective to the meeting. Apprised that evening, once again, of the suspicions of Admirals Morgan and Mulligan, this time he did not dissent, but he did suggest an organized short list of suspects be produced, just to demonstrate, if necessary, that things were not being run in a haphazard way.

Admiral Morgan's face betrayed a hint of irritation as he replied, "I got it right here, Harcourt. Been updating it every four hours for three weeks. I'll read it to you and give you a copy. Sometimes I forget that politicians spend at least a third of their time covering their asses. In my game you don't always have time for that."

"If this situation should somehow get out of hand, you might be grateful to me," replied the Secretary of State, smiling thinly.

The national security advisor grinned back, no more warmly. "Goddamned bureaucrat," he muttered. "*Now pay attention.* There are four nations that have submarines out there, which we cannot locate at present, and have not located during the entire period of the three crashes.

"One. A French strategic missile boat, 14,500-ton *Le Temeraire*, commissioned in 1999, based in Brest. She's probably on patrol in the Bay of Biscay, but we discount her as a suspect. We'd have picked her up if she'd been in the middle of the Atlantic.

"Two. The Royal Navy has a Trident SSBN out there some-where, HMS *Vengeance*. She's bigger, 16,000 tons, also commissioned in 1999. If we ask the Brits where she is, they'll tell us, but I don't think that's necessary in the light of our close association with them in this matter.

"Three. The Russians have two that we cannot locate. The first is TK-17. That's one of those 21,000-ton Typhoons out of the Northern fleet, Litsa Guba. She was damaged by fire in 1994, but they repaired her. She's a strategic missile boat. Most unlikely, but possible, although I'm damned sure we'da got her if she'd been in the area. The other is a Delta IV, K-18, 13,500 tons, out of Saida Guba, again the Northern fleet. We'll probably pick her up in the next few days. She's another strategic missile boat, and no more likely to have avoided detection than the Typhoon. But I am planning to touch base with Moscow tomorrow, just to check.

"Four. China also has one missing, her newest, 093. She's a medium-sized 6,500-ton cruise missile attack boat commissioned in 2003. Received a new missile system up in Huladao back in 1998. But she's based on the other side of the world. I suppose this is a possibility, but highly unlikely. That Chinese boat is way behind Western technology, and would be even less likely than the Russian Delta to avoid SOSUS. And I doubt the Chinese would wanna operate so close to us and so far from home. Remember, in the past two or three years, they have lost . . . er . . . some of their . . . er . . . top guys."

Admiral Morgan then paused, and he peered over the half spectacles he used for reading. He was peering at the United States Secretary of State. "The other possibility, Mr. Travis," he said, elaborately, "is called HMS *Unseen.* And for me, she's fucking well named."

"Thank you, Arnold. Just checking," he replied, brightly, still smiling.

The President then asked the critical question. "How long do you think we have, to locate and destroy this fucking submarine before the world starts to speculate, then finds out about it? "

"Not long, sir," Admirals Morgan and Mulligan answered in unison. And the national security advisor added, "In my view probably less than two weeks. I think the media will stick to their theory that there's a 'Bermuda Triangle' out on the edge of space . . . until it finally sinks in that *Air Force Three* was downed from a much lower altitude, in a very different place. Then they're going to try and connect all three crashes in some other way . . . all with big U.S. interests. No other nation harmed, except the Brits, who are considered by our enemies anyway to be the fifty-first state. All the flights were easy to locate by departure times etc. . . .

"Then there's going to be one tiny whisper out of somewhere that Concorde's pilot tried to shout 'MISSILE.' Then there'll be a tiny leak of the last call from *Air Force Three.* Then there'll be a barrage of inquiries demanding to know if there was *anywhere* the missile could have been fired from. Then the captain of that merchant ship will sell his story to a tabloid and the headline will read: 'WERE ALL THREE AIRCRAFT SHOT DOWN BY MISSILES?' Then one of the defense correspondent guys will actually wonder whether it could have been launched from a disappearing submarine.

"At which point we would have to run the risk of looking very, very foolish if we dismiss that as a possibility. That's a worst-case scenario, but we want to be ready."

"That, Arnold is not good. Not good at all." The President was frowning deeply, his face displaying profound worry. "The ramifications are simply horrific. Imagine the press arriving at the conclusion that there is a rogue submarine, undetected, out in the middle of the Atlantic, knocking down passenger airliners. The mere fact that they got to that conclusion before we did will make us look criminally careless.

"Then they will go after us, dumb-ass military, dumb-ass politicians, etc. Then there will be a real crisis of confidence. There will be calls for my resignation and probably all of yours, too. Then there will follow a world airline crisis, with some passenger carriers refusing to make the North Atlantic run. That kind of stuff can bankrupt airlines, and passengers will cancel flights wholesale.

"That will cause a stock-market crash of every industry connected with airlines. You'll see big, publicly held stocks cave in; corporations who build planes and aircraft parts will see staggering losses. Banks who are owed big sums of money from airlines and plane makers will go into a collective tailspin, if you'll excuse the pun. The whole thing could turn into your worst nightmare."

"Specially if that bastard Adnam bangs out another one," growled Morgan.

"Jesus Christ," groaned the President. "And you know the media are gonna just love it. They'll come at us like a pack of starved dogs. And they'll demonstrate all their familiar traits . . . ignorance, naïveté, innocence dressed up as ferocity. I guess they'll never learn that the games governments play are usually much deeper than the games they pretend to play."

"Nossir," replied the national security advisor. "They won't ever learn that. But they'll always love wading in and upsetting the applecart. Despite the obvious fact that any damn-fool hack can upset an applecart. That's easy. It's understanding the entire picture, then acting carefully, that's hard. And anyway, the press don't have time for that."

Admiral Dunsmore, the Chairman of the Joint Chiefs, spoke next in his usual calm and thoughtful way. "Despite our general disapproval of the way the media are about to behave," he said,

"I think we can be sure they won't do much tomorrow. They'll be too busy handling the news story. But we should take very definite steps to keep the lid on this for as long as possible. No good can possibly come out of a public uproar.

"So far as I can tell, we have two objectives. One, to seek and destroy HMS *Unseen* before she strikes again. Two, to bottle up the situation, tight, until we do so. Even then we might never be able to announce what has happened."

"Expertly stated, Scott," said the President. "Please continue."

"Thus I think we should have patrols organized around Iceland and right across the GIUK Gap. We should keep the *John C Stennis* group in the area and have them work east from 30 West, then move south for maybe 200 miles before heading west again. That way we might just push *Unseen* into an area covered by SOSUS. I would also like to see three more frigates up there, and I suggest Joe Mulligan and I have a strategy meeting as soon as possible.

"In regard to keeping the story tight, I think we should have our ambassador in Dublin pull a few strings to ensure the Irish understand that it was *our* Vice President who died, *our* two senators who were lost, that the aircraft was U.S. military, and that the entire matter is regarded as classified by both ourselves and the UK.

"I think we should also prevail on the Brits to shut up that merchant ship captain. That may take a threat, but Whitehall is very expert at that. I believe we have the black-box recording from Concorde under tight control, so if we are careful, we might be more successful than Arnold believes at shutting this story down."

"Christ, I hope so, Scott," replied Morgan. "Also I have instructed George Morris to beef up our satellite surveillance on that part of the Atlantic, and SOSUS is already fully in the picture. Trouble is, *Unseen* is undetectable if she stays slow and deep. Even when she snorkels she's a whole lot quieter than a Kilo. And if she's being driven by Adnam, there're gonna be no mistakes. He won't even snorkel in good SOSUS water if he can help it."

"What are your instructions to our commanding officers, Joe?"

"Uncompromising and closely controlled, sir. If they locate a diesel-electric boat showing an unequivocal Upholder-Class signature, anywhere near the area, sink it."

"Christ, what if they sink the wrong one? The owners will be seriously pissed off."

Admiral Mulligan chuckled. "Sir, the Royal Navy have no diesel-electrics at sea. They only owned four of these boats. They sold one to Israel, and we know that's in Haifa. Two are out of commission in Barrow-in-Furness. The last of the four is *Unseen*. I've already spoken to the First Sea Lord. The Royal Navy has its own frigates out there as well. If they trip over a diesel-electric with a U-Class signature, *they'll sink it.*"

Arnold Morgan interjected, "Sir, it would be better to hunt the boat to exhaustion, then capture it on the surface. That way we could catch Adnam and his crew and hang the fucking Iraqis out to dry. That way no one would object to whatever reprisals we may wish to take. But we may prefer not to risk that with this bastard, sir. He's too slippery. We just might lose him."

"Yes, Arnold. I do see that. By the way, what precisely do you mean by 'hunt to exhaustion'? I'm not familiar with that."

"It's a submariners phrase, sir. It means setting out a kind of dragnet on the surface, using a mass of radar, and keeping the target submarine submerged, with his battery getting lower and lower. Every time he comes to periscope depth, he picks up a surface ship or aircraft ready to detect his snorkel mast. He has no option but to go deep and hope that the coast will be clear when he comes up later. But his battery will eventually get very low, and he'll have to come up again. He may get lucky, maybe snorkel for twenty minutes, until he is caught again. But it's not enough . . . he can't submerge for long enough to get away . . . someone'll catch him on radar. Then the real hunt is on. You bring in a surface ship, real close, something that can knock off his snorkel mast, cut off the air supply to the engines.

"Right then, he's nearly finished. He has to surface. And that's when we bang a couple of shells through his sail, as a gesture of our interest. Then we'd accept her surrender, board the submarine, and interrogate the crew."

"Well, if I was driving the submarine, gentlemen, I'd sink the surface ship with a torpedo," said the President.

"Sir," said Admiral Mulligan, "we have many ways of avoiding torpedoes if we have good prior warning. Especially if we know precisely where our enemy is located. In such a case, if our commanding officer believed there was a real danger from the submarine, we would simply attack first. Those are the orders my men have at this moment. And to me they make military sense.

"However, Arnold has political obligations. He wants to find out who the hell they are. And he's right. I'll change the orders to my COs. Delete 'sink on sight.' Substitute, 'hunt to exhaustion.'"

At that moment the President's private line rang and confirmed he would broadcast briefly to the nation at 2100. Giant television-monitoring screens were being erected all through the parkland to the south and southwest of the White House, where there were now an estimated half million people gathered in tribute to the dead Vice President and his staff.

Dick Stafford, the press secretary, was waiting outside the Oval Office, preparing to go over the speech with the Chief Executive. Clearances were being requested for the forthcoming memorial service for Martin Beckman, which would be held in the massive greystone edifice of Washington's National Cathedral, 3 miles to the northwest of the White House. The great bells of the Cathedral Church of St. Peter and St. Paul would toll for Martin Beckman throughout the night.

The President called his meeting with his advisors to a close, thanked everyone for their efforts, and approved their recommendations. He went on to say he wished he was leaving with them to work on the plan to eliminate, finally, the specter of Commander Adnam.

But that was impossible. As the President phrased it, "Guess I have to stay right here and mind the store." And as Bob MacPherson added, lingering behind for a few moments, "Minding the store might be a lot better than helping these guys. They've got an uphill struggle . . . and if they fail to catch him, and he hits again, heads are gonna roll."

Meanwhile the three admirals were all headed in different directions . . . Morgan to Fort Meade, Mulligan to COMSUBLANT in the Norfolk yards, and Dunsmore to his house along the Potomac. Arnold Morgan would spend the entire evening with Admiral George Morris, watching the satellite reports, praying for a breakthrough, just a sighting of the missing British diesel. They would also watch the Presidential broadcast, and then, sometime after midnight, the national security advisor would call his old sparring partner in the Kremlin, Admiral Vitaly Rankov, chief of the Main Staff, the third most powerful man in the Russian Navy. It was a call to which he was not looking forward.

The evening passed swiftly. Arnold Morgan and George Morris pored over charts, studied photographs, tried to get into the mind of Ben Adnam. Which way would he go? Or was he still lurking five hundred feet below the surface, right above the Atlantic Ridge where SOSUS might not be quite so efficient? Every two hours satellite reports came into Fort Meade. At 2035, shortly before the President's broadcast, a picture from Big Bird confirmed that Chinese submarine 093 was cruising east through the Shanghai Roads. Neither of the American admirals was surprised.

The Presidential broadcast highlighted the television coverage, which was relaying routine messages of condolence from heads of state all over the world. They were all sympathetic, all complimentary, all despondent about the future of world harmony without Martin Beckman. But none of them contained the pure cry from the soul that was echoed in the words of the President of the United States.

No one would ever forget his unscripted concluding passage. *"I never once briefed Martin on any issue that involved the poor and the underprivileged . . . there are no words to convey to such a man the depth of the despair of the Third World. He needed no words, no paper, no files, no parchment, no rules to play by . . . because his rules were written on his heart . . . and I don't quite know what we'll do without him."*

On the following day, no fewer than eight major East Coast city tabloids printed their front page edged in black. The tone of the media, was for once, pure shock, as if none would dare to offend one single citizen, with a smart-ass, tasteless headline. The *New York Times* led the way with two massive lines, straight across the top of page one, which read:

MARTIN BECKMAN, OUR MAN OF PEACE, DIES IN MYSTERIOUS CRASH OF *AIR FORCE THREE*

The *New York Post* stated simply:

DEATH OF THE PRINCE OF PEACE

Almost all of the broadsheets divided the front pages into two stories, one dealing with the actual demise of the aircraft, the evidence, the height, position, and speed, whatever quotes there were. The second, much bigger story, was devoted to Martin Beckman, and how a huge, dangerous shadow hung over the world because of his death.

Arnold Morgan had to wait until 0800(EST) to reach Admiral Vitaly Rankov in Moscow. He made the call from his office on the old secure line into the Kremlin. The Russian officer greeted him in English with polite reserve, concerned, as he always was, that when Morgan called there was trouble, somewhere, for someone.

"Arnold, a nice surprise to hear from you. And how are things at the hub of the world's last remaining superpower? Not so good today, ha? I am very sorry, Arnold. He was a very special man."

"Yeah, Vitaly. It's too bad. Left a big gap here. Everyone liked Martin."

"But what about the aircraft, Arnold? My God, it was nearly new, wasn't it? What went wrong?"

"Who knows, old buddy? Damn thing just crashed." The American was struggling to get out of this drift in the conversation. He wanted only to check on the whereabouts of the two missing Russian submarines. But Rankov was making that awkward.

"But how did it crash? There's nothing up there to collide with, right? That's three bad crashes, all unexpected, in the past five or six weeks. All unexplained. What's going on, Arnold? Is that what you called about?"

The admiral knew he was walking a road that would cause him to level with Vitaly Rankov, and although he did not particularly wish to do so, he was not unduly bothered by the prospect. Rankov was the former head of Soviet Naval Intelligence, and he knew about secrets. Also he might be able to help. The two men had cooperated before.

Nonetheless, Admiral Morgan elected to keep his powder dry. "It was not exactly what I called about, Vitaly. But I would appreciate you marking my card if you could."

"Very well, Arnold. How can I help?"

"According to our surveillance, there are two Russian submarines we cannot see or hear. I don't want to know *specifically* where they are or what they're doing. But I want to ask you to tell me roughly where they are, unless, of course it's a state secret, and then, of course, I'll understand."

"I doubt it, these days. Which two?"

"Northern Fleet Typhoon TK-17. Northern Fleet Delta IV K-18."

"Wait a minute."

Admiral Morgan held on the line, drawing little submarines on his writing pad, as he usually did in times of stress. But in less than four minutes the Russian was back.

"The Typhoon's in the Pacific, way south of the Bering Strait, heading for Petrapavlosk. You'll probably pick her up there on overheads tomorrow. The Delta IV's in refit in the Baltic. Covered dry dock in St. Petersburg. That's why you can't see her. What else? I am anxious there should be no misunderstanding between us."

"Not much really. Pretty routine inquiry."

"Arnold, dear Arnold. On the day after your Vice President is killed in the crash of no less an aircraft than *Air Force Three*, probably the best-maintained passenger jet in the world . . . you get up at God knows what time to call me to ask about a couple of submarines that are doing no harm to anyone, especially the one that's in hospital? I have leveled with you, my friend. Now you must level with me; otherwise, a very useful friendship for both of us will begin to lose its foundation."

"Crafty Russian motherfucker," murmured Morgan, but not quite softly enough, not on the new crystal-clear international phone lines. He heard at the other end a roar of laughter from the giant ex–Soviet international oarsman.

They both laughed, and Morgan knew he had to say something, although he was not sure precisely what that ought to be.

Admiral Rankov saved him a lot of trouble. "Arnold, you don't think someone shot those aircraft down, do you? And if the answer's yes, you couldn't possibly think it was us, could you?"

"Vitaly, I do think someone shot them down. But I never thought you had anything to do with it. I now know you could not have had anything to do with it."

"Why? Because the two submarines are now accounted for?"

"Yes."

"Then you believe the aircraft were shot down by a missile launched from a submarine?"

"Yes."

"Jesus. Who has such a submarine? Not us."

"Nor us. But someone has. You haven't fitted a surface-to-air system on someone else's boat, have you?"

"If we have, no one's told me."

"Well, Vitaly old buddy, the last time there was an almighty calamity, the one involving our aircraft carrier, you'll recall it all started with a missing submarine of yours."

"I'm unlikely to forget that."

"Well, if you have anything in the North Atlantic and it happens to trip over a diesel-electric boat with engine lines from a couple of British Paxmans, do me a favor, will you? Sink the sonofabitch, before it knocks out another airliner."

"Arnold, is this classified information? I presume you do not wish a word of this to get out?"

"Vitaly. It's as secret as any secret I have ever confided in you. Don't let me down, will you?"

"I would not dream of it, my friend. Basically you are telling me that someone stole or hijacked the Royal Navy's Upholder-Class boat that went missing a year ago? Is that what you're saying?"

"Correct."

"And he's somehow converted it to have an antiaircraft missile, and now he's out there, causing havoc?"

"Correct. And remember, if they can hire one of yours, they can surely steal one from the Brits."

Admiral Morgan could not, of course, see it, but there was a broad smile beginning to decorate the Russian's face. "Arnold, what kind of security do you have on *Air Force Three*? You do, of course, have missile jammers, decoys, and not just some kind of chaff?"

"No, we never went that far."

"Arnold, I'm surprised. You really want to get that security beefed up. It's a damned dangerous world out there. As *you* once told *me*, old comrade, stuff happens."

"All right, Rankov. All right. I'm hearing you. Don't give me a difficult time. I've got enough trouble. But if you should see or hear anything in the area between 20 West and 30 West on the jet flight paths, lemme know, will you?"

"Absolutely. I'll put our two North Atlantic patrol submarines on alert right away. Just one thing, though, before you go . . ."

"Uh-huh?"

"Remember . . . stuff happens."

012130MAR06. 57.49N, 9.40W. Depth 300. Course 90.
Speed 8. *Unseen* runs quietly east in deep water.

Commander Adnam's task for his Iranian paymasters was over, the revenge of the Ayatollahs on the Great Satan complete. Three strikes. An eye for an eye. And now the former Israeli commanding officer was alone in his cabin, wondering whether he would find his reward of the final $1.5 million in his bank account. The Iranians had paid the first $1.5 million in three installments, without a murmur. The question was, would they now cut him loose? Or, more likely, have him assassinated and save the cash? *I know what I'd do if I were the head of the Iranian secret service*, he said to himself. *I'd execute Benjamin Adnam forthwith.*

He sat with his loaded service revolver on the small table before him, his big desert knife sheathed on the belt beneath his jacket. He was writing a letter to his trusty navigation officer, Arash Rajavi. It read as follows:

My Dear Arash,

We have traveled far together in the short time of our acquaintance but, as you know, for many reasons I have to leave you. This letter is to confirm what you already know, that I enjoyed serving with you, and regard you as potentially a great submariner. I do believe this is a very good boat and will do much to further our cause.

During your long journey home, please try to remember all that I have taught you. Keep your speed down to less than 8 knots all the way, run close to the coast of Ireland, get into the Bay of Biscay, staying inshore all the way round. Then run down the coast of North Africa to your refueling point. Your next stop is at Code Point Delta, 200 miles off the east coast of Madagascar, and after that I want you to make slowly for the coast of Somalia and Oman, and stay inshore where you will be much safer. In so doing you will be well clear of the American CVBG.

Until we meet again, my friend, may Allah go with you. Commander B. Adnam."

He took the letter and sealed it in an envelope, on which he wrote carefully, "To be opened by Lt. Commander A. Rajavi after my departure. Commander B. Adnam." It would not be long now.

The telephone on his desk rang almost immediately, as he finished. It was the navigator reporting their position, and Commander Adnam ordered the Officer of the Watch to take *Unseen* to periscope depth. He put down the telephone and began to change into the wet suit he'd kept from their swim in Plymouth Sound. Over that he put on extra layers of the cold-weather clothing provided for the bridge watch-keepers in the North Atlantic. The gear rendered him as close to immune from cold, wind, rain, and snow, as made no difference.

The commander placed his sheathed knife-belt around his waist and stored in the zipped pockets of his jacket a large envelope of cash, his revolver, his compass, his handheld GPS link, a small chart, and his paperweight, the one he had used to stun the would-be assassins when he left Iraq. He carried two sealed bags in which were stored civilian clothes and shoes, his passports, papers, a substantial supply of food and mineral water, his binoculars, and a flashlight. Then he pulled on his fur gloves. He had no need of a hat. The jacket had a tight fur-lined hood rolled into the collar. He concluded he could survive for several days in the open, should that become necessary.

The CO picked up his bags and made his way to the control center, where there was already activity. The fishing boat was signaling about a mile off their port bow. Ben ordered them to surface and make their way toward the boat. The night outside was frigid, but the sea was calm, and the skies were clear. "We'll make a straight ship-to-ship transfer," he said. "Put the fisherman on your starboard side . . . deck crew to their stations." Then he turned, removed his right glove, and asked his senior officers to enter the control center.

He said that he had been privileged to fight with men such as they. "And I believe you will all become very fine submariners. You have learned thoroughly and learned quickly . . . and I shall miss each one of you, although I have high hopes that we shall meet again."

Then he paused, and an immense sadness settled upon him as he prepared to part from the men with whom he had lived and worked for so long. For a moment he seemed lost for words, but then he extended his right palm, and, echoing the words of another commander, he said softly, "I should be obliged if each of you would come and take me by the hand."

And as they did so, they each understood the meaning of the word "camaraderie," as perhaps only fighting men can, those who have faced danger together, but somehow come through it. Most of these young Iranians had been with their Iraqi-born leader for well over a year. Most of them had gone into the water with him in the outer reaches of Plymouth Sound on that black night when they had stolen the submarine. It was not yet clear in their minds that they were the most hunted men in the world. But they knew it was not over yet.

By now the deck crew was preparing to secure *Unseen* alongside the still-moving, aged, rusting 200-tonner, *Flower of Scotland*. And there was urgency in their every move. Out there were the search ships of both the United States Navy and the Royal Navy. And the Iranians intended to be on the surface for the minimum time. It was understood among them that they would dive the submarine and, if necessary, leave the commander in the water should they be threatened.

And now the fishing boat was lowering big fenders very low, its engines reversing, the captain himself throwing a looped continuous line over the rail to the submarine for the CO's bags. Commander Adnam had his life jacket on, and they were hitching two lifelines to his belt. Transfers of this type can be extremely dangerous in the dark in mid-ocean, and there was tension in the air.

The wide gangway was pushed out under the rail of the fishing boat, and the submarine's deck crew hauled it over. They had just made it secure, when, somewhat to Ben's surprise, a submarine officer he had seen several times in Bandar Abbas walked across and joined him on the casing.

"Good evening, Commander," he said. "I am Lieutenant Commander Alaam. I was responsible for hiring the boat; you will return it to Mallaig. The skipper knows the way."

"But I understood you were coming back with me," replied Adnam.

"Change of plan, sir. I am taking over *Unseen* all the way home."

"I see. But I have not briefed you."

"I presume you have briefed someone, sir."

"Of course. The navigation officer, Lieutenant Commander Rajavi, is in a position to take command. But the matter is nothing to do with me. I should speak to him immediately if I were you."

"Yessir. Good-bye, sir."

Commander Adnam turned once more to face his deck team for the last time. "Allah go with you," he said.

"And also with you, sir," replied one of them.

And with that Benjamin Adnam walked across to the *Flower of Scotland* and ordered the skipper to let go all lines and head due east with all speed. He stood on deck in the biting wind and watched *Unseen* pull away, running south. One minute later she was gone, beneath the dark waters of the North Atlantic in which she had caused such havoc.

Then he turned and went immediately to the bridge and asked Captain Gregor Mackay to join him alone on the deck. His request was simple. "I want you to stop this ship immediately and hand over to me the rigid inflatable you have on the stern, I want her filled with petrol, and ready to go in five minutes. Also put a full four-and-a-half-gallon jerry can in the boat. Do it yourself, no one else."

"I canna do that," said the captain, in a broad Scottish brogue. "I dinnae even own the ship."

Ben smiled at the old familiar accent he had heard so often during his days training at Faslane. He pushed away a million memories of the Scotland of his younger days and returned quickly to business, a subject he knew sits easily with any Scotsman, especially a fisherman. "How much is the Zodiac worth? She's a 15-footer, right? With a 60 h.p. outboard?"

"Yessir. I suppose £6,000, sir."

"Then if I give you £10,000 in cash, you'll be well ahead, correct?"

"Yessir."

"Then hurry, man," snapped the commander, reaching into his bag for the cash and watching with some satisfaction as the fisherman from the Western Isles moved aft and began to fill the tank with gasoline.

Seven minutes later, the ship was stationary, and the Zodiac was in the water, secured by a painter to the port-side rail. Commander Adnam handed over the money, and Captain Mackay counted it out very carefully. "Aye, sir, I think 200 of these 50-pound notes adds up very nicely."

Ben grabbed his bags, threw them down into the rubberized Zodiac. He climbed over the side, dropped onto the firm GRP deck, revved the engine, slammed her into gear, and took off into the night. Captain Mackay watched him go, half in amazement, half in ecstasy. "That young man is in a very great hurry," he muttered. "But it was a pleasure doing business with him."

Ben Adnam moderated the speed as soon as he had put 200 yards between the Zodiac and the *Flower of Scotland*. He checked his global positioning system, then the compass, and settled into a steady 15 knots, which he would hold in an easterly direction for a little over two hours. He did not yet refer to his map. Instead, he made himself comfortable on the long rubber seat behind the wheel, pulled up his hood, and watched the lights of the fishing boat, heading southeast, over his right shoulder.

The night was bitterly cold, but still clear as he moved swiftly across the calm sea. There was a slight swell, but the Zodiac rode that perfectly, the silence of the seascape broken only by the high-pitched whine of the well-tuned outboard. So far as Ben could tell there was no other ship in the vicinity, save for the

Flower of Scotland, the lights of which he could still see 2 miles away.

He checked his watch, which was still set for Greenwich Mean Time, and saw that it was 2320. He glanced again at the running lights of the fishing boat; then he turned back toward the east, where a rising moon was casting a thin silver path on the sea, lighting his way.

Nonetheless, the mighty red-and-orange flash that lit up the sky over his right shoulder still turned the night into day. Two seconds later the thunder of the blast split the night air as the *Flower of Scotland* and her three-man crew were blown to pieces by a bomb that detonated right behind her engine.

Ben Adnam watched the burning wreckage scatter downward onto the water. Then he shook his head, shrugged, and kept heading east.

He knew it was a bomb. A torpedo from *Unseen* would have caused quite another kind of explosion, more muffled, less spectacular. And yet he was curious. Because he saw in his mind the tense, worried look there had been on the face of Lieutenant Commander Alaam. He remembered the way there had been no time for even the warm exchange of greetings so prevalent in the Muslim world. No time to discuss anything, not even to deliver the congratulations of their masters. Not a word about the success of the operation. Not even civility. Not even approval, far less warmth.

The Iranian, in Ben's view, had been a man on the edge of his nerves, taut, dry-mouthed, and desperate to get away. He had been too overwrought even to offer a reasoned explanation for the change of plan. In Commander Adnam's view, he might as well have carried a placard with him which stated he had just booby-trapped the *Flower of Scotland* in order to kill their redundant employee, who knew too much.

But Ben Adnam was still curious. "I wonder why," he asked the empty ocean. "After all that I have done, some people still assume that I may be a fool?"

So many lessons, for so many people. "Especially Captain

Mackay," he mused. "That was a hard way to learn there's no such thing as a free lunch."

His own situation was, however, only marginally better than that of the late master of the *Flower of Scotland*. Betrayed first by Iraq, and now by Iran, he felt the horizons closing in. He understood the reasoning of the Ayatollahs—that he, Benjamin, was just too much of a liability. If they offered him shelter and perhaps more work in Iran, it would be a only matter of time before someone put together the pieces that made up his murderous six-week reign of terror in the North Atlantic.

The Americans were plainly not going to sit still and forget about the acts of mass destruction he had perpetrated. There would be men in the Pentagon and the CIA, perhaps even the White House, who would never rest until he was caught. He knew, too, the icy cunning of the British military, who would eventually learn of his whereabouts and come after him.

The Ayatollahs would be crazy to harbor him; he had always known that. It was nonetheless an emotional, if not intellectual, shock, that they had attempted to execute him quite so summarily, within a couple of hours of his leaving the superb submarine he had acquired for them. *On reflection*, he thought, *I'm glad I played it safe. I just hope my crew is as lucky.*

He had experienced the feeling of desolation when he had walked from Baghdad almost two years previously. But that night it was a hundred times worse. Because he could not go back to the Middle East, where he was wanted as no Arab had ever been wanted. Three powerful governments, Israel, Iraq, and Iran, had all made determined attempts to assassinate him. He had to face it. There was *nowhere* for him to go. He was, as usual, on his own.

For the moment, he must concentrate on survival in the short run. He could feel the chill of the night upon his face as the Zodiac ran on toward the island. He pulled out his chart, and he checked the GPS and the compass. He held the little boat steady on course zero-nine-zero and, facing the east, prayed silently to his God to forgive him.

The trouble was, he needed to get into his bag for the flashlight, and he needed time to look at his chart, just to check. Rather than attempt to hold his course during those routine navigational procedures, he switched off the motor and stopped. And there, solitary in the gusting chill of the Atlantic, Ben Adnam once more studied his bearings. He had already programmed in the way points, and after two minutes of checking, he kicked over the engine and headed east again, course, zero-nine-zero.

As expected, the GPS told him he was about 15 miles west of the four lonely, uninhabited islands of St. Kilda, which sit in gale-swept isolation, at the mercy of the open Atlantic, 50 miles west of the rest of the Hebridean Islands, and 110 miles from the Scottish mainland. They are the most westerly point of the British Isles, save for the great granite slab of Rockall, which lies another 180 miles closer to North America.

Commander Adnam was headed for the largest of the St. Kilda group, named Hirta, which is these days referred to simply as St. Kilda, separate from the trio of tiny neighboring islands of Soay, Boreray, and Rona. The combined population of the four is easy to calculate. Zero.

Before the 1800s the only way out to St. Kilda from the Scottish mainland was in a rowboat pulled by the men of the Isle of Skye. It took several days, and nights, and even today it can be impossible to make a landing in the massive seas that have battered the islands since the dawn of time.

Ben knew the problems, and he knew how swiftly the weather could change out there. He could feel the wind freshening a little from the southwest, and he thanked his God it was not from the southeast, because a gale from there renders the only landing place on the entire island, Village Bay, unapproachable. He had been to St. Kilda once before, during his submarine training with the Royal Navy, but they had not landed, and, so far as he knew, no British Navy warship had ever put into Village Bay. Not even in the deep water on the outer edges.

He just had to pray the weather held and that he could get into shelter unobserved. Instinct was telling him to open the throttle fully and go for it. But that would use too much gas. And, besides, much more important in his mind, it would betray panic, a lack of professionalism. Ben Adnam despised amateurs.

He shined the flashlight on the chart again, noted the depth of the water, and the precise position of his way points along the route to the beach. He noted once more that the southeastern tip of St. Kilda was separately named Dun, a high, jagged promontory, three-quarters of a mile long. The chart showed that there was a channel between Dun and the main part of the island. But it was very narrow, and shallow at low water, strewn with rocks. At one point the chart was showing zero depth at low tide, and the former commander of HMS *Unseen* had long assumed he would go right around the long headland of Dun, despite the extra twenty minutes running time that would add to his journey into Village Bay. If he revved the propeller on the rocky floor of the Dun channel, he knew he would be finished.

With the slight rise of the wind, the night grew a little darker, as lower clouds drifted northeastward out of the Atlantic, a high thin layer of cirrus, covering the moon. But none of it worried Ben. He knew everything he would see in the dim, diffused light. And he recognized the cloud for what it was, the precursor of an Atlantic low, bringing rain on a southwest wind, with reasonably warm temperatures.

Commander Adnam was satisfied he had his mission under tight control, including the weather, his precise course and position. Not for him the nagging dread of less experienced helmsman at the dead of night with no radar, that of being swept against the cliffs or the rocks, in a following sea, which he had.

He stayed deliberately on the southerly edge of a planned track that would take him within a mile of the terrible black cliffs of St. Kilda. But he would see them in the dim light, even if the GPS failed.

The Zodiac went on for another fifty minutes, 12.5 miles, planing comfortably at just below 15 knots. Then he cut back the engine and chugged forward quietly, just at idling speed. Suddenly, he could see the shape of the island—bang in front, a monstrous cliff, topped by a massive 1,000-foot mountain peak, glowering out over a shallow bay. He could also see yet another peak, even higher, way back beyond the first one. He shined the light on his chart. "That's it," he murmured. "I'm looking at the twin peaks of Mullach Mor and Mullach Bi." He checked the compass and saw that the GPS had not let him down.

He stopped the engine and poured half the contents of his spare gas can into the fuel tank before setting off again at 5 knots. After ten minutes, he slowed right down, and turned inshore, and there, about 100 yards off his port bow, he could see the great rock stack of Hamalan, close to the tip of the Dun headland. He ran on for another 200 yards, then turned northeast in the dark, then right around into Village Bay, setting a course of three-four-two on his handheld compass.

The Bay itself measured a mile across from Dun to its northern point. But the British had built a military base along that northern shoreline, and used it periodically as a missile-tracking station for the rocket range at Benbecula on the main Hebrides Islands. According to Ben Adnam's guidebook, the British Army made a foray to their base every two weeks, when a couple of soldiers would land and stay for two days, checking the island over, particularly their electronic equipment.

Commander Adnam thus headed quietly into the western edge of the bay, where the chart told him he could land and secure his boat behind a rocky outcrop and out of sight of the north shore. He would then proceed on foot to the military base, which he hoped would be deserted, with a store full of gasoline. If there were soldiers in residence, he proposed to move into one of the original old islanders' cottages, which were currently being restored by the Scottish National Trust and the Scottish National Heritage in the summer months, and wait out the soldiers' forty-eight-hour tour of duty. He had sufficient food and mineral water to last him at least that long.

He ran without incident onto the dark shore of Village Bay. Given the calmness of the sea, he was surprised at the rough water breaking onto the shore. He steered the Zodiac right in, but heaved the engine up as the bow hit the shingle. As it clicked into its secure position, he darted forward with the painter in his right hand and jumped off the bow into a few inches of water.

He waited for the next wave to come in and lift the much heavier stern, moved left, and heaved the stern right around, with the raised rubber bow now headed to sea. He knew from long experience that even the smallest waves can wash right over the stern of a Zodiac, and quickly fill it with seawater and weed. The problem was, that the stern, with the suspended engine, was very heavy, and that was the part he had to pull. So he attached the anchor line to the wooden transom, and every time the sea lifted the boat, Ben pulled on that line, until the Zodiac was on relatively dry shingle. Then he wrenched it around and dragged it farther up the beach into the shadow of the rocks, where it would not be seen unless someone fell over it. It remains a sailor's mystery why it is so difficult to haul a 15-foot rubber hull backward, but hardly any trouble to pull it forward.

He leaned on the rocks and opened one of his bags, devoured a cheese sandwich and swigged greedily at a bottle of water. He was in the lee of the wind, but it was still cold, and he pulled on his hood again as he set off toward the military camp. Ben moved quickly over the beach toward the old church and manse, where St. Kildans had often spent nine hours a day on Sundays, before they finally evacuated the place in 1930 after a thousand years.

The old white-painted church actually stood just beyond the camp, but it provided excellent cover from which to observe the military buildings. And the submariner stayed low, finally coming off the beach some 40 yards beyond the Army huts on the north shore. He reached the moonlit shadows of the church and edged around them until finally he faced the camp.

There, to his irritation, he saw lights in two rooms, and as he drew nearer he could hear the unmistakable hum of a generator. As if to confirm his worst fears, there was an Army Land Rover parked right outside the door. No doubt. There were two soldiers, at least, in that building.

Ben swiftly reassessed his options.

A) He could check out the building, break in and kill both men immediately, drive his boat over, fill it with gas, and leave. But that would be messy, and the murder of two British soldiers would quickly cause an uproar he did not need, as soon as the landing craft returned, probably the next day.

B) He could hide his boat, and himself, until they all went away in a couple of days. Then he could break into the store and steal the gasoline. But that ran the small risk that the Army landing craft, which would probably come in during daylight, might somehow see the Zodiac as it crossed the bay. Or, the soldiers in residence might find his boat. That option was no good either. Too slow. Too many risks.

He looked again at his watch. It was 0200. He moved back into the shadows, checked his chart, and went to Plan C. He would make his way back to the boat, deflate the inflatable sides, and pile shingle over and around it to disguise it from anyone approaching by water. Then he would find the main street, to the north of the camp, and get into one of the houses for better shelter overnight. The next day he would get around to his boat before it grew light at around 0900, and wait out the short daylight time until around 1500. Then he would go to work.

By 0300 the boat was impossible to identify, and, carrying his two bags, Ben Adnam found his way to the line of village houses shown clearly on the map and shoved open the door to the one with the freshest paint. Inside it was cold, but out of the wind, and there was a sofa set in front of a fireplace. Ben decided not to risk a fire, but he spread out luxuriously upon the sofa and fell asleep. He clutched his big desert knife in his right hand, which rested on the floor.

He awakened at 0800, ate a sandwich, drank more mineral water, and slipped out of the house into the chill of a March morning in the outer Hebrides. He pulled up his balaclava and left the road, moving cross-country back to the boat, staying out of sight and range of the Army buildings. Nothing stirred, save a gaggle of puffins on the beach and a passing gannet that had been fishing in the shallows.

At 1100 he heard the Army Land Rover rev up and drive away. He could see two soldiers occupying both front seats. As they left, driving to the west, Ben carefully headed for the camp, and there, beyond the church, was the building where the lights had been on. There was nothing. Just silence. No sign of life.

"Just the two of them," said Ben to himself. "Excellent." And he made his way back to the boat, where he waited out the daylight hours, watching the jeep return at around 1400.

At 1700, Lieutenant Chris Larkman and burly Corporal Tommy Lawson, both of the Royal Army Service Corps, were playing cards in front of the electric fire that warmed their spartan room, when the young officer put down his losing hand and walked slowly over the to north window.

"Anything the matter, sir?"

"No. Nothing. I just thought I saw a light, way up there on the headland, the Oiseval side."

"Well, sir, unless it was a plane crash, I'd judge that as totally unlikely." The accent was flat, East London, in contrast to the harder public-school tones of the commissioned man.

"Very unlikely, Corporal Lawson. It must have been a reflection through the window."

"Yessir. As a matter of fact I'm very pleased it was nothing because I'm about to take command of this game."

"I wouldn't doubt it, Corporal. Nor would you if you could see the load of rubbish I'm playing with."

"Right, sir. 'Ow about that," he replied, laying down the ace, king, queen, and jack of spades, plus the other three kings.

"Christ, Corporal. That's a lot too good for me . . . hey . . . wait a minute. I could have sworn I just saw that light again."

"Where, sir? Let me 'ave a look."

The thirty-two-year-old Lawson joined the twenty-five-year-old officer at the window. In the way of the British Army, it was the young elite assisted by the old stager, a combination upon which the British Army was built. Chris Larkman, whose grades at Bryanston had not been good enough to put him through a top university, had struck up a lasting friendship in the Army with the former failed bricklayer who now shared this remote island with him. And they would represent a formidable fighting unit, Larkman and Lawson, should push come to shove. The slim athletic, former Hampshire County rugby fullback, and the rough East Ender with iron in both fists.

Lieutenant Larkman's wealthy parents were bitterly disappointed that their son should have ended up in the RASC—"So much nicer in a good Guards regiment"—but Chris was happy, and he was considered by his superiors as a man destined for higher rank. Lawson was going nowhere, but he was fine where he was, a natural-born corporal, tough, bossy, sharp, irreverent, and a bugger when riled.

He stood by the window with his superior, peering into the black night, up at the great escarpment of Oiseval, which rose fairly smoothly on the landward side, then ended with terrifying suddenness to seaward, like a giant apple sliced in half. The black cliff plunging down five hundred feet, almost sheer to the jutting deepwater rocks below. It was only half as high as some of the other cliffs on St. Kilda, but it was a hell of a sight from both top and bottom.

"There it is, Corporal . . . look . . . up there . . . to the right . . . three flashes."

"Where, sir . . . You mean 'igh up?"

"Right. Keep looking. Pretend you are staring up at the very top of the headland. Keep staring."

Three minutes went by, and then Lieutenant Larkman saw it again. *"Did you see it, Corporal? Three flashes."*

Tommy Lawson was silent, which was unusual and brief. But when he answered he was deadly serious. "Yessir. Yes I did. That was not some fluke of nature. Someone's up there, sir. And if he 'asn't landed in a bloody parachute, quite frankly I don't know how the fucking 'ell 'e got up there, do I?"

"Do you think it is definitely a person? Not some meteorite or something."

"That, sir, is a bloke. A bloke wiv a fuckin' light, right? Otherwise, he wouldn't be shinin' it, would 'e?"

"No, I suppose he wouldn't."

"Well, what's 'e fucking doing up there then? That's what I wanna know, don't I?"

"Yes, that's rather what I want to know, too. We, Corporal, had better find out."

"Well, sir. We've really got two choices. We can either take the jeep and get up there, wiv lights, and flush 'im out, or rescue 'im, as the case may be. Or, we leave 'im up there all night to freeze 'is bollocks off."

"I don't think we really ought to do the latter. We are in charge of the place. There is quite a lot of sensitive equipment here, and I am inclined to think we should just go and sort it out?"

"I think that is the correct military assessment for an officer of your class, sir. And I'm 'ere to do as you tell me. 'Owever, I must say, meself, I'd probably take the bollock-freezing option, wouldn't I?"

"Okay, Corporal. Coats on. We don't need weapons. Bring two flashlights, and let's get out there. Warm the engine over, will you? I'll shove a petrol can in the back . . . You know the gauge has never worked on this bloody thing."

"Right, sir." Corporal Lawson headed for the door, jangling the keys to the jeep. He opened it and kicked over the engine, which started with a roar. The lieutenant was right behind him, with a gas can from the store.

The breath of both men was white on the freezing night air, and as the corporal walked, he glanced again up to the highest escarpment of Oiseval. And there it was again. Three short flashes. But this time it was followed by three longer ones, and then, immediately, by three more short ones. "Sir, I think we're seeing an SOS up there," said Tommy Lawson. "Which means it's got to be an aircraft of some kind. There's no other way anyone could be up there . . . Might be a Navy chopper or something. But we didn't hear nothing, did we?"

"No, we didn't," replied the lieutenant. "Nothing at all." And there was a worried frown on his face as Corporal Lawson drove

the jeep over the rough terrain beyond the camp, heading northeast across the rising ground, up toward the light.

The total distance up to the summit of Oiseval was less than
half a mile, but it was rock-strewn, and Lawson had to pick his
way through the boulders. They were making about 5 mph and
the Land Rover lurched and roared its way up the steep hill to
the top. Every few minutes they saw the flash of the light above,
and as they drew closer they had to make a wide detour around a
sheer rock face that even their vehicle could not handle.

Finally, they were within sight of the highest point and saw
the flashlight again, dead straight ahead, to the east, on the brink
of the cliff. There was no sign of wreckage, and the headlights of
the Land Rover were beginning to shine out over the ocean far
below.

"What I don't want to do, is to drive this fucking thing over
the edge, right sir?"

"Right, Corporal. Actually, I think we should stop here and
wait for the light. Keep the engine running and the main beam up
so that whoever it is can see us. He can't be far away, but it's so
damned dark."

"Yessir. And it's a bloody long way down if anyone misjudges
it."

They waited for five minutes. And there was nothing. "Perhaps 'e's fainted, sir . . . or died."

Chris Larkman was about to agree, when the light flashed
again, directly opposite the officer's left shoulder. Not more than
30 yards away. There was no sound. Corporal Lawson heaved on
the hand brake, took his flashlight, and opened the door. "'Old it,
sir. I'll come round."

The corporal stood outside for a few moments, fastening his
big winter jacket and pulling on his gloves. Then he slammed the
door on the driver's side and walked to the back of the Land
Rover, and as he did so, Ben Adnam came out of the night like a
demon and slammed the paperweight into the area behind Lawson's right ear. The big East Ender crumpled to the ground, and

Chris Larkman never heard a thing above the noise of the engine. And through the steamy Perspex of the rear window, he never saw the Iraqi commander drag the corporal's body back around to the driver's side.

Lieutenant Larkman waited. Then he called out, "Corporal Lawson? Everything okay?" But no reply came back, and Chris tightened his belt and pulled down his hat. Then he opened the door and stepped out onto the frozen peak of Oiseval, instinctively moving to the back of the jeep, in the direction he had seen the corporal walk.

Commander Adnam was waiting. The young lieutenant thought he saw a shadow and made to turn, but he was too late. The former master of HMS *Unseen* banged the paperweight hard into the area behind the officer's right ear, and he, too, crumpled to the ground.

It took Ben Adnam a full ten minutes to haul both unconscious men back into the front seats of the Land Rover. But he managed in the end, let go the hand brake, slammed the driver's door shut, and heaved against the open window.

The Land Rover began to roll forward, its headlights still on. It gathered speed slowly, and was traveling at only around 10 mph when it plunged over the precipice, its engine still running, all the way down, until it crashed into deep water 500 feet below. Ben heard it hit the ocean, and doubted whether anyone would ever find it. Finally alone on St. Kilda, he was extremely busy. He checked his watch. Lieutenant Larkman and Corporal Lawson had died at 1741. The commander turned back toward the military camp far below, and, snug in his cold-weather gear, using the big flashlight he had borrowed from Tommy Lawson, made his way down to the British Army's fuel store.

It took him fifteen minutes, and he made a visit to the living quarters before he went to work. He noticed a label on a suitcase. "Lawson T. 23082826. Corporal. Royal Army Service Corps."

Ben stood by the electric fire for a few minutes and decided to make himself a cup of tea in the small kitchen. He sat down in the one comfortable chair and sipped the hot, sweet brew, thinking about the journey he must now make—140 miles at 15 knots. Over nine hours running time if he made no mistakes. The sea remained calm enough. Perhaps the low front, which he had feared, had just drifted by on its way to Iceland and the North Cape. He'd need a lot of gasoline. But right now he had a lot of gasoline.

He returned to the kitchen and washed and dried his cup, carefully placing it back on the shelf where he had found it. There were two dirty cups in the sink, and the arch terrorist considered a third might be a clue to the forthcoming Army investigators. Also, he wanted no fingerprints left behind.

Leaving the lights and heater switched on, he went outside, still using Lawson's flashlight to save his own. The fuel store was open and inside there was a 1,000-gallon tank of diesel on which the gauge showed half-full. This was not good news since it would not power his outboard. But he found a stack of four-and-a-half-gallon gasoline cans in a lean-to shed at the back—the fuel for the Land Rover, stored in the fresh air, for safety.

Ben left immediately, heading along the shore toward his boat. Once there he cleared the stones away, reinflated the buoyancy bays, and hauled the boat the short distance to the water, where he manhandled it into the light surf breaking in from the Atlantic. He paddled out into deeper water and let the engine down. He primed it, using the rubber bulb on the fuel line, and hit the starter. Captain Gregor's Zodiac fired the first time, and Ben drove it easily across the bay to the flat landing place right below the church.

He raised the engine and beached the Zodiac. Then he jumped out and spun the boat around, bow to sea, with the stern and raised engine hard aground. He guessed the boat would float and drift on the incoming tide inside twenty minutes, so he had to move fast. He jogged back to the store, returning more slowly with two heavy fuel cans in under fifteen minutes. There was an extended tank under the seat of the Zodiac, and it took the whole nine gallons.

Two journeys later he had another three cans on board, giving him 13 gallons more, which would, he knew, be plenty to carry him over the water to the little Scottish fishing port of Mallaig. He still had six big sandwiches left and three bottles of water, but he had not taken extra food from the soldiers' kitchen, great though the temptation had been. Commander Adnam regarded himself as a professional military man, not a sneak thief, and his principles did not permit him to take as much as a piece of cheese, unless it was essential to his survival. He was curiously obsessive about the whole concept of acting professionally. Indeed he had his own private definition. "Professionalism has nothing to do with money. It involves the total elimination of mistakes."

And thus far, he considered he had made none. The Iranians plainly believed he was dead, an error of judgment that had also been made briefly by Iraq, and for much longer by Israel and the United States.

The Army landing craft would arrive the next morning at the earliest, and the officers would be faced with a complete mystery involving the disappearance of a lieutenant and a corporal, plus one Land Rover, green in color, property of the Royal Army Service Corps. Unless they were prepared to spend years combing every yard of the treacherous deep waters beneath St. Kilda's cliffs, they would *never* know what had become of the missing men. Nor would they ever know that Commander Adnam had ever visited the island. There was, he knew, no trail. There had been no fighting, no gunshots, no blood, nothing broken. No one had seen him. At least no one who was still alive. And he was not injured. Better yet, he was mobile.

He paddled the Zodiac out into deeper water before lowering the engine and running swiftly to the east, across dark Village Bay, out into the open North Atlantic, toward the main Western Isles, and, 100 miles beyond, the Scottish mainland fishing village of Mallaig.

B EN ADNAM CLEARED THE OUTER REACHES OF
Village Bay just before 2100 on the night of Thursday, March
2. It was still calm, but there was an unmistakable Atlantic swell.
However, the waves rolling in from his starboard hip were fortunately long, with smooth tops, and the Zodiac could quarter
across them with ease.

The commander was more than happy with the conditions,
even though they would take his full concentration for hour after
hour. He was, after all, warm, dry, relatively comfortable, and so
far as he knew, not immediately wanted by anyone. It was his
former submarine they were after. Ben just had to keep heading
east in the dark, keeping a sharp eye out for fishing boats, and
restricting his speed to a relatively easy 15 knots. He was well
practiced at keeping his speed down, and he wore a lean smile in
the night as he steered along course zero-nine-seven, going for
the Sound of Harris, 40-odd miles distant.

The Zodiac was a very good boat, and it zipped effortlessly

through the mild hills of the Atlantic. It steered easily, and Ben could check the GPS without cutting his speed.

At 2300 he ate another sandwich, leaning back in his seat, staring into the dark and listening to the perfect running beat of the outboard engine, as the Zodiac climbed the retreating swells, flew along the tops, then raced downhill into the troughs.

Less than an hour away Ben would enter the central seaway through the islands that form the outer Hebrides. This is the Sound of Harris, which separates the Isle of Harris to the north from the sprawling archipelago of North Uist to the south.

The Sound of Harris is around 5 miles wide at its narrowest point, but it is scattered with small islands and hunks of rock too big to be ignored but too small to be named. Commander Adnam would have to be very careful in the sound, because though the tide would be quite full, the chart showed it was studded with dangerous obstructions, difficult to see, particularly those just beneath the surface.

The Zodiac drew only about a foot when it was running fast, on the "stump" of the engine's wake, but he could not risk losing his propeller, and Ben hoped there would be some moonlight south of Harris, to light his way through the rocky seaway.

And in this he was lucky. The moon was high at midnight as the GPS link flicked to 57.48N, 07.15W. He knew that the tiny uninhabited island of Shillay, a 116-acre slab of granite that marks the southern entrance of the sound, lay somewhere to starboard. He elected to run southeast for a couple of miles in the hope of seeing it, and after eight minutes he picked it out on the freezing moonlit ocean, a half mile off his starboard beam, jet-black vertical cliffs rising out of the water.

He thanked Allah for the GPS, and slowed the Zodiac to a halt. The three hours running had used seven gallons, and he tipped the entire contents of one of the army cans into the tank, knowing he could run for another three hours before refueling again. Then he pressed forward once more, heading southeast, where the northern headland of the island of Berneray awaited him 6 miles farther on.

He passed the headland shortly after 0030, then braced himself for the really tricky part of the run through the sound—picking his way through the cluster of tiny islands southeast of Killegray that guard the eastern entrance. There is often a buildup of ocean swell right there, and the islands are low and hard to see in the dark. Ben elected to keep well southeast, and when he saw the island range in sight, they were a lot closer than he had expected. He crept past them carefully, and met with relief the wide expanse of the Hebrides Sea, which separates the Western Isles from Skye. Almost immediately the ocean seemed to flatten out.

He was not unfamiliar with these waters, because of his months in the Royal Navy, and he knew that the Hebrides are to Scotland very much what the Great Barrier Reef is to eastern Australia, sheltering the mainland from the winter rage of the open ocean. One way or another, he was glad to be in calm seas with a full gas tank, west of the historically romantic Isle of Skye, headquarters of the powerful MacLeod Clan. And as he turned more toward the south he found himself singing quietly, that most haunting of Scottish airs, an air he had once learned by heart from local people around the Royal Navy submarine base of Faslane, which had been his home long ago . . .

> Speed bonny boat, like a bird on the wing,
> "Onward" the sailors cry;
> Carry the lad that's born to be king,
> Over the sea to Skye.

And, like Scotsman all over the world, he saw clearly in his mind the most famous image in the long and bloody history of that country, that of twenty-four-year-old Flora Macdonald and her men, rowing the Catholic Charles Stuart—Bonnie Prince Charlie—to safety, across these very waters, after the crushing defeat of the Jacobites at the Battle of Culloden, on Drummossie Moor, in 1746.

From his position at 0100 it was 25 miles to the coast of Skye, and he considered that if Flora and her men could row it, his

Zodiac ought to make it without much trouble. He pulled down his hood, tucked behind the Perspex windshield to kill the wind, and pressed forward on a course of one-six-five. Two hours later he was right off Neist Point at the top of Skye's Moonen Bay, and thus far he had not seen a ship.

Ben eased his speed and tipped the contents of both remaining gasoline cans into his almost empty tank. That would give him 10 gallons for the final three hours it would take him to cover the 48 miles down to Mallaig, from where Lieutenant Commander Alaam had chartered the *Flower of Scotland* four days previously.

He'd make it, of that he was sure, and once more he pushed open the throttle, settled the Zodiac into its cruising position, and began his run down the long dark coast of the sprawling 400,000-acre Isle of Skye.

It was 0500 when he crossed Soay Sound in the shadow of the towering Cuillin Hills, which rolled down to the sea on his port side. Ben could barely see them, but he could feel them somehow blocking out the horizon to the northeast. Twelve miles ahead he would see the lighthouse at the Point of Sleat, and from there it would be a straight 5-mile run across the Sound of Sleat to the port of Mallaig, which was, of course, one fishing boat light.

Ben knew there were clear identifying marks on the Zodiac that linked it to the *Flower of Scotland*, and he wanted to make the port before daylight. For all he knew it might be crawling with police and coast guard in search of the missing fisherman. He picked up a red marker buoy a half mile outside the harbor and followed the lights in, carefully filling his Army gasoline cans with seawater and lowering them over the side before he arrived.

Right outside the harbor wall he cut his engine and rowed in with his paddle, staying right in the shadow of the moored boats. Then he made for a mooring at the far end with a small rowboat attached. He tied up the Zodiac and transferred his bags to the 10-foot wooden dinghy, jumped aboard, and rowed the 100 yards to the stone jetty, fastening off the painter with a bowline on a ringbolt.

Then he climbed the steps to the dock side, which was lit by one small streetlight. It was the first time he had stood on inhabited land since *Unseen* had left Bandar Abbas five months previously. Carrying his two bags, Ben found himself in an unspoiled little fishing port, a total jumble of fish-curing sheds, fishing baskets, herring boxes, netting, and gear. Out close to the approach road was a big steel rubbish bin, half-full of cardboard boxes.

Commander Adnam ducked in behind it, and with huge reluctance began to pull off the wonderful cold-weather Iranian Navy clothing that had protected him for four days. He doused himself liberally with deodorant talcum powder, which was all too plainly an essential part of his kit. In the other bag he had a dark grey, heavily wrinkled suit, clean shirt, tie, socks, and shoes. He had no coat, no scarf, and no hat, and the temperature was about 4 degrees above freezing, with a light wind. Nonetheless he could not wander around the West Highland town looking like Scott of the Antarctic, and reluctantly he packed his foul-weather gear into one of the bags, jammed it into one of the cardboard boxes, and crushed it down to the bottom of the trash bin. Then he picked up the other bag and began to walk into the town, toward the railway station, hoping it was not Sunday. He had lost count of the days of the week, but his guidebook told him there was a restored winter train service on weekdays leaving Mallaig for Fort William at 0800, in a little over one hour.

The walk seemed as cold as the desert at night at that time of the year. But Commander Adnam could deal with that. He quickened his pace, followed the signs to the station, and was gratified to discover it was Friday morning, March 3. He was also cheered to find a low, hot radiator in the waiting room, and he thankfully sat on it, having purchased himself a single ticket 130 miles south to Helensburgh. It was 35 miles to Fort William, where he would change trains.

At 0730 the train pulled into the station from a siding, Mallaig being the end of the line. It was warm and quite busy, but Ben Adnam found an empty corner. He guessed accurately that it would not remain empty for long since it was a Friday morning and there were people on board plainly going to work in Fort William. With his dark beard, rumpled suit, and no coat, he hoped he would be mistaken for a penniless Highland poet or some kind of a wandering minstrel. Anyway, he did not think he much resembled the usual image of a terrorist foreign Naval officer who had just wiped out three of the most important transatlantic jet aircraft on behalf of the Islamic Republic of Iran. Nonetheless, he did feel uncomfortably conspicuous.

Ben Adnam had never traveled as far north on the West Highland Line, but he had been to Fort William once with an old girlfriend. Actually, she had been his only girlfriend, and he remembered it as if it had been yesterday. He remembered, too, the old Scottish garrison town, standing rock-steady in the shade of Ben Nevis, the highest mountain peak in the British Isles.

They had stayed in a lovely hotel, Ballachulish House, which dated back to the eighteenth century, and overlooked Loch Linnhe and the Morven Hills. Fort William held many memories for Ben Adnam, and he tried not to think of them, for they represented another world, to which he no longer belonged. They were days of remembered laughter and love. But after a brilliant, if unorthodox career, there was but one preoccupation for him. And it overwhelmed every other concern he had. Survival. Nothing else.

The train pulled out of Mallaig station on time, heading south, then east, across the top of Loch Shiel and on into the Highlands. It reached Fort William before 0900, and the Glasgow train was waiting. Ben grabbed a copy of *The Scotsman* from the kiosk and found an empty compartment. The train left immediately, but he saw nothing of the first fifteen minutes of the journey, because it took him that long, searching diligently, to ascertain there was, as yet, no mention of missing trawlers or soldiers.

That task complete, he took the opportunity to clean himself up properly in the men's room, before going back to his seat. He was at last free to stare out of the window at the breathtaking scenery as the train ran along the River Spean, with the great pinnacle of Ben Nevis 4,500 feet above them to the right. After 15 miles they turned down the Glen, all the way along the eastern shore of Loch Treig and through the mountains to Rannoch Moor. From there it was southward all the way, right down the northern end of Loch Lomond, and past Loch Long to the Gareloch. The route took them right past Faslane, the Rhu Narrows, and into Helensburgh.

The final miles were laden with memories, and the commander thought of his months there, of long-lost colleagues, and perhaps, most of all of his Teacher, Commander Iain MacLean, the cleverest man he had ever seen in a submarine—the stern, beady-eyed martinet who had taught him how to sink a big warship and how to evade the most relentless of pursuers. He tried, as he always tried, to fight away the memories of the great man's daughter, the soft-spoken Scottish beauty who, to his everlasting regret, he never had time to love, far less to marry.

Helensburgh Station looked the same, gray and dour. A few passengers were waiting for the Glasgow train, but basically the place was deserted. It was midday when it arrived, and Ben was one of only five people disembarking. It was a little warmer there, certainly warmer than it had been out in the Hebrides Sea earlier in the morning, and Ben Adnam was heading for what they still called in that area, a gentleman's outfitter.

He stepped out into the small resort town, which slopes up from the Clyde, and the wide streets seemed little changed. He knew precisely the shop he required, and he was inside and out again with two dozen pairs of undershorts and socks, plus ten shirts, and a half dozen ties. He next headed for a country sports shop down a small narrow throughway off Upper Colquhoun Street, and in there he purchased a thick Scottish sheepskin coat, two cashmere sweaters in olive green and dark red, a cashmere scarf, and a trilby hat. To this he added two country tweed jackets, two pairs of dark grey trousers, and two pairs of cords, one tan and one dark green. Shoes were more difficult, but he went for a couple of pairs of brown loafers with thick leather soles and a pair of black brogues. He wore one of the sweaters, and the sheepskin and the trilby and, feeling considerably better, stepped out again into the cold, headed for the Royal Bank of Scotland, having just punched a serious hole in his last £1,500. At that moment he wished he had not been quite so generous to Captain Mackay, who had, unwittingly, wasted it anyway.

Ben had always retained a bank account in Scotland, under the name Benjamin Arnold, and he made a point of keeping a minimum of £20,000 there, in case of an emergency, such as the one in which he found himself. No one at the bank knew him any longer, and he had to provide identification in order to collect 1,000. He checked the balance of the account, which was correct, and inquired briefly if there had been any mail addressed to him in the past three months. There had not, nor had he expected there to be anything. Since the Iranians had made a valiant attempt to blow him to pieces on board the *Flower of Scotland*, he considered it unlikely they would have deposited his final payment of $1.5 million. He was right about that. They hadn't.

He left the bank, once more feeling a sense of desolation, and wandered through the town in search of a cab. That took him ten minutes, and by the time he arrived to spend the weekend at an old haunt from his Faslane days, the Rosslea Hall Hotel in Rhu, it was almost 1300.

At that precise time, a Royal Army Service Corps sergeant, George Pattenden, was stumping around the military camp on the island of St. Kilda making one loud and noisy demand, "Right, then. Well . . . where the fucking 'ell is everyone, then?"

Back on the beach, Captain Peter Wimble, R.C.T. was still holding the landing craft in the shallows near the church in readiness for the two soldiers, Lieutenant Larkman and Corporal Lawson, to move down the beach ready for evacuation. This was unusual in itself because everyone knew by radio the ETA of the landing craft, and thus far in his two-year tour of duty in the Hebrides, Captain Wimble had never yet arrived without the two departing men already standing on the beach ready to go.

On this Friday lunchtime, Sergeant Pattenden had leapt onto the beach and yelled. When no one showed up, he had, with con-

siderable bad grace, walked up to the camp and been mildly surprised that the lights were all on, the generator was still running,
but the jeep had gone, and of the lieutenant and the corporal
there was no sign.

"Funny," he had muttered. "That's bloody funny. Where the
fuck are they?" His irritation was plain, since it was obvious his
landing party could not return to base at Benbecula without the
men they had come to take off St. Kilda. Larkman and Corporal
Lawson could not just be left behind with limited supplies.

At its longest stretch, the southwestern shore, the island
stretched for 3 miles, from Soay Stack to the tip of Dun. At its
widest point, from Gob Chathaill on that long shoreline, east to
the Oiseval, the island measured almost 2 miles. But its coastline
was a largely unapproachable panorama of towering black cliffs,
riddled with caves, no beaches, and fairly high mountains in the
interior. It was not a desperate place to search, if you had a half
dozen Land Rovers. But Sergeant Pattenden knew they had virtually nothing. And in Army terms that meant they would have to
walk, and there were only two hours of daylight left.

The sergeant headed back down to the beach to report the situation, and the young captain, a friend of Chris Larkman's,
immediately ordered the landing craft to be made fast at the jetty
farther along the bay. Then, he said, two parties of three men
each, would begin a search, one on the Ruaival side of Village
Bay, the other up on Oiseval.

They kept going until 1630, when it became hopelessly dark,
then returned aboard, radioing to their Hebrides HQ the distress-
ing fact that Lieutenant Larkman and Corporal Lawson were
missing. Everyone knew the weekend was shot to pieces. There
would be no going back until Chris Larkman and his corporal
were found. Everyone had the most terrible feeling of foreboding, because there was really nowhere they could be unless
they'd gone over the edge of a cliff.

Captain Wimble decided they would be more comfortable at
sea, and all six men spent the first night in the landing craft
anchored off in the bay.

In the morning, back alongside, they set out once more to scour the Atlantic island.

By lunchtime the situation was judged to be critical, and two Army helicopters were dispatched from Benbecula. They combed the area for two hours, searching above the walking troops, clattering along the shoreline, gazing at the cliffs through binoculars, using infrared sensors. By dark, which fell at 1640, there was not a sign of the missing men, or their Land Rover, and the two choppers had to return to base for more fuel.

Back in the huts the search party had sleeping bags, food, and supplies. Plus a new Land Rover that had been brought over in a second landing craft. The Army also replaced the fuel cans borrowed by Commander Adnam. But, with a heavy heart, Captain Wimble accepted that Chris Larkman and Corporal Lawson were dead, although he had no idea what had become of them. But he knew Chris, and he knew that something terrible must have happened. The ex–Rugby player from Hampshire was a very solid citizen in Wimble's view, and Lawson was a cool, experienced, cockney soldier. It was, to Captain Wimble, inconceivable that either of them could have done anything ridiculous. He just could not imagine what had happened. Neither could anyone else.

Monday morning, March 6, found Ben Adnam still ensconced in the Rosslea Hall Hotel, still resting, but shaved and comfortable, operating under the name of Ben Arnold. His plan was to lie low for a month. He needed to find a quiet place, miles from anywhere, where he could rest, think, and walk, regaining his composure and fitness. Because just then, with his mind in a turmoil, he judged himself to be "no good to anyone." He could not even go home. He *had* no home. There was not even an office he could call. Any phone call, any journey, was, for him, fraught with peril. All he needed was time to think, because he required, unlike other men, a completely new life. And that, he guessed, might be pretty hard to come by.

Five months in a submarine had played havoc with his sense of well-being. He was anxious to get into shape and bought himself a new pair of training shoes, a track suit, sweatpants, and a guidebook to the Highlands. What he really needed was a guidebook to the universe, because the boundaries of this earth were extremely confining to an ex–Navy officer with Ben Adnam's track record.

He studied the guidebook all through his dinner in the hotel. And by 2200 he had drawn up a short list. Ben retired to his room at 2245, poured himself a glass of whiskey, and sat down to make a decision. Half an hour later, he made it. He would rent a car for cash from a local garage. And he would drive up to a little village named Strachur, on the Cowal Peninsula. And there he would check into Creggans Inn, right on the eastern shore of Loch Fyne. It was a place he had been to, long ago, and he remembered it well, with its awesome views across the lonely water. They had dined there on the night he had passed his Submarine Commanding Officers Course. So far as he could recall it was possibly the happiest night of his entire life.

He was not experienced in matters of the heart, and every instinct he had told him there was no point ever going back. Nothing was ever the same, or could ever be the same. There were so many things he had never said, wished he had said, and would never say. And returning to the place where once they had been so content would make matters, probably, appreciably worse.

She was gone. And she had been gone for several years—five at least since they had spoken. He knew she had married a wealthy Scottish landowner. They had seen each other twice since then. But surely a return to Creggans could do nothing except enhance his sadness and highlight the fact that life held little promise for him. The longer he was alone, the worse the depression became. Few people had ever compiled such a personal record as he had . . . rejected and betrayed by the only three employers he had ever had, all of whom had tried to assassinate him. He had no home, no future, no love, no relatives nor friends. And a past that would surely devour him in the end.

Nonetheless, he picked up the telephone and booked himself into Creggans Inn for a month. He informed the receptionist that he was a South African, mainly because he always carried a South African passport, along with those of Iran and Turkey. For this journey he also had a four-year-old British passport, but had not, thus far, used it.

He checked out of the Rosslea Hall Hotel when the garage brought his car, for which he gave them £300 in cash, the other £300 due when he returned it in a month. It was a six-year-old metallic blue Audi A8, with 70,000 miles on the odometer, but it ran well, and the garage mechanic had not even bothered to check his British license, which had been carefully forged for him in Egypt a few years previously, under the name Benjamin Arnold, like his Helensburgh bank account and two of his passports.

It was a little over 30 miles around the lochs to Strachur, and Ben drove it slowly, especially the first part, running north up the east bank of the Gareloch, the dark familiar waters in which he had so often driven submarines. He ran through the Argyll Forest Park along the A83 much quicker, before slowing down again, dawdling along the bank of Loch Fyne, looking for the big white house on the far bank, where once, and once only, he had been a guest. That, too, he remembered as if it had been yesterday.

He checked into the renowned warm and comfortable inn and sat by the fire in the bar. He had chicken sandwiches for lunch and sipped orange juice, while he read *The Scotsman*. And in the pages of that venerable journal, on a misty Monday morning, he found two items that took up a considerable amount of space.

The first was on the front page, from which the unsmiling faces of two soldiers stared out. On the left was Lieutenant Christopher Larkman, and on the right was Corporal Tommy Lawson. The headline read:

OFFICER AND CORPORAL MISSING
IN ST. KILDA MYSTERY

The story went on to detail the Army search that had been going on throughout the island all weekend. It quoted the officer in charge, Captain Peter Wimble, confessing that everyone was completely baffled by the disappearance of the two men with their Land Rover. "They did not have a boat," he said. "Anyway, it's more or less impossible to land on St. Kilda at this time of the year without a military landing craft. Which means they must be either on the island or in the ocean. And we now know they are not on the island. Which, I am afraid, leaves only the ocean. Though how, or why, or where, we cannot say."

The story concluded with the statement that the Army did not believe either of the two men could still be alive, but that the search would continue along the shore, beneath the cliffs, weather permitting.

The second item, inside on page three, concerned a missing fishing boat, the *Flower of Scotland*. And the newspaper treated it as another mystery, that the harbormaster at Mallaig had lost contact with the boat in the small hours of last Thursday morning, March 2. This was not altogether unusual, since radio failures can occur anytime. But there was now concern for Captain Gregor Mackay and his crew, even though that very experienced master often fished deep, lonely waters out toward the Rockall Bank.

The situation was regarded as sufficiently serious for a sea-and-air search to be initiated, and the newspaper revealed, "the Royal Air Force were expected to send out two Nimrods at first light on Monday morning."

It was, however, the latter part of the story that interested Ben Adnam. According to the Harbormaster, the Zodiac tender from the *Flower of Scotland* was located on the outer edge of the Mallaig harbor on Friday morning. It was parked on a mooring used by a lobsterman with a small boat, and that lobsterman knew it had not been there when he had left the previous evening. Even more baffling, the lobsterman, Ewan MacInnes, who had spent all of his life in Mallaig, knew Gregor Mackay well and had seen him leave, two nights previously "with a foreign-looking laddie" on board. Ewan had watched them clear the harbor. The stranger was standing on the stern, he said, "right by the Zodiac."

Now, Ewan MacInnes was not, apparently, the world's most

reliable source. A cheerful, bearded man of fifty-five, he had a reputation as a hard drinker and a bit of a romancer. But the coast guard had grilled him, the police had grilled him, and the local newspaper reporter had grilled him. And, despite the assertion of a local landlady, that "Ewan had spent half the day in here drinking, before he sailed," the lobsterman was adamant. No, the Zodiac had not been on his mooring when he left, "for the plain and obvious bloody reason that it was on the bloody stern of Gregor's boat, where it always bloody well is."

Yes, said MacInnes, I saw it leave. And yes, the foreigner was standing next to it. And, "What's more, I can tell you what he was wearing, a dark blue jacket, looked military, with a fur hat . . ."

The Scotsman plainly believed the fishing boat was gone. On an inside feature page they ran a big speculation piece on "yet another disappearing trawler." And they cited the ever-lurking menace to fisherman: Royal Navy submarines prowling beneath the surface. For the moment, the newspaper was prepared to disregard a different sort of menace, one which the Royal Navy also had to deal with. For now, the features department would concentrate on the age-old problem of an underwater warship hooking into a trawler's net and dragging it down, stern first, to the bottom.

They named all of the trawlers which had apparently suffered this fate in recent years. And they mentioned the Navy's reluctance ever to accept responsibility for these mishaps, unless the evidence was overwhelming. The problem was that no submarine can see the lines that hold the net, and there was a rule to deal with that . . . all trawler captains are supposed to station a man with an ax, on the stern, while the boat is running through the submarine roads around the Clyde estuary. If the net snags on a periscope or a mast, the drill is to sever the lines instantly and let the net go. The Navy, subject to an internal investigation, had long made it clear that they would bear the cost of new gear.

Out at sea, in the open waters of the Atlantic Ocean, however, the issue was more complicated. A trawler could be dragged down by a submarine owned by either the Royal Navy, America, or Russia, and no one was ever much the wiser. It sometimes took a full week before anyone even realized the fishing boat was gone. And this was most certainly the case with the *Flower of Scotland*.

The Scotsman had a "house list" of former Royal Navy commanders, retired but still Scottish residents, who were always good for a pithy quote. And on this occasion they took delight in quoting the former Polaris commanding officer Captain Reginald Smyth. "Oh, Christ," he told the reporter, in his usual languid drawl. "Another one? Bloody bad luck, hmmmm? That's the trouble with Scottish fisherman, they're usually pissed (drunk). Couldn't trust any of 'em to swing an ax straight—they'd probably chop their dicks off."

Pressed further by the reporter, Captain Smyth added: "Seriously, the chances of a submarine catching a fishing net are millions to one against. The ocean's a very big place. But until those trawlermen understand thoroughly that it *can* happen, there'll be accidents. If they want to avoid them, they *must* have an axman on the stern. The submarine cannot see them, and it cannot feel them if it snags the line. Only the trawler can tell something's wrong . . . and they've got about five seconds to swing the ax. It's damned rare, though. You can understand them not always bothering."

The captain got his photograph in the newspaper for that piece of intelligence. The italicized caption beneath it was a simple "quotation": *Drunken fisherman have themselves to blame.* Three weeks later Reg Smyth received a mild rebuke from the Admiralty.

Ben Adnam was contemplative. He finished his chicken sandwich and ordered a cup of coffee. And he gave due consideration to the conclusions that might arise from the evidence of Ewan MacInnes. *If he is believed*, he considered, *then it will become obvious that someone got off the fishing boat and somehow found his way back to Mallaig. But that would be impossible given the gasoline situation. Which means, I suppose, that MacInnes cannot be believed. But a good detective would wonder. He might even wonder whether there might be a connec-*

tion between the Zodiac and the missing soldiers. I hope not.

Ben drank his coffee. Then he went up to his room and changed into his get-fit kit. He was next seen pounding along the A815 road along the loch, bound for the tiny village of St. Catherine's, 4 miles away. Alas, he never made it. Ben gave out after 2 miles and was forced to lie down on his back on the wet grass to catch his breath. He walked back, feeling sick and sweating like a Japanese wrestler. Five months with no exercise can reduce anyone to middle age, even a man as fit as Ben Adnam once had been. And the realization of his condition made him doubly determined to get back into top shape.

Every morning for a week, he arose at 0600, pulled on his running shoes and track suit, and pounded his way toward St. Catherine's. Then he tried again in the afternoon. On the fifth day he made it. On the seventh, he made it there and back. By the end of the second week, he was running effortlessly to St. Catherine's and back, twice a day, timing himself. He also took charge of his diet, eating only fresh fruit, and cereal for breakfast, grilled fish and salad for lunch, fillet steak or roast lamb, and green vegetables for dinner. Temporarily he cut out all dairy products, and drank just a half bottle of Bordeaux with his dinner.

By Wednesday, March 29, one year to the day since he had stolen HMS *Unseen*, he felt that his body was back in shape. That day he abandoned the soft option of running along the A815, and instead took to the hills, running for miles in the mountainous foothills of Cruachnan Capull, which rises 1,700 feet above the loch, opposite the Duke of Fife's Inverary Castle. For the first time in a year he felt, lean, hard-trained, and ready, if necessary, to kill to survive.

And yet . . . something had happened to the mind of Benjamin Adnam. For the first time in his life he questioned the things he had done. For the first time he asked himself whether they were right? Was he really the obedient instrument of Allah, fighting for a holy cause? Or was he just the pawn of power-crazed earthly leaders, who answered to the same god as the citizens of the United States: the god of money and possessions?

He believed in the triumph of Islam, and he believed in the cause of Fundamentalism. And yet . . . no man had ever done more than he, risked more than he, been more successful than he. And where had that put him? Nowhere. He was a total outcast throughout the Middle East. His massive contribution to the *Jihad* against the West had turned him into an Arab who was essentially stateless, with a price on his head in several countries. And the great Nation of Islam could, it appeared, offer him nothing. Not even loyalty. It could offer him only death, death by assassination, not death in battle, or in glory. Death in some back-street building at the hands of fourth-rate hired murderers. Was that a fit ending for Benjamin Adnam?

For the first time the commander began to reflect on the crimes he had committed. He now asked himself, *Were they crimes*, those massive blows he had struck against The Great Satan? Not if they were executed on behalf of Allah for the greater understanding of his word. But how could he now think that? The rejection by Iraq and then by the most learned Ayatollahs of Iran must surely mean that Allah was displeased. Otherwise, his humble disciple Adnam must have received some reward, or recognition, or even an *honorable* death and the eternal peace of the life hereafter.

But he had received nothing. Except treachery. And he had been responsible for the deaths of so many people, most of them entirely innocent. Thousands of American sailors and aircrew on the carrier, a packed Concorde airliner, Starstriker, the Vice President of the United States plus his entire staff. "My God, what have I really done?" The darkness came blood black for Ben Adnam on the night of March 29.

For hour after hour, his dreams were interrupted by the searing crash of high explosive, and he awoke frequently, cradling his own head low against the pillow, sweating, trembling at the impact, haunted by his own most terrible actions against humanity. He was afraid to go to sleep, afraid even to close his eyes, because the images were too stark, too real. He could not look at the burning men in the ships he had smashed, and the engulfing red tide of his dreams was not the heavenly sunset of his aspirations. It was too dark for that. And the screams were too loud. Twice he awakened, fighting to break free of the plastic body bag that was dragging him endlessly to the bottom of the Atlantic, weighted down by a concrete block.

He stood up, drank some water, and mopped his face with a towel. Sheer exhaustion drove him back to bed, to fitful sleep once more. But it did not last for more than a half hour. Before dawn broke over the peaceful waters of Loch Fyne, he had thrown himself violently to the side of the big double bed, gripping the sheet, trying with desperation to break free of the Army Land Rover as it plunged toward the water . . . gaining speed . . . down . . . down . . . down.

At 0600 on March 30, the great terrorist Ben Adnam was breathless; he was shaking like a leaf; and he thought he might be losing his mind.

While he lay quivering in his bed, on the eastern side of the loch, there was a flurry of activity on the western side, about a mile and a half to the north, in the wide sweeping front drive of the big white Georgian mansion owned by Rear Admiral Sir Iain MacLean.

The admiral was making an early start, and he had five passengers to fit into his Range Rover: his trio of black Labradors, Fergus, Muffin, and Mr. Bumble, and his two granddaughters, Flora, age six, and Mary, age nine. The evacuation was not easy because the youngest of them, the eighteen-month-old Mr. Bumble, had made a rush for the loch pursued by Flora, who had fallen onto the wet grass and wrecked her trousers and coat, while ridiculous Mr. Bumble was doing a fair imitation of Mark Spitz in the freezing water.

Lady MacLean arrived with towels, grabbed the dog from the shallows, carried him wriggling to the Range Rover, and threw him in the back with the others. Flora made her own way back, giggling and trying to restore her clothes, which was plainly impossible.

Sir Iain said he had no time to wait, because the plane would probably be early into Glasgow from Chicago. He told Flora that only God knew what her mother would think of her, covered in mud, but that her stepfather would almost certainly laugh. Lt. Commander and Mrs. Bill Baldridge did, after all, live on a vast ranch in the state of Kansas, surrounded by grassland and the miles and miles of mud that goes with grazing pastures in winter.

This was the first visit Bill and Laura had made to Scotland since first they had left together in the winter of 2004. Sir Iain had twice visited them in Kansas, but there had been terrible family scars caused by the brutal court battle that had taken place over the children.

Laura MacLean, mother of two, had, at the age of thirty-four, left her banker husband, Douglas Anderson, for the American Naval officer to whom she was married. The MacLeans and the Andersons, lifelong friends, had banded together to make the girls wards of the court in Edinburgh, and absolute custody had been granted to their father.

The judge had made it perfectly clear at the hearing that if Laura insisted on running off with her American lover, it would be a very long time before she would see the girls again. As the Anderson lawyer had pointed out, these girls were daughters of Scotland, granddaughters of a famous Scottish admiral on one side, and, on the other, of one of the most important landed families in the country. There were critical questions of inheritance to consider. No, the court would not permit them to be taken to the American Midwest, from where they might very well not have returned.

It was Admiral MacLean himself who had begun the healing process. He told his disapproving wife, Annie, that he could no longer bring himself to turn his hand against the daughter he loved. He added that he didn't give a bloody fig for Douglas Anderson, whom he considered an extremely dreary man, and that he liked Bill Baldridge very much and was determined to do something about the situation.

Assisted by the fact that Douglas wound up in the London tabloids, having an affair with an actress from Notting Hill Gate in London, the admiral moved to have the court order overturned. And he succeeded, citing the facts that Lieutenant Commander

Baldridge was the son of one of the biggest ranchers in Kansas, that he had a doctorate in nuclear physics from MIT, that he had been one of the leading weapons officers in the U.S. Navy, and was a personal friend of the President of the United States. "And, perhaps more significantly, of mine," he added with uncharacteristic immodesty.

The admiral enjoyed firing a powerful torpedo, and the judge decided that without his support the court order was essentially worthless. Yes, the girls were free and entitled, and could by rights visit their natural mother during any and all school holidays. And now, the imminent arrival of Bill and Laura, on this day, was an occasion of great excitement. Because they were staying for ten days, then taking Flora and Mary to Kansas for the first time, for the remainder of Scotland's long Easter break.

The other objective to be achieved was a reconciliation between Laura and her mother. The two had hardly spoken since the custody case ended, since Lady MacLean felt that poor Douglas Anderson had been dealt a cruel and unnecessary blow. But he had married the actress, and things were rather different, particularly since Douglas was fond of saying publicly, albeit self-protectively, "Natalie is a lot prettier than Laura, and a lot less bloody trouble."

Sir Iain thought he was a lousy judge, a man to be pitied. But his wife, reversing course, had leapt to the side of her absent runaway daughter like a tigress defending her young, and began making no secret of the fact that, finally, she supported her daughter's decisions. Both Sir Iain and Laura were hopeful that in the next few days the deep family rift would be healed.

The Range Rover made it to the airport a half hour early. They parked the car and headed for the international exit gate. Bill and Laura, traveling first-class, were among the first out. Bill, wearing a big leather cowboy jacket over a dark grey suit and tie, his rolling gait straight from the High Plains, was unmistakable.

Laura followed him through the door. She looked slim and quite stunning in a long, fitted, dark green suede overcoat with matching trilby hat and burgundy leather boots. Iain MacLean had never seen her look so well, nor so happy. The girls fell into her arms, and the two ex–Navy officers shook hands warmly. "She looks marvelous," said the admiral quietly. "I was quite worried about her a couple of years ago. Thank you, Bill . . . for looking after her."

The Kansan grinned. "And thank you, Admiral, for being so goddamned decent about the whole thing . . . neither of us could help it, you know. It just happened, and it wasn't a mistake."

"No. I know it wasn't."

Laura introduced the girls to their new stepfather, and for a few moments they just gazed up into the deep blue eyes of the six-foot-two-inch Midwesterner who looked like a young Robert Mitchum. In the end, the elder daughter, Mary, asked earnestly, "Sir, are you really a cowboy like my father says you are?"

"Yes, ma'am," said Bill, grinning. "I sure am . . . ridin' them dogies home, out there on the prairie . . ." This caused the little girl to fall over with laughter.

"And you're really my stepfather?"

"Guess so, Miss Mary. Sure hope we git to ride the range together sometime."

"Stop it, Bill," Laura admonished, laughing. "Mary, ignore him. He really doesn't talk like that at all."

"Jest cain't wait to git back in the saddle agin," added the lieutenant commander.

With the introductions complete, Laura kissed her father, and they walked back to the Range Rover, and the frenzied barking of the Labradors. The 55-mile journey took them almost two hours, thanks to the morning traffic in Glasgow. Bill regaled the girls with tales of Wyatt Earp and the Dalton brothers, never once dropping his cowboy act. He told them about the prairies, and the fact that his mother was on the board of the cowboy museum in Dodge City, "where I'm sure gonna take both you girls, once I git you fixed up with a couple of six-shooters . . . jest in case we meet any cattle rustlers on the trail."

Even Sir Iain was laughing by that time, and it was not until they headed north up the bank of the Gareloch that Bill suddenly offered his hand to Mary, and told her in a completely different accent, "Just kidding, Mary. Lieutenant Commander Baldridge. United States submarine officer by trade. You can call me Bill."

Mary looked quite disappointed. "Hmmmm," she said, "I wish you were still a cowboy."

"Well," said Laura, "I'm glad we got that little charade over . . . he's so silly, Daddy. He's actually been practicing his cowboy act in case we meet any of your stuffy friends."

"Good idea, Bill," said the admiral. "Give 'em the full Wyatt Earp."

It was just before ten o'clock when they arrived at the house, and the admiral moved in to deal skillfully with the tensions that remained between his wife and the visitors from the United States.

Bill did his part here, too. "I just wish you could find some time to come over and visit us, Annie," he said. "I've always thought you would like it, and my mother would love to meet you at last."

Lady MacLean smiled. It was a smile that did not quite ask for forgiveness, but almost. It had been so much easier for her husband, who had liked Bill from the very start, and indeed had worked with him on a Royal Navy mission. And even she had to admit that Laura's second marriage had worked out, that she had never seen her daughter so happy, nor in such a bloom of health. At the end of the winter, too. "Kansas certainly seems to agree with Laura," she said. "I am sure it will be fine for me as well. Iain loves it there as you know . . . and I hope you'll find it in your heart to forget the bitterness of the past . . . it was such a shock for us all, you know."

"As far as I'm concerned, the past is already forgotten," replied the rancher, gallantly. And turning to Mary, he added, with a conspiratorial wink, "Yes, *ma'am*." Which again reduced the little girl to helpless laughter.

"He's a cowboy, Grandma," she said. "That's how they talk."

"Only sometimes," said Annie. "Don't forget. I've known him longer than you."

"Yes, but he's *my* stepfather," she said.

"And he's my son-in-law," replied her grandmother.

"Easy, girls. Hold your fire. I don't want y'all to start fightin' over me."

"*There!*" yelled Mary, triumphantly. "*I told you that's how they talk . . .*"

At that point Admiral MacLean assumed a loose command. He suggested Annie organize some coffee, and he sent Angus, the red-bearded butler, upstairs with the suitcases, calling after him, "The blue room in the front." Then, turning to Bill, he added, "There's a big double bed in there now, so don't look too forlorn."

"Oh, right. I forgot. That's my old room. I haven't been in there for what? Four years?"

"Must be. It was 2002 wasn't it, when he got the *Jefferson*."

"It was also 2002 when we got him, wasn't it?"

"Well, it was 2002 when the Mossad thought they got him."

"Oh, I think they got him, sir. Did I ever tell you the President presented me with Adnam's little submarine badge . . . the one he received from Tel Aviv?"

"No, you didn't. And will you *please* stop calling me sir whenever we touch on Navy matters. I'm Iain, plain, simple Iain. Do you understand me, Lieutenant Commander?"

"Yessir."

"Excellent."

Both men laughed easily. "As a matter of fact, Bill, the President told me he'd given the badge to you. I talked to him at the wedding. I must say he was very impressed with the way you identified the problem, then hunted the submarine down."

"Actually I hunted the man down, rather than the submarine. We'd never have found that, not without a tip-off."

"No. I suppose not. They are the devil to find, those diesels, eh?"

"Sure are . . . I miss it all sometimes, you know, Iain . . . that's not a complaint. Laura and I are very happy running the ranch, and it'll be great having the girls there for a vacation . . . but there are times . . . times when I see an item about the Navy in the newspaper and think about how I would tackle it. There's not a better life when you're single, and free, and the issues are international . . . and you feel you're helping to run the world."

"I know, Bill. I miss it, too. I suppose we all do after we leave. But some of us never quite take off the dark blue, eh?"

"Not quite, sir," said Bill to the senior officer, who this time raised no objection.

By midday, on the other side of Loch Fyne, Ben Adnam had somewhat recovered from his tortured night. He had opened the curtains wide at first light and slept in bright sunlight for most of the morning, missing breakfast altogether. He decided on a quick cup of coffee, which he sipped downstairs in front of the fire. Then he decided to attack his all-time record of fifty-one minutes to St. Catherine's and back.

This required him to reach the halfway turning point in twenty-four minutes—six minutes per mile—because the second half was always slower. And he set off along the loch, running hard on the flat surface of the A815.

The trouble was, his heart simply was not in it. And he found himself dawdling, looking at the water rather than his watch, and he jogged into St. Catherine's five minutes late, which in his mind defeated the object of the exercise. So he sat on a stone wall looking across at Inverary, while he caught his breath.

And once more his thoughts returned to the darkest side of his life, to the monstrous acts of destruction he had perpetrated. And again he was haunted by the one question he could no longer answer: "For Whom Did I Do It?" And he was afraid there was no answer, because there was no one to whom he could defer in the matter of his deeply held religious beliefs.

He did not doubt Allah, nor did he doubt the Prophet, nor indeed the Koran. His worry was that he had performed his great tasks without Allah approving what he was doing. He had been taught that the senior clerics of the Muslim faith, the mullahs and the Ayatollahs, were not in direct touch with God, but were merely teachers, learned men who were there to study the Koran and to guide their fellow Muslims in the words of the Prophet Mohammed. He understood thoroughly that all Muslims must find their own faith, because there can be no direct word, through the mullahs or the Ayatollahs.

He could not possibly defer to the President of Iraq, for whom he had operated for most of his life. And, despite feeling very much at home in Iran, the clerics of that country had not hesitated to cut him off from his reward, the minute it suited them.

Who, then, was he? Just a terrorist who would operate for anyone? Was he some kind of an international criminal? A hit man? A mercenary? Because, should that be so, he was uncertain whether he could live with it. Ben Adnam was a man who believed in his own higher calling. And that profoundly held philosophy was in ruins. He did not know what to do, nor where to go. And there was one problem that would not go away: He was, without question, the most wanted man in the world.

He gazed across the flat, dark, shining waters of Loch Fyne. It was almost 2 miles wide at his present location. But it was a very bright, cold, cloudless day, and Ben could see for a long way. Snow still shone on the high peak of the "submariner's mountain," The Cobbler, 9 miles to the east, and Ben could see it up across the huge pines of the Argyll Forest. It reminded him, as everything in that place did, of days long past, especially those days when he had returned to the Clyde estuary in a Royal Navy submarine, watching for the mountain to signify that they were almost home.

Now he had no home. And The Cobbler was still there. And so was all the grand and glorious scenery on the other side of the loch, the steep lightly wooded foothills that sloped up to Cruach Mohr, which he could also see, towering over the land behind Inverary Castle.

Directly across the water was the great white mansion of his Teacher, the father of the only girl who had ever loved him. Alone in his desolation, Ben stared at the far bank, trying to see the house where once she had lived, but there were trees to the north of the grounds, he remembered, and it would be hard to catch a glimpse of the building.

It was strange how he was suddenly drawn back to the memory

of Laura MacLean, just when he was not only the most wanted, but also the most unwanted, man in the world. They say that men about to face a firing squad, or the noose, or the electric chair, often cry out "Mummy" as they go to meet their Maker. And Ben wondered if that might not be the reason he so yearned for Laura. Was it just a helpless, despairing cry for unconditional kindness. Although he was not sure she could deliver that anymore. The brutal truth was, there was no one else.

And he sat on the wall, in the sharp chill of the early Highland spring, knowing that she was far away with Douglas Anderson, but unable to tear himself away from the sight of the place where once she had lived. He felt like a jilted lover, the kind who cherish a masochistic desire to stand secretly and watch the home of their former wife, or girlfriend. Just for a glimpse, just for even a thought-flash of remembered joy, and passion. In the desperate million-to-one hope of a chance meeting, and instant reconciliation, the ungrasped straw of the terminally hopeless.

Wearily, Ben picked himself up and turned back down the loch, running hard, trying to drive the demon of Laura from his soul, as if he ever could. But he had to get back to the inn. He had ordered lunch for 1345, homemade soup and a grilled Dover sole, and he needed fuel. In the afternoon, before dark, he would attack his St. Catherine's record again. And then he would concentrate. If he could.

The bar was fairly empty, but the fire was crackling, and the landlady was unfailingly cheerful. They talked for a while about his work in the South African mining business. And he explained why he was here after a lifetime in the perfect climate of Pietermaritzburg. "My grandfather was a Highlander," he told her. "And my wife died recently. I just wanted to come here for a month and feel my roots, visit a few little villages in the area. Someone told me how beautiful Loch Fyne was, and someone else told me about this place. Here I am, for another few days . . . rested and fit. And I've enjoyed every moment of it."

He liked the people who owned Creggans. They were never intrusive, and allowed him all the space he wanted. They worked on the old Scottish theory that if a man wants company, he'll ask for it. There's never a need to intrude. To some visitors this private, standoffish view of the world is precisely what leads to Scotsmen being describe as dour. But to Ben Adnam it was a godsend. And in a few days he would vanish from this place forever, remembered, he hoped, by very, very few people.

He decided to cancel the afternoon run and instead to take the car and drive the 28 miles up to the northern point of Loch Awe, the thin, 23-mile long serpent of Highland water, at the head of which stood the fifteenth-century castle of Kilchurn, and the great brooding mountain of Ben Cruachan. It stood 3,700 feet above the loch, and Ben was resolved to walk to its peak someday, to claim what was widely regarded as the best view in Scotland. Ben climbs Ben, as it were. But probably not that day; and he put his binoculars in the car in case he just wanted to look down at the magical waters of the heavily wooded, deepwater fisherman's paradise. In the back of his mind he also thought he might have a further use for the binoculars on the way back. But it was a thought he refused to recognize.

There was little traffic, and the Audi made short work of the journey. Ben gazed at the towering bulk of the mountain and decided to walk quietly around the castle instead. He climbed the stairs to the huge turrets and tried to imagine the force of the gale that had destroyed one of them, on that terrible night after Christmas in 1879, when the Tay Rail Bridge in Dundee was also demolished. He inspected the old turret, and then he walked to see the view from atop the castle, right down the long, straight waters of the loch. It was, as the guidebook said, truly spectacular.

Finally, he returned to the car, to drive, he knew, to the east bank of Loch Fyne, to look across the water to the house where Laura used to live.

It was growing dark by the time he arrived at his observation post on the edge of the road. A soft tallow mist was already gathering in the central channel of the loch, and it would obscure his view of the grandiose MacLean mansion. But it was still pretty good. The high-powered glasses magnified the far bank many times, and Ben could see the lawn running down the water. He and Laura had walked along that bank before dinner on the one night he was invited.

Ben focused, and he could see the lawn clearly. He could also see two or maybe three figures moving toward the loch. But it was too far. He could not make them out, and he guessed it was his old Teacher, Commander MacLean, perhaps with his wife and an early-arriving weekend guest. He remembered the family did a lot of private entertaining. But what Ben really wanted to know was the whereabouts of Laura. And he had no way to overcome the obdurate stupidity of that thought. His mind ranged over a succession of ludicrous options associated with such a reunion.

1) Take out Douglas Anderson, and maybe she would come with me, to where?

2) Try to charm her, persuade her to see me. No possibility. We both knew it was over the last time we met.

3) Kidnap her, and beg for a second chance.

Forget it, Ben. It cannot happen . . . but if I could just see her . . .

He stared across the water, at the green of the MacLean lawn, and wondered again where she was. Never had he known himself so acutely irrational. But he had nothing else to do, and he had no idea where to go.

The end of the afternoon on the other side of the loch saw the admiral, Bill, and Laura, dressed warmly, strolling back across the lawn after a long walk down the shore. Both of the visitors had found the conversation riveting, because Iain MacLean was telling them in a perfectly matter-of-fact way, that he and Arnold Morgan both believed that Ben Adnam was still alive. At that point in the talk, Bill Baldridge almost fell into the loch.

"*Alive?*" he said. "How could that be? The Mossad took him out in Cairo, didn't they? Jesus, I've got his badge, Admiral Morgan's seen the documents, so've the Israelis. They've got his passport. They have his personal Navy record, the one he owned, with his entire career on it."

"All true," replied Admiral MacLean. "The trouble is none of them have seen the body. You'll remember that Ben was, apparently, assassinated by two people who'd never laid eyes on him. They left with the dead man's papers, but the Egyptian police took the body, and it was cremated. As Admiral Morgan is rather fond of saying, the Mossad have no idea whether they took out Ben Adnam or Genghis Khan."

Bill laughed. But he was thoughtful. "And what gave rise to this sudden desire to exhume the Israeli commander?"

"Ah, that's another story," replied the admiral. "I'll tell you at dinner. Come on, let's go in and have some tea . . . we've walked far enough for one day."

"Do you really think he's still alive, Daddy?"

"Quite frankly, yes I do."

"Try to remember, darling," said Bill soothingly. "Should he call, don't forget to let us know."

Dinner that night was a re-creation of the feast Bill had enjoyed when first he had come to visit the admiral back in 2002, the time when he had first met Mrs. Laura Anderson. There was a magnificent poached salmon, with mayonnaise, potatoes, and peas. A bottle of elegant white Burgundy from Mersault and a superb bottle of Lynch Bages 1990 were set in the middle of the table. Bill remembered two things about his first dinner at the MacLeans—one that the admiral never served a first course with salmon, because he believed everyone would much rather have "another bit of fish if they were still hungry." Two, the admiral preferred to drink Bordeaux with salmon, as did Laura, which left Lady MacLean to deal with the Mersault.

Of the many other differences between the previous time and this one, the most striking was the lack of a view. In that hot July when his heart raced at the very sight of Laura, he had been able to see right down the loch while they dined, and he recalled Sir Iain pointing out through the window the little village of Strachur over on the Cowal Peninsula,

On this occasion it was just as charming but different. There was a glowing log fire in the 50-foot-long dining room, and the big patterned brocade curtains were drawn. Lights were switched on above the six paintings that hung from the high walls, three ancestors, one nineteenth-century racehorse, a stag, probably at bay, and a pack of hounds in full flight. Otherwise, the only light in the room came from the eight lighted candles, set in obviously Georgian silver holders, which Bill thought probably came with the house.

As before, he sat next to Laura, facing Annie MacLean, the two girls having had an early supper in order to watch television in Laura's old nursery.

The salmon was as good as the last time, when it was the best Bill had ever tasted. The Lynch Bages was perfect, and the admiral was amusing, recounting tall stories about Arnold Morgan's visit several months ago.

"What precisely did he come here for?" asked Bill.

"Well, I think he wanted to get away for a week or so with that extremely attractive lady he plans to marry."

"Kathy? Yes, she is very beautiful, isn't she?"

"Absolutely," said Sir Iain. "I told him she was probably a bit too good for him really. And he took it very well, for him."

"But what else, Iain? Tell me more."

"Well, Bill, I suppose you, if anyone, is entitled to know this. And so indeed is your wife. I have been wondering whether to break this to you gently or just to come straight out with it. And I've decided on the latter course. Arnold Morgan and I think that Ben Adnam has stolen, and now commands, the missing Royal Navy submarine HMS *Unseen*, and that he has been sitting in the middle of the Atlantic, underwater, banging out jet airliners, including Concorde, Starstriker, and *Air Force Three*."

As showstoppers go, that one went. Laura choked on her Lynch Bages, and Bill dropped his fork on the table with a clatter.

But he recovered, quickly. "Oh, nothing serious," he said. "I was thinking it might be something important."

"Oh, no," said the admiral, "very routine. Just the sort of thing he might do, don't you think?"

"Well, assuming he managed to jump off that Egyptian funeral pyre, I'd say most definitely. Right up his alley. Any evidence, or are you and Arnold going in for thriller writing?"

"Actually, there isn't much evidence, except circumstantial. But there's a lot of it, and, very curiously, Arnold and I stacked it up quite separately, on different sides of the Atlantic, and arrived at precisely the same conclusion."

"Might I ask when Arnold arrived here?"

"Yes. Last May. A few weeks after *Unseen* went missing. He came here with a real bee in his bonnet about it. And his reasons, as you would expect, were pretty good. He considered first that the submarine had not been found by the Royal Navy, despite the use of God knows how many ships, all the most modern sonar, and underwater diving equipment in a relatively narrow, shallow section of the English Channel. It was obviously not there. He thus reasoned that it had left its exercise area, and that it had been deliberately driven out of that area by someone else. Not, he decided, by the British lieutenant commander who was in charge.

"Therefore, he considered the ship had been either hijacked or stolen, and he went for the second option. *Unseen* sent all the right signals back, as soon as she left Plymouth; therefore, her CO knew what they were and he knew how to send them. Ben Adnam? I taught him all that; I even taught him how to drive an Upholder-Class boat, which *Unseen* is."

"Hmmmm," said Bill. "And then . . . ?"

"Well, she vanishes and is never heard from again. But then the Concorde falls out of the sky, for no reason whatsoever. The most brilliantly maintained aircraft on the North Atlantic suddenly vanishes without a word. Then, a matter of days later, Starstriker falls out of the sky on her maiden voyage. A brand-new, tried and tested prototype that Boeing swear by, an aircraft that's been under guard for weeks, no passengers, just crew, falls straight into the Atlantic without a word. Same place, 30 West, right on the Mid-Atlantic Ridge, the very best place in all the ocean to hide a submarine.

"And then *Air Force Three*. Virtually new. Flown by one of the best pilots in the United States Air Force. Vanishes, and I hear on the grapevine, there were smoke trails spotted, of the kind that might fit a missile."

"One major point, Iain. *Unseen* has no weapon that would fire such a missile. Neither does any other submarine in the world. Such a system would have to be custom-made and fitted . . . I think."

"Well, Bill, I think Arnold believes the Iraqis found a way, and did fit such a system. I intended to ask you what you thought might be feasible."

"I suppose one of those advanced Russian SAMs might do it . . . maybe the Grumble Rif. It'd have to be radar-guided. Heat-seeking wouldn't do it, because the supersonics would be going too fast. Come to think of it, you could probably adapt the submarine's regular radar just to a part of the system, the launcher and the missiles. Then you could catch the aircraft coming in . . . just in the normal way. Then send the bird away right off the casing, to the correct altitude, and let the missile's own radar in the nose cone do the rest. Couldn't miss if it was done right."

"One problem, Bill. I wanted to ask you. If it was Iraq, and we know Adnam is an Iraqi, *where?* That's what's exercising Arnold and me, *where* could they have made the conversion. They have no submarine facilities."

"I don't see that as a major problem, because I think such a system could be bolted onto the deck. You could get most of the high-tech work completed inside the submarine. If you could hide her for a short while, alongside a submarine workshop ship . . . well, I'm saying you might get it done without even going into a dry dock, so long as there was a crane on board. Remember, Adnam got ahold of a submarine before when he needed it. I guess he could have done it again.

"No, I think the biggest problem for Adnam would be getting a crew. There are no submariners in the Iraqi Navy. And there would be no way to train them. And he surely could not have persuaded an entire crew of Brazilians to go along with the scheme. Did Admiral Morgan have any ideas on that? Or did he just assume Adnam found a way, like he did with the Russian Kilo?"

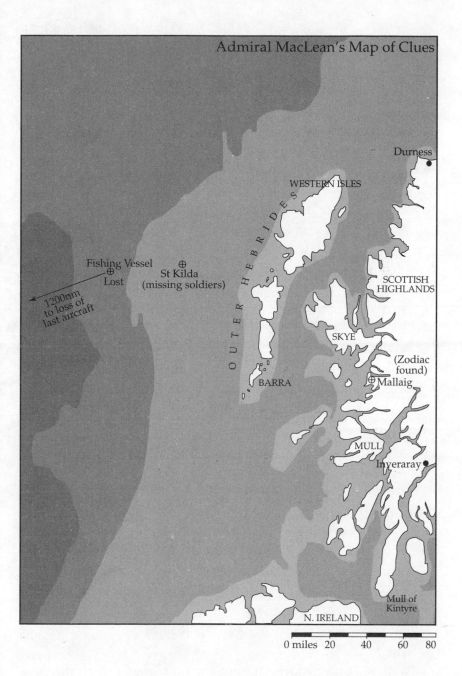

Admiral MacLean's Map of Clues

Durness

WESTERN ISLES

O U T E R   H E B R I D E S

SCOTTISH
HIGHLANDS

Fishing Vessel
⊕
Lost

⊕
St Kilda
(missing soldiers)

SKYE

1200nm
to loss of
last aircraft

(Zodiac
found)
⊕ Mallaig

BARRA

MULL

Inveraray

Mull of
Kintyre

N. IRELAND

0 miles 20   40   60   80

"He didn't mention any of that. I thought perhaps he might know something he was not prepared to share with me. Anyway, Bill, that more or less brings you into line with our thinking. But the problem of finding it is very tough. And there have been a few developments around here that I've been pondering, probably stupidly, just because I've got a bit too much time on my hands these days. Let's just finish our coffee, then we'll go over to the study and have a glass of port, and I'll show you a few things . . . Laura, you wouldn't pop over and put a couple of logs on the fire in there, would you?"

"Only if I can come over with you and have some of that port," she replied. "How about you, mum?"

"Oh, I won't, dear. I'm off to bed. It's been rather a long day, so don't keep your father up half the night."

"No danger of that . . . Bill and I would like to be a-l-o-o-o-o-ne in the room where we first fell in love . . . I'll send Daddy packing, don't you worry."

Everyone laughed, and they helped take the cups and dishes to the kitchen before crossing the hall to the book-lined study, in which Laura was blasting the fire with bellows. Then she thoughtfully poured three glasses of Taylor's '78 and sat in the left-hand chair, leaving Bill and her father to sit closer and study an atlas he had obviously been using recently.

Sure enough, he handed the heavy book to the Kansan, holding it open to a map of the eastern side of the North Atlantic. "You will see on there, I have made a succession of crosses placed in circles . . . well, the one on the far left is the place where the two supersonic jets went down. The next one, more easterly, is where you lost the Vice President in *Air Force Three*. The next two are more recent . . . very up-to-date. You see the one about 35 miles west of St. Kilda?"

"Got it."

"Well, we have reports in the Scottish papers this month of a mysterious incident . . . a fishing boat just vanished somewhere out near there. And there were a few rather baffling circumstances attached to it. My next cross is exactly on the island of

St. Kilda, where, a couple of days later, two trained British soldiers, an officer and an experienced corporal, just vanished, and they haven't found 'em yet.

"My fifth cross is in the harbor of Mallaig, where there may be yet another mystery. The tender from the lost fishing boat, a 15-foot Zodiac, suddenly turns up on someone's mooring a couple of days later, and everyone is saying the chap who discovered it, a lobsterman, was a habitual drunk and ought not to be listened to. He says the boat had been on his mooring just a few hours. The police say in the newspapers, it must have been on the mooring for days.

"Bill, quite frankly, if you are a fisherman, I don't care how pissed you are, you'd know if someone had parked a bloody great rubber boat on your mooring four days ago, or last night. I think the lobsterman ought to be listened to."

"Mmmmmm," said Bill, studying the map intently.

"And now I'm going to leave you with this thought . . . follow my crosses . . . look at the dates . . . see how they move in a steady easterly direction . . . a chain of circumstances . . . leading to what? Ben Adnam? I wonder. Let's regroup in the morning . . . breakfast 0900 I think. Good night, you two . . . oh, and Bill have a look at the little book there . . . the one about St. Kilda. I think you'll find it interesting."

Laura walked across the room and removed the atlas from Bill's lap, folded it, and placed it, with exaggerated firmness, on a shelf. She then took from a side table a CD, walked over to the player, and turned it on.

"*Rigoletto*," he said.

"The first one we ever listened to together, my darling," she whispered. "Right here in this room, nearly four years ago . . . Placido Domingo as the duke, Ileana Cortrubas as Gilda."

And as the rhapsodic sounds of Verdi's overture rang out, dominated by the glorious violins of the Vienna Philharmonic, Laura walked to her husband, sat on his lap, and hugged him as she always did, as if she would never let him go.

"I love you," she said. "And it happened in this room. When I had known you for about three hours. I've never doubted it, and I would change nothing."

"Nor me," said Bill.

"Nor I," she corrected, laughing at his inability to deal with "me" and "I." And then she kissed him as she always did, softly, with her hands in his hair, and her touch electrified him as ever.

"Same bedroom tonight," she said. "How lovely. How unbearably romantic."

Neither of them knew that beyond the deep red curtains of the study, out under the tall hedges beside the road near the main gate, was parked a metallic blue Audi A8, its driver finding an unbalanced peace just in being there.

March 31, 2006.

BY 0100 THE DOWNSTAIRS LIGHTS WERE OUT IN THE locked, silent MacLean household. The three Labradors were asleep in the big kitchen near the Aga, but they had, at the insistence of the admiral, the complete run of the house through-out the night hours, should an intruder decide to press his luck. However, this had never happened, since most burglars were aware that the average Labrador is a bit of a Jekyll and Hyde, once dark has fallen and a house is quiet. From a cheerful, bois-terous companion, he turns into a suspicious, growling watch-dog, likely to go berserk at the slightest sound. That huge neck of his powers jaws that can snap a lamb bone in two. The reason the British police do not use Labradors in confrontational situa-tions is their instinct to go straight for a man's throat.

Ben Adnam was unaware of these canine subtleties, and at 0115 he stepped out of his car and walked softly down the drive toward the house. He did so for reasons that were beyond him. He just wanted to be close to the building where once he had been near to Laura. The trouble was, the black, burly Fergus was unaware of his motives, and, with ears that could hear a shot pheasant hit the ground at 200 yards, he heard a footfall on the gravel drive. He came off his bean bag like a tiger, barking at the top of his lungs, racing toward the front door, pursued now by the even bigger Muffin, and Mr. Bumble.

The noise was outrageous. Upstairs, the admiral awakened and walked out into the corridor, where Bill was already standing in his dressing gown, with all the downstairs hall lights on.

"What's the matter with them?" he asked.

"I don't know, Iain, but when dogs react like that in the middle of the night it's always because they heard something."

And even as they spoke, they heard the unmistakable sound of a car pulling away, heading up toward the village of Inverary, fast.

"Probably someone was lost," said the admiral. "It's pretty dark out there."

The dogs were quiet now, and Sir Iain turned out the lights. "See you in the morning Bill, 0900."

"Yessir," said Bill, against house protocol.

Commander Adnam shot through Inverary at almost 70 mph his headlights on full beam. He might not have had much success at beating his all-time record to St. Catherine's and back. But he set some kind of a mark for the Scottish all-comers Inverary–Creggans Inn run. Right around the north end of the loch, pedal to the floor. He used his key to slip in the side door and went immediately up to his room. And there he lay exhausted on his bed, wondering exactly who was at home in his former Teacher's house, and where Laura was.

Would he ever see her again? And what had he been doing, lurking in the night shadows, like some burglar? He did not know. Except there was nowhere else where he could connect with anyone, even in his mind. It was as if the aura of the MacLeans, a family that once had almost liked him, had created a roomful of memories. And to sit in his cold car outside the house was to sit in that room. The alternative was so lonely, so frighteningly isolated, that he did not believe he could face it for much longer.

He knew one thing, however. For the first time in his life, he was in danger of losing his grip. Because there was nothing for him to do. He was friendless, stateless, and certainly homeless. And his ungrasped straw was Laura.

Ben did not sleep at all that night. Partly because he was afraid to do so, because of the nightmares. But mostly because he knew he had to move and seek out a direction. The problem was he could not even make a phone call, because there was no one he could call. One false move, and he would be arrested and possibly deported to the United States, where he was undoubtedly Public Enemy Number One. If they nailed him, they would not, he knew, bother with murder or life imprisonment. He would face a charge equivalent to treason against the state, and that, he guessed, meant the chair.

He drank just coffee at breakfast, in sharp contrast to the splendor of the spread that was prepared at the MacLeans. The admiral loved fish for breakfast, so long as it was served after 0900, and Angus had prepared both kippers and poached haddock, for two, since none of the female members of the household had yet made an appearance.

Bill had never had fish for breakfast, but he entered into the spirit and tasted his first kippers, ended up having two pairs of the rich, smoked Scottish herrings.

Over China tea, and toast with locally made chunky marmalade, he and the admiral settled down to chat about the Great Theory. The atlas was already open on the table. "Well, Bill," said Sir Iain, "what did you come up with?"

"Not much really. I was tired as hell, and Laura wanted to play some opera for sentimental reasons. By midnight I thought *Rigoletto* was driving HMS *Unseen*."

The admiral chuckled, and produced some newspaper clippings. "Here," he said, "read this one . . . it's got the stuff in it from the lobsterman, the stuff they have all, apparently, dismissed as unreliable. I'd be glad if you'd read it."

Bill did so slowly. "Well, Mr. MacInnes was pretty definite, wasn't he? I mean about the Zodiac suddenly showing up in the small hours of the morning. And he was also pretty definite about the new guy on the fishing boat, the one wearing the military jacket."

"Wasn't he, though? Very definite. And I can understand why. That chap has lived all his life in Mallaig, where his father was also a fisherman. The sight of that harbor is unchanging. *Anything* slightly out of the ordinary would register, even to a man who's had a few drinks. He's probably seen Gregor Mackay's boat pull out of that harbor a thousand times . . . but on that particular day he noticed something different, a new face . . . strange clothes. A man standing on the stern by the Zodiac, where MacInnes had never seen anyone before. To him, that would be a major departure from the norm. As if you reported to Boomer Dunning's *Columbia* and found a Zulu warrior at the periscope."

Bill laughed, but he was very serious. And he interjected, "Like seeing a sheep on my land. We've never raised them. Just cattle."

"Exactly so, Bill. That man, even through the alcohol, remembered. If I were the investigator, I'd regard the drinks as a plus, not a minus."

"I think I would, too, Iain. So what you're saying is that someone got off the fishing boat, in the Zodiac, and drove it all the way back to Mallaig. Christ, it's gotta be, what? A hundred and sixty miles?"

"At least . . . more like 175, I'd say."

"It couldn't carry that much gas, could it?"

"Easily. If it had four of those four-and-half-gallon jerry cans. Then it might."

"Well, let's assume, it did. What does this have to do with the man commanding the rogue submarine?"

"Only that someone may have got off the rogue submarine."

"Onto Gregor Mackay's kipper ship?"

"Possibly."

"You think he was out there recruiting?"

Sir Iain laughed loudly this time. "Bill, I love that American sense of humor . . . but that's not really what I meant. I meant maybe Gregor's boat had been hired to go out and *take* someone off the rogue submarine."

"But who could have hired it? The Iraqi Embassy?"

"No," replied the admiral. "But how about the foreign-looking laddie in the Navy jacket standing by the Zodiac."

"Jesus, I've been so busy making jokes, I never really thought about that."

"Well, son-in-law. Think."

"Right. I'll do it. One question. How far from the place *Air Force Three* went down was the *Flower of Scotland's* last-known position?"

"I've calculated it, Bill. The VP crashed at 53 North, 20 West. The *Flower's* last known was around 57.49 North, 9.40 West, about 490 miles. That's the distance between the final hit on *Air Force Three* and the place where the *Flower of Scotland* vanished."

"How about timing?"

"The Boeing was lost around 1300 GMT on Sunday, February 26. The harbormaster at Mallaig lost contact with Captain Mackay on the night of March 1."

"So the submarine had six days to get there."

"It would have done, my boy, if February had more than twenty-eight days in this non–leap year."

"Christ, I'd forgotten about that. So it had only a little over three and a half days?"

"Correct."

"You got a calculation on that, sir?"

"Uh-huh. Four hundred ninety divided by three and a half is 140 miles a day. Divide that by 24, and you have a nice quiet little running speed of 5.8 knots. Just about reasonable for a submarine creeping away from a crime to a meeting point, wouldn't you say?"

"Just. But then what? Ben gets off, pinches the Zodiac, and

somehow sinks the fishing boat? I can't buy that. If Captain Mackay had come all the way out to meet him, why didn't Ben just travel to Mallaig with the boat?"

"Well, I agree, Bill. It's all a bit far-fetched. But in the middle of it all, we do have one incontrovertible fact—the fishing boat did vanish. I suppose Ben, or whoever it was, could have shot the crew dead, left in the Zodiac, and lobbed a hand grenade on board as he went. But that's unreal, reckless thinking. Not at all like him. Too noisy. Too likely to be discovered. What if someone heard the explosion? He could not afford that."

"And how about the gas for the outboard? There's no chance there was enough for 175 miles. And the trawler's diesel fuel would not work in an outboard. Which puts Ben in the middle of the Atlantic in the middle of the night with no fuel. Don't like it, sir. Doesn't stack."

"Not quite. I agree. And the disappearance of the trawler is something I don't really have an answer for. But Ben would know how to sink a boat . . . if he was prepared to kill the captain and the two crewmen."

"Only to be stranded himself, Iain. Stranded absolutely nowhere. And no way to get anywhere."

"Ah, but Bill. There is something you have forgotten. Someone got somewhere. Someone got the Zodiac back to port, right back to Ewan MacInnes's mooring, on the morning of March 3. That's when he says it arrived. You see, I believe him."

"All true. But how? They don't usually run on air."

"No. They don't. But it would be nice to ask the two missing soldiers, don't you think? St. Kilda is only 35 miles from the *Flower of Scotland*'s last known. Ben could have made it to there."

"Jesus, sir. So he could. I wonder if they've noticed missing gas, or missing gas cans."

"I imagine they're too busy looking for missing soldiers . . . but it's food for thought, don't you think?"

"It sure as hell is."

"What I can't work out, is what happened to the fishing boat? But I can work out that Ben Adnam, having planned his evacuation from the submarine, might have been the man in that Zodiac, for whatever reason. So he goes to the military base at St. Kilda, takes out the two soldiers, steals as much gas as he needs, and arrives in Mallaig a couple of days later, on the morning of March 3, when Ewan MacInnes noticed Gregor Mackay's tender on his mooring."

"Admiral, for a story with as many holes in it as that one . . . you make out a very good case. Tell me your conclusion."

"I think Ben Adnam was in Scotland. I actually think he might still be here . . . and what worries me is what he might be planning. I mean it would not be beyond him to take a shot at a Trident submarine. I just don't know, but Arnold Morgan and I both think he stole HMS *Unseen*. And God knows what he might do next."

"Be kinda interesting if he stole a Trident and blew up half the world, wouldn't it?"

"Extremely. The trouble is there are really only three people in this world who understand the man and his capabilities. I, who taught him. You, who caught him. And Arnold, who's paranoid about him."

"Mmmmmm . . . one thing, Iain . . . picture this yourself. You're in a 15-foot boat climbing through the Atlantic swell. It's freezing cold, you're all alone in the pitch-dark heading for an uninhabited rock called St. Kilda. According to your little book the place is surrounded by huge black cliffs and is just about unapproachable in winter. How the hell could anyone manage a safe landing under those circumstances?

"You'd get swept onto the rocks and drown and no one would ever know."

"Not Ben. He's been there before. At least he's been close enough to have a good look at Village Bay in the southeast, right from the fin of a submarine."

"He has? How do you know that?"

"I was there."

On Monday morning, April 3, Ben Adnam checked out of the Creggans Inn and drove to Helensburgh. He paid the second cash installment on the car and asked if he might keep it another week. He'd pay £150 extra if it was less than a week, £300 if it was more. "As long as you like, sir. Just keep us informed if you want it more than two weeks."

Ben picked up more cash at the Royal Bank of Scotland and requested they provide him with two credit cards, a VISA and an RBS bank card, plus a couple of checkbooks. He expected, he said, to be going on a journey, and he would be wiring £50,000 into his account that same day.

The bank was more than happy to oblige an excellent, if frequently absent, customer like Mr. Arnold, and agreed that his business mail would be held there at the Helensburgh branch until further notice. The bank would deduct credit-card bills from his account automatically. He could pick up both cards in a few days.

The commander then set off for Edinburgh, a drive of 70 miles, straight through Glasgow and on to Scotland's capital city along the M8 motorway. He located and checked into the Balmoral Hotel, at the eastern end of Prince's Street, right above the Waverley Railway Station. And, in the absence of a credit card, left a deposit of £500 with the receptionist.

He checked into his room and immediately left the hotel, walking swiftly up The Bridges to the nearby offices of *The Scotsman*, with its new computerized reference room in which, for a fee, readers can sit in a small cubicle and pull up on the screen clips and pictures from any news event that the newspaper has covered. There is a further charge for printouts and copies, but the place is a fountain of information, and the Iraqi terrorist wished to bring himself up-to-date with world events that had taken place in the long months he had been at the helm of HMS *Unseen:* particularly those events in which he had personally been involved.

He began by pulling up the stories on the missing submarine itself, and there were many of them, around the time Ben and his men were running south down the Atlantic a year previously. But the news of *Unseen* died out quickly, as the Royal Navy's search came to nothing. There was a routine "WHATEVER HAPPENED

TO UNSEEN?" But there was no knowledge, no progression of the facts. No one had speculated anything even close to the truth. At least, not in *The Scotsman* they hadn't.

He then pulled up the stories on Concorde and was shocked at the amount of coverage, pages and pages of feature articles, reams of pictures, identifying the victims, their families and the crew who died out over 30 West in the North Atlantic. There were, in addition, two sprawling features over two pages on two separate occasions speculating on the "Bermuda Triangle" out on the edge of space—detailing an eminent scientist's view that the hole in the ozone layer might make supersonic flight impossible in years to come. Ben permitted himself a thin smile at that one.

The Starstriker catastrophe received matching coverage, with a proportionate rerun of the "Bermuda Triangle" theme. One scientist felt that it was more or less decisive. And agreed with the Greenpeace spokesmen, that all supersonic flights should be suspended until a thorough investigation was completed.

By then it was 1700 and the reference room was about to close. Ben put on his sheepskin coat and stepped out into the chill Edinburgh afternoon, walking slowly back to his hotel, alone as perhaps he must always be, the great terrorist with nowhere to turn.

The following morning he was back in the reference room by 1000 reading through the accounts of the death of the Vice President and the crash of *Air Force Three*. He found the account of the merchant ship captain, who saw the wreckage falling from the sky, and who talked, initially, of smoke trails. But there was no follow-up to that. The captain, a former Royal Navy officer, had either not been pressed for more detail or, thought Ben, had been told to shut up.

The fact was, there was no mention of missiles. No connection anywhere with the possibility of anything being fired from a submarine. He had accomplished his task with the maximum of publicity, the maximum of terror, and the minimum of identification. Commander Adnam considered he had completed his task for the Islamic Republic of Iran impeccably. And the best they could do was to refuse to pay him, then try to have him murdered. Ben shook his head.

Next he pulled up the stories on the St. Kilda soldiers. Still no sign of them. But he was somewhat unnerved by the testimony of Ewan MacInnes, the man who *knew* someone had driven the Zodiac back from the *Flower of Scotland*, and who categorically saw that idiot Lieutenant Commander Alaam standing publicly on the stern of the departing trawler.

Ben Adnam thought that was an example of amateurism at its worst. And he was gratified to see that no one had expanded on the observations of the lobsterman. It seemed to Ben that no one believed the man.

In the next hour he pulled up everything he could find on the Iranian Naval Headquarters at Bandar Abbas. There was very little, certainly no mention of the big dry dock in which they had converted *Unseen*. No mention of terrorism, nothing on missiles, not a word about Iran purchasing new SAM systems from Russia. He checked, too, the military news from Baghdad, and that was just about nonexistent. Just a small item about the Pentagon checking into the possibility of test-firing surface-to-air rockets somewhere down in the southern marshes.

So far as Ben could see, neither he nor anyone else was under direct suspicion for the atrocities that had taken place in the middle of the Atlantic. Which might have meant he could make a clean getaway, except that he had nowhere to get away, to or from. And, as ever, his thoughts returned to Laura MacLean.

And he gazed at the computer, afraid to slide back down into the well of maudlin introspection that had consumed him for several days. But afraid more of being alone. He told himself to get up, and get out, and think, and make a plan. But the memory of her perfect face stood before him still. He stared back at the keys and willed himself to leave the newspaper offices. But then he punched in the name of MacLean—*Admiral Sir Iain, by now, I guess*. And within seconds the file jumped onto the screen, and Ben scanned down the list. One item popped right out at him: DAUGHTER'S DIVORCE AND CUSTODY CASE.

He ran the cursor down, pressed ENTER to retrieve, and a stack of reference material became available. Not quite so much as that on the crash of Concorde, but more than he found on the missing *Unseen.*

Ben could scarcely believe his own eyes. It was all there, and he scrolled down the computer pages, reading with amazement the story of Laura's split with her Scottish banker husband, Douglas Anderson.

He considered the entire thing so out of character. Laura? On the front pages of the newspapers in a terrible scandal that ended up in the High Court in Edinburgh? In his anxiety to devour as many facts as possible, Ben skipped over the part about the man with whom she had run off. It took him ten minutes, paging back through the reports, to find his name, Lt. Commander Bill Baldridge (Retd.) of the United States Navy. "At least I outrank him," muttered Ben.

There was very little in the paper about the divorce itself, because that was heard *in camera,* as these personal matters often were in Scotland. The newspapers printed the name of the man cited by Mr. Anderson, but very little more. The real public uproar had erupted over the custody battle for Laura's two children. So far as Ben could tell, the American had come to the court and been photographed but, of course, took no part in the case. The rights and future entitlements of the little girls were discussed by the judge, the lawyers, and the two very influential families.

Laura's barrister had pleaded her case valiantly, but reading the reports in retrospect it was obvious that the judge was never going to allow Laura's daughters to leave Scotland while they were so young. And, to Ben's amazement, Laura had left without them.

In an unguarded moment, in reply to a reporter's question about when she would return, she had turned around, and snapped, "I never want to lay eyes on this damned place, ever again."

Douglas Anderson had been very dignified throughout the whole proceedings and said nothing outside the court, except that he and his family, assisted by Admiral Sir Iain and Lady

MacLean, had a duty to raise the little girls in the best possible way, and to ensure that their inheritance was properly managed.

So that was it. Laura was gone. And, save for a short mention in *The Scotsman* that the American had become a farmer in the Midwest after leaving the Navy, there was no further clue as to where Mr. and Mrs. Baldridge lived. Ben assumed they were somewhere together, and married, since all of this had taken place in the winter of 2003/4, over two years ago.

An appalling melancholy swept over him. For he knew that the United States was the most dangerous place on earth for him. That was where he would be executed, summarily, if they found out who he was. And Commander Adnam did not underestimate the men in the Pentagon. He knew they were incredibly smart, absolutely ruthless, and would think nothing of "stringing up some towelhead terrorist." He had met Americans, right here in Scotland, men from the Holy Loch Base. He knew how they talked and what they thought about serious enemies of the U.S.A.

For the first time, ever, he believed he would never speak to Laura again.

With a sad heart, he turned off the machine and walked bareheaded out into the cold, rainy streets of Edinburgh. But he did not mind the rain, because it obscured the tears that ran silently down his face. It was the first time the forty-six-year-old Benjamin Adnam had wept since he was a child in the village of Tikrit, on the banks of the Tigris River.

He did not want to return to the Balmoral Hotel, because that was just another prison. There was only his empty room, and he was frightened of the solitude. He actually thought he might break down completely. And so he kept walking, heading, for no reason, for the great ramparts of Edinburgh Castle, which glowers over the city.

It was 1235, and he turned into the High Street, walking west up the long rise to Castle Hill, which leads up to the massive granite edifice which has symbolized the innate defiance of Scotland for more than 850 years. Ben had been here once before, in 1988 with Laura, and he stood staring up at the Outlook Tower, just as the castle's 1300 cannon shot crashed out over the city, as it did every day except Sunday.

There was a considerable crowd of tourists awaiting the sound of the cannon, and a predictable number of "oohs" and "wows" as it happened. Ben stood still at the sound of the sudden shot, and his muscles tensed. It was the reaction of a military man, in a military place. Although no armed forces have been garrisoned in the castle since the twenties, it was once home to the great Scottish regiments: the Black Watch, the Royal Scots, the Seaforth Highlanders.

In the Middle Ages, the castle was besieged constantly, mostly by the English. It is impossible to remove the overtones of blood and valor from such places, and Ben Adnam felt more at home there, in those stark, bleak vales of distant courage and gallantry, than he ever did in the Balmoral Hotel. Ben imagined the clash of steel and the thunder of the guns, as he walked slowly along the stone walkways to the twelfth-century St. Margaret's Chapel, the small stone-arched place of worship inside the castle. These days it is nondenominational, and used only by visiting military, but once it was an important Catholic church.

Ben opened the door and stepped inside, gazing at the five magnificent stained-glass windows behind the altar. Before him were images of St. Ninian, St. Columba, St. Margaret, and St. Andrew. But Ben had no interest in them. He walked to the bright, beautifully colored window dedicated to Sir William Wallace, the great Scottish national hero of the thirteenth century.

This, Ben knew, was a real man . . . William Wallace, who had led his renegades to kill the Sheriff of Lanark, and then to defeat the English governor of Scotland, Lord Surrey, in a brutal battle near Stirling . . . William Wallace, the man who finally drove the English out of Scotland altogether. Ben knew that in the end Wallace had been executed for treason. Nonetheless, he died bravely at the age of only thirty-three, and Commander Adnam stood in front of the window and bowed his head in front of Scotland's most noble terrorist.

He stayed for just a few minutes, then walked outside, where it was still raining, and, within him he felt the old resolve surge again.

He gazed out northward across the gray expanse of the city, toward the wide waters of the Firth of Forth, and beyond to the ancient kingdom of Fife. He thought back to the days of Wallace, and the undaunted fearlessness of the man . . . the audacity it must have taken to move in and ruthlessly attack the enemies of his country.

Suddenly, for the first time in a month, Ben believed he was thinking clearly again. The face of William Wallace had seemed to look kindly upon him, and the example of the long-dead martyr of freedom seemed to galvanize his spirit. In a flash of inspiration the commander knew where he must go, and what he must do. It was his only chance, and it was a chance that might lead him simultaneously to Laura. But first he had to find her.

He turned from the castle and headed back downtown, hurrying along the High Street, then turning back along The Bridges to his hotel. He arrived there and found a telephone book with listings for the border country. *The Scotsman* had always quoted Douglas Anderson as, *"Speaking from his estate near Jedburgh last night."*

"Anderson . . . Douglas R.—Galashiels Manor, Ancrum, Roxburgh . . . that's it." Ben Adnam wrote down the address and phone number, then debated the merit of making the call and decided against it. The telephone has a disadvantage, he decided. The person on the other end is able to say, politely, "No. I'm afraid I cannot help, and I'm extremely busy at the moment. Good-bye." Which is essentially the end of the campaign.

No, he concluded, *I'll go to Galashiels Manor and talk to Mr. Anderson in person, if he's there. I'll make up some story to persuade him to give me Mr. Baldridge's address.* Having decided, Ben had a quick cup of coffee in the downstairs vestibule, ordered his car from the garage, and set off out of Edinburgh, southeast to the Borders.

He drove quietly out past the city limits and onto the A68. It was 28 miles to the Galashiels area, down a long winding road, past the western edges of the Lammermuir Hills. There, on the high ground, were some of Scotland's finest grouse moors, in particular those of the dukes of Roxburgh, and those of Sir Hamish Anderson, the magisterial father of Douglas.

Commander Adnam sat behind the wheel, glancing occasionally at the cold bleak winter home of the game birds, and reflecting upon his forthcoming tactics. He would pretend that he knew nothing of the divorce and that he had come to visit Laura and her husband as a result of a long-standing invitation.

In the end he wanted just one thing from the banker—the American address of Lieutenant Commander Baldridge. And if Mr. Anderson should prove difficult, it might be necessary to force the information from him, which might mean he would have to silence him permanently before leaving. But that was a course of action the commander was quite prepared to take. Old habits tend to die hard among terrorists. And Ben Adnam knew that for the rest of his life, if he was to evade capture, he might have to take such actions. Because for him, one witness as to his possible identity was one too many. That would signify, quite simply, the end of his life.

He reached the junction with the Selkirk–Kelso road and continued on straight for the 6-mile run down to Ancrum. The afternoon had turned suddenly bright, as the rain cleared swiftly away to the northeast, and, after a couple of miles, Ben stopped in a desolate stretch of green hilly countryside and checked his map. He was inside a triangle, bounded on three corners by Selkirk, Jedburgh, and Kelso. Twelve miles away to the southwest was the cashmere and knitware town of Hawick.

Right there he was in the heart of the great border tribes of Scotland, the men once known as the Border Reivers. Their lawless reign of terror had flourished along those lonely hills for 350 years, until 1600, because England regarded the entire region as "ungovernable." Ben himself had just seen, in the past 20 miles, signs that remain of them still—ancient castles, stately homes, fortified farmhouses, ruins of historic abbeys, remains of watchtowers built as fortresses with walls 7 feet thick. There were remnants of abandoned hamlets in remote valleys, remnants of a cruel and turbulent history in which the warring tribes of England and Scotland had fought each other savagely over four centuries. Many of their descendants still lived in the area: families with names like Nixon, Armstrong, Graham, Kerr, Maxwell, Forster . . . and Anderson.

But it was quiet there as Ben Adnam drove south, almost eerily quiet. For these borderlands represent the center of one of Britain's last wilderness areas, a land of vast moors, forest, hills, rivers, and streams. And the Iraqi ran on down to Ancrum, stopping just short of the tumbling River Teviot, for hundreds of years a silent haven for salmon fisherman. Ben actually drove past the village green and on out to the other side before realizing his mistake and turning back.

He stopped and turned around, drove back to the village shop, where he inquired as to the address of Mr. Douglas Anderson. "Take the road to Nisbet," he was told by the gray-haired, tidy Scottish lady behind the counter. "And on your left you will come to a graystone gateway with carved granite lions on the posts. Turn in there . . . the drive's about half a mile long. Mr. Douglas is in residence, I believe. By the way, if you get to the Memorial, you've gone too far."

The commander found the road to Nisbet and drove out through the rolling country traditionally hunted by the duke of Buccleugh's foxhounds, next to the vast lands owned by the marquis of Lothian. He found the lion gates and turned into the drive, making his way between long lines of towering spruce trees on either side. The house itself was gray stone with four columns on the front portico. The oak doors stood 12 feet high.

Ben parked the car, walked up the four steps to the entrance, and rang the bell. An elderly butler, dressed in striped trousers and a black jacket, answered the door, and Ben asked if he could possibly see either Mr. or Mrs. Anderson. His English was impeccable, and the butler recognized this to be so and invited him to step inside. Then he asked who he should say was inquiring.

"Tell them, Mr. Arnold. Ben Arnold from South Africa."

"Very well, sir."

When he returned he was accompanied by a dark-haired,

youngish woman of medium height and quite striking good looks. She wore a deep red silk shirt, tight black pants, and high heels. Her lavish lipstick matched her shirt. She looked like an actress to the tips of her dark red fingernails.

"Good afternoon," she said. "I'm Natalie Anderson. My husband is rather busy at the moment, I wonder if I could help . . . I don't believe we have met?"

The commander smiled and offered his hand. "No . . . no we haven't. I'm Ben Arnold . . . and this is all rather embarrassing."

"It is?"

"Well . . . it is. You see, I thought Mr. Anderson was married to a lady named Laura."

"Not anymore," said Natalie, laughing. "They were divorced two years ago. I've been married to Douglas for more than a year now."

"Oh . . . I see. Then that makes it even more awkward."

"It does?"

"Well, yes. You see my wife and I met and became quite good friends with Laura Anderson in Cairo several years ago. We live in South Africa, but we exchanged addresses and promised to meet if we ever were in the same place . . . my wife arrives tomorrow, and we're staying in Kelso. So I thought I'd do a recce, and arrange a dinner or something . . ."

"Well, Mr. Arnold . . . that sounds lovely . . . but since none of us knows each other probably out of the question."

"Oh, absolutely. And I apologize for taking your time."

Ben turned to leave, but he hesitated and looked back suddenly, and said, "I say, I'm sorry to be a bore . . . but do you think your husband would have Laura's address? At least my wife could send her a Christmas card and let her know we tried."

Natalie smiled, and replied, "I'm sure he would. Let me go and get him. I have to go to Kelso myself now, so I'll say good-bye and send Douglas to see you."

Ben waited, feeling the hilt of his desert knife in the small of his back, wondering how he would feel when he confronted the man who had taken "his" Laura. In less than two minutes he found out. Douglas Anderson, a tall, heavily built man, wearing a country suit with thick, long socks and plus fours, came marching across the hall, the steel tips on his highly polished brown brogues clipping on the stone floor.

"Good afternoon," he said, in an accent that betrayed every vestige of the polished, landed Scottish banker. "I hear you've got your wires a bit crossed. I'm Douglas Anderson."

The two men shook hands, and Anderson immediately looked at his watch, and said, "What is it . . . five o'clock? Tell you what. You've come a long way . . . how about a cup of tea?"

"Well, I hate to intrude, but that would be very nice."

"Come on in here," he replied, leading the way into a warm, comfortable drawing room with a log fire. "You can tell me about meeting Laura."

Ben followed him in. "Cairo," he said. "Maybe eight years ago."

"Yes . . . I remember she did go there once for a brief holiday with a girlfriend. Annie, wasn't it?"

"Yes, I believe that was the name of Laura's friend. But anyway, my wife Darlene got on very well with Laura. They went shopping together, hired a couple of camels and rode out around the pyramids. I used to call her Laura of the Desert. We were all staying out at the Mena House Hotel near Giza."

"Absolutely. I remember her telling me about the place."

"Anyway, we lost touch, but we always kept her address, and now I'm here on business for a few days and Darlene's flying into Edinburgh tomorrow. I thought we might all get together . . . but it really was a bit embarrassing meeting the new Mrs. Anderson like that. I suppose I should have called and saved everyone a lot of trouble."

"Think nothing of it, old boy. I'm glad of the company. Natalie's gone to her bloody aerobics class, and I'm alone for a couple of hours."

The butler brought in the tea, and Douglas Anderson poured it. "Sugar . . . ?"

"No thanks. Just a splash of milk."

"And how about you, Ben? What's your line of country?"

"Mining. Copper and coal. We have holdings in both. I'm here to see several bankers in Edinburgh, but I thought it would be nice to stay out here for a few days in the country. I say, I'm really sorry about you and Laura . . . she seemed such a nice girl."

"Oh, yes. She was. Damned nice family. Daughter of a very eminent admiral, you know. It all happened so damned quickly. I never knew what had hit me. She suddenly met this bloody American, here in Scotland, and announced she was buggering off with him. Shook me up, I can tell you."

"Well, Douglas, you look to me as if you've made a satisfactory recovery," said Ben, smiling.

"Haven't I?" said Douglas, laughing loudly. "I was a bit bloody lucky really, landing a beautiful younger woman like that . . . she's only twenty-eight now. I'm forty-five. She keeps me young, and I've taught her how to catch a salmon. Not much of a deal for her really. But she seems to like it up here . . . and we have nice holidays."

"Where did this bloody American come from?"

"Well, that's all been a bit secret, Ben. You remember that United States Navy aircraft carrier that got itself blown up about four years ago? Well, apparently the Pentagon thought it might have been hit by some fucking Arab in a submarine, and this Baldridge Johnny—that was his name—was over here trying to find out who he was. Apparently Laura knew the chap they all suspected . . . an old boyfriend, I think, when he was training here. Nothing serious, of course . . . just some bloody foreigner learning how to drive a submarine. Her father was the Teacher at the base at that time."

"Hmmm. Did they find him?"

"Don't think so. I never heard any more. Except my wife had cleared off with the American investigator. Left me high and dry. My luck changed in the summer . . . my mother's on the board of the Edinburgh Festival, and we had a group of the actors and directors out here for dinner one evening. Natalie was playing the lead in the main theatre. I drew her next to me at dinner, and we never looked back."

"Well, Douglas, you have been very kind. The only thing I wondered was, could you possibly let me have Baldridge's address? I think my wife would like to send Laura a Christmas card or something, and let her know we did try to get into contact. She'll be very disappointed to have missed her."

"No problem, Ben. Natalie mentioned that . . . and I have it right here. Baldridge Ranch, Burdett, Pawnee County, Kansas, plus the zip. My daughters are going over there in a few days for the first time. I did hear that Laura and her husband might show up here . . . but I think they're bringing the girls back after the Easter holiday. No one tells me much . . . not now I've remarried. I believe American Airlines are in command of the outward journey."

Ben stood up and offered his hand. "Douglas, I'm sorry to have taken your time. It has been most enjoyable, and I wish you every happiness. You have a very lovely wife."

"Thank you, Ben. I'm glad to have met you. I hope you have a nice stay in Scotland, and please give my regards to Darlene, whom I nearly met."

They both laughed, and Ben took his leave, walking out into the dark, and starting the car, heading out through the spruce trees, and the A68 back to Edinburgh.

Admiral Sir Iain MacLean answered the telephone in his study just after 1800.

"Oh hello, Douglas. How nice to hear from you."

"Yes . . . well it's been a bit of time, hasn't it? We don't seem to run into each other so often these days. How's Annie . . . and the American branch of the family?"

"Oh, they're all fine . . . Bill and Laura are here actually."

"Oh, they are? I thought the idea was that their mother would bring the girls back."

"Well, it was. But they had a change of plan, decided to come over for a few days, and take the girls to Kansas. Then they'll fly them up to Chicago and put them on the direct flight back to Edinburgh. You don't want to speak to Laura, do you?"

"I don't think so, Iain. Tell you the truth, I was just looking for an excuse to have a chat for a few minutes. Nothing very important. But I had a rather unusual visitor this afternoon, looking for Laura."

Iain MacLean's voice went ice-cold. "You did? Who was it?"

"South African chap. Nicely dressed, expensive sheepskin coat, driving an Audi. Told me he and his wife had been friends with Laura about eight years ago. But the address he had was mine. He thought we were still married."

"What did he look like, Douglas?"

"What do you mean, what did he look like? Perfectly ordinary sort of chap, well-spoken, in the mining business."

"No, Douglas. What did he *look* like."

"Well, he wasn't all that tall. I'd say a bit less than six foot. Quite broad, well built."

"What kind of coloring?"

"Oh, dark. I took him for a South African Jew. Black hair, curly, cut short."

"Did he tell you his name?"

"Yes. But I can't remember . . . the surname anyway. His first name was Ben."

Admiral MacLean's mouth went dry. He said, "Just a minute, Douglas . . ." He poured himself a glass of mineral water before continuing.

"Was there anything else about him that you noticed?"

"No, not really."

"Did he say where he and his wife met Laura?"

"Yes, he did. Cairo. Laura went out there with her girlfriend Annie about eight years ago. Stayed at the Mena House out near the pyramids. According to this chap, they all met there and exchanged addresses. I just thought it was a bit strange. You know, Laura never mentioned anything about a South African couple to me, and I just wondered if the chap rang any sort of a bell with you."

The admiral was silent for a few moments, hearing about ten thousand bells of pure alarm ringing in his head. But he said, quietly, "No, Douglas. She never mentioned anything to me . . . I was going to ask you if you had told him that Bill and Laura were here, but of course, I forgot, you didn't know."

"No. But I think I mentioned they were expected sometime soon. You know, bringing the girls back from America . . . that sort of thing."

"Did he say how long he and his wife were planning to be here?"

"I think he said a week or so. His wife arrives in Edinburgh tomorrow."

"Well, Douglas. I thank you for ringing. Sorry I can't help much. I hope to see you soon."

They said their good-byes. But without putting down the phone, Admiral MacLean instantly made another call, transatlantic to Washington, straight to the White House main switchboard.

"Would you connect me to Admiral Arnold Morgan, please."

"Certainly, sir. Who shall I say is calling?"

"MacLean. Admiral Iain MacLean in Scotland."

"Admiral Morgan's office . . ."

"May I speak to the admiral, please. This is Iain MacLean in Scotland."

"Morgan. Speak."

"Arnold, it's Iain."

"Hey, Iain, old buddy. How ya bin? Anything hot?"

"Hottest. He's here."

"Who? No. Jesus Christ. You at home?"

Morgan paused for a few seconds, gathering his thoughts . . . no secure line.

"When you say he's here, Iain, do you mean the he I think you mean? And do you mean he's in the country, in your house, or in your study?"

"The very one, Arnold. He's trying to find Laura. He turned up at her ex-husband's house this afternoon looking for her."

"JESUS CHRIST!"

"Look, Arnold. I have been fairly certain for some weeks now that he was in Scotland. Can you get hold of a chart of the North Atlantic, the eastern side?"

"Yeah, wait a minute." It took two. Then, "Got it. I am looking at it."

"Right. Get a pencil and mark with a cross the following positions . . . yes, that's it . . . two on 30 West, one on 53 North, 20 West . . . right . . . where the airliners went down. Right, now put a cross at 57.49 North, 09.40 West . . . that's it . . . now one at 08.35 West, same latitude. Now one at the port of Mallaig on the coast of Scotland opposite the southwest corner of the Isle of Skye."

The admiral then pointed out the progression of his thoughts—the lost fishing boat, the missing soldiers on St. Kilda, the Zodiac suddenly turning up in Mallaig. "I believe," he said, "that our man got off *Unseen* at 09.40 West, made his way to St. Kilda for petrol, then got to Mallaig. I have no idea what he is doing—but today a man turned up at my former son-in-law's house looking for Laura. The description fitted Adnam as I remember him. But he claimed to have met her in Cairo. And I know that she and Adnam once went there together. No one was supposed to know, and no one but he *could* have known. It was him all right, and he's on the loose here."

"Did he give an indication how long he was staying in Scotland?"

"No. But my idiot ex-son-in-law did tell him Laura was expected at the end of Easter, so I imagine he'll stay around here for a couple of weeks. But you could never be sure. For all I know he's going to get back on the submarine and hit something else . . . but I thought I'd better keep you up to speed."

"Iain, I don't need to tell you I'm delighted that you did call. I'm just wondering if there are any further checks we ought to make. Where are Bill and Laura now?"

"They're here, I think, for another five days."

"Let's get 'em the hell out. Back to Kansas. And I think I'd better get a general alert out to watch for Adnam at all airport entry points in the United States. I cannot imagine that he would come here, where he is most wanted as an international criminal. But, now he knows she has gone off with an American, he might try to get to her in the States. Wish we knew what name he was traveling under."

"Douglas—the ex–son-in-law—had a name but forgot it."

"Don't forget to congratulate him for me on that."

"I won't. Do you have a decent picture of Adnam for your checkpoints?"

"I'm not sure . . . but I think I can get one from David Gavron."

"Okay, Arnold. I won't keep you any longer. If you don't have any luck with the Mossad, we have a good picture of him when he was here . . . eighteen years ago, but it might help."

"Good. We'll talk later."

Commander Adnam drove north, his mind churning. Laura was coming to Scotland, but what good would that do him? She would be at MacLean's house, and the admiral would recognize him instantly. He could not keep the white mansion under surveillance, and she might only be there for a couple of days. No, if he wanted to talk to Laura, and her husband, the place to go, perhaps in the next week, was Kansas, their permanent home.

The United States of America was also, he believed, the only place to which he could go, the one country whose natural self-interest might just make him too valuable to kill, if he played his many high cards correctly. Because Benjamin Adnam was not merely the most wanted man in the world, he was also one of the most knowledgeable. He knew many Naval and military secrets of Israel, Iraq, and Iran. He understood their attitudes, hopes, and fears. With him, Benjamin Adnam, on its side, the United States would have a supreme, strategic asset. Just so long as he could convince them of this before they took him out.

He knew he had to go in at the highest possible level, and that might not be too simple. He had not a single contact in the U.S.A. Unless—and the thought struck him suddenly—Mr. Baldridge took him there. The man entrusted with running to ground the perpetrator of the *Thomas Jefferson* disaster would be a man in touch with the highest members of the current Republican administration in Washington.

The sheer simplicity of this trail to a new life struck Ben as so utterly convenient it must be impossible. But the logic was as straight as a line of longitude. If he could find Laura, he would find Baldridge, and if he found him, he might be able to swing some kind of a deal. Either way, the former U.S. Navy officer would most likely prefer to put the great Iraqi terrorist in front of some very senior people, rather than the local sheriff.

The main problem was, surely, how to get into the United States of America without being apprehended by the immigration authorities and swiftly handed over to the merciless agents of the CIA. He believed the straight London–New York, or London–Washington was very tight at the immigration desks. And he decided to find another, quieter route into the customs halls of the Great Satan.

As he drove back past the rolling hills of Lammermuir, Commander Adnam weighed up the factors that ranged against him: the fact that Lieutenant Commander Baldridge had spent time with the MacLeans meant they all knew who he was; he felt reasonably sure Douglas Anderson would have alerted the admiral that someone had been inquiring for Laura; knowing the mind of old MacLean, Ben was prepared for anything. *My Teacher will remain consistent, missing nothing, not then, not now.*

In Ben's view, he had to get out of Scotland and into another country without his British passport being freshly stamped. From there he would try to make his way unobtrusively into the United States. There was only one country from which he could pull off such a move . . . Ireland, because he would not need a passport to get in. Not from England or Scotland. If MacLean had alerted his American friends, they would be keeping a rigid watch on passengers coming in from London, Manchester, Edinburgh, or Glasgow. But perhaps not quite so stringently from Shannon.

Bill, Laura, and the girls arrived back from Edinburgh shortly after 1900. Laura had signed a stack of legal papers in her solicitor's office, and Bill had countersigned several as well. It was beginning to look as if she would be granted full custody and that Douglas would have the girls for vacations only. Admiral MacLean's powerful intervention with the judge had worked a miracle, and it seemed increasingly likely that they would ulti-

mately attend their new stepgrandmother's alma mater, Welles-
ley College, outside Boston, Massachusetts.

The admiral met the Range Rover as it drove in, with Laura at
the wheel. He told Mary and Flora to run along to the kitchen,
where their grandma and Angus had their supper ready. He then
suggested that Laura and Bill join him in the drawing room for a
drink before dinner because there was something he needed to
discuss.

They could both see the concern on his face, and they both
noticed he was silent as he poured three glasses of whiskey and
soda. The admiral wasted no time beating about the bush.

He mentioned that he hoped Bill liked the Scotch, a single
malt distilled locally, but that the subject he wanted to discuss
was very pressing.

"Ben Adnam showed up this afternoon at Douglas Anderson's
house," he said. "He was looking for Laura, who he apparently
thought was still in residence. Douglas called to let me know—
the description fitted, and he told Douglas that he and his wife
met you in Cairo . . . the Mena House Hotel actually . . . bit close
to the bone, eh?"

"God, Daddy. I didn't know even you knew that."

"Well, I didn't until about two years after the event. But I tend
to come stumbling along a bit behind the rest of the world.
Nonetheless, the Cairo clue was decisive. It had to be Ben."

"Correct. It had to be Ben. And you say he was looking for me?"

"According to Douglas, he was."

"But why?"

"Oh, it's hard to know really. But chaps in his line of country
lead very strange, lonely lives. And when they finish their various
projects, it's nearly impossible for them to return to anything
normal."

"Yes. I suppose so. Do you think I'm in any danger?"

"Possibly. I mean when a chap has already killed several thousand people, you don't quite know what his state of mind may
be. Especially if he's been fired, or, for some reason, feels
unwanted. All kinds of odd thoughts can pop into such a dis-

turbed mind. I mean, it's not completely beyond the realm of possibility that he might have gone to the house intending to kill Douglas and kidnap you. Let's face it, he might be planning to kill Bill right now, and kidnap you. Either way, we are going to be very careful indeed until he is caught. I've had a talk with Arnold Morgan, who is concerned for your safety. He thinks you should leave Scotland immediately and return to Kansas . . . that's the morning flight to Chicago tomorrow."

"You think it's that serious, Iain?" asked Bill.

"Actually, no. But you can't be too careful with this man. So it is serious enough for me to have changed your reservations, and organized a Navy car and escort to get you into the airport with the girls by 0900 tomorrow."

"Does Adnam know where we live in the States?" asked Laura.

"I don't think so. He did not, after all, even know you were not married to Douglas anymore. But I'd better bloody ask. I should have thought of that when he rang. Must be getting old."

"What's Admiral Morgan doing?"

"Stepping up security at all airport points of entry, looking for Adnam, in case he should try to enter the U.S.A. If I know Arnold, it'll be quiet but thorough. I just called him back. He's organizing a Navy helicopter to run you from Chicago to Kansas, and for the time being there'll probably be some military security at the ranch—firstly to protect you, secondly to catch this bastard. We now think there's no doubt he was somehow responsible for all three of those aircraft crashes."

"Do you think Ben might be planning to kill my husband, Daddy?" said Laura.

"Well, we have to work on the theory that he might be thinking along those lines. Dementia can easily enter the mind of a mass murderer . . . but I don't think so. Because there's an edge of hysteria in that type of thinking . . . murdering husbands in order to run off with their wives. Doesn't sound like Ben to me. He's too cold-hearted for that, too reasoned, too clever. In my view he may have wanted some kind of favor from you, but he might have turned very unpredictable if you had refused him help. None of us know where his professionalism ends and his madness begins.

"And we can take no chances. Commander Adnam must for the moment be treated as a rabid dog. Simply because he has been operating on an entirely different wavelength from most of the human race for a very long time. He may be unpredictable now in his actions. Maybe even irrational. But we do not want to assume anything. And the quicker we get you both home, with the girls, and under the personal protection of the President's national security advisor, the better I shall like it."

"Have you told Mummy anything?"

"No. And I see no reason to worry her unduly. You can leave that to me."

They finished their drinks, and Bill and Laura went upstairs briefly to change before dinner. They went into the bedroom that overlooked the loch and the ex–lieutenant commander was quite surprised at his wife's reaction. She threw her arms around him, and he could feel deep within her an uncontrolled trembling. "He really scares me, darling," she whispered. "There's something so absolutely terrible about him. And to think he's out there somewhere. He found Douglas, and he could find this place. My God, he's been here before. For all we know he's out there watching."

"Ben Adnam is not the kind of man to be scratching around in some field, watching a house like some kind of a pervert," said Bill. "That's not him at all. He operates to carefully drawn-up plans. I'd be surprised if he came anywhere near here. I mean, Jesus, your father knows him. So does your mother. This is the last place he'd show up."

"I suppose not. But if Daddy and Admiral Morgan are worried, then I ought not to take this lightly. I'll get Angus to start packing up the girls, and my things, while we're having dinner."

"Okay, I'll make my own arrangements. But I'll tell you one thing—I would not want to be searching for Ben here in Scotland because I'm guessing he's on his way out of here right now."

"Why?"

"Well, he now knows you don't live here. He has played that card and lost. He has a Mr. Anderson who knows him, and he'll know that a routine phone call from Douglas either to your father, or to you, will stir up a hornet's nest. In my view he'll be on his way out of the country instantly."

"But where will he go?"

"That's the question, Laura. Maybe back to the Middle East. Maybe to Switzerland to collect money. Maybe South Africa, which he mentioned. But not, I suspect, to America, where he's the most wanted man in history, having just murdered our saintly Vice President, and a half dozen politicians."

The farewell dinner at the home of Admiral MacLean was deeply traditional. Annie served Scottish smoked salmon from the Tay, with a bottle of Olivier Leflaive's superb 1995 Puligny-Montrachet. The thick Angus steak fillets were accompanied by a 1990 Châteaux Lafleur from Pomerol.

"It took a bit of courage to risk steak on a world expert beef-producing rancher from the Great Plains," said the admiral. "I hope we've measured up."

"Fantastic," said Bill, swallowing luxuriously. "And this is probably the best glass of wine I've ever had."

"Yes. They all got it right in Bordeaux in 1990," agreed Sir Iain. "Took five years for it to come right again. By the way, I'm really sorry you all have to go tomorrow, but I think it's for the best."

"I agree. And now we got Morgan on the case, I would not be surprised if they picked our man up very soon."

"I hope before he does any more damage, Bill. I still have it in my mind he somehow took out those two soldiers on St. Kilda. Otherwise, they'd still be there. Imagine that, two lives for a few gallons of fuel. I suppose that's how you become, in his business . . . in the end."

"Guess so. And of course those guys always believe they are in the military, and to kill a couple of enemy soldiers hardly counts."

"Well, he knows you were in uniform, doesn't he?" said Laura.

"I hope he doesn't think you hardly count. Because if he does, I'll hunt him down, and I'll kill him in cold blood."

Laura Baldridge did not have even a semblance of a smile on her face when she spoke those words. Her parents both looked quite shocked.

BEN GUESSED THAT ADMIRAL MACLEAN KNEW THE identity of the mysterious visitor to Galashiels Manor that day. That meant there would be some kind of security in place, and that he should avoid airports in big cities, like Edinburgh, Glasgow, London, and Dublin. His every instinct told him to stay rural, in his unobtrusive car, to travel alone and be seen by as few people as possible.

He studied his little map throughout an excellent dinner of cold smoked trout and roast pheasant. And by 2230 there was no doubt in his mind. The way to Ireland was through West Wales to Fishguard, and into the Emerald Isle via the quiet southeastern Irish port of Rosslare.

He would not need a passport, if he was British, and he resolved to spend some time with a travel agent before leaving Scotland. The one right around the corner from the hotel, in the High Street, he decided, would do just fine.

He slept late the following morning, read the papers downstairs in the hotel lounge, and drank three cups of coffee. Then he checked out, left his bag with the concierge, and asked for his car to be brought up at midday.

Inside the travel agent's he studied a pile of brochures dealing with travel to and from southern Ireland. He bought himself a single ferry ticket from Fishguard to Rosslare, sailing at 0315. He intended to stay in Ireland for a few days organizing a B-2 multiple entry business visa into the United States, and then to leave via Shannon for Boston, the two closest points on the North Atlantic route.

There was one excellent reason for this. The U.S. immigration authorities have a fully staffed operation in Shannon for checking passengers straight into the U.S.A. Thus passengers go through the American desk in the sprawling Irish airport, their passports are stamped, and the Shannon–Boston flight becomes essentially an internal journey, as if it were Chicago–Boston.

Ben Adnam reasoned he had ten times the chance of slipping through the U.S. desk in Shannon, with a return ticket and a new American business visa, than he ever would in an American port of entry, where the CIA might already be watching every incoming passenger from Scotland and England.

He arranged for and prepaid his Dublin hotel, which he understood was just a short walk from the U.S. Embassy in Ballsbridge. He strolled back to the Balmoral to pick up the Audi, phoned his bank and told them to send his credit cards overnight to the Berkeley Court in Dublin. Then he tipped the doorman, slung his bag on the rear seat, and set off south out of Edinburgh, heading for the long, lonely A7 road that runs down through Galashiels and Hawick, 100 miles to the English border city of Carlisle.

It took him a couple of hours to get to the grim Scottish wool town of Hawick, trailing a line of three trucks in pouring rain for most of the way. Thankfully, Ben watched them peel off in the middle of the town, and was pleased to hit the open road, south of the great cashmere center.

It had stopped raining, and Ben was able to drive fast down the almost empty winding highway as it followed the tortuous course of the Teviot River for mile after mile, through spectacular border valleys and hillsides. South of Langholm, the A7 picks up a new river, the Esk, and again follows its twisting course through the stark border mountains, the grazing fields for cattle and sheep, deep green below the level of the road.

At Longtown the Esk swung away to the west to its long estuary at the head of the Solway Firth. Ben pressed on south for 6 more miles, before joining the fast, wide M6 motorway, which would take him almost 200 miles into the Midlands of England, the backbone of his journey.

He reached Penrith, the gateway to the Lake District by 1530, the Audi now cruising at 80 mph east of the long rolling hills that guard the high waters of Ullswater, Haweswater, and Lake Windermere. He refueled at the Tebay service station, picked up a sandwich and a cup of coffee, and drove on south.

From there the M6 skirts the waters of Morecambe Bay opposite Barrow-in-Furness, recent home of HMS *Unseen.* But the relentless southward progress of the freeway offers no opportunity for sightseeing, and Commander Adnam just kept driving through northwest England, past Lancaster, past Blackpool, Preston, Southport, and Wigan, past Warrington, Manchester, and Liverpool, past Newcastle-under-Lyme, Stoke-on-Trent, and Stafford. All the way to Birmingham, where the M6 splits into the M5, the fast road to Bristol, 90 miles farther south. Ben made it by 2100, crossing the great span of the Severn Road Bridge into Wales twelve minutes later.

He paid the toll and pulled into the Magor service station where he refueled, parked, and found a quiet table near the window for supper. He glanced at the plates of the other diners, careful to select food that would not fix his presence in the memory of the waitress. Bewildered, as always, by the eating habits of the English public, he ordered fish, chips, fried eggs, and baked beans like just about everyone else.

With Bill, Laura, and the two girls now well on their way to Chicago, Admiral MacLean and his wife had a peaceful, elegant dinner of grilled river trout, new potatoes and spinach, accompanied by a bottle of Sancerre. They each had a glass of port at the table while they finished the final edges of a full Stilton cheese.

Lady MacLean retired early, but the admiral was very restless. Finally having moved over to his study to read the newspaper in front of the dying log fire, he stood up and dialed the number for Galashiels Manor, which was answered by the butler.

"Oh, good evening, Beresford. This is Iain MacLean. I wonder, is either Mr. or Mrs. Anderson still about?"

"Oh, good evening, sir. I'm very sorry, but they've gone to France for a few days. But Mr. Douglas will be in London next Tuesday, I believe."

"Oh, that's a pity. Still it wasn't important. Just a quick question I wanted to ask him . . . will he be staying at the club?"

"I believe so. But I could not be sure."

"Very well, Beresford . . . thank you anyway . . . good-night to you."

There was a very worried frown on the face of the admiral as he made his way to bed.

Ben Adnam checked his watch. It was almost 2230 as he pulled onto the slip road from the service station and entered the M4, which runs almost the entire length of the South Wales coastline, way beyond Swansea and into West Wales. It was pitch-dark, and beginning to rain again. The motorway was busy, and the Iraqi found the Welsh-language road signs highly confusing. It was a language that made Arabic look simple, and he stuck to the middle traffic lane, not going too fast, watching the big white lettering that signified he was passing Newport, then Cardiff, then Pontypridd, then Bridgend, Maesteg, Port Talbot, Neath, and Swansea. This was the old industrial heartland of Wales, the southern end of the steep valleys, from which they once mined the finest shipping coal in the world, Welsh anthracite.

Ben Adnam had learned much about rugby football while studying in Scotland, and he recognized the names of those towns and mining villages, almost every one of them with a place in the folklore of world rugby. Beyond Swansea he watched for the signs for Llanelli, the West Wales mining town reputed to have produced more world-class stand-off-halves than all the rest of the British Isles put together.

Ben had watched the Royal Navy play rugby several times and remembered meeting three of the massive tight forwards, all of them submariners, all of them from Wales. Irrationally he wondered if they might be living near there, and whether their lives were less lonely than his. He would have given anything for a conversation, with anyone, even with Able Seaman Berwyn James, the big, cheerful 1988 Navy forward from Neath, whose neck measured 24 inches, whose forehead was nonexistent, and whose IQ was only a shade higher than plant life. Ben remembered Berwyn well.

The M4 ended to the northeast of Llanelli, and he sped down toward Carmarthen, slashing through the rain at 75 mph He'd have liked to cruise at 90 mph plus, which the car would have managed with ease, but this he did not do. Leaving an inevitable trail, which must be uncovered within a month, maximum, was one thing; getting arrested by the police for speeding on that night would have been crass.

The roads were deserted down there in West Wales, and now the signposts were beginning to pinpoint the port of Fishguard. Ben raced past St. Clears at midnight, still heading due west. At 0030 he turned north at Haverfordwest, for the last 15 miles of the 560-mile journey. Cardigan Bay and the ferry port lay due north before him. The fish and chips lay heavily upon the stomach of a weary Commander Adnam.

The traffic, even in the small hours of the morning, grew much heavier, and Ben found himself in a convoy of trucks all trundling up the narrow, winding road between fields of unseen sheep, to the ferry. Those last 15 miles took him forty-five minutes, and the rain and spray made it impossible even to contemplate overtaking. The line of traffic meandered through ghostly quiet Welsh villages like Tangiers, Treffgarne, Wolf's Castle, Letterstone, Newbridge, and Scleddau before the trucks turned left along the country road that bypasses Fishguard and leads down to the port.

Ben decided to go straight into the middle of Fishguard and look for a gas station, and at 0115 he drove into the desolate town square and began to follow the signs to the ferry. He was surprised at the height of the town, which seemed to be perched on a giant headland above the cold waters of the Irish Sea. He could see the harbor lights, way below, down a steep, curving road, and out to the west of the harbor wall he could see the huge lighted bulk of Stena Line's massive car ferry, the *Beatrix Königin*.

There was one gas station open along the wharf, and he filled up the Audi to ensure that when he arrived in early-morning Ireland he had a full tank for his journey. Then he made his way to the ferry, showing his ticket at the kiosk and collecting his boarding pass. The route took him through the customs shed, and a police officer stepped from the shadows and beckoned him to stop. Ben did so and wound down the window.

"British passport, sir?"

"Yes."

"Straight ahead." The officer did not ask to see it.

Outside the ferry-port shop a line of half a dozen early arrivals waited in their cars. But Ben got out and went inside to buy a cup of coffee. But he did not linger. He tipped in a couple of small packets of sugar, stirred, and returned to the car, where he sat and sipped, and contemplated the world that lay ahead of him.

At 0210 they called the drivers forward, and, in a long, snaking line, they made their way a half mile along the dock, with the harbor waters to their right and the streetlights of Fishguard high above to the east. Seamen ordered each of the 27 cars into a designated place, deep in the hold, balancing the weight on the port and starboard sides of the nine-deck-high ferry.

The trucks boarded ten minutes later, by which time Commander Adnam had made his way, following the signs, to the executive lounge up on deck eight. It was warm, deserted, and comfortably furnished. He sank into an armchair and drifted off to sleep before he even had time to remove his coat. He did not stir until the ship was under way, reversing out of its berth, then moving forward, to the north, around the long harbor wall into the easterly waters of the Irish Sea. Subconsciously Ben could tell they were just leaving. He could easily pick up the changing beats of the engines, as the *Beatrix* settled onto her westerly course, running through the sheltered waters, with the rugged, towering cliffs of the wave-washed coast of Pembrokeshire a mile off their port beam.

He sensed that the rain had stopped, and he walked out onto the windswept upper deck, staring over the rail at the strange moonlit coast of Wales, feeling again the old familiar rise of the ocean beneath the keel. He had already studied the route on a map he bought in Scotland, and he leaned forward on the rail, peering into the darkness for the lights of perhaps another ship.

But that part of the Irish Sea was deserted. And he waited alone, watching for the flashing light of the lighthouse on Strumble Head, which he knew was the end of the land, the point where the giant ferry would enter the rough open waters of St. George's Channel, where the great Atlantic swells roll in from the southwest.

He felt the waters before he saw the light, felt the angle of the ship increase just slightly as she pitched slowly forward, then rose with the wave, hesitating, then angling down, the foam white spray slashing out wide from a great curl of water off her bow, as she drove her way westward.

Now he could see the light on Strumble Head. Four short flashes, then a seven-second gap, and four more.

The commander walked back inside, feeling, curiously less tense than he had all day. The feeling of the open sea, where he was used to being the acknowledged master, had a calming effect. It was, he understood, home. The only home he had ever had. And, possibly, the only home he ever would have.

He sank back into the armchair and closed his eyes. Sleep engulfed him immediately and when he next awakened it was a little after 0530. Along the wide companionway at the end of his lounge was a big right-angled ship's bar that served alcohol, soft drinks, coffee, and biscuits. A few passengers were scattered, mostly sleeping, at various tables. No one was speaking.

Ben strolled along and sat at one of the high barstools, and ordered black coffee and a small package of shortbread, which had a Scottish tartan emblem on the wrapper. He remembered them from Faslane, and he munched them slowly, thinking again of his days training with the young British submarine officers at Commanding Officers' Qualifying, all of them under the all-seeing but fair eye of the young Commander MacLean, the Teacher. He smiled despite himself, despite everything.

Five more minutes went by before his daydreams were interrupted. An unshaven young man, no more than nineteen, dressed in a cheap, black-leather jacket, jeans, and running shoes, came and sat one stool away and ordered a pint of Guinness. Except that he just said, "stout," pronouncing it "stoht," but the barmen knew what he meant, and, slowly allowing the creamy head to settle, placed the glass of jet-black Irish nectar before the young man.

"Good lock," he said, then, turning to Ben, added, "Will you have a jar?"

It was not until that moment that Ben realized the young man was extremely drunk, and would be a bit lucky to make it to the car deck, never mind the road out of Rosslare. "No, I won't thank you," he said. "It's a bit early for me."

"Early? Jaysus, I t'ought it was a bit late."

Ben smiled. The Irishman was a handsome kid, with black hair and a narrow, serious face. He smoked deeply, taking inward breaths that pulled the tobacco fumes deep into his lungs. Ben judged him to be a man with a lot on his mind, despite his youth.

"Now what might you be doing on this terrible bloody ship at this time of the night?" he asked with that disarming frankness of the Irish.

"I missed the earlier ferry, and had to hang around Fishguard," replied Ben. "How about yourself?"

"I've been attending to a bit of business. Late finish. Had to get down from London on the train. Takes for bloody ever. You change at Swansea."

"Should have got a plane," said Ben.

"Not worth it. Costs a fortune. And I live in the south. Water-ford. When I'm there, like. Someone'll pick me up at Rosslare."

Ben had not had a harmless chat like this for literally years. It was against everything he knew. Idle chatter. Loose thoughts. Leaving an impression upon another person. Matters that are for-bidden to men who work undercover. He had to stop himself spilling out any salient facts, and he told himself to tell only lies. That way he would be more or less immune to indiscretion.

"What line of country are you in?" asked the Irishman, but before Ben could answer, he leaned over, quite suddenly, thrust out his hand, and added, "Paul, Paul O'Rourke. You don't live in Ireland, do you?"

Ben shook his hand, and said, "Ben Arnold. I'm from South Africa. Mining's my trade."

"Oh, roight. I'm in politics meself." And he drew deeply on his Guinness.

There was silence between the two for almost a minute, then: "Now then. You, sir, I can see, are a man of the world, so you'll not mind my mentioning this. But there's been a lot of trouble in your country over the years . . . you know, the poor native blacks striving to get some of their lands back from the whites who took it away. What do you think about that? About a people who were savagely dispossessed, and are trying to assert themselves, to get a dacent loife?"

"Well," said Ben, "we don't quite look at it like that. You see there were almost no indigenous blacks in South Africa when the whites settled it. They have arrived from the north over the years, trying to get work in a country built from scratch by Euro-peans, Dutch, and English."

"Jaysus. I t'ought the buggers had always been there."

"Paul. You thought wrong. South Africa was always white."

"Is that why it's so bloody rich, unlike the rest of Africa?"

"I suppose so. All its industry was built by the whites. My own corporation employs thousands of black workers . . . but I'm not saying we didn't make mistakes. We did. We should have provided more opportunity, years ago, to bring the best of the blacks onside, into white society. Apartheid was never right. And it turned out to be very damaging."

"I read a lot about it in college," said Paul. "Before I dropped out. I was doing a degree in world politics at UCD. But I missed the part about the blacks being itinerant workers, visitors to the white state."

"Well, that's what they were. And that's how most of 'em got there in the beginning. Streaming over the borders from places like Nyasaland. And, of course, many more immigrants came over from India."

Again there was silence. Then Ben asked quietly, "And what was it, Paul, that was so pressing in your life, you decided to abandon your university degree?"

"Oh, not much really. I just got caught up in politics."

"What kind of politics? You thinking of running for office sometime?"

"Perhaps sometime I might. But I got into the more practical end of t'ings."

Ben sensed that Paul O'Rourke was about to say more than he should. He watched the boy, smoking nervously, gulping great swallows of Guinness, his hand trembling slightly.

"My people are Republicans," he said. "We've always believed in a united Ireland. My dad was an activist, so was his dad, and his."

"What kind of activists?"

"Well my great-grandda came to Dublin with Michael Collins from Cork in 1916. He died in the fighting at the post office; the English gunned him down. My great-uncle was wounded, but he got away. He was with the group that retreated to Bolands Bakery. I t'ink about it every time I go to Dublin . . . they never had a chance against the English artillery . . . but Jaysus, the lads were brave on that day . . ."

Ben nodded, said nothing. "My whole family is Sinn Fein," said Paul. "It just means in Gaelic, 'Ourselves Alone.' We want Ireland to be one country, with no English here at all . . . that's why there's the IRA . . . that's our military wing."

"I know," said Ben. "Are you a member?"

Paul was silent. Shook his head, then said, "Let's just say I'm sympathetic."

He gulped some more Guinness. "I don't think you'd understand, Mr. Arnold," he said. "We're from different sides of the tracks. You belong to the rich ruling class. I belong to an organization struggling to break free from a cruel and wicked oppressor."

"You think the English are cruel and wicked?"

"We've nothing to thank them for. They raped and pillaged this country for centuries. And by whose right? The right of their bloody guns, that was their only right. But you'll find that England's first colony is destined to be her last. And it may be our guns that finally put an end to it."

"When did you first get interested?"

"I t'ink I must have been about thirteen. There was a little party at my granddad's house down in Schull on the Cork coast, and some English people were invited back from the pub. I remember they were all singing songs, each person taking turns . . . and when it came time for the Englishmen to sing, they did 'It's a Long Way to Tipperary.'

"At that moment my grandfather went berserk. I was standing right next to him, and he smashed the flat of his hand down on the table, and shouted, 'I'LL NOT HAVE THAT SONG SUNG IN THIS HOUSE . . . I'LL NOT HAVE IT! DAMN YOU . . . DAMN YOU TO HELL!'

"Well, the party broke up right then. Everybody left, but the next day I asked my dad what had upset Grandpa so much. And he told me that song was an English marching song, and the Black and Tans used to sing it."

"Who were the Black and Tans?"

"Oh, that was the English occupying army in southern Ireland, before we drove them out. My dad told me they had shot grandpa's mother and both of his sisters when he was about fourteen years old down in Cork. He said Grandpa stood on the doorstep of the house, covered in the blood of his own dead mother, and he could hear the English soldiers marching off, singing 'It's a Long Way to Tipperary.'"

"Does that mean you want to become a terrorist, a soldier of the IRA?"

"I'm not sure. And I can't explain it. You'd never understand what it feels like to be prepared to die for something you believe in, Mr. Arnold. I hate the English, and so does everyone in my family. They'll never be forgiven for what they've done in Ireland. And it's up to just a few us to get the last of them out of here. And the best way to do that is to bomb their bloody country until they leave."

"I should be careful, Paul. It's a lonely life you're considering. Hunted by the English, the feeling that every man's hand is turned against you. And the constant danger of high explosives and British Army marksmen. Worse yet, you end up not daring to trust anyone."

"I've already studied the subject pretty carefully, Mr. Arnold. I'm brave enough, and I think I might be smart enough . . . I have helped in a few missions, but never in a real way. My father commanded an IRA squad, but he never told us what he had done."

"Well, I think you should take it very carefully, Paul. It's a big step. And you'll have a lot of time to regret it if it turns out to be wrong for you. Also, you might get killed."

"Ah, you say that because you can't quite understand what it's like to believe in something and be ready to die for it. It burns right into you, the hatred, and the feeling of being right, being justified. All terrorists are men apart."

"So they are, Paul," replied Benjamin Adnam. "So they are."

1600. Wednesday, April 5.
Office of the National Security Advisor.
The White House.

Admiral Arnold Morgan was on the secure line to CIA Headquarters, Langley, Virginia.

"Yeah. Well, I don't know where the hell he is, or where the hell he's headed. But I know he was in Scotland last night. And I have no real reason to suspect he may be trying to get into the United States, but he might be . . .

"Yup. I got a picture the Mossad wired for us. Yup, it's on the way over. Excellent quality . . . well, I'd be inclined to get some guys into the main airports of entry from Britain . . . flights from the northern airports, Edinburgh, Glasgow, Manchester . . . just because they're nearer to his last-known position. Yeah, but we'd better watch flights in from London Heathrow and Gatwick. Just in case he heads south first. The Brits are watching all those airports.

"Yeah . . . I've sent a physical description. Remember he's a Navy officer . . . usually looks smart. And he speaks with a very correct British accent. But remember, too, he's no fool and is unlikely to oblige us by looking like a gentleman . . . right . . . right . . . well, I guess New York, Washington. Possibly Philly . . . possibly Boston . . . maybe Chicago.

"Yeah, alert immigration, the passport guys, for anyone fitting this description . . . okay . . . no I'm not sure . . . for all I know he might be going back to the Middle East . . . but he could be coming here . . . yeah, possibly Kansas . . . right . . . no . . . I don't think he'll have a visa . . . he won't have time to get one. No . . . he'd forge a passport . . . but the modern U.S. visas are almost impossible to forge accurately . . . I'd guess he wouldn't dare to try that . . . too big a risk. If he does try to enter the U.S.A., we're looking for a guy with no visa, traveling just as a visitor, for less than ninety days.

"Okay . . . let's stay right on top of this . . . remember, this bastard is the worst terrorist in history . . . and, if he comes here, I want the fucker caught. So does the President . . . so don't screw it up."

Arnold Morgan banged the phone down, yelled for coffee. Then yelled for Kathy O'Brien. Three seconds later, when the door didn't open, he strode toward it, snapping, "Dumb-ass broad!" just as the President of the United States entered, chuckling, "Who me?"

"Christ, no, sir. Sorry. It's just that bastard Adnam really gets to me. I've no proof, and it's a real long shot, but he just could be on his way here."

"Hell, that we don't need."

"Not if he plans to blow up another warship or a goddamned aircraft, or even an airport . . . he really spooks me . . . I just think the fucker might do anything."

"I agree. If your theories are right, we might be in big trouble. Yet again. We gotta catch him, Arnold. What's the latest?"

"Well, I just heard from Iain MacLean in Scotland."

"Oh, yeah. What does he think?"

"Well, it was Iain who alerted us Adnam was in Scotland. He thinks he's trying to locate Laura."

"Jesus. You don't think he's trying to kill Bill, do you?"

"Hell. I hadn't even thought about that. But when a guy's killed as many people as Adnam, you don't know what he might do."

"We must find him, Arnold. Christ, he's just killed the Vice President, among others. You got Langley on the case?"

"Absolutely."

"Keep it tight, Arnie. We gotta get him. Use as many people as it takes. How 'bout Kansas? You think we need guys out there?"

"Not yet. He probably won't even come here. I don't want to alert the entire country. Right now I thought we'd just get a tight grip on all the incoming flights from Britain. We got good photos, good description . . . we might just have a shot at picking him up."

"Okay, buddy. I'll leave it to you. Keep me informed."

"Aye, sir."

Back on the *Beatrix Königin*, Ben Adnam had said good-bye to Paul O'Rourke and was making his way down to the car deck. They had passed the flashing light to port that marks the channel into Rosslare, and now they were reversing, beyond the harbor wall into their berth on the Irish quayside. It seemed to take forever, but at 0710 on Thursday, April 6, Commander Adnam drove the rented Audi out onto Irish soil, making his way through the dock to the kiosk in front of the customs shed, which was completely empty.

All of the cars from Fishguard just drove straight through, following the "Exit" signs, up the steep hill and out onto the main road to Wexford and, one hundred miles north, Dublin. It was growing light, and Ben could see he was driving over a long, flat coastal plain, with only few houses and little traffic. Thankfully, the fleet of heavy trucks from Wales was far behind, and Ben settled down to drive fast, along the wide, lonely Irish roads, up to Enniscorthy, then to Ferns, and Gorey and Arklow, through the Wicklow Mountains to the southern suburbs of Ireland's capital city. Given the speed of the first part of the journey, he anticipated it would take him two hours. But as he proceeded north up the east coast, the rain began again, and the traffic grew heavier.

By the time he reached the outskirts of Dublin he was in a rainswept morning rush hour, bumper to bumper all along the N11. Up ahead he could see his landmark, the towering aerial tower of Ireland's television station RTE. He was looking for the next right after that, at the Catholic church, and he finally turned into exclusive Anglesea Road at 1000.

Five minutes later he crossed Ballsbridge, swung right again into Shelbourne Road, and ran down to the Berkeley Court Hotel in Lansdowne Road. He drove straight in to the rear parking lot, checked in, and crashed onto his bed on the fourth floor. Exhausted. Hungry. Too tired to eat. But safe. And anonymous. In a new country, in which he had never even shown his passport.

Ben slept until midday, picked up the credit cards he had asked to be sent, and left the hotel in a light drizzle. He took a cab to Grafton Street and used his Royal Bank of Scotland credit card to purchase a raincoat and an umbrella in Brown Thomas, Dublin's excellent answer to Harrods and Saks Fifth Avenue.

Then he walked back up to St. Stephen's Green and picked up a cab from the rank. He had it drive him to the great round building of the American Embassy, which sat in its own grounds behind a black wrought-iron fence at the end of Shelbourne Road. He walked through the small gateway, crossed the cobbled courtyard, and walked up the slope to the visa office. He explained to the duty guard that he wanted to pick up application forms for a B-2 multiple-entry business visa.

The guard waved him through the security X-Ray, and at the counter the Iraqi terrorist was the only person seeking help. The Irish lady was polite and genial. She gave him the form and pointed out that he must fill it in carefully, explaining that he must pay the fee into the Irish Bank along the road and collect a receipt. He must also provide a photograph, passport size, and acquire a letter from his bank or employer to confirm that he was a man of substance and would not be entering America in order to receive welfare payments.

Ben thanked her and took a cab back into the center of the city to the office of the Royal Bank of Scotland. There he explained to the manager that he was an established client of the bank, at the Helensburgh Branch, and would like a letter explaining that he had run an account from there for many years, and that it currently contained a sum well in excess of £50,000 sterling.

The manager said he would fax the request to Helensburgh immediately and that Mr. Arnold should call in tomorrow morning and collect the letter of recommendation, which would be marked for the attention of the U.S. Embassy.

Ben picked up another cab and returned to the Berkeley Court, retired to his room, and worked on the long, detailed form, electing to use his British passport, into which the coveted B-2 businessman's visa would be stamped, valid for ten years. The notice in the embassy specified it would take two working days. But the lady behind the counter had explained that if he could return the completed documents the following morning, Friday, they would almost certainly be ready after two-thirty on Monday.

Faced with a lonely weekend in rainy Dublin, the commander walked slowly back to the hotel, reflecting that when he entered the United States, officials would not be looking for a man with a visa. He suspected that at Shannon Airport, they might not be looking for anyone at all.

But first he must ensure the visa was issued. And back in his room he checked every question carefully, ensuring that all of his answers were those of a stable, well-to-do Scottish businessman from Helensburgh . . . Ben Arnold, mining executive, with interests in the South African coal and copper fields. Currently residing in Dublin for six months. He had invented his address, invented his profession, invented his corporation, invented his name, forged his British passport. The only truthful document he would present to the American consular officials would be the letter from the Royal Bank of Scotland.

The next morning, when he picked it up from their Dublin office, it was precisely as he wished—*"To the American Embassy, Dublin. This letter is to confirm that Mr. Benjamin Arnold has had an account with us for more than 15 years, and that his current balance shows in excess of £50,000 sterling."*

He walked to a supermarket, where he had four passport pictures taken in a machine. Then he stopped at the Bank of Ireland and paid the fee of sixteen Irish pounds, collected his receipt, and strolled the quarter mile to the embassy. There he placed his British passport, his signed application form, his photograph, his letter from the bank, and his receipt for the fee, into a brown envelope, and deposited it in the polished wooden drop box. As he left, the American security guard smiled, and said, "After two-thirty Monday, sir. It should be ready."

He then walked over the wide bridge that spans the River Dodder, toward the headquarters of the Dublin Horse Show. He crossed the road to a shopfront marked Ballsbridge Travel and went inside, requesting a business-class round-trip ticket from Shannon Airport to Boston on Tuesday, April 11. He was looked after by a trim, pretty Irish girl named Loraine, who checked and accepted his credit card, and booked him on the Aer Lingus Flight that leaves Dublin at midday and arrives in Shannon twenty-five minutes later. But Ben planned to drive from Dublin, leaving early in the morning and making Shannon by 1100 to check in and arrange for the return of the car to Helensburgh.

He took his ticket and walked back to the hotel. After a light lunch, he traveled by taxi out to the suburb of Clonskeagh, to spend the afternoon at the Islamic Center and Mosque, a truly stunning religious and educational establishment founded in 1996 by Sheikh Hamdan al Maktoum of Dubai, for the 7,000 Muslims who live in southern Ireland, mostly in Dublin.

The mosque is a magnificent stone building set beneath a vast copper dome. It holds 1,200 people, and Ben Adnam answered the Friday evening call to prayer, kneeling with several hundred of the faithful, begging his God for guidance and forgiveness.

All through that long weekend, the commander went back and forth from the Berkeley Hotel to Clonskeagh. He read the Koran in the library, attended prayers throughout the day and early evening, and on the Sunday afternoon succeeded in gaining a private audience with the imam, a wise and considerate Egyptian sheikh whose teachings had brought comfort to many of his countrymen.

Ben Adnam was unable to reveal the truth about himself, but he tried to explain his predicament, that he had worked for governments, carrying out their bidding, because he believed in their motives. He spoke of his betrayal by those governments, and tried to define his current dilemma, and his desperate need to attain the understanding of Allah.

The imam was thoughtful and encouraging. But as with all Sunni Muslims, he stressed that Benjamin must continue to nurture his own faith, that no one could help him with that. But he assured the weeping ex–Naval commander who knelt before him, that Allah was merciful, that in his opinion, Allah would not damn him, and that in the fullness of time, subject to prayer and devotion to the teachings of the Prophet, Benjamin would one day be welcomed into the arms of his God.

By night Ben slept only fitfully in his luxurious bedroom in the Berkeley, fighting off the persistent nightmares, awakening in the dark, and spending hours trying to reconcile the brute instincts of the international terrorist with his devout and pious yearnings to be closer to the kingdom of Allah. The result was always confusion, as the images before his mind, images of death and destruction, raced on with the glancing speed of all disconnected dreams.

At 1430 on Monday he walked into the consular section of the United States Embassy. The guard waved him through the security X-Ray, and told him to go straight to window three. The lady behind the glass recognized him, and smiled. "Mr. Arnold?" Ben nodded, and she handed him an envelope in which was placed his passport and the letter from the bank.

Outside in the courtyard, beneath the great fluttering Stars and Stripes at the top of the flagstaff, he stood for a moment and opened it. Taking up one full page in his passport was the official entry visa to the United States of America, printed along the ornate lines of a banknote, in green and pink with a wide yellow band across the great Seal of the United States. Ben's photograph, name, and passport number faced the predatory head of the American bald eagle. The visa, the B1/B2, was good for ten years, until the year 2016.

The next morning, Tuesday, April 11, six days after Arnold Morgan had alerted all entry points, Ben Adnam checked out of the Berkeley at first light and headed southeast out of Dublin, bound for Shannon Airport and then Boston.

He took the city route, running along Dublin's Grand Canal to the Crumlin Road, and heading southwest through County Kildare, past Naas, and on to Roscrea and Limerick. The road was empty throughout the second half of the 130-mile journey, and Ben pulled easily into the precincts of Shannon Airport at 1050.

He parked the car in the long-term parking lot, took the key, and paid a fee of £28 that was good until late Saturday. He taped the key to a piece of card he had brought with him, and placed it, with the parking-lot ticket, and a check for £1,000, drawn on his Helensburgh account, in an envelope addressed to the garage in Helensburgh. The accompanying note read:

"Sorry about the distance. But I had to go to Ireland. The Audi is in the long-term car park at Shannon Airport, bay M39. I expect you'll have to send someone over, so I enclose

enough money to cover expenses and inconvenience. Thanks for cooperating—Ben Arnold."

He was sure the Scots mechanic would be irked at the prospect of the journey, but equally sure the extra cash bonus would undoubtedly make it worthwhile.

He purchased two Irish airmail stamps inside the airport and mailed the envelope from the box next to Hertz rental desk. It was, he thought, an easy way to avoid a mysterious missing Audi in Helensburgh, which ultimately turned up at Shannon airport, the same Audi that perhaps Douglas and Natalie Anderson had seen parked in their drive. His 1,000-pound payment to the garage might prove beyond measure in covering his trail for the next couple of weeks.

He checked his bag at the Aer Lingus desk and was directed to the business-class lounge. At 1300 he was escorted by a stewardess down to the line of United States immigration desks, through which the transit Dublin passengers had already passed. There were only 23 passengers beginning their journey in Shannon, only two of them business-class: Ben and a vacationing travel agent.

Ben moved through first. The uniformed officer was American, and he leafed through the passport, without looking up. "Purpose of trip?"

"Business. Meetings in Boston first, then New York."

"Ah-hah. How long do you intend to stay in the United States, sir?"

"Maybe three weeks. No longer."

The immigration official looked through a large black book with clipped-in computerized pages. Found nothing, took his stamp, and confirmed in Ben's passport that he had entered the United States on April 11, 2006, at the port of Shannon. In the space that was marked "Admitted until . . ." the officer just wrote "*B-2.*"

Essentially, the world's most wanted man was in the U.S.A. "Enjoy your flight, sir," said the immigration man, handing him a customs form to be completed for Logan Airport, Boston.

Same time. 1300. Tuesday, April 11.
Loch Fyne, Scotland.

Admiral MacLean was still trying to track down Douglas Anderson. He called Boodle's in St. James's and was irritated to find
the Scottish banker was not in residence at his club, and further-
more was not expected. Then he called the Connaught Hotel,
then Brown's, with the same lack of success.

Finally, supposing that Douglas and Natalie had stayed
another couple of nights in France, he called Galashiels Manor
again, and asked Beresford to please ensure that Mr. Anderson
called him on a matter of some urgency. Whatever time of the
day or night he received the message.

1400. April 11.
International Arrivals Building. Logan Airport.

Dick Saunders, the CIA chief at the Boston Station, had been on
duty since 0700. In company with two field officers, Joe Pecce
and Fred Corcoran, they had been combing passenger lists for
incoming flights from Great Britain, especially from Scotland.

Right now was the busy time, with big jets trundling in off the
Atlantic every five minutes until 1500: the morning flights from
Europe. There were British Airways 747's from Glasgow, Edin-
burgh, and Heathrow. There was American Airlines from
Heathrow, and a North Western out of Gatwick. Virgin had one
from Manchester. They were all interspersed with flights from
Paris, Frankfurt, Madrid, Rome, and one from Dublin-Shannon.

The three CIA observers would have their work cut out for
them, as they had had every day for the past week, since the
order had come down from on high to try to find a traveling Arab
named Ben Adnam, probably from Scotland, maybe from England, no visa, probably under an assumed name. But each agent
had a good photograph, and they placed themselves strategically
in the glassed kiosks with the immigration staff, making it well-
nigh impossible for *anyone* to walk through who looked *any-*

thing like the dark-skinned foreigner in Naval uniform in the photographs held by the CIA men.

Their problem was that Ben Adnam did not have to pass through the glass kiosks into the United States. He had already completed that formality back in southern Ireland. Aer Lingus Flight 005 came in on time, 1410, and, along with the rest of the passengers, Ben walked straight through the immigration area, down the steps to the customs hall, and collected his bag.

Admiral Morgan's last line of defense was field officer Pecce, who was down in the hall, standing at one of the main-desk search centers watching the incoming passengers from Edinburgh. Ben Adnam walked right by him, 25 feet to his left, with his head held high, bag in hand. He handed his customs form to the officer, who initialed it, and told him to present it at the door. Half a minute later he was out in the arrivals hall, taking his time, walking with his bag toward the exit.

He turned left outside the international building and headed for Terminal D, where he hoped to locate either American or United Airlines. He decided on a direct route to Kansas, and bought a ticket, no longer terribly concerned about leaving a trail.

Thus, with just one change at Kansas City, Missouri, he flew straight to Wichita, and from there took a small local flight down to Dodge City, the old Wild West town in the southwest of Kansas, a 45-mile car ride from the big ranch run by Bill and Laura Baldridge. Arnold Morgan had not yet ordered a team in to protect Bill's household.

Ben arrived at Dodge City airport on the evening of Thursday, April 13. He rented a dark red Ford Taurus station wagon for a week, using his Scottish credit card and his British license. And he was checked into a new hotel out near the airport before 2100.

At that precise time Bill and Laura were sitting alone beside the big fire in the living room, half-watching the television news, half-reading magazines. They had dined earlier that evening with both of Laura's daughters and Bill's mother, and they were each sipping a glass of port, a habit imported from the home of Iain MacLean in faraway Scotland.

Bill's days were busy in the early spring, keeping track of the herds, which his brother Ray tended on a day-to-day basis, and watching the beef markets, deciding when to buy and what to sell. The warmer weather sometimes came late to the High Plains, and it was often frosty and still freezing cold when the master of the great Baldridge spread marched out onto the frozen ground before first light. Sometimes he was so tired in the evenings he could have crashed into bed at seven o'clock, but he treasured the peaceful later hours with his beautiful Scottish wife, and they always stayed up until around eleven-thirty.

They had both talked to her father this evening, and he was unusually tense, explaining to them that he still thought it possible that Ben might try to get into the United States, despite Admiral Morgan's dragnet around the points of entry.

The veteran Royal Navy submariner begged Laura to be careful, and when he spoke to Bill he practically forbade him to allow her to be alone at any time of the day or night.

"I don't need to tell you how dangerous, or how mad he may be," said Admiral MacLean. "But I intend to ask Admiral Morgan to get some heavy security into the ranch within the next twenty-four hours. I simply do not consider it worth taking a chance."

By 2130 Ben Adnam had completed a study of a detailed map of the counties that surrounded Dodge City. And there, just west of Burdett, he noted in red letters the symbol "B/B," then, in parenthesis (Baldridge). It looked as if the main ranch buildings were right off Route 156, where the Pawnee River and Buckner Creek converged before winding down to the Arkansas River. The Scottish newspaper that had described Lt. Commander Baldridge as a farmer was right. Ben figured there were thousands and thousands of acres out there in the flat grazing land that straddles Pawnee County and Hodgeman County. "About twice the size of Baghdad," he murmured. "It could be hard to find the house, but you couldn't miss the land."

Ben, dressed in his dark track suit and soft, black running shoes, left the hotel, with his bag, at around 2145, driving fast out along Route 50 from Dodge City. He turned north up 283 to Jetmore, then east, 23 miles to Burdett, the little town that sits almost on the border of Pawnee County. He checked the road signs every few minutes. They stayed consistent. There were no turns. He was running dead straight along 156.

Ben drove through the little township of Hanston, which he guessed was his halfway point from Jetmore. He checked the reading on the speedometer and resolved to start slowing down and searching after 10 more miles.

Instinct more than navigational skill guided him, and approximately one and a half miles before he reached Burdett, he made a sharp right turn into the pitch darkness of a south-running country road. Way out to the left he could see lights, and as he came to a bridge he slowed and stopped, winding down the window, and hearing the unmissable sound of a flowing river not far below. *Too far. That's the Pawnee*, he thought, *in full flow at this time of the year after the winter snow, melting down from the Rockies. Like the Tigris at this time, back home. Different mountains, same sound.*

He reversed the car, swinging backward into a gateway and heading back to Route 156, where he took the next right turn, into an equally dark country road. But there were lights dead ahead now, floodlighting the great iron gates and archway of the B/B Ranch. He could see that the entrance was closed, and that the post-and-rail fence ran right up to stone pillars guarding the entrance. He caught sight of two carved wooden longhorn steers on each post but kept going, driving at 50 mph past the B-Bar-B, where Laura lived.

He kept driving for a mile. The fence had ended, and Ben could see a clump of trees on the edge of the frosty road. He pulled off onto the grass shoulder and parked behind the trees. Then he pulled on an extra sweater, leather gloves, and a dark woolen hat. He checked that his big desert knife was firm in the back of his leather belt and, after locking the car, began to jog back to the main gates of the Baldridge Ranch.

It took him eight minutes, but before he got there, he cleared the fence and made his way cross-country toward the distant lights. The moon was up, and very bright, and he wanted to come into the ranch compound behind the buildings, with the shadows in front of him, rather then behind. This was difficult, and he realized he would have to circle the ranch buildings in order to achieve it, but he did not want the clear, pale light of the moon in his face.

He reached the buildings and flattened himself behind them. Inside he heard a sharp thud on the wall, followed by another. *Stables*, he thought. *And the horses have heard me.*

He began his circle around to the main house, creeping silently through the shadows with the soft, light steps of the Bedouin. He hoped to God no one would see or hear him, because he was not intending to kill anyone, except perhaps Baldridge, if he had to. If it became obvious that Laura would leave with him. There was a corner of Ben's brain that was not functioning in any way accurately, or even rationally. And the master of all these Kansas acres was right in that corner.

Ben made his way softly into a place where he could observe the house, with his back to the moon. His plan was to take Bill and Laura by surprise. There was no point walking up to the door and trying to be reasonable. For all he knew this damned cowboy would gun him down in cold blood. No, he had to take control. And to do that, he must put them both on the defensive. That way he could see how the land lay.

He planned to enter the house through an upstairs window in which the curtain was not drawn, the sure sign of an empty guest room. The trouble was none of them were drawn right now, unlike the downstairs windows. And he could see light crossing the hallways between the rooms. He had seen one room on the farside of the house with a drawn curtain but no light, and he guessed, correctly, that Laura's daughters might be asleep in there.

He waited for a half hour, until 2345. The curtains were being drawn by a figure he could not identify, and he made his move. He slipped quietly across the yard and climbed easily onto the roof of an outbuilding. From there he swung up onto a second-floor balcony, then went higher, to a gently sloping roof leading up to the one window with still no drawn curtain.

Crouching on the sill, he inserted his knife between the sliding panes and flicked the catch back. At that exact moment Laura Baldridge walked in, switched on the light, and saw the big blade of the desert knife jutting upward in the gap. She also saw a dark figure in the light, and she yelled at the top of her lungs . . . "BILL! BILL! COME QUICK! THERE'S SOMEONE BREAKING IN!"

Outside on the roof, Ben Adnam nearly died of shock. Two dogs were barking furiously below. He ducked low and moved higher, the only way he could go, up toward the chimneys.

Bill Baldridge unlocked the gun cupboard in the back hall, selected a D.M. Lefever 9FE shotgun, and snapped two 16-gauge shells into it, cramming four more into his jacket pocket. He took the stairs two at a time and found Laura pressed against the passage wall outside the spare room.

"Right in there," she whispered. "I saw Adnam close against the window with a big knife . . . it was Ben . . . I know it was him . . . if we don't kill him, he'll kill us. Jesus, wait here, I'm going for a shotgun. This is bloody ridiculous."

"I guess there are advantages in marrying a girl whose family trade is war," he smiled. "She doesn't lose her nerve that easy."

At the same time Laura was going to get a shotgun, it was 0600 of the next day in Scotland and Douglas Anderson was awakening in Waverley Railway Station, in a sleeping car, on the overnight express from London. The red light on his cellular phone was flashing, and he pressed the button for his recorded messages. There was just one. The familiar voice of Beresford informed him that Admiral MacLean wished to speak to him on a matter of the utmost urgency, and would he call him at whatever time of the day or night.

Douglas was usually somewhat unnerved by the admiral, and he did precisely as he was asked, awakening Sir Iain on a misty Scottish morning just before dawn.

But the great submariner awakened fast, asked his former son-in-law to hold for one moment, pulled on his dressing gown, and hurried downstairs to his study.

"I say, Iain, I'm awfully sorry about the time . . . but the message did say . . ."

"Don't worry about that, Douglas. I'm delighted you made it . . . and I did want to ask you something very important, and I wish I had been able to reach you before . . . you remember that South African chap who called to see Laura the other day . . . did he, by any chance, ask where Laura lives now? I don't mean just America . . . he didn't ask for her address, did he?"

"Yes, he did. He said his own wife would very much like to send her a Christmas card, just to show they had tried to make contact in Scotland . . . I wrote it down, in full, on a piece of paper for him. It seemed a reasonable request."

Admiral MacLean's heart missed a beat. But he steadied himself while Douglas went on, calmly, "The ranch in Pawnee County, Kansas, correct? I remember it . . . sounds like something out of the Wild West."

"Yes . . . so it does. Thank you, Douglas. I'm sorry to have been a bother." And with a pounding heart, Admiral MacLean replaced the receiver. "Fuck," he said, uncharacteristically. Then he picked up the phone again and placed a call to Admiral Arnold Morgan's office in the White House, where it just after 0100.

The main switchboard patched him through to Kathy O'Brien's house immediately, and the national security advisor awakened instantly.

"Iain . . . hi. This has got to be important."

"It is. In the last few minutes I found out that Adnam is almost certainly on his way to the Baldridge Ranch. He's walking around with their complete address and zip code in his pocket. That's what he went to Anderson's house for . . . Arnold, trust me. He's on his way . . . My God, he's capable of blowing the house up."

"Holy Topeka!" grated the admiral, slipping into Kansas mode. "Leave it with me, pal. I'll have a team of heavies in there inside two hours."

He rang off, called the CIA duty officer, and told him to put him through to Frank Reidel, the Agency's chief military liaison man. They connected in less than sixty seconds, and the admiral wasted no time with explanations. Just told Frank to get a half dozen heavily armed hard men by helicopter to the Baldridge Ranch in Pawnee County, Kansas, IMMEDIATELY. He told them they knew the way in the control room at McConnell Air Force Base, Wichita. No, he did not care if they used civilians, agents, U.S. Marines, Navy SEALs, or King Kong. Just so long as they moved fast . . . who are they looking for? . . . an escaped Arab terrorist, Benjamin Adnam, Commander Benjamin Adnam. Certainly armed. Extremely dangerous. Preemptive action if necessary. But try to keep him alive."

Then Arnold Morgan called Bill Baldridge and waited with mounting concern while the phone rang and rang before an answering machine picked up and requested that he leave a message.

It was just a few minutes after midnight back in Kansas, and Laura was heading downstairs at breakneck speed to the gun cupboard in search of the shotgun, left to her by her grandmother, the countess of Jedburgh. Bill Baldridge went into the small office next to his bedroom and spent five minutes adjusting the zones on the burglar alarms, activating the entire downstairs area, but only one part of the upstairs system.

He positioned himself on the main landing, in the shadows near the big fireplace along the corridor from his old bedroom. If Adnam was to enter the house, he would have to come through one of two rooms on the second floor, or else the alarms would go off, floodlighting the house, alerting every ranch worker and the local police.

Bill believed Laura. It had to be Ben, and his plan of action was clear. If the Iraqi came through either of those bedroom doors onto the landing, he would gun him down like a prairie dog, no questions asked. If he tried to gain entry through the downstairs doors or windows, the alarm system would surely frighten him off.

However the five minutes he had taken resetting the zones was critical. Out on the roof, Ben Adnam had been scared, but not unnerved, by being spotted. And like a good submarine commander, he elected to press home his attack while the enemy was in disarray. He moved from the chimneys, back down the roof, and opened the window where he had prised open the catch.

Laura, in her haste, had not relocked it, and Adnam climbed through, crossed the room, and turned out the light, positioning himself behind the door of the empty third-floor spare room. It was Bill he wanted, because that way everything else would fall into place when Laura could see clearly who the master was.

Ben stood breathing hard after his exertions, gathering his thoughts, trying to work out what he wanted most, Laura, or access to the United States national security chief. The problem was confusing him. He knew he wanted Laura more than anything he had ever wanted. But he sensed that was his heart. His brain was still a small voice in the background, telling him, whispering *If you kill Bill Baldridge, you'll probably have to kill Laura . . . you'll never get out of this state, never mind this country, alive . . . they'll hunt you down and send you to the chair . . . don't be a fool . . . negotiate with Baldridge . . . because that way may lie sanctuary, and a life . . .*

And yet . . . he longed for Laura. The memory of her touch and her laughter, and their love for each other, was as vivid that night as it had ever been. Ben Adnam would have cut off his right arm to have her just once more. And at 0004 he stepped through the doorway into the upstairs corridor, his desert knife clutched in his right hand.

One floor below him, Bill leaned against the wall, his rifle cocked, watching the two doors along the southern corridor. Ben saw him first, the glint of the barrels of the Lefever, which was not so much an advantage as a clarification. The Iraqi's task was plain, he had to descend thirteen steps without being heard, at which point Bill Baldridge was his.

Downstairs he heard Laura yell, "Where do you keep the shells for this damned thing . . . ?" Bill, standing not fifteen feet below Commander Adnam, shouted back "Cupboard by the back stairs . . . top shelf . . . right-hand side . . . leather box . . ."

Ben took three steps downward while Lieutenant Commander and Mrs. Baldridge communicated. And he pressed himself against the wall deep into the shadows of the upper staircase of the big, heavily timbered ranch house. He pressed on down three more steps. Bill took a pace forward, then another, peering down over the balustrade to the first floor. Then he stepped back into his original position.

Ben Adnam was just 7 feet away now, and suddenly, as if emerging from the dark tunnel of his own self-pity, all of his old sense of cold-blooded reason came flooding back. He wasn't going to kill Baldridge. But he pounced noiselessly, with a menace that was guided by cool intent. And Lt. Commander Bill Baldridge felt the cold steel of the Iraqi's wide desert knife pressed hard against the left-hand side of his throat.

"Good evening, Lieutenant Commander," said a British voice. "I don't need to tell you it would take me less than five-thousandths of a second to sever your jugular, do I?"

Bill Baldridge said nothing.

"But, actually, I do not intend to do that. Now, walk carefully and place your gun on that chair."

They both moved four paces across the hall, close to the corridor that Bill had been guarding. He put the loaded shotgun down.

"Excellent," replied Adnam. And, with a move that absolutely astonished Bill, he removed his big desert knife from Bill's throat and placed it on the chair also, right next to the Lefever.

"There," said Ben Adnam. "I have not, of course, come to kill you. I have come to claim your attention. Because I want to bargain for my life . . . I believe you know who I am, and I should like to think we can now talk on equal terms."

As it turned out, that might have been possible twenty seconds earlier. But it was no longer possible. Because suddenly, jammed hard against the base of Commander Adnam's skull, were the two cold rings of steel of the 29-inch barrels of a loaded 12-bore Purdey sporting gun that had once belonged to the Ninth Earl of Jedburgh.

"Hello, Ben," said the soft voice he had traveled across the world to hear. "If you keep very still, I may not blow your head off. But if my husband tells me to do so, I shall not hesitate. I expect I'll be given the Congressional Medal for my marksmanship."

Ben Adnam froze. But he kept his composure. "Hello, Laura," he said. "What a nice surprise. Are you sure you know how to use that thing?"

Bill Baldridge, whose childhood heroes had been local men like Wyatt Earp, Bat Masterson, the Dalton brothers, and Wild Bill Hickok, was amazed by the coolness of the conversation between the Scottish heiress and the Arab assassin.

He was, for a few seconds, speechless. Then he heard Laura say, "Ben, both my grandfather and I could hit a high pheasant flying downwind at 50 mph with this particular gun. I assure you, I am even better with a closer target." And she shoved both barrels a little harder into the dark curly hair at the base of the skull of her former lover.

Bill, like the commander, by now believed she might actually do it. And he stepped forward to confiscate the knife and reclaim his own gun from the chair. But he took the greatest care to stay well clear of the front of Adnam's face, just in case his wife got carried away.

Then he spoke for the first time. "Commander Adnam," he said, "step through that door over there, turn left, and face the wall with your hands on your head. If he makes one move, Laura, kill him. Or I will."

Ben walked forward slowly, Laura's magnificent shotgun, bearing Purdey's classic rose-and-scroll pattern engraving, still rammed against his head. Inside the office, Bill searched him carefully, warning Laura, "This man is lethal . . . he could kill the pair of us with his bare hands in under twenty seconds . . . keep that ole Purdey rock solid against his brain, and keep your finger on the trigger . . . twitching."

"Don't even think about the mess you'll make," said Laura to Ben. "I was going to have this carpet changed anyway, and the room's being redecorated next month."

Bill couldn't help smiling, but the deadly nature of the game kept him focused. He moved behind his desk, keeping his own gun trained on Adnam, who was still standing, pressed against the wall. Bill held the weapon straight with one hand and pressed a button on the telephone with the other.

Then he picked up the receiver. "Ray . . . hi . . . yeah, sorry it's so late . . . but we got a big problem right here . . . I want you to come over right now, dressed and armed . . . your shotgun . . . and some rope . . . round up McGaughey, and Razor . . . and make it quick."

He turned off the burglar alarms, walked around, and stood next to Laura. No one spoke, no one moved for eight minutes, until, with a crash of the front door, the big, prairie-hard Ray Baldridge came clumping in, accompanied by the veteran herd manager, Skip McGaughey, and the ranch hand and groom, Razor Macey.

"Up here, guys!" yelled Bill. They heard the three men climb the stairs, walking along to the light in the office. Ray came in first, holding a shotgun and a lariat. McGaughey had a six-shooter in his belt, as did Razor.

"Hey, little brother, you got a visitor?"

"He's a bit more than that . . . this is the bastard that killed Jack, sank the *Jefferson*, and God knows what else. Make him secure, willya, treat him like a steer. . . ."

The very mention of Bill and Ray's brother, Captain Jack Baldridge, who had been Group Operations Officer in the lost U.S. aircraft carrier, four years previously, galvanized the Kansan cowboys.

Ray eased Laura away, took Ben by the back of the neck, kicked his feet from under him, and dropped expertly down on one knee, his other shin rammed into Commander Adnam's throat as he lay prostrate.

Ray wrapped the rope tight around the Iraqi's wrists behind his back, looped it around and through, and did the same to Ben's ankles. Houdini himself would have been there for life. "He ain't goin' nowheres," said Ray. "You want me to put a hot branding iron to him?"

"Not yet," said Bill. "Depends a lot on how he behaves. Can you put him in that chair? I wanna talk to him."

They manhandled Ben upward and sat him down, facing Bill. Laura stayed behind the chair, as if trying to avoid gazing upon the man she had once loved.

"What do you want, Ben Adnam?" said Bill. "What the hell do you want?"

Ben smiled. "I want you to get me in front of the President's highest national security officer. I have much to say, and much to sell."

"Are you kidding?" replied Bill. "They'll put you in front of a firing squad in about twenty minutes. After the crimes you have committed. Not just against the U.S. But against humanity."

"Maybe they will. But perhaps not. Do you know of anyone else who knows as much as I do—and who has also deliberately placed himself in your power?"

Bill Baldridge looked pensive. "No, offhand, I guess I don't."

And he picked up the telephone again and dialed the number of the main switchboard in the White House, where it was not yet 2:00 A.M. on the morning of Friday, April 14.

Everyone in the room heard Bill's terse request. "Hello . . . this is Lieutenant Commander Bill Baldridge in Kansas . . . please connect me right now to the President's national security advisor wherever he is . . . yes . . . correct . . . Admiral Morgan . . . Admiral Arnold Morgan . . ."

None of them noted the narrow smile on the face of Commander Adnam as the White House operator prepared to awaken the admiral for the second time that night.

E VERY SEAT WAS OCCUPIED IN THE SLEEK U.S. AIR
Force C20 Gulfstream 4 as it raced at 450 knots above southern Illinois toward the Missouri border. Admiral Arnold Morgan
was next to Deputy Director of Central Intelligence Stephen
Hart. Opposite them sat Frank Reidel, the associate director of
Central Intelligence in charge of military support, the link man
between Langley and the U.S. Joint Command.

Next to Reidel, was the Secret Service agent with the communications system connected directly to the Oval Office. Behind
them were two other armed Secret Service agents, plus an armed
U.S. Marine staff sergeant with his corporal. The Gulfstream
seated only eight.

They flew to the north of St. Louis and picked up the mean-
dering Missouri River as it swerved through Jefferson City. At
1003, two hours out of Andrews Air Force Base, Maryland, they
cleared the eastern border of the state of Kansas, flying 30,000
feet above the old cavalry outpost of Fort Scott.

Twenty minutes later, they began their descent, sliding swiftly down out of gray clouds that scattered cold, spring showers over the eerie rolling contours of the Flint Hills, the last remaining expanse of tallgrass prairie in the United States. Arnold Morgan was tired. He'd been awake half the night, ordering hit squads, canceling hit squads, talking to Iain, and Bill, even Laura, ensuring that the Iraqi prisoner was tightly bound, was under the heavy guard of three armed Kansan cowboys, supervised by a former lieutenant commander on his own intelligence staff.

He stared out of the window on the starboard side of the aircraft, gazing at the geographic phenomenon below, 6 million acres of bluestem grass, rising and falling in jagged, uneven granite hills, none of them more than 300 feet high, right across the otherwise clean, flat, billiard table of central Kansas—north–south—from the Nebraska border 200 miles to the state of Oklahoma. A good steer gains two pounds a day grazing down there. That bluestem is the finest nutritional pasture for raising beef cattle on earth.

The Gulfstream continued to lose height, until it shrieked down across Butler County and headed into McConnell Air Force Base, on the outskirts of Wichita. It touched down on the runway at 1038. The door was opened immediately, and all eight of the men from Washington were escorted directly to a waiting Army helicopter, a howling Sikorsky Black Hawk, its rotors already running.

The transfer took less than four minutes. Seat belts were tightened, the door was slammed shut, and the helo clattered into the sky, flying to the south of the city before altering course to the northwest, low over the Great Plains for more than 100 miles, straight toward the southern border of Pawnee County. The pilot knew the way—he'd made the journey several times before, twice on Bill and Laura's wedding day.

Bill Baldridge spotted the Black Hawk over 10 miles out. He could see it, a faint dot low on the horizon, drawing ever nearer, moving over the prairie at 250 mph—a mile every fifteen seconds. Soon he could hear the steady thump-thump-thump of the rotors, and he could see the downward blast of air flatten the pasture as Arnold Morgan came barreling out of the sky to meet the terrorist he had loathed for so long.

Bill signaled the Black Hawk to land on the lawn to the west of the main house, 50 yards from the barn in which Ben Adnam was still securely tied like a steer in the Flint Hills Rodeo. He had been there for nine hours, guarded by two of Bill's ranch hands at all times. He'd slept on a pile of straw with a couple of horse blankets to keep out the cold. And during the night Ray Baldridge had stopped by specifically to let him know that for what he'd done to his brother Jack, Ben'd be "goddamned lucky to survive the night . . . someone's gonna kill you, that's for sure . . . might be my mommy, might be Bill . . . might be any of the guys around here . . . just don't count any on waking up, hear me?"

With that Ray had gone off to bed. He felt better for having gotten that off his chest, and he felt he had achieved his objective, that of frightening Ben Adnam to death. But that he had not done. The Iraqi commander knew he was safe until this Morgan character arrived, but after that . . . well, it would be a journey into the unknown. Ben Adnam knew that if the top national security man in the U.S.A. wanted him dead, then dead he would quickly be. But at least he knew he was safe, relatively, until midmorning.

He also heard the U.S. Army Black Hawk come shuddering into the B/B ranch. And he heard the shouts of the Americans out beyond the heavy wooden walls of the horse barn. Then he heard the sound of the rotors die away, and almost instantly there was a shaft of light through the small barn door, which was set into the huge dark red double doors that were opened only for tractors.

By then both of Ben's "jailers" were on their feet. The big, rangy Skip McGaughey, his gun leveled at the Iraqi's head, and young Razor Macey, toying with his six-shooter. First man through the door was Bill Baldridge, wearing a sheepskin rancher's coat, Stetson, and high boots with spurs. Right behind him came a smaller, thickset man wearing an expensive dark blue overcoat and a wide-brimmed dark brown trilby hat. Ben noticed his piercing blue eyes immediately, the craggy face, scowling expression. *That's Morgan*, he thought. *That's the national security chief, the man I'm looking for.*

Almost before the CIA chiefs and the Secret Servicemen were in the door, Adnam's assessment was confirmed.

"Is that the sonofabitch over there, Bill?"

"Yup, the one trussed up like a steer. The other two are my trusted herd manager, Skip McGaughey, and my groom, Razor Macey."

Admiral Morgan walked over to them immediately.

"Good to see you, men," he said. "Been keeping an eye on this bastard, have you?"

"Yessir. Most of the night."

"Did he behave himself?"

"Yessir. Never gave no trouble."

"Guess that makes a fucking change," growled Morgan. "If he steps outta line, shoot that sonofabitch right between the eyes, right?"

"Yessir."

By then the Marine staff sergeant was inside the door, blocking it completely. His corporal was patrolling outside. The Secret Servicemen formed a posse at the end of the line of open horse stalls. Ben was in the third one along, next to Bill's beloved Irish-bred bay hunter, Freddie. The two CIA men flanked Admiral Morgan as he made his way across the wide stone walkway toward the man who had sunk the *Thomas Jefferson*, blown both Concorde and Starstriker out of the sky, and obliterated *Air Force Three*, along with the Vice President of the United States and all of his staff.

Arnold Morgan gazed down at the arch terrorist, still tied by the ankles, his wrists behind his back.

"You've caused us a lot of trouble," he said carefully. "Too much for any one man to have created. And I've waited a long time to meet you . . . now gimme your correct name, rank, and country . . . ?"

"I'm Commander Benjamin Adnam, sir. Islamic Republic of Iraq."

"Is that an Iraqi Naval rank?"

"Nossir."

"What is it, then?"

"Israeli, sir."

"Did you serve in the Israeli Navy?"

"Yessir."

"Were you an Iraqi spy working undercover?"

"Yessir."

"And now?"

"Iraq, sir. I returned to work in Iraq."

"Iraqi Navy?"

"Nossir. Intelligence."

"Commander Adnam, did you sink the *Thomas Jefferson*?"

"Yessir."

"Did you also command a stolen Royal Navy submarine in the North Atlantic earlier this year?"

"Yessir."

"And did you cause that submarine to fire surface-to-air missiles that brought down three civilian aircraft?"

"Yessir."

"And was that submarine operating under the command of the Islamic Republic of Iraq?"

"Yessir."

"Then might I ask what the hell you are doing in the one country that wants you dead more than all the other countries in the world put together? And why have you made it so easy for us to nail you, right here?"

"Yessir. I have come here to bargain for my life. I have unique information that I believe has a value to you. You are correct to notice that I made my trail here relatively easy for you. But not so easy that you got here first. And I expect Mr. Baldridge will confirm I have shown no sign of being a serious threat to anyone. I am here to meet *you*, sir. Because you, of all people, will realize I am of more value to the United States of America if I'm breathing than if I'm not."

"And what gives you the idea I couldn't get any information I may need, out of you, for nothing?"

"You probably could get much of it from me—but not all of it.

Not without my conscious, willing cooperation. And perhaps we should talk about that. I would, however, ask you to remember that I have always been prepared to die for my country and my beliefs, sir. That is the one thing that has never changed. You'll either employ me, or I'll quite happily die with my secrets."

"I guess we'll see about that . . . Bill, can you take me to the house for a cup of coffee, before I get angry with this fucking towelhead?"

"Sure can, Admiral . . . how is it you like it?"

"Black, asshole . . . I mean former asshole . . . with buckshot." Both men laughed, and Bill put an arm around the wide shoulders of the great man as they headed for the house, accompanied by two Secret Servicemen.

Bill called back, "I'll send coffee out for everyone in a minute . . . guard that bastard . . . he's dangerous."

Inside the house Bill led the way to the big log fire in the hall, and suggested the two agents might like to go into the kitchen, where his wife Laura was, with the housekeeper Betty-Ann Jones. But at that moment Laura came into the hall, dressed in snappy Western garb, light brown suede tailored trousers, white shirt, and a dark green Indian-patterned waistcoat. She walked straight over to the admiral and kissed him on the cheek. "Arnold," she said. "How lovely to see you. Will you stay for a couple of days?"

The admiral slipped his arm around her waist. "Wouldn't you rather I got rid of the world's most dangerous man for you?" he said. "Can't stay this trip . . . we're outta here by five at the latest . . . will you invite me again?"

"Of course . . . did Bill tell you how we caught the Iraqi?"

"Not yet. I'm ready though."

The former submarine commander then recounted the adventure that had taken place the previous evening, culminating with the pivotal moment when Laura had rammed her grandfather's Purdey into the back of Adnam's head, with a view to blowing it off.

"She told him she expected to get the Congressional Medal of Honor for marksmanship," chuckled Bill.

"Damn right, she would," said the admiral. "And any other award she wanted. . . . What happened then . . . your boys just moved in and made him secure?"

"That's it. Tied him up good and tight. And kept him under guard till you guys showed up. What now? You taking him back?"

"Yup. I wanna have another little talk with him in a minute. He seems ready to tell us anything we want to know right now."

"That's how I'm reading it, Arnold. He told me last night he wanted a deal, and for his part he would disclose anything we wanted."

"And in return for that he wants his life."

"Guess so. But I'm getting the feeling he's been betrayed by Iraq. Otherwise, he woulda gone straight home to Baghdad and kept his head down. Also, I have to say that before Laura made her dramatic entry with the Purdey, Adnam had essentially turned over his weapon. He had placed the knife on the chair. He was unarmed. He was actually surrendering."

"Hmmmm. Bill, let's go through this thing the way we used to, back in Fort Meade. Let's think this through, item by item. I'm going to write down a list of the certain facts . . ." And with that, the admiral pulled out his little notebook and pen, and wrote down his prime thoughts thus:

1. ADNAM, DESPITE KNOWING THAT ALMOST ANY AMERICAN WOULD KILL HIM AS SOON AS LOOK AT HIM, HAS GIVEN HIMSELF UP, LAYING AN OBVIOUS TRAIL TO THE B-BAR-B IN THE PROCESS.

2. HE DOES NOT APPEAR PARTICULARLY REPENTANT.

3. HE PERHAPS DOES NOT GREATLY VALUE HIS LIFE.

4. HE MUST KNOW A GREAT DEAL ABOUT THE MIDDLE EAST—NOT ALL OF WHICH CAN BE OBTAINED WITHOUT HIS CONSCIOUS COOPERATION.

5. THE HISTORY, AND THE FINE DETAILS, WILL BE OF QUESTIONABLE VALUE. AGENTS TEND TO BE TOLD ONLY WHAT THEY NEED TO KNOW. BUT THIS ONE IS SPECIAL,

*HE WILL KNOW MORE THAN MOST, AND HIS REAL VALUE
IS LIKELY TO LIE IN THE FUTURE.*

6. *HE HAS OUTWITTED ME, ARNOLD MORGAN, EVERY INCH
OF THE WAY. CHRIST! I'VE JUST FUCKING WELL
REPORTED TO HIM! CAN I NOW USE HIM? IS THAT WHAT
HE IS REALLY OFFERING?*

7. *OR, IS THIS SOME OTHER TORTUOUS PLAN, INTENDED
SOMEHOW TO FUCK UP MY LIFE.*

8. *MIGHT THIS SONOFABITCH BE ON A SUICIDE MISSION TO
KILL THE PRESIDENT'S NATIONAL SECURITY ADVISOR?
(N.B. KEEP SAID SONOFABITCH MANACLED, AND
DISARMED, FOR NOW).*

"That, Bill, is how I see this equation at the moment. But one thing is immediately interesting . . . do you think he might tell us where to find that goddamned submarine?"

"Dunno. But I think he might. If, as I suspect, the Iraqis have dropped him."

Betty-Ann brought in the coffee, and the two former U.S. Navy colleagues sat companionably in big leather armchairs, which had Kanza Indian blankets thrown over them.

"Seems real strange, after all these years, to think Ben Adnam's out there in that barn, eh?" Admiral Morgan was thoughtful. He sipped the hot coffee, then he asked Bill, "Do you think we could, under any circumstances, use this bastard for our own purposes?"

"I think it would be a political impossibility. Christ, if the public ever found out precisely who he is, and even half of what he's done, we could end up with the first lynch mob of the twenty-first century."

"Hmmmm. I wonder what he knows? I wonder if he could put a finger on any of that germ-warfare activity that's been going on in Iraq. What about their agents in this country and the UK?"

"I'd guess he knows more than they think. Whether he tells us may depend on how badly they've pissed him off. My own view,

Arnold, is that his great value to us will be to give us a first-class psychological profile into the Iraqi mind-set."

"I agree. I am certain they've pissed him off real badly; otherwise, he could not possibly have contemplated coming here. Not even to see your beautiful wife, the thought of which has been scaring the life out of me these past two or three days."

Bill grinned. "Bet he never thought she'd nail him with the earl of Jedburgh's pheasant gun," he said, smiling.

"No. I wouldn't think that was any part of his plan . . . but the question is, do we think Adnam is just too risky, too treacherous, too big a liar even to consider doing business with? I must say, Bill, my immediate instinct is to kill him now. Although I could be persuaded to wring him out first, then eliminate him. But . . . *but* . . . *but* . . . *but* . . . I wonder whether the bastard isn't too valuable for that."

"Admiral, comfortable and pleasant though this is, let's get back out there, and you have another go at him. Let's ask him about the submarine . . . the part that was worrying my father-in-law . . . that and the fishing boat."

"Okay, old pal. Let's get out there and see how forthcoming he is."

It was raining lightly, and both men put on their hats for the short walk to the horse barn. Inside they found the two CIA chiefs working on a detailed report of the journey and the preliminary interrogation that had already taken place. Everyone had coffee, and Ben Adnam was still sitting on a bale of straw, tightly bound. There had been no further conversation since the admiral left, and no one was untying the Iraqi until Morgan gave the word which, understandably, he did not seem inclined to do.

The admiral moved in very quickly. "Commander Adnam, there is no submarine in the world equipped to fire short-range, accurate, surface-to-air missiles fast enough to bring down a supersonic aircraft. How and where did you convert HMS *Unseen* to possess this capability?"

"We did it at sea, out in the Atlantic near the equator in the doldrums."

"What kind of missile system?"

"Russian in origin. But we did not get it directly from them."

"Exactly what missile system, and who did you get it from?"

"That information is for sale only, sir. Not for money, you understand. For my life."

"How did you know it would work? Did you test it?"

"Yessir."

"Where?"

"Down in the marshes in the south of my country, east of Qal At Salih."

"How?"

"We test-fired four down there. Then once more in the Gulf on live aircraft. Pilotless, of course."

"Of course. Perish the thought you should kill someone." Admiral Morgan was trying unsuccessfully to avoid the sardonic.

"Did you hit it?"

"The test was successful, sir."

"How did you make such a huge alteration to a submarine out in the ocean?"

"It was not huge, sir. We simply modified the regular radar in the boat to locate the target at long range. We then had ample information to fire the missiles into a steady, oncoming target at a known cruising height. The actual launcher was bolted onto the deck, behind the fin." Adnam spoke his apparent secrets with the finesse of a man who knew his captors were going to find out anyway. And he added, as an apparent statement of good faith, "I could show you how to achieve something similar anytime, should you decide to work with me."

"Thank you, Commander." But the admiral turned to Bill, and speaking as if there was no one else in the barn, he exclaimed, "Can you believe this crap? I'm just getting a high-tech lesson in submarine weapons conversions from a fucking Marsh Arab . . . Jesus Christ."

Everyone laughed. Even Adnam. "Sir, I'm not from the marshes. My home is farther up the Tigris on the edge of the desert."

"Oh, Jesus, yes . . . so it is. The situation just fucking worsened . . . I'm being told how to put an advanced weapon onto an American nuclear boat by a fucking Bedouin."

Then he turned back to the Iraqi. "Right," he muttered. "Now listen, I know you're probably some fucking Von Braun of the Desert, but I wanna dead straight answer, right here . . . did you really lower that huge missile launcher over the side of a supply ship on a crane and manhandle it into position, seal it, and sail for the North Atlantic?"

"Yessir. Yes we did. In less than two days."

"Jesus Christ. Whose idea was it?"

"Mine, sir."

"How did you come up with such an invention?"

"It was not an invention, sir. The Israelis came up with it several years ago. And they had such a system made and tested. I merely stole a copy of the plans back in 1999 and adapted their ideas on a much grander scale."

"Was that HMS *Aeneas*?" asked the admiral, displaying as usual his encyclopedic memory for ships and previous conversations.

"Yessir. Yes it was."

"Hmmmm. And then, what . . . you just set off for the Atlantic and sat there on 30 West awaiting your prey? . . . And how did you get away? To Scotland?"

"Again, sir. That information is for sale. Also, I have no intention of informing you of anything that may incriminate me with another country."

"In your shoes, pal, I'd dispense with the formalities and start trying to make a few allies. Before I agree to anything I'm gonna need a lot of information. Give this bastard some coffee someone, while I confer with my former employee."

The admiral and Bill walked out of the barn together, leaving everyone else inside except the Marine corporal on guard outside the door.

"Okay," he said to the former lieutenant commander, "he's telling the truth so far, right? But I really want to know more about how Iraq got that Kilo in 2002, and how they got that Upholder out of Plymouth . . . Christ, to the best of my knowledge no one has ever stolen a submarine before. At least not from a major Naval power. And this man has stolen two!"

"Well, he said he would not tell us anything that would incriminate him outside the U.S. I suppose we can't blame him for that. I think we should try him on the technical problem of driving the submarine, training the men, and above all, what the Iraqis now plan . . . and where the hell they are taking *Unseen* right now."

"I'll try him on the theft, but he'll duck that, I'd guess. The real issue for me is, who's driving it now and where the hell is it?"

They walked back inside the barn, and Arnold Morgan returned immediately to the fray. "You wanna tell me how you got the submarine out of Plymouth?"

"I drove it, sir."

"How many crew did you have?"

"Forty, sir."

"All Iraqi?"

"Yessir."

"Who trained them to drive a British Upholder-Class diesel-electric?"

"I did, sir."

"Where?"

"Iraq, sir."

"How?"

"I used a full-scale model."

"Who built it?"

"We did, sir?"

"Based on what?"

"Plans, sir. Plans of the Upholder-Class."

"Where did they come from?"

"I presume England, sir. I was never told."

"What do you mean, you were never told? How did you know they were genuine?"

"Because I've driven an Upholder-Class boat, in Scotland, and I know they were."

"What about all the Brazilians on board? How did you get rid of them?"

"I won't incriminate myself with another nation, sir."

"How about the Royal Navy officers? What happened to them? Are they still alive?"

"I won't incriminate myself . . ."

"Yeah I know," interrupted the admiral. "How did you get into the exercise area, and out again, without being discovered for thirty-six hours?"

"I found the Orders in the CO's office, and I just kept sending in the right signals at the right time."

"*Jesus H. Christ!* This is unbelievable. How far from the area were you when you decided to miss the diving signal?"

"About 300 miles."

"And from there you just headed south, around South Africa and back to the Gulf of Iran?"

"Nossir."

"Whadya mean, NOSSIR? Did you take *Unseen* into the Gulf of Iran?"

"Nossir. The supply ship serviced us at sea in the Atlantic. I stayed with the submarine when the missile system was fitted."

"Very well . . ."

The admiral then conferred for the first time with Stephen Hart and Frank Reidel, discussing briefly the formalities of the arrest. Admiral Morgan suggested that since Adnam was plainly a seagoing military enemy of the United States, he should be taken into custody under the direct auspices of the U.S. Navy. The Central Intelligence Agency would then be entrusted to undertake the debriefing, working in conjunction with the U.S. Joint Command.

Frank Reidel thus became a key man in the operation, working as he did as the senior liaison between the CIA and the Pentagon. All three agreed that the matter ought properly to be kept under the tightest imaginable secrecy rules throughout. The admiral thought the interrogation should take place at the CIA Headquarters in Langley, Virginia, and that the commander from Iraq should thus be held securely during the entire time, under the normal procedures governing the arrest of an "enemy of the United States."

In point of fact, he would be held more securely than anyone had ever been held before. Guards from the U.S. Marines would supervise his captivity, night and day, though they would never be told who they were guarding. Accommodations would be organized by the Central Intelligence Agency.

The admiral then returned to Commander Adnam and addressed him formally. "Commander, on behalf of the government of the United States of America, I place you under arrest. Your crimes against this nation and against humanity are of a dimension to deny you any rights whatsoever, under any treaty ever entered into by the member nations of the UN. You will be held on an indefinite basis until it is decided whether you should stand trial or simply be made to disappear.

"At this stage we shall not be working with any other nation, but you may assume that Her Majesty's Government in London will be informed in due course that we are presently holding the Iraqi terrorist who destroyed Concorde Flight 001 in February. Do you understand me?"

"Yessir."

"Okay. Untie his hands and someone feed the fucker. Bread and coffee . . . don't want him to get too comfortable. Bill, I'm gonna beg Laura for a roast beef sandwich, then I'm gonna sit in the kitchen and annoy her for a half hour . . . maybe we can send down to the local town for lunch for these guys."

Bill Baldridge and Arnold Morgan returned to the house, both men heading for the kitchen, where the dark-haired daughter of Admiral Sir Iain MacLean was supervising the production of sandwiches. "Just us, Laura," said the admiral. "The rest of the crew are eating out . . . in the barn, that is . . . I don't expect you to feed half of Washington. In my view you've already done quite enough."

"Well, Admiral that's very kind of you. Now . . . why don't you and Bill go and sit by the fire in the hall. I'll bring lunch in, and perhaps I might join you for a while."

"That's the only reason I came out here," said the admiral. "I just wanted to have lunch with you . . . these other ruffians can take care of the business."

Laura laughed. "Will I assume Benjamin will not be joining us?"

"That'd be safe." Arnold Morgan chuckled. "By the way, have you called your father?"

"Yes. I did that at around two this morning . . . right after Ray and Skip tied Ben up and carried him over to the barn for the night. It was eight in the morning in Scotland, so it was not too bad."

"What did Iain say?"

"Well, he was just so relieved we were both safe—but he laughed like hell when I told him I'd captured Ben with Grandpa's shotgun . . . and he did ask me to pass on his best regards to you and Kathy."

"But not to Ben?"

"Certainly not to Ben." She laughed.

"Do you realize, Laura, your father and I called this one almost a year ago? We both somehow sensed that if *Unseen* had been stolen, there was only one person who could have done it—just one person in all of this world that audacious . . . that damned clever. And right now he's out in the barn."

"What will happen to him?"

"Now that is the question. Men like him, and there aren't many . . . I really mean spies like him, even without his operational brilliance . . . they rarely get executed. They just know too much. They are too useful alive."

"But surely a man who has committed such shocking crimes, brought that much grief to so many families . . . surely he must be executed."

"Not necessarily. What would execution achieve? Although Bill does not quite agree with me . . . yet." And he smiled at the proprietor of the B/B.

"He's just too darned notorious, Arnold. There'd be a public outcry if you were found to have him kept alive."

The admiral nodded, was silent for a moment, and took a sportsman-sized bite out of his roast beef sandwich. After stirring his coffee and taking a couple of swigs, he spoke. To Laura.

"What would *you* say to Ben if he said he would finger Saddam Hussein's old germ-warfare plants . . . the ones that could wipe out half the Middle East . . . or Europe . . . or the U.S. if you would spare his life? What *would* you say? I'm not saying he could. I'm just making the point. If we execute, we get nothing. If we wring him out, we might get a whole bunch of Christmas presents. What would you say?"

"I'd spare him. And take his damned knowledge and use him as long as he was useful. Not a day longer."

"And that, my dear, is why agents like him rarely get executed."

"There are no agents like him," said Bill. "He's completely different. He's a one-man demolition squad. And he's brought endless desolation to endless families."

"But there is one difference."

"What is it?"

"Hardly anyone knows who he is, or what he has done. The public do not even know the *Jefferson* was hit by a foreign terrorist. We've never admitted it. Neither do they know there was a lunatic sitting in the middle of the Atlantic knocking down passenger aircraft. Certainly not that same lunatic. In the collective minds of 250 million Americans, including the press, and all but a few of the military, no one knows the bastard even exists."

"True," said Bill Baldridge. "It just seems such a gigantic secret to keep under wraps . . . and if he somehow escaped and got out from under our control and did something dreadful . . . like blow up the Pentagon or something . . . then it would all come out . . . that this administration had been working under cover with the most evil terrorist in the history of the world, and now look what's happened? . . . You'd end up more reviled than Ben."

"That is indeed a risk. But I'd cope with my disgrace in the private knowledge that I had probably saved thousands of lives and that I had acted in accordance with my beliefs and my conscience."

"You're a big man, Arnold Morgan," said Laura. "Just don't let him get out of your control."

"Not I," said the admiral. "And when I'm done with him, I'll probably still have him eliminated."

"That's my man," said Bill. "And that's the way to look at it. Ben Adnam deserves nothing. Certainly not fairness. Ask the friends of Martin Beckman."

"The biggest problem with Ben," said the admiral, "is his unbelievable cleverness. When you think about it, he's been a couple of jumps ahead of everyone in all his projects . . . ahead of Israel . . . ahead of me . . . I suspect ahead of the Iraqis . . . certainly ahead of the U.S. Navy . . . and the Royal Navy . . . and, even now, of the entire U.S. government. Remember, he came here determined to get in front of people in high office to plead for his life . . . and he did it. First time. He was a couple of jumps in front of the immigration authorities . . . a couple of jumps ahead of the CIA guys . . . certainly a couple of jumps ahead of me, again."

"He wasn't always far in front of me," said Bill, quietly.

"No, he wasn't. But he was far enough. You did identify him. And basically caught him, or at least you caught his ship, but only with his help. You and Laura's dad, between you . . . the problem is, is he just too clever, and too devious for any of us to work with?"

"Probably," said Bill. "But you have to try and wring him out. And then decide, I guess, what further use he can be."

"That's about it," said the admiral. "And now I think we have to get him out of here." He rose from the armchair and put on his coat. He and Bill headed for the door, and twenty minutes later the Black Hawk was revving up and ready to go. All eight men were strapped in, Ben Adnam securely bound on the floor between the Marine staff sergeant and his corporal.

Bill and Laura watched them rise above the ranch and then above the prairie, and the sun came out briefly as the Army helicopter set a course southeast and clattered away toward Wichita, where the Gulfstream 4 awaited. About a dozen people in all of the

world knew that the United States was in control of the arch terrorist who had caused havoc above the North Atlantic.

0930. Three Days Later, Monday, April 17.
The Memorial Garden.
CIA Headquarters, Langley, Virginia.

Admiral Morgan, Stephen Hart, and Frank Reidel were seated
together on the wrought-iron garden bench in front of the pond.
It was one of the first warm spring mornings, the third day of the
relentless grilling of Ben Adnam by the CIA's professional inter-
rogators, some of whom had been flown in from the Middle East
to test, and retest the validity of the Iraqi Intelligence officer's
information. Thus far he had neither cracked, nor so far as they
could tell, lied to them in any way. But on the previous evening,
tired and battered by the endless questioning, the commander
had said something to Morgan which he plainly believed was a
critical card.

"Tomorrow, Admiral, I will give you something that will show
you once and for all that I am sincere in my desire to switch my
allegiance to your country. I have told you my price is my life,
but tomorrow I will write something out for you. Then you can
decide for yourself my usefulness to you."

The second night of interrogation had ended at 0230, long
after Admiral Morgan left. Commander Adnam was due to reap-
pear at 1015, and the admiral and the two CIA chiefs had agreed
to meet here, in this outdoor cradle of American patriotism and
loyalty, to discuss tactics.

It was peaceful in the garden. And the constant cascade of the
falling water broke the silence and muffled their words. Admiral
Morgan was reflective as he stared at the fieldstone wall around
the pond. It was inlaid with an almost obscure bronze plaque on
which were inscribed the words:

IN REMEMBRANCE OF THOSE WHOSE UNHERALDED
EFFORTS SERVED A GRATEFUL NATION.

Whenever he read them, a chill went through Arnold Morgan, and he thought again of the terrible dangers unknown American agents had faced over the years. And he wished, irrationally, that he could somehow meet them again, right there, and rise to his feet, and shake the hand of every last one of them. They were his kind of people. Hard, unsung heroes, concerned with the well-being of their country, never personal glory.

The three men chatted for twenty minutes, trying to decide what course of action to take. Whether to eliminate the mass murderer in their midst and say nothing, thus avoiding the awkward problems of having to alert the general public to the known danger they had been dealing with since 2002, and risking exposure as complete incompetents. Or to come clean, admit everything, and put the terrorist on trial for crimes that carried a compulsory death penalty. Finally, there was the enticing prospect of saying nothing, utilizing Adnam to carry out a few harrowing strikes against the Islamic Fundamentalist regimes of the Middle East.

All three options had support. But it was the latter one that intrigued them most.

At 1005 they returned to the main building and made their way up to the interrogation room. They all picked up coffee on the way, and were sitting down when Commander Adnam was escorted in by four Marine guards. He was handcuffed, but free to walk in the direction the guards indicated.

Once seated, the bracelets were removed while he placed his hands on the table in front of him, where there were pens and writing pads. He immediately began to write neatly at the top of one of the yellow pages. His message was short, and he requested it be torn out and handed to Admiral Morgan.

"201200APR06 18.55S, 52.20E. Refueling."

The admiral looked up sharply, and snapped, "*Unseen*?"

"Yessir."

"Indian Ocean, right? Whereabouts."

"Two hundred miles due east of Madagascar."

"No bullshit?"

"Nossir. This is another way to help convince you of my worth."

Admiral Morgan left the room and charged straight into the office of the deputy director. He grabbed the secure line and told the switchboard, "GET ME ADMIRAL MULLIGAN RIGHT NOW . . . EITHER IN THE PENTAGON OR WHEREVER HE MAY BE."

It took five minutes to locate the Chief of Naval Operations, who at the time was on board the cruiser *Arkansas* in the navy yards at Norfolk, Virginia. And the conversation was brief.

"You secure, Joe?"

"No."

"Go to SUBLANT right now and call me secure at Stephen Hart's office, Langley."

There were very few people those days who gave orders to Admiral Mulligan. None who spoke to him quite like that. But he and Morgan were old friends, and Joe Mulligan knew that was just Arnold's way. And he also knew the edge of gravity in the voice of the national security advisor when he heard it,

The admiral left *Arkansas* immediately, and a waiting Navy staff car took him on the short drive to the headquarters of SUBLANT. Reconnected with Arnold Morgan, he had to stay right on top of his game to keep up with the President's right-hand man, who he knew was now deep into the interrogation of Commander Adnam.

"Joe. I'm not saying we've cracked him. But he's just come up with something . . . the position of HMS *Unseen* at midday this Wednesday. She's gonna be in the Indian Ocean, which seems about right given she probably left the North Atlantic at the end of February . . . he has her position 18.55 South, 52.20 East. He says it's 200 miles due east of Madagascar. I'm just looking at a map now . . . it's 1,500 miles from DG . . . can we make it? . . . 1200 Thursday, April 20 . . . yeah . . . yeah . . . okay Joe, I'll leave it with you. Let's go . . . I'd prefer them alive . . . but I'll take 'em dead if necessary."

CRASH. The phone went down like a sledgehammer as Morgan marched resolutely back to the room where Ben Adnam was being systematically wrung out. Or at least a substantial group of people were trying to wring him out, the trouble being that Ben Adnam gave the impression of telling nothing that he did not want to tell.

Admiral Mulligan conferred quickly with COMSUBPAC, Vice Admiral Alan Cattee in Pearl Harbor, formally requesting that USS *Columbia* be released to Black Ops Control. They opened up a conference line to the Battle Group that operated around the 100,000-ton Nimitz-Class carrier *Ronald Reagan*, which was stationed off Diego Garcia for a few more hours. The vice admiral did the talking, on the secure line, and was patched through to Admiral Art Barry, who commanded the Group.

The former captain of the *Arkansas* checked his watch, which said almost 2000, nine hours ahead of Washington. He confirmed *Columbia*'s position, and said, "She's ready to go anywhere. To make that location by midday on Thursday, she'll need to clear DG by midnight. Leave it with me."

Commander Mike Krause and his crew had already had a long day, testing a new sonar fitting, out in the deep water south of the American Naval base. He and his XO, Lt. Commander Jerry Curran, had dined together on board, but some of the crew were ashore, on base but ashore.

The U.S. Navy is trained to move quickly. The entire crew was located, and was on board the submarine inside two hours. At 2345 Commander Krause signaled the engineers to answer bells. Up on the casing, still warm in the hot tropical night, the deck crew prepared to cast her off. The Officer of the Deck ordered, "*Let go all lines . . . pull off . . .*"

And the tugs began to haul the jet-black 7,000-ton Los Angeles-Class nuclear boat away from her jetty.

"Engines backing two-thirds . . . the ship is under way . . . ahead one-third . . ." The commands were succinct as always, spoken calmly from the bridge by Mike Krause, the tall New Englander from Vermont, who had previously served as the Executive Officer in *Columbia*.

And now the great bulk of the nuclear boat moved forward down the channel, running fair at 12 knots, out toward the open water of the Indian Ocean, which surrounds the island of Diego Garcia. America's sole operational Navy base in this part of the world is situated bang in the middle of absolutely nowhere, 1,000 miles south-southwest of the tip of the Indian subcontinent, 7 degrees south of the equator, 1,600 miles east of the Horn of Africa. It feels like the hot end of the earth, and the nights are dark and silent. It is not the favorite place of United States Navy personnel.

Commander Krause ordered a course of two-two-five, heading southwest away from the Chagos Archipelago, a group of towering underwater peaks that rise up from an ocean depth of 16,000 feet between DG and the southern end of the Carlsberg Ridge.

Navigation Officer Lieutenant Richard Farrington, who stood on the bridge with the captain, put the total distance to the search area at 1,587 miles. *Columbia*'s two nuclear-powered turbines, which generated 35,000 horsepower, would have to drive her at a high-speed 27-knot average, twenty-four hours a day, to give them a chance. That meant well over 600 miles a day, which the commander thought was touch-and-go, even with no stops. Six miles off the island, he ordered her deep *"Make your depth 400 feet . . . all ahead flank . . . steer two-two-five."*

Columbia thus raced toward the southwest. On the first day her objectives were simple; she wanted to be over the line of 70 degrees longitude by midday, and out over the north end of the Mid-Indian Ridge by midnight. On Wednesday it was even simpler; she needed to be across the Nazareth Bank, south of Mauritius, and the 60-degree line of longitude, before midnight. That would give her a reasonable ten-hour run to the search area. All of that assumed there would not be the slightest problem in running. The only slowdown factor would be periodic moves to the surface for GPS checks and satellite comms.

And they very nearly made it. A CO_2 scrubber went on the

blink after twelve hours, which cost them ninety minutes fixing it and ventilating the boat afterward. But they were only two hours late at the Nazareth Bank, and they made good speed into the area west of the 53-degree line of longitude, where *Columbia* came to periscope depth. Lieutenant Farrington had them bang on 18.55 South, and at 1139 on Thursday morning, as they slowed down to come to periscope depth, they picked up some odd noises directly ahead. Through the periscope they thought they saw something about 10 miles off their port bow . . . but it was difficult to identify.

The captain himself finally expressed the view that it could have been the fast-disappearing fin of a submarine, beam on. They just caught a glimpse, and it was gone. POSIDENT was very difficult. It could have been an Upholder-Class submarine, but it had disappeared before he saw it, just as *Columbia* had come to periscope depth. The fact was they were too far away to do much about it. Except watch and proceed cautiously in the same direction, using passive sonar for the moment. Active was not an option, for fear of alerting their target.

But they never saw it again. *Columbia* continued her careful approach, the sonar revealing nothing. And it was with great reluctance that the American team had to admit to themselves they had missed their quarry. The carbon dioxide scrubber, which allowed them to breathe, had cost them the mission.

For half an hour they moved forward, now steering course three-one-five. Still on passive, still watching the screen for the slightest indication. But it was to no avail. HMS *Unseen* possessed all of the most diabolical attributes of stealth and silence that were common to the Russian Kilo. If she stayed slow at around five knots, she was literally impossible to hear. And *Columbia* was hearing nothing. The only information Mike Krause and his sonar team had was that the submarine was probably an Upholder, clearly the tiresomely named *Unseen*. She had showed up right on time at 18.55 South, 52.20 East, her last-known position. And she was last seen heading north 200 miles off the east coast of Madagascar. Destination unknown.

The CO knew that he probably could open up on active sonar and pick up his fleeing opponent. But that course of action had its dangers. *Unseen* was a very quiet, possibly hostile submarine, and she could be within 10 miles of him. He had been told not to sink anyone without POSIDENT, and he could not swear that he had it. And there was the possibility of a preemptive shot against him, at short range, with short notice. Mike Krause was not too happy about any of that.

And it was with some irritation that the CO came back to PD at 1300 and accessed the satellite to inform SUBLANT he had traveled flat out, but had been too late. By about fifteen minutes. To give chase now on active sonar, Mike Krause felt he needed new rules of engagement. Caution was his watchword. He was no Boomer Dunning.

By now Admiral Morgan had joined Joe Mulligan on the line to Alan Cattee in Hawaii, and news of the near miss spread an aura of gloom, lightened only by the fact that Ben Adnam had certainly provided data.

Nonetheless, Admiral Morgan decided to test him again, and he went back into the interrogation room and barked at the captured terrorist. "Sonofabitch was not there . . . the goddamned ocean was deserted . . . you told me there would be a fueling tanker in the area and my team found nothing. If you're bullshitting me, Adnam, you might be spending your last day on this earth."

If Adnam's nerve was going, he betrayed nothing. "Admiral Morgan, I gave you the best information I have. But you know and I know that a refueling point can change at any time. The time and position can be pushed forward or back. My reading of this situation is that the submarine had already fueled and gone by, and is still proceeding north for possibly another 3,000 miles, into the deep waters of the Arabian Sea toward the Strait of Hormuz."

He was uncertain of the precise destination, but he knew the projected route. When he had left *Unseen* the plan was to run north in shallower coastal water toward Oman. He thought it unlikely that Iraq would be able to keep the submarine, and that they might scuttle it in the Arabian Sea. Alternately, he believed it possible they might sell it to another Middle Eastern country, possibly Iran, which had superior submarine facilities, and which might pay very highly for such a boat.

"It's a pretty goddamned hot property for that, isn't it," grunted Morgan.

"True, but ships can be altered. And Iran has excellent facilities for working on submarines. I do not, however, have firm information about their intentions. The plan was always that I should leave the ship in the Atlantic. When my mission was complete."

Either way, Commander Adnam had indicated that the newly refueled *Unseen* would make for a point 400 miles east of Mombasa. From there he said it would run up the long coast of Somalia, past the Horn of Africa, and across the Gulf of Aden into the national waters of Oman, west of the ops area for the American CVBGs.

Admiral Art Barry's Battle Group was steaming north under the clear skies of the southern Arabian Basin, way south of the Gulf of Oman, in depths of more than seventeen thousand feet. The giant carrier *Ronald Reagan*, pitching heavily forward, through great ocean swells, at over 20 knots, was surrounded by a formidable arsenal of Naval firepower, two cruisers, three destroyers, four guided-missile frigates, a nuclear submarine, and a big fleet replenishment ship.

SUBPAC sent a signal to Admiral Barry that arrived at midnight. In broad terms it detailed the possible route of HMS *Unseen* as supplied by her former commanding officer to Admiral Morgan. Admiral Cattee had been advised that *Columbia* was planning to follow that route in the hope of catching the fleeing Iraqi captain. The stolen Royal Navy submarine was expected to make the final 300 miles into the Strait of Hormuz on her battery; thus she could be expected to come shallow to snorkel-charge, maybe twice, when she was between 500 and 350 miles south of the strait, close to the Omani coastline.

Admiral Mulligan suggested that Admiral Barry conduct a search in that area beginning in two weeks . . . on May 10. The ideal solution, so far as he was concerned, was to hunt the submarine to exhaustion, force her to the surface, then board and search, identifying precisely who they were and who had controlled her operations. Then sink her. No word was mentioned about her precise activities over the past three months. But Art Barry was quite sure about the tone of the signal. Urgent.

And he sent immediately for his destroyer escort squadron commander, COMDESRON, Captain Chuck Freeburg, and his Group Operations Officer, Captain Amos Clark from North Dakota. The three men ordered coffee and pondered the charts. It was no problem to arrive off the Omani coast in plenty of time; the question was whether to take the entire force, or just peel off three destroyers or frigates and send them on alone.

Admiral Barry thought they might need fixed-wing aircraft as well as helos for such a search. This would mean the whole force would move over to the western reaches of the Arabian Sea. That decision was up to him, and he made it quickly. Everyone would go to help find the Royal Navy submarine that was causing so much angst at headquarters. "Jesus," said Captain Freeburg. "Right here we got the CNO and COMSUBLANT acting on information from Arnold Morgan. That's not big. That's monstrous. Guys, we better find this sucker."

The trouble was the sheer size of the new search area. Basically the Americans would have to take a NW/SE line 500 miles from the strait, and conduct their search in a seascape of almost 200,000 square miles. The fixed-wing aircraft would be crucial to the operation, and the carrier itself would need to operate from the center of the area.

Admiral Barry made his course adjustments and reduced the speed of his flotilla. Meanwhile, nearly 3,000 miles to the southwest, Commander Krause searched in vain for a sign of the vanished *Unseen*. But there was nothing.

On the morning of May 4, the first two Lockheed S-3B Viking ASW aircraft roared off the deck of the *Ronald Reagan*, heading in toward the Omani coast, cruising at 300 knots. Both of these Navy ASW aircraft could carry four Mark 5 depth charges, or four Mk 46 torpedoes. But today their mission was not to destroy, just to locate.

Like *Columbia*, they found nothing. And they searched for three days in relays. But on May 7, one of them picked up a radar contact 400 miles to the south of the strait. The Viking came in low and dropped sonobuoys, but the contact had long since disappeared. To the trained Navy pilot, that meant one thing . . . the submarine was snorkeling when it picked up the radar of the aircraft, which caused it instantly to slip away beneath the surface. But the Viking pilot was definite. He had it. The clue was strong, the contact was snorkeling 180 miles east of the Omani port of Al-Jawarah.

The Americans knew two facts. They had interrupted and hopefully prevented the submarine's full battery-charge, and from now on it must be continuously harassed. *Unseen must* come to periscope depth again soon, probably within 100 miles. Art Barry's pilots were ready. They got it again, surprisingly, 110 miles to the north, and this time they had a guided-missile frigate within strike range: Captain Bill Richards's 4,000-ton Oliver Hazard Perry-Class USS *Ingraham*, patrolling 15 miles to the east.

Right now *Unseen* was 90 miles east of the southern tip of the island of Masirah, and again she picked up the Viking's radar and instantly vanished below the surface. It was early in the afternoon, and the Americans knew the submarine would be forced back, within hours, to charge that battery. And, on his way in, at high speed, was Captain Richards, the former XO of the destroyer *O'Bannon*, his face still terribly scarred from flying glass from the same nuclear blast that had destroyed the *Thomas Jefferson*.

He ordered *Ingraham* to her maximum 29 knots and the sleek, heavily armed frigate, with her crew of 206 at battle stations, came swiftly into the main search area, just to the north of *Unseen*'s last known.

The Americans now had a hot datum. They had two radar fixes from the Viking. They knew the submarine's speed of advance, 5 knots, and they knew her course, zero-four-zero, which would probably go to zero-zero-zero as she struggled north, now in desperation, toward the Gulf of Oman, gateway to Gulf of Iran. Essentially they had 270 miles to catch her before she turned into more populated narrow waters, patrolled by the navies of Oman and Iran.

Captain Richards had an excellent intelligence assessment from Langley. *"Your target has acoustic characteristics of Brit U-Class. Mission: hunt to exhaustion, board, POSIDENT submarine, arrest crew. Shoot only in self-defense."*

Tactics for the frigate commander were clear. He must use every available asset to flood the quite limited area with fixed-wing, helicopter, and surface-ship radar. That way *Unseen* could not come up without being detected. That way Captain Richards could home in for the final moves in this elaborate and lethal game.

At 2205 the rogue submarine was forced to periscope depth by her dying battery. Again she put up her snorkel mast, because by then she was gasping for air—air to flow through the diesel generators while she tried to restore her electric power. *Unseen* was like a drowning whale, and the American harpoonists picked her up instantly on the radar screen of their patrolling helicopter. The U.S. pilot began tracking the submarine, reporting her every move back to *Ingraham*.

Captain Richards reacted swiftly, ordered his sonar active, and sent his own helicopter in to assist. *Unseen* picked up the American's electronic beam immediately, but her latest fifteen-minute battery charge was insufficient. The battery had been just about dead flat a half hour previously. Time was running out for the stolen submarine.

Lieutenant Commander Alaam ordered *Unseen* deep. But he knew it must be for the last time. The submarine was simply running out of power, and the American frigate was very close. *Unseen* was caught in the classic chess position—Morton's Fork—when the rook checks the king but threatens the queen at the same time. If *Unseen* stayed deep, it would run out of power completely. If it came to periscope depth, the Americans would force it deep again or blow its mast away. If it came to the surface, the Americans would capture them all and execute them. There was no escape. Lieutenant Commander Alaam must have known. This was checkmate.

Captain Richards knew his opponent was trapped.

Five minutes later, at 2255, *Unseen*'s lights and other systems suddenly wavered. Lieutenant Commander Rajavi reported the battery was at zero percent charge. Flat, that is. So flat you could barely see it sideways. And shortly before 2300 Lieutenant Commander Alaam ordered *Unseen* to periscope depth to try to snorkel for the last time.

Captain Richards, 4,200 yards off her starboard beam, picked her up before the submarine's diesels had even started. And he ordered his Italian-built OTO Melara 3-inch gun into action. Sixty seconds later they had blown off the top of *Unseen*'s ESM mast, ending all communications. They had blasted the periscope, rendering the submarine "blind," and they had obliterated the snorkel mast, making further recharging impossible at PD.

And now *Unseen* was finally forced to the surface. She came rising out of the dark Arabian Sea, the water cascading down her hull, but there was no sign of her crew. The American helicopter circled the submarine and, with the aid of flares, photographed her unique missile system from several angles. But the pilot reported no activity.

The frigate commander ordered two Mk 46 torpedoes to be readied in tubes one and two. Then he sent an immediate communication to the Flag, explaining that *Unseen* is stopped on the surface with a flat battery, no communications and no periscope. Engines not running, so probably all hatches shut. He believed boarding might be difficult. The crew has not surrendered, nor even come to the bridge. Indeed, it appears to be battened down inside the hull. Captain Richards was afraid the crew might just scuttle her. However, he confirmed he was quite prepared to press on and break into her, using whatever explosive was necessary, then neutralize the crew. He would await further instructions.

Admiral Barry considered this was one for the hierarchy and sent an immediate signal to SUBPAC, who appeared to be running the operation. The three American admirals, Morgan, Mulligan, and Cattee, separated by thousands of miles, spoke tersely on the conference line.

"Look, I'm not sure we need this bullshit," said Admiral Morgan. "We know exactly who these guys are. We know where they got their ship, and we know what they've been doing. We also know they're Iraqi. We've got their goddamned former commanding officer just up the road calling the shots for us."

"Right." Admiral Mulligan concurred. "And boarding is dangerous. These maniacs might just blow the ship apart with a lot of our guys on the casing. I really do not want to run those sorts of risks, because they are not necessary . . . my decision, therefore, is that we should bang it out right now, before the fucking thing breaks loose again."

"Agreed," snapped Morgan. "Go to it, Alan."

The message relayed via the satellite to the *Ronald Reagan* was, as ever, crisp. *"Cancel existing ROE. Sink your contact."*

The order reached *Ingraham* before 2330, and there was still no sign of life from the crew trapped in HMS *Unseen*. Captain Richards again sent the helo up for one final look, and something amazing happened. A figure showed up on the submarine's bridge and began rattling away at the U.S. Navy helicopter with some kind of a machine gun. It was like writing a suicide note. And the pilot wheeled away, heading for the deck of the missile frigate.

Captain Richards gave the final orders. *"Fire tube one."*

Seconds later an Mk 46 MOD 5 blasted out of the frigate and set off in a dead straight line toward *Unseen*, which was now wallowing 4,050 yards off the frigate's bow. It hit with a dull explosive thump as the torpedo punched a killer hole into the pressure hull. *Unseen*, and her Iranian crew, were gone inside a minute, sunk in water almost 3 miles deep. No one lived for more than thirty seconds. And no one in the Middle East would ever know, how and what had happened to the terrorist missile boat.

On board *Ingraham* everyone knew what had happened, that

in the course of their mission they had sent probably 50 men to their graves. No one dwelt upon the humanity of their actions, only on their sense of duty, that high and mysterious anthem of fighting men. And their world quickly fell into tune with it.

Meanwhile, back on board the *Ronald Reagan*, Captain Barry took some delight in the fact that not all U.S. carriers are prey for marauding diesel-electric submarines. "We had a bead on her from the moment we stepped up to the plate . . . that sucker never moved without us knowing," he told Amos Clark. "In the end we only needed a couple of good ASW search aircraft and a good frigate, and they were dead at first base."

"Yessir. The only time the rules change a bit is when you don't know the fuckers are out there. Sneaky little bastards." Art Barry reflected on the incontrovertible fact that all surface group commanders *hate* submarines. Especially nonnuclear boats.

His signal back to SUBPAC confirmed the destruction of HMS *Unseen*, sunk 145 miles off the coast of Oman shortly before 2400 on May 9. No wreckage. No survivors. No U.S. casualties.

The photographs wired back to HQ via the carrier arrived in the late afternoon. And after a brief study of them, the two Washington-based admirals headed home with copies, a Navy helicopter delivering Admiral Mulligan to the Pentagon, and Arnold Morgan to Langley, Virginia, where Ben Adnam was going into his fourth week of being debriefed.

He had held up night and day, through question after question, checks and rechecks, until the words of the Iraqi Naval officer were either proven true or false. Thus far he had not faltered, and the CIA was becoming more and more impressed by him. Especially Frank Reidel, who had deep experience of field officers, having been head of the Far Eastern desk for several years.

The photographs of *Unseen*, personally brought to the interrogation room by Morgan himself, showed, of course, the incredible sight of the missile launcher behind the fin. And upon this the admiral felt Adnam's story lived or died. Everything else fell into place, he knew that. But the question remained, that system.

He sat down to grill personally the former pirate CO of *Unseen*, and he kept going for four hours.

"How heavy was it? . . . what kind of crane did you use? . . . what was the name of the supply ship? . . . how many people did it take? . . . who were they? . . . where does Iraq get ahold of such engineers? . . . who trained them? . . . where are the holding bolts situated? . . . what kind of seals did you use? . . . was it pressurized inside? . . . where did you test it? . . . how many missiles did you take on the journey? . . . did you intend to commit more crimes against civil aircraft? . . . who liaised with you in London on the two departure times of Concorde and *Air Force Three?*

The admiral tried every trick known to the master interrogator. And, as the former director of the National Security Agency, that was a substantial number of tricks. But Ben Adnam held firm. He answered every question. He knew every answer. By 2200 there was no doubt in Admiral Morgan's mind. Iraq had perpetrated the atrocities, under the guidance of their hero, and Iraq must be taught a lesson. The issue would be to find one sufficiently severe.

The admiral called it a day, or a night, just before 2300. He had left his own car at Langley, parked in the director's private space, as always, and drove himself to Kathy's house, which was less than 4 miles away, across the American Legion Memorial Bridge into Maryland.

She was waiting up for him, as promised, and poured him a large rum on the rocks, as he marched wearily through the door and crashed into a large armchair without even taking his coat off.

"I am beat. Nearly," he said. "And I still love you. Even after dealing with more bullshit than a field of longhorns."

Kathy O'Brien looked wonderful. Her long red hair, just washed, fell about her shoulders. Her slim figure was encased in a dark blue silk housecoat. She wore no makeup except lipstick, and Arnold Morgan was once more amazed that she could care about him. She handed him his drink and kissed him, told him to get up and take off his coat and anything else that might make him happy. She put on some music and told him, in answer to his request, that, no, he could not have a roast beef sandwich.

"First of all, they're not good for you to eat all the time. And secondly, in anticipation of your late arrival, I have prepared a nice late dinner for us."

"Dinner! Jesus, it's the middle of the night."

"Pretend you're Spanish, El Morgano."

The great man laughed. "Do you know I've never been there, but I've always heard those crazy pricks have their dinner at midnight and then stay out drinking wine till about four."

"That's right. But they don't start work until ten, and they have a two-hour siesta after lunch. They go back to the office from about four in the afternoon to eight."

"Guess it works for them. You don't hear of many Spanish Secret Servicemen though . . . they're probably eating or sleeping or drinking . . . anyway what do we have?"

"Dining room, Barbarian . . . I don't serve picnics, as you well know."

The admiral dragged himself up, reluctant to move, but Kathy had candles lit in the elegant room beyond, which contained only antique furniture and four small oil paintings.

"Sit, and pour us some wine . . . I'll be right there." Three minutes later she came in with some perfectly cooked veal piccata, thinly sliced in a lemon-based sauce, accompanied by spinach and new potatoes. In the middle of the table was a wooden board containing a small baguette, real French brie, no butter, and big white seedless grapes. The wine was a five-year-old white Burgundy from Sancerre.

"Jesus, this was well worth waiting for. Will you marry me?"

"No," she said cheerfully. "Not while you're still employed. But I do love you."

The admiral took a large bite of veal and a swallow of wine. "That does it," he said. "I'm resigning, soon as I finish this."

"Yeah, right," she said. "Now tell me about your day, and the inquisition of Commander Adnam."

Despite the clear overtones of massive secrecy involving the entire scenario, it was plainly impossible for it to be kept from the lovely Mrs. O'Brien, who had been present when Ben's name had first come up, a year ago, and anyway, as Arnold's secretary, had taken so many calls regarding the capture of the terrorist she had lost count. Anyway, she was as bound by the secrecy laws as her future husband. And she was equally trusted.

"Well, he seems to want to stay here."

"In a casket?"

"No, as an employee. He makes the point, like most major spies who are captured, that he has information that is priceless."

"And has he?"

"He sure does. But he'd need such a thorough change of identity I'm not sure it'd be possible."

"Arnold, that could never work. Think of all the families he's destroyed, just in the Navy. Think of all those people on Concorde. How about all the families of Martin's staff? How about the memory of Martin? And Zack Carson, and Jack Baldridge. It would be like hiring the Boston Strangler."

"I know it would. But this guy has knowledge. Real knowledge. In my view he may be the most valuable agent anyone has ever caught, including all those faggot Brits who worked for Moscow."

"You're not supposed to use that word anymore. It's politically incorrect," she replied with studied seriousness.

"Not when *they* were lifting each other's shirts," he replied, chewing the veal, and drinking the white Burgundy with relish. "I'm in the past tense. An old, dead faggot is an old, dead faggot."

Kathy giggled at the admiral's unfailing, irrepressible aim at any subject. Then she said, more seriously, "I suppose you don't need reminding that you did not really catch Ben Adnam. He came here unaccompanied of his own accord, and effectively gave himself up. Plainly, he could have killed Bill, and he might have gotten Laura. But she says he never intended to kill anyone. He just wanted to get in touch with you. He's probably regretting it right now."

"The problem for all men like him, Kathy, is they end up having nowhere to turn. No one wants 'em. No one needs 'em. In the end, the only country that does want them is the one they have always worked against. Just because of what they know." He paused for a moment. Then he said, "Men too deep in national intelligence can often become outcasts, because, finally, they just have no one to talk to."

Kathy gazed at him quizzically. Then moved adroitly. "Are you really planning to use Ben on a long-term basis?"

"I do not have that authority. The question is, will I recommend something of the sort to the President of the United States?"

"Well. Will you?"

"Kathy, that's the second item to which I don't have an answer."

"What's the first?"

"Whatever would happen to me, without you?"

THE FINAL BARRAGE OF QUESTIONS FIRED AT BEN
Adnam by the President's national security advisor concluded the principal interrogation of the Iraqi terrorist. He was
still under the control of the CIA, and under twenty-four-hour
guard by the United States Marines, but he was now moved to a
CIA safe house 15 miles south of Washington, west of the
Potomac River.

He posed, obviously, the most enormous problem. The simple
solution was to get rid of him, quickly, professionally, and illegally. The best solution was to use him in every possible way to
guide U.S. military dealings in the Middle East. But the moral
solution was to put him on trial, to answer publicly for his horrendous crimes against the American nation and others. Arnold
Morgan hated Solution Three.

He hated it because it opened a zillion cans of worms. It
would bring in the British judicial system to deal with the downing of Concorde; it would let the media run riot all over the
world; it would cause desperate problems for the airline industry

because the media would go on and on about "Could This Happen Again?" And, worse yet, it would cause U.S. government and military authorities to admit what had happened to the *Thomas Jefferson*. And that would cause the media to go collectively berserk for about six months, possibly threatening even the President's term in office.

In the interest of a quiet life, Admiral Morgan knew that Solution One was the simplest answer. Just get rid of the sonofabitch. Very few people in the States even knew he existed, never mind what he'd done. If he should suddenly disappear, the problems would vanish with him. *There is no other Ben Adnam. We have solved everything. Why not just proceed as if nothing has happened? Ben who?*

The trouble was, Arnold Morgan did not operate like some other military and political careerists. He operated only in the specific interests of the United States of America. And he knew, as surely as he knew the sun rises in the east, Ben Adnam had real possibilities. He knew of no one else in the world, indeed he had never met anyone in his long career, who could in such a short space of time have completely outwitted the entire political-military establishment of the United States. Not just once, but twice. Not to mention the Brits, the Russians, and the Israelis. Arnold Morgan reckoned Adnam was as close to priceless as makes no difference.

Arnold Morgan knew as well as anyone about the restrictions all governments place on classified information. But Ben Adnam was not just any old intelligence officer. Ben Adnam was some kind of a military genius, and in Arnold Morgan's opinion he was likely to have found out *anything* he really wanted to know. In his present plight, Adnam had two commodities to sell. Knowledge, and lateral-minded cunning. And Morgan's instinct told him the Iraqi was unlikely to come up short. Certainly Adnam would probably know more than Langley about all kinds of matters in the Middle East.

Before Ben Adnam had left Baghdad he had deposited the full story of his operations in three different safe-deposit vaults in

Europe. The written account was split into several parts, no one of them complete. He had allowed the CIA to check out one part of one deposit in Paris. Neither the CIA, nor Arnold Morgan, who had spent a lifetime in the dogged pursuit of such data, was disappointed. The admiral could not bring himself to have commander Adnam eliminated; nor could he risk him going into a public trial before a jury. Admiral Morgan already knew, he wanted to "run" him.

Which was why, broadly speaking, he and two Secret Service agents were driving fast down Route 1 to the Woodley Hills district, the admiral himself at the wheel. Arnold Morgan sensed there was something in the nature of a showdown in the air between him and Adnam, because sooner or later someone was going to have to decide something. Right now the admiral did not know what course of action to advise the President, but he would by the end of the day.

They pulled into the tree-softened driveway that led through languorous lawns turning green with the advance of spring. At the end was the big, white, gabled house that represented the most unlikely-looking prison in the U.S.A. Only the presence of two uniformed Marine guards inside the glass of the front porch betrayed the secret nature of the location.

Admiral Morgan parked and walked into the house, nodding at the two guards. Inside, two CIA field officers met him and took him into a living room that enjoyed rural views out to the trees, and three more guards. Sitting in an armchair, reading the *Washington Post*, despite his manacled wrists, was Commander Benjamin Adnam.

He wore a blue shirt, dark grey trousers, and brown loafers, all of which he had bought in Helensburgh two and a half months before. He stood up immediately upon the arrival of the national security advisor and nodded a greeting. "Admiral", he said calmly.

"Commander," replied Arnold Morgan, unable to bring himself to reduce to the ranks the submarine genius he wanted to hire.

He turned to the Secret Servicemen and the CIA field officers who had accompanied him into the room, and said curtly, "I'll let you know if I need you."

One of the CIA men nodded to the Marine guard, who was plainly ready for this instruction, and, before leaving, he hand-cuffed the prisoner both to the chair, by the wrist, and to the table, by the ankle. Ben Adnam was not going anywhere, even if he had anywhere to go.

"I want to talk to you about your future, if any," said the American gruffly.

"I'd be glad to join you," said Adnam, smiling.

"We won't waste each other's time on trivialities, because we both know I could have you eliminated anytime I think suitable. And, like Laura Baldridge, I'd probably get a medal from a grate-ful nation."

"If you say so, Admiral."

"However, I would like to touch base with you on the ques-tion of a trial, should my government decide to charge you either with crimes of mass murder against the state, or alternately war crimes against humanity. What would your reaction be?"

"I should plead not guilty to everything. I should deny ever having been in anyone's Navy. I should say I was just trying to get a job here. Then I would leave you to persuade the Iraqis to give evidence against me. You could ask them to swear I was the world's greatest terrorist acting on their behalf. Or you could try Israel, get them to admit in front of that beleaguered nation that their military had been made to look absolutely ridiculous, by me, for the biggest part of twenty years."

Arnold Morgan shook his head, frowning.

Then Adnam added, "You could, of course, try to nail me with the Royal Navy submarine, the one you have undoubtedly hit by now, illegally, in international waters, drowning the innocent crew, as if you were a group of gangsters. That would probably go down very well in the United Nations. And in your press, which has been told nothing of all this. Personally, I would not really know. You see, I've never been in a submarine. I'm in the mining business myself."

"We could bring in evidence from Scotland," growled Morgan. But he was only testing the waters.

"Where's that, Admiral? I've never even been there, as my passport will show. You have only one witness, that fool Anderson, whom any good lawyer would rip to bits."

"You have told me plenty, Commander. And the CIA."

"Yes. Your methods of torture, like some Third World despot, have been very effective. You and your henchmen could make a man admit anything. On the other hand, real evidence, as you know, is very hard to find. I can't help thinking a public trial is not in anyone's best interests. And you will never get anyone to admit I had anything to do with downing those aircraft."

Admiral Morgan had always known that the cooperation of Benjamin Adnam was only good while the man made his plea for life. Once that was achieved, and he was put on trial, things would be very different. And in his soul Arnold Morgan knew this man never would, never could, come to public trial. The ramifications, on all sides, were just too difficult. No good could possibly come of it. Not for anyone. Especially not for the United States of America.

"Should we decide to take a more agreeable route, and make you a clandestine employee of the government, what would your expectations be?"

Benjamin Adnam restrained even a cautious smile. He had after all planned for this moment for weeks and weeks. This moment represented his entire reason for being in the U.S.A. But he spoke slowly.

"Admiral Morgan, I would plainly need a new identity. Which I imagine you would have little trouble providing. I would also need somewhere to live and some money. The Iraqis treated me less than generously.

"I imagine you would wish me close to Washington, where my knowledge could best be put to use."

"Would you wish to become a citizen?"

"I think I would leave that to you."

"Do you put a high price on your worth to us?"

"I always put a high price on my worth to anyone."

"Have you considered that you might owe us something."

"Nossir. I work for money. Or else I leave. If I can."

"Try not to forget Option One."

"I have not forgotten it. But if you are planning to exercise that, then we ought not to be talking at all."

"No we ought not. But lemme ask you this, how much money do you think we should pay you?"

"Sir, that depends how long I stay, and how long you would wish to employ me."

"How long would you like to stay here in the United States?"

"Until I die."

"Which could be tomorrow."

"But I hope, and think, not."

"Why? Are you not our most intractable enemy?"

"Was. Not anymore. And, I doubt it has escaped you, there are very few places I can go. In my trade you tend to have a downward spiral of friends, a spiral that ends up running out."

"Commander, I understand that very well. But I would like to pursue finances for a moment. If, for instance we wanted to employ you over a ten-year period, there's no way we'd give you a substantial lump sum before that time was up. Just in case you decided to vanish. However, we might think about a monthly arrangement with perhaps a capital sum accruing to you each year, which you could not, of course, touch."

"What if I wished to buy a house here?"

"No problem. We'd own it until your service time was up."

"Then, under such circumstances, I would expect to accrue money at the rate of $1.5 million a year, on top of my normal living salary. The interest to come to me."

"Uh-huh."

"After all, I can probably show you how to get Iraq out of your hair permanently. What would that alone be worth?"

"Commander, you do not need to waste your time convincing me of your worth. I know it. That's why we're sitting here."

"Excellent. We could probably make a very good team. You

remind me in many ways of my Teacher. Different style. Same analytical mind."

Despite an uneasy feeling that he was being patronized, the admiral smiled. He stood up and walked to the window. Then he turned around quite suddenly, and said, "I wonder how wise it would ever be for me to turn my back on you."

"Admiral, I have nowhere else to go. That's why I'm here."

"That's why we're talking. I guessed your situation. The only catch may be that you are already working for someone else."

"Admiral, if you can trust me long enough to make a deal, I give you one promise. I can prove my former employer became my enemy, and I will do so to your satisfaction, as soon as we seal our arrangement. If I fail, you may either execute me, or I will take cyanide."

"Accepted. The burden of proof is on you. That's between us. And now I'm outta here. Hope you get a decent dinner. We'll talk tomorrow."

"Oh, Admiral, just one thing you should know before you go . . . I forgot to tell you, I have written out my *whole* story, you know the aircraft carrier, and the passenger airliners . . . with suitable backup material, to be released to the media by my Swiss bank, if I should disappear, or die. You know, if I fail to report to them every six weeks.

"I've arranged for the material mainly to go to foreign newspapers . . . the UK, France, Germany, and of course, the *Washington Post*. I thought that might deter you from executing Option One . . . the fact that I might come back to annoy you . . . from beyond the grave, as it were. How will the President laugh off the decision to take out three Iranian submarines when Iran had done nothing? How will you excuse your lies about the loss of the *Jefferson*? Your more recent cover-up over the airliner 'accidents' will seem like kid stuff in comparison.

"Matter of fact, I think you should be extremely relieved you did not go to Option One in the first hour before we had time to talk . . . anyway, see you tomorrow."

The admiral scowled, headed back out to his car, walking

resolutely, his chin stuck out in front of him, looking as if he were about to declare war. He was behind the wheel, with the engine running, before the Secret Servicemen had time to scramble out of the house and join him. Admiral Morgan did not like being outwitted, as he suspected he was by the Iraqi. Generally he preferred the driver's seat.

He drove on to his lunch appointment, first heading north to the Richmond Highway. From there they went farther south, away from the city, for another nine miles, where the admiral turned first onto a secondary road, then onto a shaded woodland drive, at the end of which was a majestic white Colonial house.

He told his Secret Service detail he would be two hours. One of them should go and find their lunch, and one should bring the communication system inside. Both agents knew they were at the private residence of Chairman of the Joint Chiefs Admiral Scott F. Dunsmore. They also knew he could not possibly have purchased this spectacular property, overlooking the Potomac River to the Maryland Heights, with his Navy salary. The scholarly Scott Dunsmore, it was well-known, was from a Boston banking family. He had also been the cleverest admiral in the Navy. That, too, was well-known.

And now he stepped out to greet his old friend Arnold Morgan, and they stood chatting for a few minutes below the tall, greening trees, some still in blossom. A couple of bobwhite quails called, from quite close in the woodland, and above them the sky was clear blue. The idyllic rural scene contrasted darkly with the grim, subversive, and murderous subject they were about to discuss. Standing there in the lovely grounds of the house was to postpone the enormity of their decision . . . what to advise the President when they met him in the White House at 1600. The subject, as it had been so many times before, was Benjamin Adnam. Scott Dunsmore had suffered the shuddering distinction of being Chief of Naval Operations when the *Jefferson* was sunk.

Inside the mansion the two admirals retired to a high summery room that faced out directly to the river and the distant

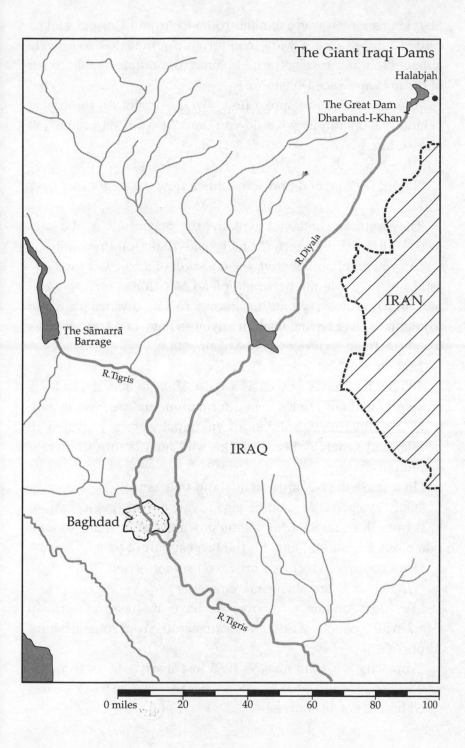

The Giant Iraqi Dams

Halabjah

The Great Dam
Dharband-I-Khan

R. Diyala

IRAN

The Sāmarrā
Barrage

R. Tigris

IRAQ

Baghdad

R. Tigris

0 miles   20   40   60   80   100

Maryland shore. It was a familiar room to Arnold Morgan, and he settled himself into a wide, comfortable armchair expensively upholstered in a rose-patterned chintz, the unmistakable touch of the urbane Grace Dunsmore.

Admiral Dunsmore spoke first. "Well, Arnold. As the brains behind this operation, what do you think? Do we shoot him, jail him, or hire him?"

"Hire him . . ."

"Right. Let's go and find some lunch now we've got that over with."

They both laughed, still avoiding the magnitude of the subject. "Well, what did he say?" finally asked Admiral Dunsmore.

"As you and I both feared, the question of a trial is a total disaster area. He told me he would plead Not Guilty, drag the trial out, and reveal everything he knows to our disadvantage. He would deny ever having been in anyone's navy and leave it to us to get the Iraqis to turn evidence against him."

"Fat chance."

"Which he knows as well as we do. He also added that he is now certain, thanks to his own information, that we have demolished a submarine illegally in international waters, drowned 50 people, and generally behaved like wild men before the world community."

"In a sense the bastard's right about that as well."

"Only in a sense . . . and he also says we won't get a scrap of help from the Israelis, who will be unwilling to be made to look ridiculous, because of him, for the biggest part of twenty years."

"He's got that right, too. Christ, you sure it *is* him?"

"Of course. Laura MacLean, remember?"

"Yes. Just kidding. Of course we have his passport. British, right? With a couple of South African stamps from Johannesburg Airport?"

"Yup. That's it. And he says he'll just leave it to us to prove who he really is and what he's done. He also said he'll say we tortured him to get an admission."

"Which confirms what we both think. He's a clever little bastard, and a trial is out of the question, correct?"

"Correct. It would be a huge embarrassment to the government and cause an uproar in the airline industry. The liberal media would have the best time since Watergate, bringing down this excellent administration."

"Anyway, Arnold, we could just find him guilty ourselves and . . . er . . . dispense with him. It seems absurd staging some kind of a trial in order to seek revenge, with his life, against so many thousands of others. It's not even a hundredth of the way toward a reasonable deal."

"Absolutely. Which brings us to the real issue. Do we unload him, right now, and act as if nothing's happened? Before you answer, I must tell you he has written out his whole story, the *Jefferson*, the aircraft, the submarine, and all, and has instructed his Swiss bank to release it to the media should he not report in every six weeks. God knows what else he has up his sleeve, but my instinct tells me to kill him would be damned nearly as bad as putting him on trial."

"Sounds like it, Arnie. Except it might be worse."

"Which brings us to the much more difficult, but more fruitful course of 'running' him, using him for our own purposes?"

"Well . . . 'running' him is certainly the most appealing if you don't care about your career. As I don't, since I'm retiring at the end of this President's tenure. You don't, because you're probably unsackable, and, anyway, you and Kathy have much to look forward to in retirement . . . with *your* pensions."

"I don't think the President cares either. He's halfway through his second term . . . so I suppose we should all act in the best interest of the country, and if it goes wrong . . . we just take it on the chin and retire gracefully from the fray.

"That means we 'run' him," said Arnold Morgan. "And that's a hell of a challenge. He actually said this morning he could show us how to get Iraq out of our hair for good. Christ, he'd be useful, with all of our dealings in the Middle East. And he's not expensive, relatively. And he says he wants to stay here. Nowhere else to go."

"The danger is, of course, he might still be working for Iraq."

"I know. And I did bring that subject up. And his reply was quite strange. He said he would prove to us conclusively that Iraq plainly tried to kill him. He also said that if he failed to prove it, he was quite prepared to take cyanide."

"Hmmmm. If we were dealing with a normal person, that'd be impressive. But with Ben Adnam, there's almost always going to be more to it than meets the eye. . . ."

"I know. I'm just trying to think what that might be. All the evidence I have tells me I am wasting my time, which, paradoxically, is why I want him on our team."

Lunch passed swiftly, as the two American admirals wrestled with the problem of the captive terrorist a dozen miles away. By the time they had worked their way through ham and cheese omelets and salad, they had agreed that Ben Adnam must live, for the moment. But a new problem emerged. Who, eventually, would 'run' the ex–Israeli submarine commander on a day-to-day basis? "Aside from the fact he needs a rock-solid Navy background, whoever it is has to be as clever as Adnam."

"Maybe impossible. I shouldn't think his Teacher would make himself available. But he'd do fine."

"How about his Teacher's son-in-law?"

"Bill? Can't see that happening. He's got that cattle operation to run, and he's quite recently married. I shouldn't think he'd want to up sticks and move to Washington. And Laura seems very happy out there in the wide-open spaces."

"I know. Think he might do it, say for six months, while we get ourselves organized with a permanent guy?"

"Well . . . Arnold, the first six months will probably be the most difficult. I don't think Bill would consider it, but you never know. I guess he might."

"Okay. Let's get back to the factory and see if the President has any strong views. If he does, this could become strictly academic. After we finish there, we'll make a new plan."

"Done."

"Hey, Scott, thank Grace for a delicious lunch, will you? I caught a glimpse of her, but she looked like she was leaving."

"She was. So are we. I'll ride with you. My car's meeting me at the White House."

At 1600 precisely, Admirals Morgan and Dunsmore presented themselves to the President of the United States. He awaited them in the Oval Office and rose to greet them with his usual affability.

"Good to see you both. Thanks for coming. How's our terrorist?"

"He's not bad, sir," said Arnold Morgan. "A bit awkward, as you'd expect, but nothing we can't deal with."

"Good. Now, I believe we are going to touch base on what to do with him?"

"Yessir. And it's a very touchy subject. And I am not sure how deeply you want to be involved. If you wish, you can, of course, lay down the law right away. But I would not really advise that. And I wonder whether you might not consider whether the President actually needs to be involved in the nitty-gritty of our decisions with some foreign terrorist . . . all I'm saying, sir, is that you don't have to, if you don't want to."

"I hear you, Arnold. And I thank you for your consideration. Could you give me a very private rundown on the situation right now?"

"Scott's damned good at that, sir. When I arrived at his house this morning, he just said, 'Right. Are you gonna shoot him, jail him, or hire him?'"

The President chuckled. "That's why he's Chairman of the Joint Chiefs. He never gets involved in trivia."

"Exactly, sir. Anyway, the most complicated area is the prospect of a trial for either crimes against the U.S. or crimes against humanity. In our opinion, it is a political nightmare, a no-win situation, and anyway, Adnam told me he will deny everything . . . he did not think Iraq would be anxious to give evidence on our behalf."

"I've already thought of that," said the Chief Executive. "Forget a trial. It would take a year, and it would drive everyone mad. It would probably drive me out of office. The left-wing media would kill us, especially if the beans somehow got spilled about the *Jefferson*."

"Exactly, sir. It's a total nonstarter. Especially since no one really knows what happened to either the carrier or the civilian airliners. And no one in this country knows Ben even exists. Just us, and our most trusted people."

"Which means his removal would be extremely simple, hmmmm? No one would ever know anything."

"It's not quite that simple sir. He seems to have made quite elaborate arrangements for substantive disclosures as to our activities in the event of his sudden disappearance and failure to communicate. The hard way is the only way we'd ever find out for real. So, making him disappear might ultimately prove as embarrassing as putting him on public trial.

"We already believe he is a mine of information. We also know, to our considerable cost, that he has a brilliant mind. And I would dearly like to use him. He could change our lives in the Middle East."

"I see. He seems to have thought it through, doesn't he? The question is, do I need to know, or care, if you decide to remove him, or if you decide to use him."

"I think not, sir," said Admiral Dunsmore. "Let's just suppose for the moment we have the man who hit the *Jefferson*. My own view is that it is unnecessary for you to be involved, *unless* we decide to go to trial, *or* if we decide to take any military action, in revenge, against another nation, based on information provided by Adnam. I don't think we could avoid your involvement then."

"I understand, Scott. And I realize you two do not want to have him executed privately. Rightly. Quite apart from the political consequences of postmortem exposure, it might be a waste of a major asset. Not to mention a purely futile act of revenge on our part. The crimes committed were so monstrous, there could

be no proportionality anyway. Not with one man's life. Therefore, my conclusion must be that I need not be involved at this
stage. I will leave the fate of the mysterious Commander Adnam
to the offices of my military commanders. But you will inform
me, Arnold, should we consider a strike against anyone."

"Absolutely, sir."

"One further point, before you go. Are we now certain that
the airliners were knocked down by Iraq?"

"Yessir. Yes we are."

"I would personally consider it very remiss of us if we failed
to make known our extreme displeasure to that pariah of a government."

"Understood, sir. I will keep you informed."

The two admirals rose and said good-bye to the President,
returning down the long corridors to Arnold Morgan's office.
Kathy O'Brien was at her post, on the telephone, and offered just
a small wave of greeting as they arrived. "Coffee," murmured her
boss. "And hold all phone calls for a half hour."

Inside his office, the admiral took off his coat, and exclaimed,
"Jesus Christ! Did you hear that last remark?"

"I sure did, Arnold. He wants us to hit Iraq, obviously not publicly, but it sounded like he expected something impressive."

"Fortuitous, huh? We just happen to have the very man we
need to guide us through those tricky waters."

"Isn't it, though? Benjamin, old buddy, I think you just got
yourself a job."

"He might have, Scott. But I'm not sure what exactly he meant
us to do. Bomb Baghdad? Take out a few streets? Knock down
some missile sites in the desert? Hit their main seaport? Maybe a
military airfield? A few oil wells? What do you think?"

"I'm not sure, but I presume he's looking for something like
their strikes against us. Too awful to be admitted, too much of a
loss of face. And too secret for anyone to know *quite* who was
responsible."

"Guess so. But it's a tall order."

"No doubt, Arnold. But it was very Presidential. He is a man

who just hates to see this country humiliated in any way whatsoever. And no one gets away with it. Not indefinitely."

"Iraq got away with the *Jefferson.*"

"Not anymore. Not by the sound of things."

"We better start thinking about plans. It just seems overwhelming at the minute. I'm not sure where to start . . . but this is
military, Scott, and you're the Chairman of the Joint Chiefs . . . I
think this ball's in your court . . . and I'm waiting for your creative
input."

"You think I'm a film director? Well, I'm not. Basically I'm an
organizer. And this is what I propose. I think we have to get
someone in here who's going to work with Adnam on an initial
plan, subject to your striking a deal, and reminding him of his
words about Iraq."

"Right. Who?"

"Bill Baldridge. For the following reasons. He's in deep
already. He's damned smart. He knows Adnam, and you and he
work very well together. He and Laura would certainly come to
Washington for a few days if we make it quick and urgent. She
could come and stay here with Grace, if necessary. Or else we'll
put 'em in a hotel. That way the three of you can try and thrash
something out. We'll pay Bill a fee; and if the mission is successful, it may just give us the opening to persuade him to 'run'
Adnam for another six months."

"Can't fault any of that. Who's gonna call Bill, you?"

"No, you. Tell him Adnam's balls are on the line. He said he
knew how to deal with Iraq. Now we're giving him the chance to
prove it. That might just titillate the master of the B/B sufficiently."

"Yeah. I guess it might at that . . . leave it with me Scott . . . I'll
call him later. I'll check how the herds are. See if they can manage without him for a few months."

Two hours later, at 1900, speaking from Kathy's house in
Chevy Chase, Arnold Morgan made contact with the former submarine lieutenant commander in Kansas. Baldridge listened
laconically to the proposition, made a lot of "Uh-huhs," "Is that

rights?" and general "Get outta heres." But in the end he did not turn it down.

He just said, "When?"

Arnold Morgan replied, "Now," which was his favorite word.

Bill Baldridge said, "How long?"

Arnold replied, "A week, max."

"Okay. You sending transport?"

"Yup. Tomorrow morning, 1000. In front of your house."

"We'll be there."

"See ya." And the admiral clenched his fist and gritted his teeth. "Now something *will* happen," he muttered. "With Commander Adnam and Bill working as a team. Just so long as we watch, monitor, and check every step Adnam makes. Maybe, one of these days, we'll even come to trust him."

But he was pleased with the Kansan's response, and he visibly brightened. "KATHY! Drinks . . . then we're going out for a little celebration."

1600. May 12. The White House Lawn.

The helicopter from Andrews Air Base touched down lightly, leaving its engines running for immediate takeoff down the Potomac. Laura remained on board, while Bill disembarked and was given a pass by the Secret Service agents and escorted into the West Wing. Arnold Morgan came to meet him in person. "Hey . . . good to see you. Grace is waiting at the house for Laura. You and I will be there by seven. We're all having dinner there, and we're all staying overnight."

Bill followed Arnold down to his office, where his briefing began. And Admiral Morgan explained everything, the potential deal with Adnam, the hopelessness of a public trial, the consequences and wastefulness of executing him. And the President's expressed wish that a strike be organized against Iraq.

Bill was particularly interested in the avowed statement from the ex–Israeli submariner to Admiral Morgan the previous day that he could rid the United States of the menace of Iraq.

"Christ. What do you think he has in mind?"

"Who knows. But when he does have something in his mind, we know, to our cost, that he is usually not joking."

"Ain't that right."

By 1800 the helicopter was back, miraculously bearing Admiral Dunsmore. The three old friends, in company with two Secret Service agents, took off from the White House in good time for the seven o'clock rendezvous with the ladies. Only Kathy O'Brien was absent, but she had to hold the fort, first thing in the morning, in Admiral Morgan's office.

The flight was swift, and the pilot brought them in over the Potomac before dark, touching down on the wide back lawn above the river.

There was a chill in the air, as there often is in the late spring on the East Coast. But Scott Dunsmore said that the cool weather would not deflect him from his plans. He was cooking outside tonight, come hell or high water. It would be the first barbecue of the season, and he intended it to be memorable. Therefore, he expected a full attendance around the gas grill while he perfected a flawless butterflied leg of lamb, just the way his cook had taught him during his days in the surface Navy as a Fleet Commander.

The fact that the huge leg of lamb was already carefully cut by Grace's butcher, and carefully marinated and half-cooked in the oven by Grace herself, did not discourage Admiral Dunsmore from claiming full credit, in advance. Grace mentioned that it would be a real shame if he burned it, like he did the last one, on her birthday two years ago.

"I was under a bit of pressure then," said the chief of the entire Pentagon. "They'll be no mistakes tonight. Let's get in there for some drinks . . . then you'll see me in action, putting a forty-minute charcoal finish to this banquet."

Laura, who had not met the Dunsmores, was captivated by them both. Grace had been charm itself during the late afternoon, and the arrival of the admiral, the most powerful man in the United States Armed Forces, was something she had viewed with some trepidation. Even though both her father and her husband had always told her that Scott was a prince of men, and she would like him, as she had liked all of those high-ranking military Americans she had met. Even Arnold Morgan, who was not precisely everyone's cup of tea.

Now, as Admiral Morgan assumed, always, that everyone had coffee black, "with buckshot," Admiral Dunsmore assumed that anyone who had endured a long day would be revived by the dark smooth taste of Johnny Walker Black Label Scotch with club soda. And with this drink he was something of an artist: in the high summer he allowed two cubes of ice in a tall glass, with a lot of soda. On Labor Day he eliminated the ice for the season, and then, as the days drew in and the temperature dropped, he reduced the soda water, until by Christmas, it became quite a short drink.

That night, only six weeks before the summer solstice, when the ice went back in, the drinks were medium long but warm. And, on a silver tray, he brought five Scotch and sodas into the big room at the front of the house. They each took one, and Arnold Morgan stepped forward to propose a toast.

"We are here tonight for several reasons, some of which can be talked about and some of which cannot. So I'll confine myself to proposing the health of Laura's father, and our friend, Admiral Sir Iain MacLean, who has, as before, been some way ahead of us."

They all raised their glasses, smiling at the thought of the urbane Scottish officer, who would have been mortified with embarrassment had he been in attendance. But Arnold Morgan was not prone to mawkish sentimentality. If he said Iain MacLean was out in front in his thinking, then that was so. And if it hadn't been after midnight on Loch Fyne, they would have all called him right there and then to congratulate him.

By now the gas grill was at full power, and Scott Dunsmore had the leg of lamb in prime position. Wearing sweaters, they all stood around outside, admiring the dusk over the dark Potomac, sipping their drinks and watching the Chairman of the Joint Chiefs strategically adjusting the angle of the gently sizzling lamb.

By common agreement, he had gotten it right this time. And dinner was outstanding, not least because the admiral decided to open his last two bottles of 1961 Haut Brion. "Bill and I drank a bottle to the memory of his brother right after we lost the *Jefferson*," he said. "This seems the right time to finish the vintage . . . on a high note, at the conclusion of an unhappy episode." The fact that the rare bottles were worth about $500 each was not lost on anyone. And the forty-five-year-old Bordeaux from the Graves district lived up to its towering reputation, casting a deep warm glow over the gathering. No one discussed the project that lay uppermost in their minds. Indeed, during the entire evening, it was touched upon only once, lightly, when Admiral Dunsmore raised his glass, and said quietly, "Welcome back on board, Bill."

The following morning Admiral Morgan's chauffeur arrived at 0800 to drive his boss and Bill the short distance back to the CIA safe house, where Benjamin Adnam awaited them. They both walked straight into the room where the terrorist was reading the newspaper, and Admiral Morgan wished him, "Good morning, Commander."

But he did not waste one second on formalities. "Right now," he said, "I am here to hack out a deal. And this is what I propose. I have a project, and I would like your guidance and general input. If this is deemed to be a success, we will then settle down and make some kind of a long-term agreement for you to work with us along the lines we outlined yesterday. Naturally, we can have nothing in writing, but in your business I expect you are accustomed to that.

"The project we are working on is against Iraq, and will be a one-time one-shot proposition. It will either succeed or fail. If I judge your role to have been critical, and it will be, and we are successful, we will make a one-time payment to you of $250,000 to start off your life here in America. You will not be required in an operational capacity. Only in strategic planning."

"Since I am sitting here thinking and reading the paper," replied Adnam, "I suppose I may as well earn some money for it."

But then he smiled, and said, "Admiral, I think that would be an excellent way to start off our relationship. Might save me the trouble of taking cyanide."

"Then we are agreed? You trust me sufficiently?"

Commander Adnam held up his handcuffed wrists. "I don't really have very much choice, do I? If I do not agree, you could always go immediately to Option One, despite the uncomfortable consequences for you, as well as me."

Admiral Morgan nodded. "Yes. And now I would like to talk to you, and so would Bill, whom I believe you know well enough?"

"Yes, I think so. We have a few things in common."

"Right. If I yell 'coffee' loud enough, will something happen?"

"I think so. There is a housekeeper for the agents and the Marine guards."

"I'll go and find someone, Arnold," said Bill. "But I bet they don't have buckshot."

The admiral grinned, but he was very preoccupied, and he turned to Ben Adnam, and said deliberately, "My President does not believe that Iraq should get away with shooting down three airliners, in the process murdering our oil-negotiating team, six politicians, and the Vice President of the United States. Neither has it escaped him that we, as yet, have taken no retribution against them for the loss of the aircraft carrier.

"We now propose to attend to these matters, with or without your help. But I hope with."

Adnam nodded.

"Now, you mentioned yesterday that you could offer a way for us to deal with Iraq on a long-term basis. Could you elaborate on that?"

As the Iraqi again nodded his assent, Bill came in with the coffee. Three mugs. All black. A blue tube of sweeteners on the side.

"That's one fucking miracle," said the admiral, firing the little white pellets into the coffee, somehow making the clicker sound like a six-shooter. "Now let's see if young Ben here can come up with a second."

Despite himself, Commander Adnam laughed. He thought he

might enjoy working with this American cowboy. "Admiral," he said, "one of the biggest problems in Iraq is water. We have two great rivers, the Euphrates and the Tigris. Both of them flow out of Turkey, and the Euphrates crosses Syria. Those two rivers are the lifeblood of Iraq. They are the reasons civilization flourished in ancient Mesopotamia, the old name for modern Iraq.

"The rivers still control the country's agriculture, wheat and barley, both irrigation and direct pumping. They control fertilizer plants, cement-making plants, light industry, the production of steel, the growing of dates. They control Iraq's drinking water and hydroelectric power. For centuries, when the water level dropped, and occasionally dried up in some areas, there was something close to national panic. But it was even worse when they flooded, as they often do at the end of the winter. Right back to biblical times . . . I expect you both know that Noah and his Ark were in Mesopotamia in that great flood.

"In order to control these waters, various governments have built a succession of dams and barrages and canals. These in turn helped to form lakes and reservoirs, which first of all absorb the floodwater, and secondly provide enormous backup when the rivers are very low.

"There is one at Dukan on the Tigris, others at Mosul and Al Hadithah. There is a huge one at Darband-I-Khan right up in the Kurdish Mountains on a tributary called the River Diyala. There is another at Basdush and Fathah, both on the Tigris. Another on a tributary, the Great Zab; a critical one at Samarra, the Samarra Barrage. There are several also on the Euphrates, at Habbaniyah, Hindiya, and Ash Shinafiya.

"But the most important ones are at Darband-I-Khan and Samarra. The Darband Reservoir stands at the southern end of a massive lake. It is surrounded by mountains, 130 miles northeast of Baghdad. It contains 3 cubic kilometers of water. Imagine that? A reservoir 4 miles long, 3 miles wide, and a quarter mile deep. The Samarra Barrage, about 76 miles north of the city, right on the Tigris, holds 85 billion cubic meters of water.

"If I were you, I'd blow out both those dams, and Iraq's economy would collapse for several years.

"Once you get out of the northeastern mountains, it's a flat country, and the flooding would be ruinous. But the distances are so great there would be no serious loss of life. The water would rise relatively slowly over the key areas, along the river. People would have time to get away. I know that because the government has made careful studies of the consequences of a dam failure. I've seen them. We'd just have a lot of factories that no longer worked, a lot of crops that would not grow, a lot of flooded oil fields. And a lot of flooded towns and villages. The country would be forced to throw itself on the mercy of the West."

"Jesus," said Arnold and Bill, almost simultaneously.

"The trouble is, Admiral. You don't have long. I read that winter stayed late in the mountains, which buys you some time. But if you want to strike hard, you need to do it while the snows are still melting, when the water in the reservoirs is at maximum height. I'd say you have about another four weeks maximum. By mid-June the levels really start to evaporate in the heat. All the Iraqi government studies show that flooding would be 50 percent worse if it happened at the end of the snowmelt."

"Jesus Christ," said the Admiral. Bill Baldridge looked amazed.

"I know it sounds perfect for our purposes," said Arnold Morgan. "But it would be absolutely impossible. We'd have to use Special Forces, train them, get 'em into the mountains somehow, through Turkey, then have them operate deep underwater, against the inner wall of the dams. Christ, we'd need about 50 guys. It would be like declaring war. And they might get caught."

"How marvelously old-fashioned," said Commander Adnam. "That's out of the question. Admiral, you don't use people, you use missiles. Cruise missiles."

"Missiles? Jesus, that's like a world war. We can't just stand a ship off, in the Gulf, or the Med, or somewhere, and start throwing big missiles at a couple of major Iraqi dams. The world community would go crazy with indignation. And we could never admit why we were doing it. I'm sorry, Commander, but that would be out of the question. Everyone would see a big missile launch from an American warship. The whole world would know what we had done, and we could not afford that."

"They wouldn't know if you did it from a submarine."

"A submarine . . . of course." The admiral never minded being outthought. "We could do that, maybe from the middle of the Gulf. But a missile big enough to come straight in and blow the wall of the dam right out? I don't think there is a missile big enough to do that. At least not one that would fit into a submarine."

"Not just one. How about six of them, Admiral? One after the other, all hitting the wall of the dam in precisely the same spot, until it gives way?"

"Commander, can you just imagine the scene? The Iraqi defensive force at the dam, and I'm sure they have one, standing there watching these big missiles coming in, belching fire, slamming into the wall, one after the other. It would be like Hiroshima. And, within hours, it would be world news, because there is only one nation that could send in cruise missiles like that. The United Nations would hang us out to dry . . . leave us swinging in the wind."

"Not if the missiles came in from the other side, and made their final approach in the dark, right above the water," replied Commander Adnam. "Then dropped into the water a couple of hundred yards short."

For the first time, Arnold Morgan was totally silent.

"By which time, sir, the submarine that fired them would have slipped under the water and headed out of the strait, deep and quiet . . . long gone, and no one would ever know."

"Holy Shit," said the President's national security advisor. "This is fucking unbelievable."

"No it's not, Arnold," interjected Ben. "You have a missile that would do it. But you'd have to modify it. Because it could make its final approach *under* the water."

Arnold Morgan took a deep swig of his coffee, rubbed his

chin in a gesture of rumination. "Commander Adnam, I want to say just one thing. I knew you were extremely clever, but your grasp of this kind of warfare has surprised me. Welcome to the U.S. of A."

It was Bill Baldridge who was now completely preoccupied, and he ignored the admiral's compliment to the prisoner. "Ben's thinking about the Raytheon Tomahawk land-attack missile," he said. "One of those big submerged-launch cruises. It had a special navigation system, they called it TERCOM-aided. You know, pre-programmed into its computer . . . you just bang in the way points. This is the sucker that can be launched from a Los Angeles-Class boat . . . and it has a hell of range, 2,500 kilometers, about 1,550 miles, which I think would get us up the Gulf, from Hormuz."

"Yes. Yes it would," said the admiral thoughtfully. Then, turning to Ben Adnam, he said, "Lieutenant Commander Baldridge was a weapons officer in the United States Navy. Submarines . . . nuclear specialist." The Iraqi nodded respectfully.

The admiral continued. "Didn't we fire some of those missiles at Iraq from submarines, in the Med, during the Gulf War?"

"We did. Those Tomahawks can hit just about anything within range. No mistakes. They're accurate now to within about 6 feet."

"Remind me. How many can the submarine carry?"

"Eight minimum. Later boats can carry up to twelve."

"How about this underwater bullshit?"

"That's the special part," said Ben. "I don't think it should be too difficult. The Brits solved it sixty years ago. What was he called? Burns Morris? You know, the dam-buster fellow."

"I guess you're referring to Professor Barnes Wallis," said Bill, pompously for a cowboy.

"Burns Wallis . . . Barnes Morris . . . what the hell? I refer to the World War II inventor who came up with the bouncing bomb . . . our problem is, cruise missiles don't bounce. So . . . our problem is going to be slowing the missile down for entry into the water. We'll have to use parachutes, because the speed's gotta come down from MACH-.7—about 450 knots—to 30.

Then it has to hit the water, moving through the last 200 yards, making a slow, shallow trajectory along its preprogrammed course, down to the target, somewhere near the base of the dam wall, which is probably 100 feet thick, 100 feet below the surface."

"One of those missiles wouldn't breach it?"

"No. But the first payload should smash the outside concrete layer, driving cracks maybe 40 feet into the wall. Then the second one bangs into the same exact spot, and makes those cracks wider, maybe 80 feet into the wall. Then the third one smashes in, and probably drives the cracks right through. The wall might go right then. But it'll go with the impact of the fourth one. The last two would just be for good measure, in case one of them failed. As you well know, a cruise missile of this size could knock down the White House, blow up a destroyer. That dam wall would not have a prayer against four of them, never mind six."

"How about the propulsion of the missile under the water?"

"That's not a problem. We can do it using the weapon's residual speed. Fast through the air, then into the water for the last couple of hundred yards. They turn into a kind of torpedo."

"Commander Adnam, are you sure of the extent of the damage if we hit Darband and Samarra?"

"Very sure. If you remember, there was a fierce battle during the Iraq-Iran War at a place called Halabjah, which is a Kurdish town in the southeast of their area, right up there in the mountains, a couple of miles east of Darband. The Iraqis fought like tigers for that town, after the Iranians had captured it in the winter of 1988. And they succeeded, drove the Iranian tanks back. But there were allegations that Iraq had used chemical weapons in retaking this little place up near the borders of the two countries.

"There was, however, more to it than that. Iraqi Intelligence had heard the Iranians were planning to blow the big dam at Darband, and Iraq could not allow that. And no price was too high to pay in order to stop them. Even the fury of the whole world over chemical weapons. That dam, and its massive hydroelectric plant, and the one at Samarra, very nearly represent life and death to the very fragile economy of Iraq.

"If they were both blown at the same time, it would wreak havoc. Imagine the situation after the Samarra dam had gone, massive flooding right down to Baghdad, and then another vast volume of water cascading out of the Darband mountains . . . to meet the mainstream of the Tigris just below the center of the city."

"Doesn't sound great," agreed Admiral Morgan. "How long do you estimate it would keep Iraq out of action?"

"I'd say ten years. At least that's what they thought might happen when the Iranians threatened Darband back in 1988."

"How far will the missiles have to travel to the dams, Bill?"

"Well, that's the problem . . . the eternal problem for weapons officers. Bigger the target, bigger the warhead. Otherwise, you end up kicking away at an iceberg with a toothpick. And unless you want to end up with a missile the size of the Washington Monument, you always have to sacrifice range . . . what I'm really saying is you can send a minor warhead 1,500 miles, but the same missile will carry a big warhead only, say, 500 miles. The size of the missile is finite. You either carry fuel or explosive. Every time you increase one, you have to cut back on the other. We'll have to make significant adjustments in design."

"Billy, you're not saying we can't do it, are you?"

"No, Arnie, 'course not. But I am just cautioning everyone we do have to trade a lot of range for a lot of extra bang. When I last looked at this sort of trade-off, range was *the* limiting factor for the payload. Not the other way around.

"Back in '91, we were taking a very serious look at those Iraqi dams, and for a while we thought we could knock 'em down with modified Tomahawk missiles. We were looking at two launch-area options: one at the eastern end of the Med, one at the northern end of the Gulf.

"We knew we would need a ton of missiles per dam, which meant we had to fire half of 'em from the Med. But that option required the missiles to fly at least 600 miles. And that gave us a *real* problem. We just couldn't get a big enough warhead to travel that far. Couldn't hold enough fuel if we were carrying that much explosive. Not without a complete redesign of the entire airframe and power plant . . . really a brand-new missile, because the 600-mile range was a given. The best we ever did was get it down to 30 missiles per dam. Right about then we stopped thinking about it."

Bill Baldridge stood up, paced the room, and drank some coffee. "I do seem to remember that Hughes went right ahead with the project. They completed operational trials, but no one ever told me how they came out. By the time they were ready, the goddamned war was over. But I did once hear they made a few. Shouldn't be difficult to find out what happened to 'em."

Ben Adnam nodded, already a comfortable member of the team. "It's about 600 miles from the Mediterranean to the more easterly dam, Admiral," he said. "But I have a problem with that routing, simply because it cuts down so drastically on our ability to optimize the actual route. We just don't have enough gas for a lot of ducking and diving. The bird will have to fly on a steady course almost all the way, quite possibly through heavy Iraqi radar and antiaircraft defense. That has major implications for the survivability of the weapon in transit. And it has implications all of its own—if we want to get 6 home, and we are calculating a possible loss of 2, we need to fire 9. Basically that's why I hate to launch from the Med."

The admiral looked up and nodded, a kind of rueful half smile on his face. He just said, "Uh-huh." But to himself he was thinking, *Jesus Christ, is this guy something, or what? He's only just fucking gotten here, and he's talking like a lifelong U.S. weapons officer.*

"How many of these missiles do you think we got, Bill?"

"Dunno. Hughes may have bagged 'em, for all I know. I'll check it out right away. Even if we pull it off, we'll still need two launch vehicles."

"That better not be a problem either," growled Arnold Morgan. "Because if it is, someone's in deep shit."

Bill Baldridge continued. "Look, we might get this thing done at short notice. But I have to check out, for a start, the status of those missiles. Then how many ships we have modified to launch these birds . . . and where they are . . . who's nearest our launch areas. I ought to get through with that today . . . the main routing stuff gets done by the targeting-computer team . . . and before their machine spits out all our options, we need to feed in every scrap of information . . . the topography . . . every hill and valley . . . every intelligence report detailing Iraqi defensive positions along the way . . . right up-to-date, which it always is. But I shall want to talk to Ben. He might have some input.

"The computer guys will understand right away that our 600-mile maximum flight path is the critical factor. They'll come up with options for us. Then we can start to make a few hard decisions, about the launch area and the vehicles that will fire the missiles."

"Okay, Bill. Sounds like you two are on top of this. But remember, this thing is not simply a high-tech problem. We have to give real consideration to the political side as well. We have to find a way to make some serious evasions in-flight; otherwise, these bastards may leave a trail that goes straight back to the Pentagon. We gotta try the best we can to keep 'em right off the Iraqi radar . . . we gotta try every twist and turn to stop anyone from finding out where they came from."

"And we don't want to make it too obvious where they're headed to, either," said Ben. "I suppose if you do happen to see a line of these things whipping through the skies at six hundred knots, you don't have a lot of time to do much about it. Better not to take any chances though."

"Right," said Morgan. "That's the thinking. Anyway, I'm outta here, so I'm leaving it to you two. Get the computer whizzes to do their thing, and let's take a look at the routing options ASAP. Also let's get ahold of a real good hard-copy map, so we can take a careful look and choose the right options. Second-guessing a computer is a dangerous business, but we have to get this dead right. You get any trouble with the goddamned eggheads and their fucking software . . . you know the kind of thing . . . resentment at a couple of outsiders like you and Ben . . . just use my name, and use it hard."

"You sure it might not be better for you to pave the way yourself, Admiral . . . one quick phone call before you go."

"You're right," he snapped, picked up a phone, and they heard him in action. Ben Adnam smiled a smile of pure admiration. Bill grinned wistfully, memories drifting back of stressful nights in Fort Meade with the Big Man.

"Right. Admiral Morgan, that's me. Yup, that's it . . . Iraq . . . all the way north from Basra to the Turkish border . . . right . . . take in Syria out to the west . . . right . . . that's it . . . same thing for the Gulf. And lemme have a chart of the Gulf itself . . . right . . . from the Strait of Oman right up to the northern end. Right. *WHEN DO I WANT 'EM? NOW* . . . CAR? Forget all about that. Get 'em down here in a chopper. What? *FIVE MINUTES AGO.* And tell the pilot to keep it running when he gets here, and to pick up Lieutenant Commander Baldridge and his colleague and run 'em down to SUBLANT in Norfolk."

The admiral banged down the phone, as usual, without missing a beat. "Okay, I guess you got about an hour before he arrives. Meanwhile, work on the details—and then make SUBLANT's Black Ops cell your headquarters. We'll probably want one of their boats anyway. The thing is we want this done with a high degree of secrecy, but we need to be fast and efficient. The cell has all the facilities. Get to it . . . I'll be at SUBLANT at 1600." And with that, Arnold Morgan was gone, like a Texas tornado, sweeping all before him, frightening the life out of everyone who stood in his way.

The day passed in a whirlwind of helicopter flights, harassed computer technicians, phone calls, checks and rechecks, satellite communications to the CVBG in the Gulf of Iran, clearances, and the development of a cold-blooded plan to attack the two great dams that keep Iraq alive as a world economic power.

At 1600, both Bill Baldridge and the Iraqi Naval officer were unsurprised when the door to the Black Ops cell burst open and Admiral Arnold Morgan marched in.

"Just tell me we're on," he barked. "No bullshit. No major snags."

"We're on," said Bill. "No bullshit."

"Beautiful."

"The best news first," said Bill. "We have a good choice of launch platforms. We can fire from surface ships or submarines, and we can position adequate assets in the northern Gulf or the Med, or both, without any trouble. We got two cruisers in the Med, both available at short notice. And we got two SSNs plus another cruiser out in the Indian Ocean with the Battle Group. The whole lot of 'em can fire these weapons.

"The main drawback in firing from the Med is we have to fly the weapons out there. We'd probably have to use a Fleet Auxiliary stores ship, but that would mean a long surface transit as well, and it might be pretty difficult to hide the sonsabitches.

"If you ask me, it would be a whole lot better to use the platforms in the Indian Ocean. That way we can fly the weapons direct into Diego Garcia and load 'em right there in private. Then it's 2,700 miles up to the northern end of the Gulf of Iran, leaving us a missile flight of only 400 miles to the most easterly of the dams, flying direct.

"That option would allow us plenty of indirect routing, but we'd have to conceal the launch platforms.

"That means submarines. And because of the number of weapons, that means both of them."

"Just as well they can both fire the birds, right?" grunted Morgan. "And what about the goddamned birds? Have we got any? Hughes got 'em stowed away somewhere?"

"They sure have. I could hardly believe our luck. They'd gone right through to 24 production models, on the shelf, ready to go. They're not gonna be cheap. Probably double normal cost, because Hughes wanna get their money back. And you can bet your goddamned life they'll charge us plenty to make a rush modification. But they can do it and have them ready to ship out in ten days flat."

"Well get on the horn and do it . . . NOW!"

"I already have, Admiral. In your name. You got plenty of cash?"

Ben Adnam shook his head, ruefully, at the apparent ease with which the Americans could deploy really major weapons of war, like big guided-missile nuclear submarines, and he pondered briefly all the troubles he had encountered just trying to acquire a diesel-electric submarine for his missions. Aloud he said, "I can't see much of a problem getting the submarines into the Gulf and up to the launch area around latitude 29 North. But it's not as deep as we would like up there, especially if we have to evade any opposition. And the high seawater temperature does place limits on maximum reactor power and high speeds.

"On the other hand the Iraqi Navy does not possess any real threat to an American SSN . . . except in the unlikely event they had a patrol craft lurking right in the launch area. I suppose our COs could either blow it away, or wait a few hours till it left.

"Even after we've fired off the missiles, even if the Iraqis were somehow able to trace the flight paths back to our launch area, they still couldn't do a damn thing about it. They simply do not own a weapons system capable of catching a U.S. SSN. Fortunately, they do not have any allies in the area either. I imagine the Iranians could make things quite awkward for us down in the Strait of Hormuz with their new Kilo. But I can't see them helping the Iraqis, of all people, can you?"

Bill Baldridge shook his head. "Not a chance," he said. "But, of the launch areas, the Gulf of Iran wins it hands down . . . just on the basis of the spare 200 miles range it gives us for a deceptive approach and defense avoidance. Arnold, I could only recommend the Med if you have overriding political reasons."

"Well, I can think of one overriding political reason why we should consider only the Gulf," replied the admiral, grinning. "If we let 'em go from the Med, just a little farther to the north, it would look as if they were coming in from Syria. Or, taking a slightly more roundabout route, from Israel, which would have the effect of causing a full-scale war in the Middle East, which no one needs. Let's just bag the Med and everything to do with it."

"The same thing would apply to routing the missiles in anywhere from the west," said Commander Adnam. "But I do have one thought. Surely even the Iraqis know that no one except the U.S.A. can fire this kind of a missile accurately?"

"We're not sure of that anymore," said the ex–weapons officer from Kansas. "The Brits have something similar. And the French and the Russians. Probably the Indians and possibly the Iranians. But the Iraqis are gonna look no further than the Americans, so we wanna leave them with a few nice little choices. Then we can sit back and try to let them prove it was us. Which will be just about impossible."

"If we're very careful," said Adnam, smiling. "Oh, by the way, Admiral, we did find out that the water levels in the dams are unusually high all over Iraq. It's been an unusually hard and wet winter. A lot of flooding."

Admiral Morgan stood up. "Right," he said, with an air of finality. "That's it. I want you to set up to use the south and southeastern approach routes. Send the missiles in along the western foothills from the Iraq-Iran border. East around the Baghdad city defenses is also good sense. If anyone should say anything to us, we'll just ask politely if they are *absolutely sure* the Iranians weren't somehow involved. I don't think there's any doubt in any of our minds, the southeast route, the one the computers put up, gives us all the advantages. You'd better get back to the programmers and have 'em produce a few more alternatives, to give us a bit more variation. Otherwise, we'll have a dozen missiles all flying down a straight line like a fucking clay-pigeon shoot.

"And make sure the goddamned eggheads understand we're

using two launch platforms, firing at the same time, each SSN taking a separate dam, in case one of 'em doesn't get to the launch area right on time. We don't want one platform *almost* taking out two dams but not quite. Much better to hit one, and hit it good, and then let the other SSN bang away at a new target hundreds of miles away an hour later. The computer guys will have to work at it, because we want the individual routings deconflicted. The missiles have to arrive at the respective dams at thirty-second intervals. Both lead missiles hitting at roughly the same time. We're looking for precision."

"Aye, sir. You want me to work on these clearances right away?"

"No, Bill. We have to go right to the top on this one. Just get it set up to move into gear, real quick, as soon as I've seen the President. Keep it moving, guys. This one's gonna fly."

The admiral picked up his briefcase and decided to take just the big chart with him, the one on which Bill Baldridge had sketched out the projected route of the Tomahawk cruise missiles. Then he got on the secure line to Admiral Mulligan, warned him of the broad requirements he was about to make of the U.S. Navy, and told him to meet him in the outer office of the Chairman of the Joint Chiefs in forty-five minutes. The Navy helicopter was already running, as the President's national security advisor marched resolutely forward, preparing to teach the government of Iraq a very severe lesson.

Inside the Pentagon, Admirals Morgan, Mulligan, and Dunsmore studied the general plan. The launch platforms would be two SSNs, both 7,000-ton boats of the Los Angeles-Class, *Cheyenne* and *Columbia*. By 1800 they were ordered into the U.S. Naval Base at Diego Garcia. The loading of 14 modified Tomahawks, prepared and flown direct from San Diego, would take place on Thursday, May 25.

Both submarines would clear DG at first light the following morning, and make their way north to the Gulf, submerged and fast, stopping off for a test-firing of one missile each 600 miles out. They would clear the Strait of Hormuz, and enter the Gulf of

Iran on June 1. Moving slower up the Gulf, they were scheduled to arrive in the small hours of June 2. Launch time was dusk—021910JUN06.

Both *Cheyenne* and *Columbia* would turn south immediately after the missiles were away and head back to the open waters of the Arabian Sea, which they should reach by midday on Saturday, June 3. By which time the Iraqis should have a great deal more on their minds than the whereabouts of a couple of SSNs, should they make such a connection.

It took only a few minutes to brief Scott Dunsmore. Arnold Morgan was happy. First thing in the morning he and the CJC would go straight to the White House to obtain formal clearance on the plan from the President. Both men assumed this would be instantly forthcoming, since the entire operation was being mounted at the behest of the Chief Executive.

They arrived at 0900. They walked immediately into the West Wing, where a Secret Service agent escorted them to the Oval Office. The President was waiting, and coffee was served as soon as they arrived.

"'Morning, gentlemen," he said. "Are you going to frighten me to death?"

"Absolutely not, sir," replied Admiral Morgan. "But we are about to frighten the President of Iraq to death."

"Could I ask you to inform me of *only what I need to know?*"

"Certainly." The Chairman of the Joint Chiefs took over, formally. "In retribution for Iraq's attack on the *Thomas Jefferson*, and subsequently for their unwarranted attacks on three civilian airliners, which ended the lives of several United States citizens, including six members of Congress and the Vice President, we intend to strike against that country on Friday evening, June 2. The operation is Black. It will be conducted by the United States Navy and will involve a missile strike against two Iraqi structures. We envision minimal loss of life, but massive economic damage to that country. We estimate it will take up to ten years for them to make a full recovery."

"Christ, Scott. Are you guys taking out the two big dams?"

"Yessir. How did you guess?"

"Well, a couple of years ago it was the suggestion of our friend Admiral MacLean."

"It was a good suggestion, too. Like most of his."

"Yes. In light of the short time frame you must be using missiles?"

"Yessir. Two sets of cruises. Fired top secret by a submarine. Preprogrammed underwater missile approach from the reservoir side of both dams."

"One of them's the Samarra Barrage on the Tigris, isn't it?"

"That's right, sir. The other's about five times bigger; it's called the Darband-I-Khan."

"Ah, yes. I remember now. Well, I don't know if we'll be accused of international banditry, but I assume our policy is to say absolutely nothing."

"Correct, sir," replied Admiral Morgan. "We'll just let those bastards understand who they can fuck with and who they can't. But we cannot allow the flag of this nation to be fired upon by anyone. Not without massive retribution from us."

"My sentiments entirely. These rogue regimes are gonna learn it the hard way. They either play by the very fair rules laid down by us, or we'll make them wish they had. By the way, might I judge from the expeditious manner this has been set up that we received help from an . . . er . . . unusual source."

"You may, sir."

"Thank you, gentlemen. I'll look forward to the evening news a week Friday."

021840JUN06. USS *Columbia*. 28.55N, 49.48E.
Periscope depth. Course 315. Speed 5.

Commander Mike Krause, conscious of the critical nature of his mission, and of the proximity of the sea bottom to his keel, had checked on the underwater telephone. Commander Tom Jackson's *Cheyenne* ran quietly 500 yards on his starboard beam, same course, speed, and depth. Both SSNs were on top line to fire. Tubes ready. A hundred checks have been made, the missile men had completed all the prefiring routines and settings. There must be no mistakes, barring missile malfunction or enemy action. The preprogramming was immaculate. The big self-guided Tomahawks were ready to do their catastrophic job.

At 1845 precisely, Commander Krause ordered, "*Stand by tubes one to six.*"

Then, "*TUBE ONE, LAUNCH.*" And the first of the specially modified SLCM Tomahawks blew out of the submarine, slid up to the surface, and roared into the black night sky, adjusting course at its cruise altitude of 50 feet above the water, heading north, a fiery tail crackling out behind for the first few seconds of its flight. And then it hit flying speed, and the gas turbines cut in, leaving no telltale trail in the sky. Nothing could stop it. At least nothing in the maritime armories of the Gulf nations.

Within four minutes, the remaining five missiles had screamed onward and upward, all under the control of the launch sequencer. All fired at exact, but different, intervals, each one designed for the specific route of each Tomahawk. No matter what the route variations, the big cruise missiles would arrive on their target, from their separate flight paths, precisely thirty seconds apart.

Next the Tomahawks, in a murderous salvo of destruction, fanned out and hurtled above the dark waters of the Gulf. Though Mike Krause could not tell, they were surprisingly quiet as well as fast. Once they were over land they could scarcely be heard at all before they were already past. Too late. Much too late for the Darband-I-Khan dam.

At 1850 Commander Krause heard that *Cheyenne* had also completed her firing sequence. Commander Jackson had drawn a long-range bead on the Samarra Barrage. Missiles away, the Americans were to get out of the Gulf of Iran. Mike Krause ordered *Columbia* sharply around to the southeast, coordinating his turn with the other SSN. And the two Black Ops submarines headed off together 500 yards apart.

By dawn, both boats would be creeping softly through the Strait of Hormuz, deep, fast, and in the center of the channel, the safety separation, 100 feet in depth. Soon the Gulf of Oman would shelf away to the unfathomable sandy depths of the Arabian Sea. The Americans would angle to the right there, running south, down the coast of Oman, passing almost directly over the shattered tomb of HMS *Unseen.*

022015JUNE06. 35.07N, 45.42E.
The guard room, western
end of the great wall of the Darband-I-Khan dam.

Corporal Tariq Nayif, at the age of twenty-one, was the duty soldier charged with walking out along the wall to the halfway point and back every half hour during his four-hour watch. The eastern half of the wall was patrolled from the guard room on the other side.

Tariq's immediate superior, Staff Sergeant Ali Hasan, a veteran Iraqi combat soldier in charge of the western guardhouse, was resting until midnight. The officer on duty, Second Lieutenant Rashid Ghazi, was reading, which left Tariq out on the wall on his own. Armed with his standard-issue Russian Kalashnikov, but nonetheless alone. To his right there was low wall, and a yawning 500-foot drop to the River Diyala, to his left the still dark waters of the reservoir. The wall was well lit all the way across, and swept by a personnel surveillance radar and infrared detectors at all times. There was a television picture showing their end of the wall in Tariq's guardhouse.

Like every night, it was cool, silent, and peaceful up there in the mountains. Tariq wore a greatcoat, hat, and gloves, as he walked slowly toward the east, his steel-tipped boots making an unusually loud noise above the gusting wind that blew directly into his face. Tariq was not a Kurd, and it was beyond his understanding why anyone should want to live up here in the cold, barren peaks of northeastern Iraq.

There were other things beyond his understanding on this night, principally the fact that less than 150 yards away, already 70 feet below the surface, a big American-built cruise missile, with a thumping 500kg warhead, was quietly making its final approach to the front of the wall, to a detonation point down at the base of the dam. It was still making 10 knots through the water, and would explode with shuddering impact, 100 feet below where Tariq stood.

It hit at 2018, detonating with a massive underwater explosion, which strangely made little sound in the air. And hardly a ripple disturbed the calm water immediately beside the dam. But the force of the underwater blast shook the giant structure to its foundations, as cracks like lightning bolts ripped 40 feet into the concrete. But it held firm, and as the waters subsided there was complete silence again, save for the pounding feet of Tariq Rashid, running back to the safety of the western guardhouse to report what little he had seen or heard.

By then Staff Sergeant Ali Hasan was on his feet outside the building yelling, demanding to know what the hell was going on. Tariq could not help much there, and as he struggled to explain the dull, muted thunder, his words were cut short by a second stunning impact on the wall, well below the surface. Both men felt the reverberations of the thud on the soles of their boots. And then, again, there was silence. No attacking fighter-bombers screamed through the sky. There had been no sense of a rocket attack, or any attack. The area was undisturbed, and the lapping of the wavelets on the shore was lost against the low gusting of the wind.

Then the third SLCM nosed into the dam wall, right into the gaping hole on the north side, before it blew. And again the force of the exploding warhead lasered those lightning-bolt cracks deep into the structure, right through this time. The two Iraqi soldiers, backing away from the obvious tremor along the great wall, could not see, but one giant jagged crack ran 100 feet diagonally down the south-facing wall . . . the one that now held back 3 cubic miles of water.

Staff Sergeant Hasan, joined now by Second Lieutenant Rashid Ghazi, was just saying that there seemed to be no military explanation, that there must be some kind of an earthquake, when Mike Krause's fourth cruise missile blasted into the underwater cavern on the north side of the dam. It blew, with spectacular impact, a gigantic breach in the dam, 150 yards across. Millions of tons of concrete finally gave way to billions of tons of water. The 100-foot-high wave surged through the gap with unimaginable force, then began to crash down in slow motion, 500 feet, to the quietly flowing river below. And, of course, it kept coming, one of the biggest reservoirs in the world, followed by an entire lake, the waters rushing in behind, from a deep mountain lake bed more than 6 miles long.

On both sides, the great wall held firm for a span of around 50 yards. It was the middle that was missing, and the 3 Iraqi soldiers stared toward the east, in terror at the clear wrath of Allah. And they turned to the direction of Mecca, knelt before their God, and prayed for guidance.

Below them, the friendly River Diyala had become a raging, cascading torrent, 40 feet higher than normal, roaring down its course, southeast, toward the Tigris 100 miles away. Toward the fertile southern farmlands south of the city of Baghdad. Toward the factories down in the industrial delta of Iraq.

1857 (EDT). June 2. The CIA safe house in the Woodley district of Virginia, south of Washington.

Lieutenant Commander Baldridge, Admiral Morgan, and Commander Adnam were sharing a pot of coffee and preparing to watch the seven o'clock evening news. The only news they had was that the missiles had been launched and the submarines were on their way home.

And an aura of gloom began to descend as the summary of the content was given, and no mention was made of the havoc they expected to have broken out in the Middle East.

"I know these media bastards are parochial in outlook," growled the admiral, "but this is ridiculous."

As 1915 came and went, still no mention. At 1920 Arnold Morgan was about to call the station, but restrained himself.

At 1922, there was an interruption. "We're just breaking away from that story for a moment because of a breaking news event . . ." said the commentator with heavy emphasis. "There are reports of some kind of a natural disaster in Iraq . . . Baghdad is reported to be under 4 feet of water at the northern end of the city . . . we have conflicting reports right now . . . but one of them suggests the great dam on the Tigris, the Samarra Barrage has breached . . . however, we have another report suggesting it is the northern dam in the Kurdish mountains, the Darband-I-Khan, that has burst . . . right now we have no further information. Communications seem to have been heavily disrupted . . . but we will keep you informed of what appears to be a huge disaster in Iraq . . . now back to the gay rights march in LA."

Arnold Morgan walked across and shook the hand of Bill Baldridge, and that of Ben Adnam.

But the Iraqi seemed very preoccupied. In fact he was wondering how the floodwater was rising in a little stone house off Al-Jamouri Street, the one in the dark, narrow alleyway next to the hotel.

He hadn't seen it for two years, since May 26, 2004, the night the Iraqi President's men had come to murder him. Since then the full moon had risen above the desert twenty-six times. It had been two years, and one week. He had just missed the anniversary, which was a pity because he liked anniversaries. But Eilat smiled. *Perfect*, he thought. *Almost*.

EPILOGUE

C OMMANDER BENJAMIN ADNAM WAS GIVEN A UNITED States passport on September 18, 2006. It bore the name Benjamin Arnold, and detailed his birthplace as Helensburgh, Scotland.

For the mission against the Iraqi dams he was paid the agreed upon $250,000. With this he made a down payment on a medium-sized white Colonial-styled house quite near the Dunsmores in Virginia, on the west side of the Potomac. He purchased an unobtrusive dark green Ford Taurus and began work in the headquarters of the Central Intelligence Agency in Langley, Virginia.

A new position was created for him—Special Advisor to the associate director of Central Intelligence. This was Frank Reidel, Langley's link between the Agency and the military. Commander Adnam moved into an office adjacent to that of Reidel, a short walk from the CIA's Middle Eastern desk, to which the former terrorist was seconded on a permanent basis. The normal strict vetting procedures for employees of the CIA were dispensed with, on special orders from the White House.

Adnam had requested that he be permitted to use the rank he had earned in the Israeli Navy. Admiral Morgan ensured this was granted, and he was thenceforth referred to in the Agency as Commander Arnold.

On the first Thursday of each month he attended a private briefing on Middle Eastern Developments, inside the White House with the President's national security advisor.

His salary was $150,000 a year, but Morgan negotiated him out of an annual lump sum in excess of $1 million that the Iraqi had demanded. It was agreed that at the conclusion of ten years service he would receive a bonus of $2 million. In return for this, Morgan insisted that all the incriminating documents be returned from the Swiss bank. And he sent special agents to Geneva to pick them up.

As Arnold Morgan had guessed, Benjamin Adnam's insights into the mind-sets of the Middle East were extremely valuable. Within a matter of weeks, it was plain that he would make a major contribution in helping the Americans to ease the political crosscurrents, to calm the warring factions among the sheikhs and dictators, in the turbulent, oil-rich crucible of the Middle East.

For himself, Ben found a peace he had never known. Away from the frontiers of hands-on terrorism, separated from the high-risk work of intelligence field agent, he settled into his smooth, suburban American life with considerable ease. For the first few months, he made few attempts at befriending colleagues, but concentrated on living quietly at home, reading and watching the news and international current affairs on television. For the first time, for as long as he could remember, he was off the front line, and no one was hunting for him. At least in America they weren't.

For the moment, Ben Adnam was content to keep the lowest possible profile, and to thank his God he was out of the lethal world of international terrorism.

On one Autumn morning he was jolted into the reality of that judgment. Reading the *New York Times*, he caught sight of a story that detailed a long police chase and a minor gun battle in the Kilburn area of northwest London. It involved the IRA and the capture of a suspected cache of explosives and guns. The shoot-out had lasted only ten minutes, and only one man was hit, quite badly. His name was Paul O'Rourke, aged twenty, from County Waterford. They charged him under the Act of Terrorism, while he lay in hospital with a collapsed right lung.

Ben shook his head. "To be prepared to die for a cause" . . . and he pondered the years ahead, and how he would deal with civilian life, should the Americans permit him that permanent luxury. He had, of course, one further score to settle. That of Iran, and their brutal, if ill-planned attempt on his life. Not to mention the $1.5 million they still owed him.

One day the Iranians would pay for that. And, confident now of the goodwill of his new masters, Ben picked up the telephone and requested a private talk first thing in the morning with Admiral Morgan. *Perhaps now is the time*, he thought. The time to come clean with the national security advisor, perhaps to consolidate his position even further.

At 0900 the following day he was sitting in the West Wing, recounting in graphic detail to Arnold Morgan that the big American cruise missiles had slammed the wrong country in revenge for the dead Americans in the destroyed airliners.

He could not know how the ferocious White House admiral would react to the revelation that he had been used as a pawn in the Iraqi's grand scheme of vengeance. But he felt that Morgan would look beyond the obvious deception, and perhaps begin to ponder again the question of a big strike against Iran. The Iraqi dams had, of course, avenged the deaths of 6,000 U.S. Navy personnel in the aircraft carrier. The demise of Iraq was justifiable simply on those grounds, and that country's proven aim of producing weapons of mass destruction.

He edged Morgan along the thought process that Iran's day would surely come. Of that he was certain. In the end they would step out of line on the international oil stage of the Gulf. And then he, Arnold Morgan, could move in for the strike against the Ayatollahs that had been so long coming.

It was clear to both men that Commander Adnam's days of illusion were over. Where once there had been hope and idealism, there was now an empty place. What remained was the skilled, unique military mind of the world's most successful Islamic terrorist. And Morgan had bought that mind at a bargain price.

They were together for less than one hour, and when he left Commander Adnam was certain he had been correct in clarifying the situation. Correct in his assessment that the American admiral would appreciate knowing, finally, the full truth. And they shook hands formally at the conclusion of the meeting.

However, Commander Adnam had misjudged his man. Admiral Arnold Morgan was furious. Furious at being outwitted by the scheming terrorist every step of the way. Furious that he had once more been hoodwinked during the interrogation. And really furious that he had moved major U.S. muscle against a country that had known nothing of the acts of terrorism against the passenger aircraft. Admiral Morgan was about ready to murder Ben Adnam, and not just figuratively. It was not on the basis of some terrible attack of conscience toward any of the troublesome nations of the Middle East. But because he was sick and tired of being made to feel a damned fool in front of "this crooked fucking towelhead."

And the Iraqi was not four yards down the drive of the White House before the national security advisor was storming through the White House, on his way to talk to the President. Their conversation lasted five minutes. Admiral Morgan briefed the Chief Executive carefully, then said with icy indifference, "Sir, I've had enough of him. He's gotta go."

"I could not," replied the President, "agree more. Please don't mention his name to me, ever again."

"Nossir," he replied. And returned to his office.

It was 2200 that evening when two CIA cars and a private government ambulance pulled into the driveway of Commander Adnam's house. Three armed Marine Corps marksmen took up sniper positions, and Arnold Morgan walked through the front door alone. Ben Adnam was reading in the living room.

"Commander," said the American, "it is my duty to inform you that we have no further use for you."

"Sir?" replied the Iraqi, betraying nothing.

"We have decided to dispense with your services on the grounds that we do not trust you, and you may become an embarrassment to the U.S.A."

"Does this mean you intend to execute me, after all, for my crimes against humanity?"

"It would, with any other prisoner of your category, Commander. But you are somewhat different."

"I see. But I imagine you have men with rifles trained upon me as we speak?"

"Yes, Ben. I do. Your time is, shall we say, limited."

"I think I misjudged you today. Perhaps I should never have told you the truth."

"Perhaps not. But this day would have come anyway."

"Are you going to tell them to kill me now?"

"No, Commander. Strange as it may seem, I have respect for you. Not for your callous murder of so many people. But for the professional military way in which you did it. As such I am going to offer you an old-fashioned form of chivalry in your departure."

Arnold Morgan reached into his coat pocket and drew out a big, wooden-handled military service revolver. Loaded. And he placed it on the table between them.

"You understand, Commander, that your death in the next ten minutes is inevitable?"

"Yessir. I do. And I am not regretful. I have no further heart for a fight. I have nowhere to go. No one to speak to. My options have run out."

"So, Ben, if I may call you that again, I am offering you an honorable way out, in the tradition of a serving officer. And now I am going to leave you. I wish you good-bye, and in a way I'm sorry. But not in other ways. I will turn my back on you briefly, but if you should even look at that revolver before I am gone, the honorable option will be gone. My men will shoot you down like a cheapskate little terrorist, which I believe would not do you justice, not in your mind, nor indeed in mine. I hope you follow me? Because I regard this as personal, between us."

Ben Adnam nodded. But he never moved. And the Admiral left. The commander heard the CIA cars reach the end of the drive. He did not, however, hear the admiral disembark and stand with two agents beneath the tall trees on the edge of the road.

They all heard the veranda door slam. They heard the slow dignified footsteps walk down the wide wooden stairs, and the soft tread of the Bedouin across the gravel. And then there was silence for three minutes, before the unmistakable crash of a single echoing gunshot in the silence of the night.

When Arnold Morgan's men went in with their flashlights, the big zip-up plastic bag, and stretcher, they found the body in a damp leafy corner of the garden. Commander Benjamin Adnam, the side of his head blown away, was still in kneeling position, facing 90 degrees on the compass, due east . . . toward a distant God, in a distant heaven, somewhere out by the shifting desert sands of Arabia.